Sign up for our newsletter to hear
about new and upcoming releases.

www.ylva-publishing.com

Other books by Cheyenne Blue

Party Wall

Girl Meets Girl Series:
Never-Tied Nora
Not-So-Straight Sue
Fenced-In Felix
Almost-Married Moni

Code of
Conduct

Cheyenne Blue

Dedication

I've been watching tennis for as long as I can remember. When I was a little tacker in the UK, I'd come home from school, walk up the path, dragging my school satchel thump-thump-thump over the pavers, and push open the door. The house would be dark, the curtains drawn tight against the summer light. The only sound would be the bonk-bonk of tennis balls, followed by sedate applause. My mother would be hunched on the sofa, staring at the TV, an untouched cuppa and a Rich Tea biscuit beside her.

Wimbledon fortnight. For two weeks, us kids scrounged our own food, got ourselves ready for school, and could stay up as late as we wanted—as long as we were watching the tennis. It didn't take long for me to enjoy curling up on the couch with Mum, as absorbed as she was.

It was the days of Björn Borg, John McEnroe, Ilie Năstase, and of course Chris Evert, Virginia Wade, Billie Jean King, and Martina-the-goddess Navratilova.

Martina. Let me pause on that name for a moment in happy contemplation.

This book is dedicated to my adoptive mother, May, who, as well as being such a wonderful mother, passed her love of tennis on to me.

Acknowledgements

Once again, many people came together to push this book out into the world.

As always, the biggest thanks go to Astrid and the Ylva team for gold medal service to lesfic. Sandra Gerth was my editor this time around, and holy moly, she has tough love down to an art. She challenged me to do my best, didn't skimp on the suggestions, but also ensured that it was still *my* book at the end of the day. Her eagle eye can spot a misplaced comma at ten paces. From go to whoa, I loved the editing process with her.

Glendon from Streetlight Graphics has once again produced a glorious cover that epitomises the story. Paulette did a careful and thorough job as proofreader. My great mate Marg also found the typos that always threaten to slide past at the last moment.

Finally, thank you to the WTA tour and tournament organisers everywhere (especially Wimbledon and the Brisbane International) for the hours and hours of enjoyment.

Cheyenne Blue
Queensland, Australia

Chapter 1

VIVA'S HEART POUNDED IN DOUBLE time as she waited at the service line for the crowd to calm. If anything, the cacophony of applause and shouts grew louder.

"Quiet, please." The umpire's even tones cut through the din. "Tie breaker, 6-5, Jones. Genevieve Jones to serve."

Viva drew a deep breath and let the tension drain from her shoulders. She twitched her toe into position a centimetre behind the service line. The crowd's noise faded; there was nothing in her mind except the next point. She rocked back on her heel and flung the ball skywards.

"C'mon, Paige! Show us what you've got!"

The shouted encouragement for her opponent cut through Viva's concentration. Laughter rippled around centre court. Abort. She lowered her racquet, caught the ball, and fought down her flash of anger as she waited once again for the crowd to settle.

"Please do not call out when play is in progress." The umpire made a mark on the tablet in front of him.

Viva spun away from the service line and nodded to the ballkid for a towel. New York's humidity made the racquet slip in her hand like butter on a hot pan. She wiped her face, hands, and the racquet handle. Staring down at the strings, she refocussed her concentration and willed away the butterflies cartwheeling in her stomach. This moment, this point. *Set point.* Nothing else mattered right now. Not her grand slam title defence, not the number one ranking she stood to gain if she succeeded. *This point matters.*

Only this one. If she won this point, the match would go to three sets. She paced back to the service line, collecting and discarding balls from the ballkid.

She bounced the ball once, twice. A third time. Her grip tightened on the racquet. *This point matters. Only this one.* A fourth bounce and she prepared to swing.

"Time violation. Warning, Miss Jones."

She dropped the racquet and swung around to face the umpire.

He stared back impassively, as if daring her to react.

She closed her eyes for a second, biting back the hot words she wanted to say. She was maybe a few seconds over time. To call a violation was massively unfair. With a deep breath, she bent and picked up her racquet.

A quick glance at her peppy blonde opponent, now taking pretend swings with the racquet. Paige had a poor three-set record, especially when she lost the second set. Viva knew she could win the match—if it went to a third set. And it was still set point to her. Viva wiped the sweat from her forehead with the back of her wristband.

Two bounces, the ball toss, the swing. *Ace!* Viva whirled around with a jubilant fist pump.

"Second serve."

What? Her eyes widened, and she turned to the umpire.

"Foot-fault." The umpire leant forward and spoke into the microphone. "Miss Jones, a foot-fault was called."

The buzz of white noise in her head built to a crescendo. Viva pressed her lips together tightly and swallowed hard. She jerked around to face the lineswoman, who stared straight ahead, no expression on her face.

Viva nodded, a jerky up-and-down, and walked back to the service line. Two bounces of the ball, the toss, the swing. The softer serve kicked wide, and Paige returned it hard down the centre. For a minute, they duelled back and forth before Paige sent a backhand winner down the line.

6-6. Viva now needed two straight points to win. She stalked back to her chair for the short break at the change of ends. A mouthful of sports drink, another of water. She wiped the handle of her racquet and tested the string tension. The little routines calmed her momentarily, stilled her jiggling knee. She focussed deep inside, trying in vain to block out the pounding music that played during the two-minute breaks.

Viva returned to the service line. Someone coughed in the crowd as she prepared to serve, and she paused, then bounced the ball one more time. A clean serve down the centre line. Paige pushed it back short. Viva raced in and scooped the ball. It hit the net cord and for an agonising moment seemed to hang there before it fell back on Viva's side of the net. *Damn. That was the worst luck. That was—No!* She slammed a wall up against the negative thoughts.

"7-6, Westermeier."

If Paige won this point, she would win the match. And she now had two serves.

Viva focussed on her feet as she returned to the baseline, this time to receive.

Paige took her time to serve, bouncing the ball many times, then a bad ball toss, which she caught and regrouped.

Viva bit her lip. The umpire should call a time violation. He should— She tamped that line of thought. *Focus.*

Paige's serve was soft, almost tentative.

Viva was already in position, and her driving return clipped the baseline. 7-7. *Yes!* She jogged back to the baseline to receive and sent a cool glance at her opponent. *Do your worst, Paige.*

Paige's next serve thundered down hard and fast and unexpected.

Viva lunged for it, and the ball glanced off the tip of her racquet. A streak of pain shot into her wrist from the force, and she gasped as the joint was forced back. The racquet fell to the ground. She bent to pick it up, gritting her teeth against her disappointment. Her wrist throbbed. It was now 8-7 and a second match point to Paige. But it was not over yet. After accepting a ball, she spun around to the service line and stared down the court as she drew a deep breath and blew it out slowly.

She twitched her foot into position, the toe of her fluoro shoe behind the line. Two bounces. A third for luck. Throw. Swing. And the serve was good; she was sure it was and—

"Foot-fault."

"No!" The shout erupted from her tight throat. "Not again! No way!"

The racquet trembled in her hand, and she clenched her fingers on the handle. A glance at the umpire's implacable face. No chance of an overrule. She swung to face the lineswoman, who sat stony-faced on the chair, her neat, brown hair as short and tightly controlled as the rest of her. She stared straight ahead, as if she were waiting for a bus.

Viva glared up at the umpire. "She's wrong! You can't let her get away with this. It's match point!" A red haze built in her mind. She tightened her grip on the racquet, consumed by the urge to smash it onto the court until it was broken beyond repair.

"Second serve."

Viva tightened her lips so much that her teeth ground together. She nodded once, tightly, to the umpire and stalked back to the service line. As she drew level with the lineswoman, she flicked her a contemptuous look. "I will not forget this."

The woman didn't flinch. Her sweat-damp hair clung limply to her forehead in the heat, but she stared straight ahead without reaction.

With a final venomous glare in her direction, Viva took her place at the service line. She heaved a breath, trying to compose herself. *This point matters. Only this one.* The hyped-up crowd, now all cheering for the American, the heat and humidity of the afternoon, Paige bouncing lightly on her toes—they all receded, pushed back into a place where they were unimportant. The lineswoman's stony face intruded, and she, too, was dismissed from her mind. *Focus.*

She accepted three balls, rejected one. To lose the match on a penalty would be an unbearable indignity. Viva closed her eyes for a second, banishing the negative thoughts. Lose? *No.* She would win this. Her grip was firm on her racquet, and conviction surged in her mind. She rocked back on her heel. The silence of the crowd was absolute. The ballkids as still as lamp posts, the umpire poised in his chair. The lineswoman leant forward, hands on her knees, gaze locked on the service line.

Second service. Last chance.

Viva tossed, swung, and smashed the ball true in the centre of her racquet. It shot like a rocket, over the net.

"Out!" The call was loud and sure from the linesman at the far end of the court.

"No!" She couldn't supress the cry, not the victory shout she had imagined, more a forlorn little sob of shattered dreams. She had lost. Lost in the quarterfinals, in the defence of her US Open title. Her legs were suddenly as weak as jelly, and she sank to her haunches on court, her head bowed over the handle of her racquet. Soon she would have to face her coach Deepak and the press, but for one private moment she let the misery consume her. Only for a second. Arranging her face into a wry smile of congratulation, she sprang to her feet and walked to the net.

Paige bounded up, elation scrawled over her face. Around them the crowd surged to their feet, and the stadium rang with their cheers and applause.

For Paige. Not for her.

"Well done, Paige. Very well-deserved." She hugged her opponent around her sweaty shoulders before walking to her chair. A quick shake of the umpire's hand, and she swiftly gathered her things and stuffed them into her bag. *Get off court.* The urge to flee was overwhelming. A long shower, that was what she wanted so that the streaming water would hide her tears.

She raised a hand to the crowd and trudged to the exit. The cacophony of cheers for the winner followed her out.

———⊶⊷———

Later, much later, after she'd showered, talked with Deepak, and faced a barrage of questions from the press about her shock loss, Viva returned to her hotel room. She lay on the bed, phone clenched in her hand, staring at the ceiling. The things she needed to do marched through her head, but she ignored them. She blinked away the moisture in her eyes and focussed on the white ceiling, replaying the final tie breaker in her head. She had had the momentum, the edge. She was the better player, higher ranked than Paige, better able to deal with the pressure. Except she hadn't. The final point rolled through her head like a horror movie. Her position behind the line, the toss, the serve. *The foot-fault call.* The mental playback stuttered and halted. That call had lost her the match.

Viva picked up the TV remote and flicked through the channels until she found a replay of the match. She skipped ahead to the final point. There she was, tension shimmering in her body, her face closed-in and intent. She replayed the foot-fault call again and again. Had her toe moved over the line before or after she hit the ball? She studied the footage. It was a bad call; she was sure of it.

Her phone rang, and a glance at the display showed it was her mum calling from Australia. She ignored it. Later, she would talk to her family, cry a little, wallow in the love and comfort offered, but not yet.

She let the replay move on. The camera cut to the lineswoman who'd made the call. Olive skin, chiselled cheekbones, aloof expression. Her name flashed along the bottom of the screen: Gabriela Mendaro. Viva paused the frame, committing her face and name to memory. Her lips twisted. This woman was responsible for bundling her out of the US Open. Now she was no longer Genevieve Jones, defending US Open champion, the number one ranking within reach; now she was just another player scrambling to remain in the top ten.

Her phone rang again, and she glanced at the caller ID. Her lips twitched into the ghost of a smile. If anyone could raise her spirits, Michi could.

"Hey, partner," she said.

"Hey yourself. How are you?" Her doubles partner was usually the most ebullient of people, but her voice now held a soft, cautious quality.

"I've had better days," Viva said wryly. "Like pretty much every day this year."

Michi was silent for a moment. "It's not the end. It's just a match that you lost. You know that."

"Yeah." Viva gusted a sigh. "You're right, of course, but at this moment, it's the end of life as I know it." In front of her, the TV screen was still frozen on Gabriela Mendaro's face. She'd seen her before—players and officials were on nodding terms. "It was a bad call." She couldn't keep the bitterness from her voice.

"Maybe. It was certainly close."

"The lineswoman should've let it go. It was match point. *Match point!*"

"That doesn't make it different. If anything, on match point the calls should be tighter."

"Any call should be accurate. And that one wasn't."

"Have you talked to Deepak?" Michi's tone still had the wary hesitation of someone who wasn't sure what to say.

"Yeah. And he said I should move on."

"Of course he did. Brett tells me the same when I have a bad call. 'Don't dwell on anything,' he always says."

"I know. Deepak's right. Brett's right."

"Am I right too?" Humour laced Michi's voice. "Because if I am, that's a first."

Viva snorted. "You're *always* right, partner. It's what you do best."

"I thought my sizzling forehands down the line were what I do best."

"Those too." Viva heaved a sigh. "You're right, Michi. Of course you are. My head knows that even if my heart is yet to catch up." She moved to sit cross-legged on the bed so that she could see out of the window. "What are you doing tonight? The whole of New York is out there. Want to have dinner? It's either that or spend a dismal hour on the internet finding the cheapest flight to Montreal for the next tournament."

"The United Airlines commuter flight. Always the cheapest because it leaves when most normal people are still in bed. But I've got a better idea. Instead of flying to Montreal, let's hire a car and drive. Just you and me and the open road. Brett wants a couple of days to see his family, so now's his chance. We've got four days to get to Montreal. We can take a tour of upstate New York, visit towns with weird names, see some fall leaves, eat way too much, drink weak beer, and share a room. It'll be like old times."

A smile tugged at Viva's lips. It would be good, the two of them having fun, with no thought of tennis. Michi was a great friend. No doubt she was gesticulating at Brett right now that he needed to visit his family in Colorado.

"As long as you don't stay up until two in the morning watching horror movies, as you did the last time we shared a room."

"Promise. No horror. Well, except for my hair in the mornings."

Viva chuckled. "It's a deal. You book a car—something roomy—and we'll plan our route over dinner tonight."

"High five, partner! This'll be awesome. The terrible two on the road again."

"No Thelma and Louise jokes."

"Not even a little one." Michi's enthusiasm bubbled down the line. "Brett and I will come by your room at six, and we'll go eat."

Viva ended the call and threw the phone on the bed. The paused TV screen was still frozen on the lineswoman, Gabriela Mendaro. For a last moment, she studied the woman's impassive face, the smooth skin, the arched brows, and the keen gaze.

Michi's words came back to her: *Don't dwell.* She clicked off the TV and rose from the bed.

Enough.

Chapter 2

Fifteen months later

THE ENGINE OF THE SPORTY hatchback roared as Viva changed down to third gear for the tight bend. The tyres shivered on the gravel road, found grip, and the little car accelerated again. Outside, the air was hot and still, the gum trees drooping in the heat of early summer.

As soon as she had a clear view of the single-lane road ahead, she pushed the car even faster. There wasn't another vehicle in sight. The narrow road was a shortcut, generally overlooked in favour of the highway.

Viva turned the radio louder, singing along to the catchy tune. She had travelled this road thousands of times over the years, first as a kid, when one of her parents drove her to the nearest tennis courts an hour away to practice, then as a teenager, when she returned from the Australian Institute of Sport in Canberra. But for all the hard work and her frantic life as a professional tennis player since, the swoops and curves of the gravel road home still had the power to excite her.

She slowed for a washout, then accelerated again, leaving a choking cloud of dust. It hung in the air, a comet trail to mark her path.

Going home. Her heart sang in anticipation. She pushed aside the underlying reason; like Scarlett O'Hara she would think about that tomorrow. Right now, she was looking forward to seeing her family again and to having a cold beer. Not necessarily in that order.

The road erupted out of the forest onto the scrubby slope that descended the valley to Waggs Pocket. The sun blazed low, reflecting on the windscreen as she headed west. Viva fumbled for her water bottle and took a long draught.

Focussed as she was on a drink, she only saw the sedan at the last second. It was parked haphazardly, blocking half of the single lane, its bonnet propped open. The driver stood further out, arms waving.

Viva's hands clenched on the steering wheel, and she braked hard. The hatchback fishtailed. She double-declutched into second and wrenched the steering wheel to the right, aiming the car at the long grass on the opposite side of the road. The hatchback bounced as the suspension bottomed out. Viva swerved back onto the road and came to a halt.

Her breath hissed between her teeth in a long exhale. *Bloody idiot.* Obviously a townie. No bush person would park like that and then stand in the middle of the road to flag someone down. She would have stopped anyway to check all was okay; it was what one did in the bush.

She reversed back through the dust cloud to where the driver waited— this time by the side of the road.

Viva opened her window. "You okay?" She couldn't see the driver clearly, but it seemed to be a woman, short and slightly built.

"Thank you for stopping." The woman stepped over and bent to peer inside the car. "I did not think you were going to." With the sun behind her, she was a silhouette. Her English was fluent but heavily accented.

"No worries." Viva squinted through the dust and glare. "What's wrong with your car?"

The woman shrugged. "I do not know. It ran rough, then stalled and would not restart. It's a rental."

Viva unbuckled her seatbelt and exited. Outside, she dwarfed the other woman by a head. She stepped aside so she could see her more clearly.

The stranger moved too, and the sunlight fell clearly on her face.

Viva froze. *No.* What were the odds of that? Of meeting her here? In Australia, in Queensland, in the middle of bloody nowhere? She gritted her teeth, and for a second the uncharitable urge to stomp back to the VW and speed away consumed her. It would, after all, be fair payback. Almost.

The other woman frowned. "Is something wrong?"

Viva paced around to the other side of the stranded vehicle. She wouldn't leave even her worst enemy stranded on a remote road. "No. Let's take a look at your car."

A crease formed between her eyes. "Do I know you?"

Viva lifted the sunnies shading her face.

"Oh." Various expressions flashed over the other woman's face, like a deck of cards shuffled fast. "Genevieve Jones." Her tone exuded polite wariness.

"In person, Gabriela Mendaro. I didn't expect to see you until the Brisbane International next month. I imagine you'll be umpiring there?"

"Yes, as always. I take December away from the tour, and I usually spend it in Australia."

Viva swept a hand around the parched and withered landscape. "But here? In the arse-end of nowhere?" *Almost on my doorstep.*

Gabriela's smile flickered like fireflies. "I like the heat. It's not so different to Spain."

Viva swallowed a retort and moved around to the front of the rental car. "Is it out of fuel?" Her fingers twitched with the need to fix the ridiculously unsuitable car and get the hell out. Gabriela Mendaro was the last person she wanted to see.

And now, in light of what she'd just learnt from her surgeon, it was doubly bitter.

Gabriela blinked, as if the question was beneath her dignity. "It has half a tank."

Viva checked the dirt road, hoping some station hand would appear in a ute to save her from this discomfort. Of course, the road remained silent and empty. She peered into the engine compartment. What little she knew about fixing cars had been learnt by listening to her younger brother and his friends discussing their latest jalopy and how they might best get it on the road. But maybe this was something simple. She poked the mass of dusty wires with a finger. They remained attached, nothing hanging loose. She found the air filter and tapped it. A puff of dust dislodged. Maybe it was chockers with dust, but really, she hadn't a clue.

Gabriela moved to stand next to her. "It might be the fuel lines. Clogged."

"Possibly. That's not something we can fix here, though. The rental company probably offers breakdown service. Did you call them?"

Gabriela raised her mobile phone. "No signal."

Of course there wouldn't be.

"Where are you heading?" This wasn't the first stranded tourist she'd rescued, although none had been on this dirt track that wound through trees and grassland.

"I think I am maybe one hundred and twenty kilometres from Merringul. I thought I would stay the night there and return to Brisbane tomorrow via Toowoomba."

"More like one hundred and fifty kilometres." Around them, the day was seeping into dusk. Already, the sun touched the top of the range and a lilac haze crept over the landscape. A flock of cockatoos settled into the tree above them, and their raucous cries bombarded Viva's ears. Kangaroos would soon be grazing in the relative cool of evening, leaping across the road with nary a warning. It was not a good time to be driving.

Viva slammed the bonnet shut. "Sorry, I don't have a clue about fixing it. Your best bet is for me to give you a lift to the nearest place where you can call the rental company."

"I don't want to take you out of your way." The words were stilted, but the mellow tones were like warmth and sunshine.

"You're not. The next settlement—indeed the only settlement—along this road is Waggs Pocket, and that's where I'm going."

"What is there?"

"Not much. Couple of dozen houses, general store, fuel if Candace can be bothered opening, and a pub. My parents run the pub," she added.

The puzzled expression on Gabriela's face lifted. "Oh. I didn't realise you were from here."

"Not many people do. Even if you've read my player bio, it just mentions Queensland, no more information than that. You can call the breakdown service from the pub. You won't get a mobile signal before then anyway, and even in town it depends on which way the wind is blowing. Better to use the landline."

"Thank you." Gabriela moved to the boot of the rental car, pulled out a small case, and carried it over to Viva's hatchback.

15

Boxes filled the boot and most of the back seat of the vehicle. "Guess I'm getting my weight training in early," Viva muttered, as she dragged cartons of bottles and foodstuffs to one side to make room for Gabriela's case. She ignored the twinge in her right wrist, the bite of pain as she stretched the joint backwards.

Gabriela moved closer. "Let me help."

"I can do this." Viva's words were curt. "These are heavy."

"I'm stronger than I look." Gabriela pulled on one of the boxes. The flap opened, revealing the dozen bottles of rum inside. "I'm surprised you can play as well as you do if you drink this much."

"I told you; my parents run the pub. I was in Brisbane, so I said I'd pick up their order." Too late the crinkling of Gabriela's eyes gave away the joke.

By moving a few cartons, they were able to jam the case into the corner amongst the paraphernalia for the pub.

Viva lowered herself into the driver's seat. "Got everything? Car locked?"

"Yes, thank you."

The hatchback was not a big car, but Gabriela was not a big woman. Even so, the car seemed cramped with her in the passenger seat. It wasn't that she sprawled. Indeed, she sat neatly, as if she was lineswoman at the Open. Knees together, feet flat on the floor, her elbows tucked in by her sides. It was as if she had been packed up for shipment.

Viva started the engine and pulled away. The hatch rattled over the dirt road, and she turned the radio up to drown out the noise. The road was fading into the darkness, and a mob of kangaroos raised their heads as she passed.

Gabriela gripped the door handle. "Can you slow down a little? You have to watch for wildlife on these roads."

Viva's foot twitched on the accelerator. "I've lived here most of my life. I think I know that."

Something moved in the long grass beside the road, and Gabriela's grip tightened. "Please?"

She *was* going too fast. Viva eased the throttle, using a bend in the road as an excuse. Her gaze swept the road for bounding kangaroos or other wildlife, but she remained acutely aware of the woman in the passenger seat. Gabriela's denim shorts came to mid-thigh, revealing a sweep of olive skin. When her lips tightened and her stare locked fixedly on the road ahead, Viva slowed even more. She wasn't out to terrify her.

Once the road straightened and entered the final steep descent to Waggs Pocket, Viva increased speed again.

Beside her, Gabriela's throat worked as she swallowed hard.

Viva flashed her a glance. "Look, over there are the Bunya Mountains. It's a national park now."

A jerky movement of Gabriela's head, but she didn't glance at the scenery.

"You're not interested?"

Beads of sweat formed on Gabriela's forehead. "It's not that. I get car sick on twisty roads if I'm not the driver."

"Do you want me to stop?"

A quick shake of her head. "No. It's okay." She swallowed again.

"Sorry. You should have said. We're nearly there."

"I'll be okay if I look straight ahead and don't talk."

The temptation to increase speed or throw the little car into the corners was strong, but Viva wasn't that vindictive. She slowed to a sedate pace, turned up the air con, and directed an extra vent in Gabriela's direction.

"Thank you."

The purple light deepened as they descended into Waggs Pocket. *Town* was too kind a word for the scattered houses that spread out around the single crossroads. Viva raised a hand at Tilly, walking her three rescue greyhounds, and again at the Bartlett twins, no doubt up to mischief judging by their sudden guilty expressions. She swung around the rest area by the creek, where the grey nomads pulled up in their motorhomes, and around the back of the pub.

It was good to be home.

Viva jammed on the brakes. The rear car park was full, packed solid with veteran cars, their shiny sides gleaming with the deep rich colours of a bygone era. Jaguars, MGs, and Minis were parked neatly in rows, bonnets all facing out. Her usual spot, at the back of the car park beside the mango tree, was inaccessible. She reversed out and parked on the grass on the other side of the road. Even here, there were a few scattered latecomers.

The minute the car drew to a halt, Gabriela exited. Stretching, she drew deep belly breaths, her gaze on the line of the creek as it wound through the park.

Viva opened the boot. "Grab your case. I'm not going to unload the supplies until I can park closer." Excitement leapt in her stomach. No matter how many times she returned to Waggs Pocket, the pull of home never lessened. She didn't look back as she led the way to the pub, but she heard the snap of a twig and the crunch of gravel behind her.

Chapter 3

EVERY TABLE IN THE BAR was occupied, and the locals at the counter were squashed tight like cockatoos on a railing. Laughter and chatter rose up to the pressed-tin ceiling. Viva squeezed past the mainly grey-haired bunch of people until she could duck under the serving hatch leading behind the bar.

"Darl, I'm so happy to see you." Her mum bustled up and stretched up to press a kiss to Viva's cheek. "I know you've had a long drive and you're tired, but the British Car Club are here. There's only your dad in the kitchen—and you know what *that* means. Would you mind working the bar with Jack so I can do the meals before your father burns the place down?"

"Of course not." She pushed down the longing for a quiet night on the balcony. The British Car Club was a good-natured, enthusiastic mob who came four times each year, puttering along the highway from Brisbane, holding up the traffic for kilometres.

She whirled around to start serving and caught sight of Gabriela, who stood straight as a fencepost on the far side of the bar, taking in the crowd with a bemused expression.

Viva grabbed her mum's arm before she could disappear. "Mum, this is Gabriela. Her car broke down, and I rescued her from the forest road. Can you let her use the phone so she can call breakdown?"

"No worries, darl." Viva's mum advanced on Gabriela. "Come with me, and I'll show you the phone." She paused. "I know you, don't I? You're a friend of Viva's from the tour. I'm sure I've seen you playing."

"She's not a friend," Viva started, but then Jack bore down to sweep her into a hug.

"Sissy. About bloody time!" His grin took the sting from the words. "I hope your arm is strong for pouring beer." His nod indicated the car club people lining the bar.

She followed Jack into the main bar area and looked around. "Who's next?"

Gabriela waited by the bar, eyes straight ahead, resisting the urge to fidget. After the brief introduction, Viva's mother had been interrupted by a customer and had yet to return. At least she appeared friendly, unlike her daughter. Viva's antagonism crackled like sparks from a bushfire. Gabriela moved over into Mrs Jones's line of sight, rested her case between her feet, and waited.

Mrs Jones put a hand on the customer's arm. "I'll see you later, Stan. Right now, I have to see to Viva's friend." She turned to Gabriela. "Come with me, darl." She led the way down a hallway and through a door marked private.

"Come in." She shuffled the papers on the desk into an overflowing pile and put a rock on top. The papers fluttered in the breeze from the overhead fan. "Sit. Do you have the number to call?"

"Yes, thank you." The car rental paperwork was in the front pocket of the case, and she pulled it out.

"Of *course* you have it. You couldn't travel around the world as you do if you weren't organised with paperwork." Viva's mother tilted her head and stared at Gabriela. "I'm trying to place you. Please don't think me rude… Viva doesn't bring many friends home with her. Normally just Michi, her doubles partner. Lovely girl, Michi."

Gabriela unfolded the paperwork and smoothed out the crease. "I'm sorry, I really don't mean to be rude, but would you mind if I called the breakdown service? I don't know how long it will take for them to arrive." Part of her mind wondered when Viva's mum would figure out she was neither a friend nor a player on the tour. She hoped the car would be fixed and she would be on her way before that happened.

"I'm sorry, darl, I should've thought of that. Yes, you call right away, then go and find Viva when you're done."

"Thank you, Mrs Jones. You are too kind."

"Lindy. There's no formality around here. Even if it would be nice at times. I'll leave you to it." Lindy whirled around and was gone, closing the door behind her.

Gabriela glanced around the office. The high-ceilinged room was stifling hot, despite the fan. There were pictures of Viva on the wall: action shots, lifting trophies, one of her and Michi Cleaver during a doubles match, shoulders close together, hands lifted to their mouths to hide their whispered tactics from prying eyes. And, of course, in pride of place was a photo of Viva lifting the US Open trophy high. Gabriela remembered that photo; it had been in every paper. *Aussie girl wins the US Open.* Viva was popular with the press; her outgoing personality, striking good looks, and athletic figure saw to that.

Gabriela searched the desktop for a pen, eventually finding one under a pile of delivery dockets, and called the breakdown service number.

"No worries." The laconic voice on the other end didn't sound concerned. "We can come and get you at the Stockyard Hotel in Waggs Pocket and take you back to your vehicle. How far away is the car?"

"Maybe thirty kilometres. I'm not too sure." The twisty dirt road that Viva had driven with such ferocity had passed in a blur of motion sickness.

"No worries," the operator said again. "We'll be with you before noon tomorrow."

"Tomorrow?" Worry gave her voice an edge, and she drummed the pen on the wooden desk. "The rental company said it was usually within the hour."

"That's within the city, mate. It's different out bush. The driver has to come from Dalby, and that's over an hour away."

"He could still get here tonight. I have nowhere to stay."

"Get the pub to put you up; hotels are obliged to offer rooms to stranded travellers. At least they used to in the good old days."

"They're fully booked." She had no idea if they were or not, but she didn't want to spend more time in Viva's company than she had to. Viva seemed prickly. Gabriela was sure the reason was something past the usual reticence between players and officials. Something was bugging Viva, and Gabriela didn't want to be there when Viva let off steam.

"Sorry, mate, but I can't get the driver out any sooner. Look out for the truck late morning. Now, got a pen? I'll give you the job reference."

She wrote down the number, ended the call, and pressed the heels of her hands into her eyes. What if the hotel really was booked out? The cheery senior crowd occupying the bar didn't look as if they were going anywhere in a hurry, judging by the amount of alcohol they were putting away. Would Viva drive her back to her car and make her sleep in it tonight? Surely not.

Gabriela dropped the pen on the desk before she could snap it in two and left the office. She followed the clatter of pots and the hiss of a fryer to the kitchen and stopped in the doorway.

Dirty dishes stacked up on every surface, and three deep-fryers belched smoke. Lindy stood at a bench as she chopped vegetables with the same ferocity Gabriela had seen in Viva when she pummelled a backhand down the line.

"Put the fish in the second fryer. Turn the oven down, or the beef will be tougher than Jack's hide. Get those chips out before they incinerate. Here." Lindy spun around and deftly did all of the tasks she'd just ordered, while an older man dithered. "Ethan, you chop the salad. I'll do this. I don't know why I keep you around." The wry affection in her voice was obvious.

"Because you love me. Although sometimes I don't know why you do." Ethan turned, and Gabriela caught a glimpse of the same small nose and oval face that Viva had, topped by the same widow's peak. Ethan's face was crinkled into a grin as he ribbed his wife.

He looked at Gabriela. "Can I help you? If you're waiting for your food, we won't be much longer."

Lindy turned too. "That's not a customer; that's Viva's friend." She smiled at Gabriela. "Did you get onto the breakdown people?"

Ethan wiped his hands on a grubby tea towel and shook Gabriela's hand, pumping with great enthusiasm. "Welcome. It's always nice to see Viva's friends. What's this about the car?"

"I did reach them." Gabriela addressed them both, trying to discreetly flex some life back into her fingers after Ethan's grip of steel. "But they cannot come until tomorrow."

"I'm not surprised. There's only one bloke in Dalby to do all the calls. His foot is flat to the boards trying to keep up. Did they give you a time?" Ethan moved over to the chopping board.

"By noon."

"Be surprised if he makes that. We can't do it tonight—the car club has us busy—but maybe by late morning, we could get Jack out to have a look at it. He's pretty handy with a spanner."

"I don't want to give you extra work—"

"Jack loves tinkering with cars. If it's an old banger, there's a good chance he'll get it moving for you."

"It's a rental."

"Then don't let Jack near it." Lindy swung around from the oven, where she was basting roast meat. "If it's under warranty, his bush mechanics will make more trouble than good."

"Mrs Jones—"

"Lindy, remember?"

"Lindy, I was wondering if you have a room for tonight? I can't go anywhere until tomorrow and—"

Lindy was already shaking her head. "We're booked solid. The car club has every room taken, and half of them are camping in the park as well."

"Is there anywhere else here to stay?" Surely, even a tiny place like this would have a B&B. Even if it was a way out of town, maybe someone would give her a lift. Anxiety twisted through her mind at the thought of Viva's face when she learnt Gabriela was still here.

"No. The only other place is Darlene's, and that's booked for the car club as well. I've got a foldaway bed; I'll put it in Viva's room for you."

"Really, no. I don't want to intrude on Viva's space." Worry made her voice sharp and high, curter than she would have liked. There was no way she could share a room with Viva. The antagonism rolled from her in palpable waves. The car ride had been awkward; sharing a room would be fraught with difficulty. For a moment she wished she had never left the ease and anonymity that Brisbane offered.

Lindy pushed the roast back into the oven and closed the door. "Don't argue. Viva will be delighted. I'll do it now."

"Lindy, please, check with Viva first."

23

Something in Gabriela's tone seemed to make Lindy pause. Her gaze raked Gabriela from head to toe. "Have you had a fight?"

"No." Gabriela shifted her weight, resisting the impulse to stand on one leg, something she'd done as a child whenever anyone challenged her. "Not that. But we are not friends; we are just acquaintances on the tour. Your daughter will not be happy if she is forced to share her room with me. It's also highly inappropriate for me to do so. Can you put the foldaway bed in the lounge or somewhere?"

"There's no air con or fan. It'll be unbearably hot."

"I do not mind. I am used to the heat."

"Gabriela, don't argue. I'll do the bed now." And she was gone in a flurry of discarded apron and bustling figure.

Ethan regarded Gabriela with wry amusement. "Has my daughter done something to upset you?" He turned back to the bench and picked up the discarded chopping knife.

"No." Gabriela's sigh gusted into the room. "It's a little more complicated than that." She dreaded seeing Viva's face when Lindy told her where Gabriela was sleeping. And she couldn't—simply couldn't—stay in the same room, no matter what the extenuating circumstances. Even if she melted in the heat, she would have to find somewhere else. Somewhere away from Viva.

Chapter 4

"MUM'S MAKING UP A BED for your girlfriend." Jack smirked as he passed Viva in the tight space behind the bar. "Doubt she'll be using it, though. You could have saved Mum the bother; you know her back is crook."

"What are you talking about?" Viva poured schooners of Classic and set them on the bar. "Eleven sixty, please."

"Her back's been sore since she lifted the kegs in the cellar when Dad was in Brisbane."

Viva took the money from the grey-haired man and whirled around to the till. "Not Mum. I know that. The bit about a girlfriend. I don't have a girlfriend."

"Really?" Jack reached past her and took wine from the fridge. "Mum reckons you're acting strange enough around Gabriela that she must be your girlfriend. She doesn't buy the 'friend' story."

"She's not even a friend."

"You turn up with a tennis player in your car. It's a logical assumption."

Viva turned to the next person waiting. "What can I get you?" And then to Jack. "I barely know her. She's not a player; she's an umpire."

Jack's brow wrinkled as he poured white wine. "What difference does that make? She seems nice. A bit stand-offish, but not a lunatic. Not like the last girl you brought home."

"Chitra's not crazy. Just a little...different."

"Whatever." Jack shrugged. "You say po-tar-to, and I say po-tay-to."

"And umpires can't mix with players. Obviously, we attend a lot of the same functions, stay at the same hotels during tournaments, but even friendships aren't encouraged. An umpire must be impartial. You're not stupid. Not most of the time anyway. You should have figured that out." She snagged two packets of peanuts, added them to the rum and Cokes on the counter, and took the customer's money.

"So why was she in your car?"

"Hers is broken down by the forest boundary. I was the next car past. I could hardly leave her there for the dingoes to feast on. She's calling roadside service. Chances are, she'll be gone soon."

Jack didn't reply, but he nodded to the corner of the bar.

Gabriela stood there stiffly, her gaze following Viva as she darted around behind the bar. One of the locals, Max, seemed to be trying to engage Gabriela in conversation, but she was responding in monosyllables.

Viva sighed. Max was an off-putting sight to those who didn't know him. His bushy hair and greying beard stuck out underneath the most battered and stained stockman's hat found in the district. His enormous hand dwarfed his schooner of beer, and his singlet had holes in it. It was a good week if he'd showered in the last three days. But Max was a sweet bear of a man, who would help anyone. If Gabriela would only listen, he was probably offering to drive her back to her car to see if he could fix it.

Gabriela's smile had a tinge of desperation as she caught Viva's eye.

Viva went over. "Is roadside service coming?"

"Not until tomorrow."

"*Tomorrow!*" Viva bit down on the swearword that also came to mind.

"It's polite not to sound horrified."

"You're right. Sorry. But really, tomorrow… I didn't expect them to be fast, but I did expect them to come tonight."

"Believe me, I could not be happier either." Gabriela's expression was deadpan.

Max touched her arm, and Viva stifled a smile at Gabriela's almost imperceptible shrinking away. "Lemme take you out to your car, missy. I can probably get it going again for you. Me and Jack can fix most things."

"Thank you, but it's a rental. I should wait for roadside service."

"Max is great with cars." Viva gave a sweet smile. "He tuned my hatchback so that it goes a lot faster. You should let him try."

"Faster is not good when you're driving." Gabriela's eyes shot sparks. "Can I talk to you for a moment? Lindy has found me a bed for tonight, but—"

"Can you wait for a bit? We're so busy. Once this lot are eating dinner in thirty minutes or so, I'll be able to stop for a bit." She glanced at Max. "Don't worry about Max; he's harmless, especially if you buy him a beer."

"You watch your lip, Viva." Max grinned from underneath the brim of his battered hat. "One of these days I'll challenge you to a game of that pat-a-cake you call tennis, and we'll see who's harmless then."

"We did play when I was nine. I beat you," she reminded him.

"You could buy me a beer. Make up for the defeat." His smile was sweetly innocent. "One for me and one for your friend."

She grinned and got two beers. "You be nice to Gabriela, or I'll set Jack on you."

Gabriela's annoyed gaze followed her back to the main section the bar. Never mind, Gabriela would get over it. She was in a rural area; she would have to interact with country people.

"Give her the menu," Jack said as he passed. "Mum stops cooking in twenty minutes. You may not like her, but that's no reason for her to starve."

"You think I'm an idiot?" The comment stung. She *had* forgotten about dinner. Including her own. She scooped up a menu and went back to where Gabriela and Max were eyeing each other warily.

"Let me know what you want to eat," she said. "Kitchen closes in twenty minutes."

"Steak is good here." Max stabbed a stubby finger at the item on the menu. "Good beef. Comes from my farm. Unless you're one of those vegetarian type people?"

"No." Gabriela's smile sparkled briefly. "I like a good steak and a glass of red wine. I will take your recommendation, thank you, Max."

"Rib eye steak?" Viva asked. At Gabriela's nod, she said, "How do you like it cooked?"

"Medium rare please."

Viva wrote down the order, added her own, and put it on the peg for the kitchen.

Half an hour later, when the car club was all seated and eating dinner, the crush at the bar eased. Jack pushed Viva towards the kitchen. "Go. Find your dinner and your girlfriend and go and eat on the balcony. Standing room only otherwise."

She gave him a grateful smile. In a fit of guilt for her earlier bad manners towards Gabriela, she poured a glass of one of the better red wines for each of them and took them over to her.

She and Max seemed to be in a good-natured argument about football.

Viva touched her on the arm. "Dinner."

Gabriela took a step away from the bar. "Thanks for the conversation, Max."

"No worries. I might see you at the tennis. I'm always on the pub social club bus to the Brisbane tournament. We've supported Viva every year, since she was in juniors."

"I'll look out for you."

"You won't miss us. Look for a bunch of bright red T-shirts with Stockyard Hotel written on them." Max tipped two fingers to the brim of his battered hat and gave her a grin.

Viva led the way to the kitchen to collect their meals. Eating on the balcony with Gabriela would be awkward, but she would cope. Some polite conversation, a few comments about the upcoming tennis season, a fine steak, a glass of good wine, and then hopefully Gabriela would go off to bed.

Bed. She frowned. Gabriela had mentioned Mum had found her a bed, but belatedly, Viva wondered where. The car club usually took all the rooms. There must have been a cancellation.

She entered the kitchen, coughing as the fine drift of smoke and cooking oil caught at the back of her throat.

Her parents were sitting at the table, eating their usual strange mix of leftover food: a piece of fish, the crusty parts of the lasagne, a slice of roast beef dripping blood that was obviously too rare to serve, and a mix of salad and veggies.

"Your dinners are in the hot cabinet," Lindy said.

"Thanks." Viva loaded a tray with the plates of food, cutlery, glasses of water, and the wine, and with Gabriela following, she headed up the wide staircase.

The east-facing balcony was one of her favourite areas. Her family's living area opened onto it. The sun had set, and a cool evening breeze wafted over, keeping away the mozzies. Viva set the plates on the solid wooden table by the rail. Muted noise and the occasional shriek of laughter drifted up from the bar below, but otherwise the evening belonged to the shrill of cicadas and the occasional chirping gecko.

"That's yours." Viva arranged the cutlery. "Medium rare, as requested."

"Thank you." Gabriela perched on the chair. "You must tell me how much I owe you."

"Nothing. Consider it hospitality for a stranded traveller. And it gave me an excuse to have some wine. My one glass a week."

Gabriela hesitated. A small frown creased her forehead. "I am not allowed to accept a gift from a player."

Viva inclined her head. "Fair point. I apologise—I meant the offer only as a courtesy, nothing more. If you see Mum after dinner, she'll let you know how much."

Gabriela's smile was brief, but her face softened and lost its authoritarian look. "I appreciate the gesture anyway. And I would hate for you to miss your wine. You only have a single glass even in the off-season?"

"Discipline and habits don't fade easily."

Gabriela studied the food. "This looks good. Max really does grow the cattle, yes?"

Viva nodded. "His family has farmed here for generations. Pasture-fed cattle. No feedlots or additives. I credit his beef as part of my good health." She flexed a biceps. "Lean beef, lean muscles."

Gabriela's gaze moved to the street, as if the posturing offended her.

Apparently, Gabriela didn't appreciate her humour. Viva stifled a smile, cut a piece of her own steak, and marshalled her thoughts back into line. It seemed silly to sit in silence as they ate. She glanced across the table, while she thought of an innocuous question. "So, how are you spending your time in Queensland?"

"I rent an apartment in Brisbane from the middle of November until the end of the Brisbane International. Usually six or seven weeks. I have stayed at the same place for years. It's by the river and near the bike path. I walk a lot, cook for myself, catch up on my reading. Mainly just enjoy time alone. It's difficult to do that on tour."

There was a wistfulness in her face that tugged at Viva. "I know what you mean. Strange cities, new faces, and something happening day and night." Viva speared a piece of broccoli. "Sometimes, all I want to do is stay in my room and watch trashy TV, but instead there's someplace I have to be. It must be different for you, though. Umpires keep themselves apart."

"To an extent. We have our own friendships, mainly with other tour officials. Not players, of course; close friendships and intimate relationships are forbidden."

Viva frowned. "Actually forbidden? As in, it's a rule? I thought it was just not encouraged."

"It's in the code of conduct. Rule 8(ii), if I remember correctly."

An imp of mischief sparked, and Viva leant forward. She put down her fork and touched Gabriela on the back of the hand. Her skin was warm. "Even us having dinner together like this would be frowned upon?"

Gabriela's hand twitched under Viva's fingers. "It would." She slid her hand out from underneath Viva's touch. "Our lives are not so different, though. It is...pleasant to talk to someone who understands." She shut her mouth abruptly, as if she regretted the words.

Viva's fingers tingled from the space where Gabriela's skin had been. She picked up her fork again and cut a piece of steak. "According to the International Tennis Federation, I should have left you by the side of the road?"

"Of course not. I've seen you at pre-tournament parties, around tournament grounds, in hotels. We don't have to pretend to be strangers."

Flashes of memory tugged in Viva's mind. Yes, she had seen Gabriela, on the edge of her vision at such places. The officials stayed aloof; they had to. But there was occasionally a brief conversation, a smile, a nod as they passed in a corridor. And she would never forget a certain foot-fault call. Her lips tightened. "Rescue is one thing; dinner is another. I should have left you in the bar to fend for yourself with a toasted sandwich."

Gabriela sipped her wine. "I'm glad you didn't. This is far better. Your parents cook an excellent steak."

"It's the thing they cook best. A fitting accompaniment to my single glass of wine." Somewhere, the polite conversation had gained a familiar warmth. Gabriela was right—they had common ground, shared experiences.

Gabriela swirled the wine in her glass. "Australian wine is nearly as good as Spanish. The reds. Rioja and the Coonawarra." She sipped again, rolling the liquid around in her mouth.

"I'm not going to argue. I don't drink enough wine to be an expert. When…if…I retire, I'm going to start a cellar."

Gabriela's gaze was unnerving. As if she'd seen through the slip to the indecision that churned inside. *If I retire. When.* Her wrist throbbed in sympathy. She ignored it.

"Where will you keep it? Do you have a home somewhere?"

"No." She pushed down the defensiveness. Thirty-two and still living at home. But it was different when most of the year *home* was a suitcase and a procession of hotel rooms. "My base is here, but I've lived away since I left to go to the Australian Institute of Sport."

Gabriela sliced a piece of steak. Fork poised, she asked, "Were you very young? Eight? Nine?"

"No, I was thirteen. Quite old by today's standards."

"But it would still be hard to leave home at thirteen." Gabriela's eyes reflected an understanding.

Viva lowered her own gaze. Of course, Gabriela would know what it was like for tennis kids. She would have umpired junior matches, seen the ambitious parents pushing their offspring, seen the regimented kids from academies doing drills on the practice courts. Maybe, too, she had noticed the little kids watching the top players—hoping, dreaming that one day that would be them.

Viva shook off her introspection. "I was lucky. I could sometimes come home for a weekend, and I was in my own country. Some kids now are halfway across the world away from family. I still got very homesick, though."

"No wonder you like to come home."

"It means my family doesn't get sick of me either."

"Ah, you players are so difficult." Her smile took the sting from the words.

Viva's lips twitched in an answering smile. That was something Jack would say in jest. She studied Gabriela, the cap of brown hair, her olive skin, warm and smooth in the dim overhead light. Her movements were neat and precise as she cut lettuce into small pieces, added a tiny bit of beetroot, and placed it in her mouth. They must have been on the tour at the same time for years, travelling to many of the same countries and cities, but there was always that distance between the players and officials.

31

"Have you been an umpire for long?" Viva asked.

Gabriela smiled, showing even, white teeth. "I did this through college, took some years off to pursue other interests, but I have been a full-time umpire now for over ten years."

That was nearly as long as Viva had been a pro. A strange career, always on the sidelines, never in the spotlight. The same endless travel, but without the possibility of fame and fortune. Viva glanced again. Gabriela had a self-contained air about her. She looked like the sort of person who would be happy with her own company. Although officials often did attend the glamour events around the tour, Viva couldn't remember seeing Gabriela at any of them.

Viva picked a piece of tomato from her salad and ate it. "You must enjoy it."

"Yes. Very much. I have friends on the tour—other officials, much as you must have friends who are players. I love the travel, but by the end of the year, I long for my weeks in Australia."

"You don't go home to Spain?"

"My brother and sister have their own lives. I visit them during the European leg of the tour. That is enough." Gabriela returned her attention to her dinner. "I love them, but we don't have much in common."

Viva pondered Gabriela's response. On the surface, she didn't have much in common with her family anymore, not on a day-to-day basis, but she couldn't imagine spending a month off in a foreign country rather than rushing home to Waggs Pocket.

Gabriela smiled. "You are thinking it strange I'm not in Europe right now, yes?"

"Not everyone is close to their family."

"They are busy people with children that are the focus of their lives." She shrugged. "That is not unusual. I feel in the way when I visit, as if I'm keeping them from what is important. So I keep the visits short. It works better for all of us that way."

"Feel free to adopt Jack as your brother," Viva joked.

Gabriela smiled. "I have met a lot worse. But you can keep him."

Viva smeared mustard on her steak. Her gaydar was pinging. Maybe Gabriela had a girlfriend in Brisbane; that would be one reason she kept coming back. But if so, why was she out touring the backblocks alone?

A shout of laughter drifted up from the bar below, and outside a single car drove slowly along the road, but otherwise there was small-town quiet. Viva concentrated on her food. It was easier than thinking about the woman opposite her. For all that they mingled in similar circles, Gabriela was right. Players and officials just didn't mix. She hadn't realised there was an actual ruling against it, though. But it made sense. Could you make a match call against a partner or close friend, knowing it might cost them the match? Often not just a match, but prize money, even a tennis ranking. Would you hesitate to call a ball out in those circumstances? Of course, the larger tournaments had Hawk-Eye, the computer system used to take the guesswork out of line calls, but smaller tournaments often didn't have that backup. Hawk-Eye didn't confirm a foot-fault call either—that was purely down to an official.

Viva set her jaw and sliced a piece of her steak. Her US Open loss bubbled to the forefront of her mind once more. What if she and Gabriela had been friends when Gabriela had made the foot-fault calls against her? Would it have affected their friendship? Viva sipped from her water glass. Maybe. Maybe not. She could second-guess that one all night. But that loss, one of the most disappointing of her career, was caused in no small part by the two foot-fault calls made by a lineswoman.

That lineswoman now sat opposite her, sharing a meal with her, and she was surprisingly easy company. Attractive company too, with her thick hair in a short bob, warm brown eyes, and serious face.

No. Don't even think it, Viva.

She put her knife and fork down with a sigh. "I'll have to run an extra couple of kilometres tomorrow."

Gabriela took a final mouthful and put her cutlery together neat as tram tracks. "I should come with you after that meal."

Viva was silent. If it had been anyone else, she would have offered to take them. Her mother's words tumbled into her head: *Be polite, Viva. You don't have to like someone, but you don't need to be rude to them.* Her mother's rule, honed by many years of working in hospitality.

Viva took a sip of her wine. "Five a.m. sharp. Be ready out front." Her mother would be proud of her. "What room are you in? I can wake you if you want."

Gabriela's gaze slid away, down to the quiet road.

A dog sniffed tyres outside the hotel, and over in the camping area, a drift of laughter came in on the night breeze.

"You're lucky to have a room." Viva took a mouthful of water, to eke out the pleasure of the wine. "I would have thought the car club had them booked."

"They did." Gabriela picked at the napkin crumpled up in front of her.

"Cancellation, then."

"No. You have not talked to your mother?"

"I've been busy in the bar." She frowned. What had changed in the last couple of minutes? Gabriela was as jumpy as a kangaroo trapped in a pen.

"There are no rooms. Your mother is giving me a fold-out bed." Gabriela wouldn't meet her eyes.

"Where's she putting it?" She knew the answer from Gabriela's tight posture. "She's put it in my room, hasn't she?"

"I am sorry. I tried to stop her. She thinks we are friends from the tour."

"It's easy. You say, 'Viva's not my friend. She won't want me sleeping in her room.'" The chill in her voice could have blown from Antarctica. Damn her mother.

"I tried. She made the assumption and hurried out."

"I like my space. I'd prefer you weren't in it."

"And I would prefer not to be in it." Dark eyes flashed ire, even in the dim light. "It is more than that too. It is in the code of conduct: players and officials must not share a room during tournaments. I do not wish to push my luck outside of that. Help me carry the bed out here, and I will be out of your way."

"You'll be eaten alive by mosquitoes. Once the breeze drops, they'll be out in swarms."

"Then I will sleep in the corridor."

"It's narrow. You'll have guests tripping over you."

"In the bar."

"Illegal."

Gabriela tossed up her hands. "There must be somewhere. Otherwise, I will think you want me to sleep in your room."

"I'd like that like a bad foot-fault call." The words snapped out, and Viva threw her napkin on the table.

Gabriela's lips twisted. "You are dwelling on some supposedly bad call I gave you? Really? You must get bad calls all the time. It's part of the game. You take it and move on."

"Not this one."

Gabriela picked up her wine. "Which one?"

"You don't know?"

"I'm a silver badge umpire. I work dozens of tournaments. Hundreds of matches a year. I do not remember each one."

"I do."

Gabriela seemed to consider it, her head tilted to one side. "So this is why you have been aloof."

Viva stared out across the landscape to where the valley sides rose from the floor, the layered eucalypts silver in the moonlight. "You could say that."

"It must have been contentious. I umpire many matches."

"You weren't the umpire. You were a linesperson that day."

Gabriela propped her chin on her hand. The low light made the furrows in her forehead more pronounced as she frowned. "The US Open last year? Your two foot-faults?"

"I was defending my title. My grand slam title. Your calls were wrong. I've viewed the footage since. The first one maybe was right. The second one was almost certainly incorrect. It was match point. Your bad call knocked me out of the tournament."

Gabriela was silent. Then she said, "I cannot remember the specifics of each and every call—how could I, any more than you can remember every backhand down the line? But you need to remember two things: first, I was doing my job to the best of my ability. Obviously, the chair umpire either agreed with that call or trusted my judgement. And secondly, I did not lose that match for you. *You* lost the match. I was not the one with the racquet in my hand." She stood and picked up her plate. "This is exactly why players and umpires need to keep their distance. Thank you for the meal. I also enjoyed the company greatly up until five minutes ago. I will go and find your mother and ask her to put the camp bed anywhere at all, except in your room."

She exited, head held high, shoulders as rigid as a junior in her first tournament.

Viva watched her go. She swallowed and stared at her own plate. The remaining piece of steak now held all the appeal of a packing crate, and the food she'd already eaten sat heavy in her gut. She didn't need anyone to tell her she had behaved badly. Her own sense of self was screaming at her right now. The call wasn't correct, but she shouldn't have attacked Gabriela like that, especially not under her parents' roof.

She picked up her plate and took it down to the kitchen by the backstairs, which Gabriela wouldn't have used.

Chapter 5

GABRIELA FOUND LINDY AND ETHAN relaxing with a cup of tea in a corner of the pub dining room. The car club people had vacated and were kicking up their heels in the bar. Jack appeared to be working the bar by himself; no doubt he would grab Viva to assist when she came down.

Lindy waved her over. "Sit down, darl. It's always nice to talk to some of Viva's friends."

Gabriela approached and grasped the back of a vacant chair with both hands. "Mrs Jones—Lindy—I need to clear up something. Viva and I are not friends. We are both on the tour, yes, but—"

Lindy's eyes twinkled with kindness. "You don't need to go on. I understand if you want to keep your relationship under wraps. Over the years, Viva has brought a couple of girlfriends to visit us, and it's been the same every time. She's told you about Chitra? Such a lovely girl, but—"

"Lindy, please. It's not that."

Something in her tone must have alerted Ethan, as he squeezed his wife's hand.

It was unnerving, having two pairs of eyes staring fixedly at her, but Gabriela continued. "I'm an official, not a player. Officials and players aren't supposed to mix. So, while I know Viva from the tour, we are not friends. Certainly not girlfriends."

"Surely the powers-that-be couldn't take issue with you staying here?" Ethan said. "You didn't plan for your car to break down."

"It's more than that." She gripped the back of the chair for support. "Viva dislikes me as I was the lineswoman who called her foot-faults in the US Open last year. Please, is there anywhere else you can set up the camp bed other than Viva's room?"

Lindy and Ethan exchanged a worried glance. "We're full. And it's a health and safety thing. We can't put a temporary bed in a public area."

"How about the balcony? Isn't that your private space?"

"Yes, but…" Ethan's forehead wrinkled. "No air conditioning. Mosquitoes."

"I will be fine. Please. Viva was kind enough to rescue me. I don't want to make it harder for her than it already is." The thought of a hot balcony teeming with mosquitoes was bad, but the prospect of staying in Viva's room was far worse. Her self-confidence withered at the thought of Viva's coldness.

Lindy set her lips tightly. "That daughter of ours needs a lesson in manners."

"No, please. I understand. Don't say anything to her. If I could ask one of you to move the camp bed so that I do not have to go into her room, it will be okay." It had been okay. Until Viva had found out about the sleeping arrangements, dinner had been pleasant. More than pleasant—enjoyable. The sort of dinner she would have with a friend. And seeing Viva across the small table had been more than pleasant too. There was never time to really study any of the players on the tour. It was all about the game, about balls and line calls, double-bounces and foot-faults. Seldom did Gabriela stop to consider the player as a person. She had tonight. Briefly, Viva had been a person rather than a player. An attractive player at that. Chestnut hair, blue eyes, and tanned skin. Viva crackled with life, as if the energy in her body was barely contained, and she moved with the grace and strength of a professional athlete.

She cleared her throat, directing her attention back to Lindy and Ethan. "Tomorrow, the car will be fixed, and I will be gone. Now, what do I owe you for my meal?"

"Nothing. Absolutely nothing. It's our pleasure."

Gabriela pulled out her embroidered purse and took out two twenties. "Will this cover it? The steak was delicious."

Ethan stood and took her hand in a firm grip, closing her fist over the money. "We won't take it, but we thank you for offering. Now, why don't you sit and chat with us while we finish our cuppa, and then I'll move the bed."

⊷⊷⊷⧁⊶⊶⊶

Whoever said senior citizens went to bed early had obviously never met the British Car Club. The bar had been busy right up to closing time at eleven, and then Viva helped Jack clean up. It was nearly midnight when she climbed the creaky stairs to her room. Her mum had told her that the camp bed had been removed from her room at Gabriela's request. Her mother had also said she was ashamed of Viva's rudeness. No matter that Gabriela was an umpire, she was still a stranded visitor and, as such, deserved a friendly approach, not the cold war.

Viva's room opened to the balcony. She closed the door and turned on the air con. A quick glance out to the balcony showed her the camp bed set up near the railing, Gabriela's humped shape underneath the sheet. The ceiling fan wasn't going—maybe Gabriela hadn't found the switch. Viva padded out to the corridor and turned it on. That would stir the air and make it more bearable.

The air con cooled her room, but even though it was late, she tossed and turned. The earlier part of her day pushed into her head. The meetings with her coach, her physiotherapist, and with Dr Jacobwitz. Especially him.

"It's been eight months since the surgery, Viva." His gravelly voice echoed in her head. "You need to consider this is as good as it gets."

"No. There must be something else you can do."

He was shaking his head before the sentence was finished. "I can't, no. But I can write you a referral to Dr Singh. He works with a lot of athletes. Let him give you a second opinion."

She nodded, and the groundswell of panic pushed down again. Dr Singh would be able to do something. He must be able to.

"I'll send him your scans along with a short report, and I'll call you as soon as he has an opening. Would you be able to take a cancellation?"

She nodded, unsure if any words would get past the thickness in her throat. She took the prescription for anti-inflammatories that he held out and forced out the words of thanks.

39

And then she'd driven home to Waggs Pocket, needing the solace that her parents and her home could offer. She hadn't thought about that conversation all evening. Gabriela had pushed it out of her head. An image of Gabriela's slow smile across the dinner table intruded. Viva turned over and kicked the sheet away. For a while, she'd managed to forget that Gabriela had done her a great wrong. In the moments of conversation, when she'd seen Gabriela's long, dark eyelashes fan down over her warm, brown eyes, dinner had been relaxing.

Until it all unwound.

Viva sat up and turned on the bedside light. Despite the late hour, she couldn't sleep. She grabbed a thriller from the nightstand. Maybe reading for a bit would help.

<hr />

"Fuel injectors are shot. Totally clogged with dust. Must be a leak in the line. Did you smell petrol as you drove?" The service man slammed the bonnet of the rental car. "Bloody hot out here and bloody quiet. Lucky for you someone came along."

"Maybe a bit of a petrol smell. I assumed it was evaporation in the heat." Gabriela moved out from the scant shade of a gum tree. "Can you fix it?"

"Nah. Have to take it to Dalby to a mechanic. He'll have to strip it back. I'll take you back to that pub." He slapped a sticker on the windscreen. "At least you don't need to wait here. And I expect you'll want to call the rental place about a replacement car."

Gabriela climbed back into the ute. "Can you take me to the nearest town instead?"

The service man's face creased. "I'm sorry, love, but I've another half dozen call outs. I won't be back at the depot until this evening."

"What about the tow truck?"

He shrugged. "Maybe. Maybe not. But that would be to Dalby. Is that where you were going?"

"I was touring around, but with the lost time I now need to get back to Brisbane."

"He won't take you there. That's a three-hour drive. You'd be better off waiting for the replacement vehicle. Although, I dunno. They can take a couple of days to deliver to out-of-the-way places. If you need to get to

Brissie in a hurry, try asking in the pub. Maybe someone there could give you a lift."

The car club. Maybe she could hitch a ride in a vintage British car. That would turn this whole uncomfortable experience into something better.

But when Gabriela returned to the pub, the only vehicles in the parking lot were Viva's sporty VW and a couple of nondescript vehicles.

Gabriela found Lindy upstairs in one of the guestrooms, stripping the bed.

Lindy straightened. "Any luck?"

Gabriela bent to pull the sheet out on the other side from Lindy. "Unfortunately, no. The car needs a tow truck, and I cannot get a lift to Brisbane. Do you know of anyone driving there today? I am going to the theatre tonight; I would hate to waste the ticket. Otherwise, I will have to wait for the rental agency to deliver another car."

Lindy pursed her lips, gathering the dirty sheet and dropping it in a laundry bag at her feet. "Freddie's going later, but you'd need to be desperate." She bent to push a stray corner of the sheet into the bag. "Viva's driving there today, though. She has an appointment late this afternoon. They rang her about a cancellation. She has an apartment in Brisbane, so she'll stay over. Nice place by the river." Lindy straightened as she added, "I'll ask her if she'll give you a lift, if you want." Her tone was offhand.

Gabriela considered. Brave the unknown Freddie, share a small car with Viva for a few hours and then be out of her life once more, or stay here for another day? Viva would be gone, and her family was pleasant, but she'd been looking forward to the theatre tonight.

"I will ask Viva. I'm a big girl." She grinned to take the sting from the words.

"Ask me what?" Viva's lean and tanned body appeared in the doorway, her thick ponytail lightly swinging.

"Gabriela's car can't be fixed. It needs a tow truck. She's going to ask Freddie for a lift to Brisbane. Excuse me." Lindy gathered the linen and slid past Viva in the doorway and down the corridor.

"Freddie? Really? You'll be lucky to get there in one piece or in the next few days. Freddie has relatives scattered over half of Queensland. Any trip he takes involves a detour to visit at least a couple of them."

Gabriela rounded the bed. "Lindy said you are going today. Would it be possible for you to give me a ride?"

"Really, Gabriela." Lindy's voice wafted from the corridor. "You don't need to be so formal. My daughter will be delighted."

Briefly, Viva's lips pressed tight. "No worries. If you can be ready to leave in an hour."

"That is fine. Thank you."

Viva inclined her head as if she were royalty and stood aside to let her pass.

Gabriela found her sports bag where she'd left it on the balcony and threw in her few items. She scrunched the light singlet and running shorts. With luck, she would be back in Brisbane in time for a run along the river path before the theatre.

———— ⋈ ————

Viva changed gear with a roar, sweeping the hatchback around a tight bend. Out of the corner of her eye, she saw Gabriela's hand tighten on the armrest. Her olive skin appeared sallow as she swallowed convulsively. Guilt tossed in Viva's chest. It would help no one if Gabriela threw up in her car, and it seemed she would rather be sick than ask Viva to slow down. She eased the throttle and kept a saner pace to the highway. She rotated her shoulders, trying to ease the tension, but every glance at Gabriela in the passenger seat had her tightening up as if it were match point. Viva cranked the radio higher and tapped her fingers along with the beat.

The straight highway made for easy driving, but it wasn't until the outskirts of Brisbane when the traffic built up that Viva spoke.

"Where can I drop you?"

Gabriela's slim shoulders moved in a swift shrug. "I'm going to West End. But any train station will be fine."

"That's okay. I'm going to Wickham Terrace. If you don't mind a walk, I can drop you on the north side of the Go Between Bridge and you can walk across the river."

"That would be good. Thank you." She inclined her head stiffly at Viva. "Lindy said you had an apartment near the river. Is that on Wickham Terrace?"

"No. It's at South Bank, not so far from West End. I have an appointment on Wickham Terrace today."

Gabriela scrunched her forehead. "Wickham Terrace is where the doctors are, yes? You had a wrist injury, if I remember correctly. You were out for part of this year?"

"Make that most of this year. I haven't played a match since April." She flashed a sideways glance. "You obviously missed me if you noticed I was gone."

Gabriela's cheeks flushed pink. "I noticed your absence, of course, but I had not realised it was so long. I hope your wrist is improving."

"It is." The words snapped into the car interior, and Viva changed down a gear and accelerated through an amber light. A car waiting to turn right blared its horn. "The season's over now, but I'll be back in the new year at the tournament here in Brisbane."

"No doubt we will run into each other there, then."

Viva pulled into a bus stop, ignoring the No Standing sign. "This is as close as I can get for you. If I take the bridge, it'll take me too long to get back. I'd be late for my appointment."

"This is good, thank you. I will enjoy the walk."

Viva gave a quick smile. "No worries. I'll see you around."

"Thank you for the ride. And also for stopping for me yesterday. I appreciate it." Gabriela exited the car and slung her small bag over one shoulder.

Viva could barely hear the stilted words over the roar of the traffic.

"Please also thank your parents for their hospitality."

"I will." A bus pulled in behind with a whoosh of brakes. "I have to move. See you."

She accelerated off. In the rear vision mirror, she saw Gabriela's slight figure step back to allow people to board the bus and then turn in the direction of the bridge. Viva let out her breath in a long sigh. The car seemed big and empty without Gabriela's still figure sitting neatly in the passenger seat. It had been a strange distraction, made stranger by the fact that her parents had seemed to take to her. Her parents had been her compass for behaviour over the years. They hadn't had a problem with being pleasant to Gabriela, despite her bad foot-fault call. No one had, it seemed, apart from her. Was it fair of her to blame Gabriela? She slowed to let a driver out in front of her. Maybe not.

Viva put Gabriela out of her mind. Right now, the specialist's appointment loomed large.

Chapter 6

"Hmmm. Tell me if this is sore." Dr Singh pressed on the tendon with his thumb.

"Yes." With an effort, Viva stilled the instinctive jerk away from the pain.

"And this?" He pressed again on a different spot.

Pain bloomed, and Viva bit her lip. "Yes, but not as bad."

Dr Singh let go of her wrist. "Extend your hand back as far as it can go." He pressed again.

This time, Viva couldn't supress the gasp.

He laid her wrist gently down on the desk between them and turned his computer screen so that she could see. "It's not good news, I'm afraid. While your previous surgery was successful—up to a point—you are once again accumulating fluid in the tendon sheath. The repair is holding, but the scans show a thickening, most likely inflammatory."

"But it was fine. It seemed to be healing well."

Dr Singh peered at her over his glasses. "And how often were you playing when it was healing well?" His tone was kind. "During the recovery period, yes, there would be a definite improvement. But now you're back to a more intensive training regime, your wrist is battling to cope."

"Does this mean I need more surgery? The Brisbane International starts in a month. I need to be fit for that."

"I'm afraid surgery won't help, not in the long term." He pointed to his computer screen. "See here and here and here? Those areas are thickened—

nodules if you like. The tendon is so ropey and uneven that it's weak. There are no good anchor points for any further repair."

"Injections, grafts—"

"Ms Jones, they are not going to help you. Not in the long term."

"Then what can be done?"

"Cortisone injections. Analgesia. But this wrist is on borrowed time as far as playing professional tennis goes."

Her throat closed over, and instant tears sprang into her eyes. Everything she'd dreaded, put into words. She blinked fast to clear the moisture. "I'll seek a second opinion." Was that really her voice, so small, so defeated?

He shrugged. "Your choice. But may I remind you, I *am* your second opinion. Your usual specialist referred you to me." His voice softened. "I realise this is not what you want to hear, but I suggest you take steps towards winding up your playing career."

A cold, hard lump settled in Viva's chest. "That's it? I'm history?"

He smiled slightly. "Not history, Ms Jones. I'm not saying you can't play again. With care, regular physiotherapy, cortisone, and periods of rest, you will be able to play at a lower level. Coaching, exhibition matches, that sort of thing. I don't foresee any major problems if you are careful. But playing constantly on the tour... I would not recommend it. Worst case scenario, the tendon could degrade to the point where it compromises the use of your wrist in everyday life, or it could snap, and that would be extremely difficult to repair. You're only—" he shuffled papers in her file "—thirty-two. You have a long life ahead of you, all being well."

"But the US Open... If I can get over this, I could have a real shot at it this year. Or another grand slam."

"I'm sorry, I really am, but I don't think that's likely. As it stands now, your wrist could probably take a few rounds of high-level matches, but not the constant play over two weeks required to get you to the final of a grand slam. That's if you make it to September injury-free." He closed her file, the finality of the manila folder closing on her medical history signifying the end of the consultation. "Take some time to think about it."

"Doubles. What about doubles? That's easier on the body. Could I do that?" Even in her own ears her voice had the tinge of desperation. "I can't give up professional tennis entirely. I just can't." She pressed the heels of her hands into her eye sockets and bowed her head so that she didn't have to face the doctor as he shot down the last of her dreams.

He sighed. "Yes, doubles would be better. But not a heavy schedule."

"Thank you, Doctor." She stood. There was no reason to prolong the agony of her life falling around her feet.

Dr Singh touched her briefly on the shoulder. "Good luck. If you intend to play next month, you'll need to call Dr Jacobwitz to set up that injection. But you'll need to rest the wrist completely for a few days afterwards, so take that into account."

She left, past the receptionist, and into the hall. She stabbed the lift button with a finger, but when the doors didn't open immediately, she marched off to the stairwell. The echoing concrete flights of stairs were drab and austere enough to match her mood. Viva swallowed and stood still on the landing, hands clenching the rail. Her wrist twinged. "Fuck!" she screamed to the stairwell. "Fuck, fuck, fuck, fuck." The words echoed back to her, and she clenched her teeth at the futility of it all and stared at her hands until her mental conditioning kicked in and the threatening tears receded.

The street was busy when she exited. It was rush hour and traffic was building, the pavements jammed with office workers hurrying for trains. She retrieved her car and joined the line of traffic fighting its way across the river to South Bank. Her route took her through the fashionable suburb of West End, its streets lined with restaurants and bars, trendy shops and street art. Plenty of people enjoyed a city life and an office job. They could have dinner and drinks with friends without watching every mouthful to ensure they got a good amount of protein or carbs. They could even enjoy more than a single glass of wine a week. Maybe that was her future.

Or she could work with her parents in the pub. Live a quiet country life, working bar, cooking chips, preparing salads. Maybe people would come into the pub, see her behind the bar, and say, "Didn't you used to play tennis? Weren't you famous once?"

Viva's jaw ached with the effort of holding back a scream of frustration. Her eyes burned with tears she would not shed. She pounded the steering wheel as the car in front slowed to a stop at a light that had barely flicked to amber. As the car idled, she stared up at the apartment blocks around her.

Gabriela rented one of these. What did she do in the evenings? She didn't seem the type to stay in and stare at the TV.

The traffic moved, and a few minutes later she pulled into the underground parking of her apartment block.

When she opened the rear door of her car, an unfamiliar sports bag on the floor behind the front seats caught her attention. Viva frowned. It must belong to Gabriela. She picked it up and looked inside. Sure enough, there was a pair of running shoes and sports clothes in a brand that was not her sponsor's. She bit her lip. Soon she would have no sponsorship.

Viva left the bag on the rear seat. She would have to find a way to return it to Gabriela.

⟶ ⋄⟨⋄⟩ ⟶

Viva was at the courts at six the next morning. When Deepak arrived an hour later, she was slamming returns from the ball machine, hitting the lines with laser accuracy. Her back prickled from his intent gaze boring into her. She glanced over her shoulder to where he stood quietly at the back of the court. She drilled a ball down the line with extra ferocity. That would show him she wasn't tennis history just yet.

Deepak waited until the machine ran out of balls before coming over to her. "Good. I see you're taking the ball on the rise as we talked about."

Viva pushed a damp tendril of hair from her face. "It's easy enough with the machine. When it's Inez or Alina on the other side of the net, it's a different story."

Deepak grunted. "Inez plays pat-a-cake and waits for you to make a mistake. Alina is all strength and no finesse."

"Alina has beaten me the last three times we've played. She'll be seeded in the top five at the Brisbane International. I'll be lucky to be seeded at all." She bounced the final ball and sent it sailing over the fence to the park beyond. "I'm lucky they didn't make me play qualifiers to make the main draw." She couldn't quite keep the tremble from her voice.

Deepak moved to stand in front of her and prised her fingers from the racquet. He laid the racquet carefully on the ground and took her balled fist in his hand. He was gentle as he turned it palm up and loosened her fingers. The top of his balding head glistened in the early-morning sunshine as he

47

bent over her hand, as intent as any palm reader. His brown fingers moved carefully over her palm to her wrist. He pressed lightly.

She gasped as a streak of pain shot from her wrist into her forearm, and she jerked back from Deepak's grasp.

Deepak let go. "Come sit with me." He indicated the players' bench, still in shade.

Viva sat, picking her bottle from the ground and taking a long drink. Her wrist throbbed in time with her pulse. She twirled the bottle in her hands. Deepak would wait for her to speak first. It was a measure of their player-coach relationship that he always listened to what she had to say before weighing in. But this time, the words she should say eluded her.

Deepak cleared his throat. "You can start with the medical appointment yesterday."

She shot a glance at him from under lowered brows. Six years, he'd been her coach. A long time in the fickle world of pro tennis. They knew and respected one another. Were friends even.

"I saw a second specialist yesterday. Dr Singh supported what Dr Jacobwitz had told me: I need to retire." Saying it out loud made it more real. Viva dropped her head into her hands, unwilling to see the sympathy in Deepak's expression.

"Okay. When?"

She shot him a glance. "Is that all you have to say?"

"Viva, I know you as well as anyone. I know what this means to you."

"You can't possibly."

"Can't I? I played professionally too. I wasn't as successful as you, but that doesn't mean I felt it any less intensely when my knee took me away from the game."

"I'm sorry. That was thoughtless of me." She lifted her head again and observed him—his keen, kind eyes that saw through her frustration and anger. She dragged a breath, held it, then released it in a gust. "Soon. Now. My tendon is held together with spit and fairy dust, and that may evaporate at midnight or with a particularly hard-to-reach backhand."

"Is that the medical explanation?"

"It should be."

When the silence stretched too long, Deepak asked, "So you're announcing your retirement?"

She dropped her gaze down to her lap. "I don't think I'm ready to let go. Tennis has been my life since I was seven. It's a part of me. Here." She looked him in the eye once more and struck her chest with a clenched fist. "It's in my heart. My soul. I've given so much of my life to it, and I wouldn't change a thing. I *love* it, Deepak. My head knows I need to retire. My heart is ignoring that."

"You need to consider your health." He picked his words slowly. "If you play on another six months, you'll reach this point again, only your wrist will be worse."

"I know you're right. But I just can't make that decision yet. I need time." Tears sprang into her eyes, and she dashed them away with the back of her wrist. "I can't let go. Not yet."

"Then don't announce your retirement. Play a few tournaments, see how you go. Withdraw from a match if your wrist gives you trouble. Gradually ease your way out of tennis."

His concerned face was blurry through her tears. "That would be worse. Gradually fading away, becoming a nobody."

Deepak was silent. This was how he was, his silence letting her solve a problem for herself.

Viva turned her racquet over and over in her hand. The familiar feel of it was comforting. "I could keep playing doubles. I owe that to Michi. I can't leave her without a partner."

"She's been partnered with Paige during the eight months of your absence."

"You, then. If I retire immediately, I'm leaving you in the lurch."

"Thank you for the thought, my friend. But you need to put yourself and your health first." He hesitated. "I've thought about what I'd do when this day came. I've had offers in the past."

She nodded.

"If you retire, I'll take a break, and then I'll take up the offer of my oh-so-persistent friend to join him in his tennis academy in Florida."

"You hate the humidity."

"I'll manage. I'm here in Brisbane right now, aren't I? Ninety-eight percent humidity, they said on the radio this morning."

"You sound like you're trying to talk me into retirement." Her attempt at a laugh fell stonily between them.

"I'm not. If you keep playing, I'll keep coaching you. But you need to consider your health into the future. There's a lot of life in front of you, and it would be good to have the full use of your right hand."

Viva stared at the park outside the court. A mother jogged by with her baby in a stroller. A dog chased a Frisbee. Two middle-aged ladies power-walked their way along the path, their bright hijabs fluttering on their shoulders. A toddler chased a man, giggling as the man pretended to fall so that the boy could catch him. Everyday life was out there, beyond the chain-link fence.

She surged to her feet and picked up her racquet. "I think I need some more drills at the net."

Deepak rose and took off his tracksuit jacket. "You do. Your footwork is getting sluggish."

Her wrist throbbed. Deepak had called a halt after two hours of drills, but she'd set her jaw and said she was fine, ignoring the worry crease between his eyes.

Now she sat on the balcony of her apartment, a glass of water by her side. Cold stole into her wrist from the icepack taped to it, but it wasn't sufficient to mute the throbbing. Careful not to dislodge the pack, she went inside to look for painkillers. Her mobile rang as she was trying, awkwardly, to unscrew the lid with one hand. The caller ID showed it was her mother.

"Hi, Mum," Viva took the painkillers and the phone and went back outside. She hit the button for speaker and settled back in the chair.

"Darl, how are you? Are you at your apartment?"

"Yeah. Not long home."

"How was your day? How's Deepak?"

"Deepak's good. Same as ever. How's things at home?"

"Busy tonight, but a bit quiet generally. Mid-week, you know. Jack and your dad are thinking of painting the dining room tomorrow."

"Please tell me Jack's not picking the colour."

"His taste isn't that bad." Lindy's amusement echoed down the line. "You have to admit the lilac he picked for the bar looks fine."

"Except it wasn't lilac when he picked it. It was royal purple. It took three coats of white emulsion before it stopped looking like a brothel."

"I won't ask how you know what a brothel looks like."

"I don't, but Jack might."

"Genevieve Elizabeth Adelaide Jones! You will apologise to your brother for that remark."

"Not if you don't tell him I said it. Anyway, how's Dad?"

"Good. There's a couple of grey nomads from Melbourne in the campground, and one of them fancies herself as an artist. She asked your dad to sit for his portrait."

"Is it any good?"

"I've already told your father we won't be hanging it in the public bar."

Viva chuckled, and then the conversation halted. Her mother's expectations hung in the silence. Viva bit her lip. As always, her mother knew when Viva wanted to talk, without her saying a word. It had been the same when eleven-year-old Viva had come home in shame having got double detention for spraying graffiti on the school bike shed. When twelve-year-old Viva had said she wanted to take up the offer to train at the Institute of Sport in Canberra. And when sixteen-year-old Viva had said she liked girls. *Really* liked girls. Her mother had said the word Viva had been too tremulous to voice out loud.

"You're a lesbian?"

Viva had nodded, mute.

"We know, darling. We've known for a long, long time." Her mother's hug had pushed away Viva's nervousness, far better than any words.

Now her mother's silence washed wordless reassurance over the line.

"Mum... I saw Dr Singh today."

"About your wrist?"

"Yes." Viva bit her lip. "He says I should retire."

"And what do you want?"

"To keep playing. To win another grand slam."

The swell of voices from the bar came over the line. Laughter. The rattle of the glass washer.

"Did you practice today?" There was no inflection in her mother's voice.

"Yes. Two hours of net drill with Deepak."

"How's your wrist now?"

"It hurts," she said in a small voice. "A lot."

"Can you get a second opinion?"

"Dr Singh *was* the second opinion." Her voice was soft. "I wish you were here with me."

"Is there anyone in Brisbane to talk to? Has Michi arrived yet?"

"She's still in Colorado."

"Deepak?"

"He thinks I should retire. He hasn't said it in as many words, but I know what he's thinking."

"Come home tomorrow."

"I can't. Practice."

Her mother's silence filled the line until she cleared her throat.

Any second now, her mother would agree with Dr Singh, with Deepak. Viva wasn't sure she could stand to hear the same words a third time. "So, what else is happening?" She put an artificial gaiety in her voice.

"Nothing much. Oh… Your friend Gabriela called."

"She's not my friend."

"She asked if she'd left a sports bag here. I took a look, and there's no sign of it. Navy blue, she said, with a pale blue stripe. She said it might be in your car, so I gave her your mobile number. I hope you don't mind."

"It's here. I found it after she'd gone."

"She said she'll call. Maybe you could talk to her. After all, she's on the tour. She'd understand." Her mother's voice held an uncharacteristic diffidence.

"I've already told you; she's not a friend. Players and officials are not allowed to socialise."

"This is different, though, isn't it?" The words "when you retire" hung in the air unsaid.

A crash and then the sound of raised voices filtered through the line.

"I have to go. Sounds like a fight. Call me back shortly if you want to talk more. I love you, Viva."

"Love you too, Mum."

Viva put down the phone and picked up her water. The ice had melted. She went back to the kitchen for more and opened the fridge. Dinner. The usual, she supposed. Lean meat, lots of salad, and a bowl of pasta. She closed the fridge and picked up the leaflet that had been in her mailbox that morning. A Thai restaurant home delivery service. That was what she actually wanted to eat: red curry chicken, a huge serving of pad thai, and maybe some fried tofu. If Michi were here, staying in her spare room, hogging the bathroom to style her wild mane of pink hair, they would probably go out to eat. Michi would nudge her under the table to point out cute girls for Viva and cute boys and girls for herself. They would drink more than a glass of wine, a fact that Viva would lie about to her fitness and nutrition coach the next morning. Michi and she would come home way too late, lie on the floor, and catch up with their lives.

But Michi was still in Denver and wasn't due to arrive in Australia until the week before Christmas. It was the middle of the night in Colorado. She couldn't call.

There was no one else to talk to. No one on the tour she could trust one hundred percent not to spread the news of her possible retirement. Her parents were busy, and she had lost contact with most of the friends from her old life. Her Australian life, B.T.—Before Tour.

She opened the fridge again and took out cold chicken and salad.

Chapter 7

GABRIELA GLANCED AT HER WATCH. Five in the morning. Even in the city, the birds were singing their hearts out, a flock of rainbow lorikeets making enough racket outside her window to wake the dead. If she raised on her elbows, she could catch a glimpse of the mist rising from the river like steam from coffee. It was the perfect morning for a run.

She heaved a sigh. Her running shoes were in the sports bag that was still in Viva's car. Sure, she could run in her tennis shoes, but they had different mechanics. Running in them would not be good for her feet or her body. She picked up her phone and scrolled to Lindy's text. It was easy. She should call Viva, be polite and professional, and arrange to collect her things. Then she could go for a run. A sensible person would have called last night, immediately after calling Lindy. A sensible person would have done a lot of things.

Gabriela got out of bed. She'd go to the tennis club and put her name down on the list of people available for social tennis.

She was in luck. The head coach recognised her and invited her to hit. It was humid, even at six in the morning, and she was damp with sweat before the end of the first game. Her feet were leaden, sluggish in the cloying weather. Jorgen played a crafty drop volley to go 3-0 up. They changed ends, taking a moment to have a drink and dry sweaty palms with a towel.

Jorgen indicated a player two courts over. "That's Queensland's golden girl over there—Viva Jones. You know her?"

Gabriela looked over. Viva was hitting with her coach, feet moving fast in tiny steps to get herself into position to return the ball. Gabriela looked away. She sometimes went weeks without bumping into Viva, and now here she was again. Possibly the last person she wanted to see. Viva's frosty silence on the journey from Waggs Pocket still rankled. It wouldn't have killed her to be polite, and the loud music had made it impossible for Gabriela to attempt conversation. "Some. We bump into each other on tour, but—"

Jorgen grinned. "I know. You don't mix much."

"Exactly."

"Heard she can be a bit of a difficult one. Not afraid to question calls."

"That is why they invented Hawk-Eye. You can't argue with that."

"Doesn't stop some people, though. Back in the day when I played professionally, the likes of John McEnroe argued the calls all the time. Sometimes, I'm sure the umpires agreed just to shut him up."

"That doesn't happen now. Even without Hawk-Eye."

"It's as much of a mind game as anything." Jorgen put down his drink bottle. "Play on?"

He beat her easily, as she had known he would.

"Thank you for the game." She grinned at him. "I had a good work-out. I am not so sure you did."

"Don't sell yourself short. You're better than most of the players in this club. Did you ever play professionally?"

"I got through the early rounds of junior Wimbledon when I was fifteen or sixteen. But I was never that great. Maybe I just was not motivated enough. Stopped playing at seventeen, went to college, the usual. Played socially and on the college team, that's all."

"Maybe you just wanted a life. The likes of Viva and any top-ranked player nowadays—their life is tennis, right from their early years. What's normal about that?"

"She's good, though." Gabriela's gaze followed Viva's slim shape as she lunged for a drop shot. "And it paid off for her. A grand slam and a few WTA titles."

"For her, maybe. But there's plenty of kids on the tour now who have worked as hard as Viva but haven't made it. What's left for them when they stop chasing the dream? Working as a coach in a suburban tennis club, like me."

Gabriela punched him lightly in the biceps. "Ha! You have a few titles to your name, if I remember correctly. And as for a career—the failed players often eventually end up as officials."

"Like you."

"Like me. I left the tennis world for a few years, but I came back."

"Will we see you umpiring at the Brisbane Open?"

"Yes. I'm silver badge, so I should get some good matches." A wry smile. "Working towards the pinnacle: gold badge. I hope to get there one day."

"You'll do it. You're a good umpire, Gabriela."

"Thank you." She gathered her towels and drink bottles and stuffed them into her bag. "I will see you around."

"You want to have another hit later this week? I'm generally busy later in the day, but early is always good."

"Sure. I would like that. Thursday?"

Jorgen nodded. "See you then."

Gabriela ambled to the changing room, a route that took her past where Viva was hitting with her coach. The sports bag tickled in her mind. An accidental meeting such as this was better than having to call Viva to arrange pick-up. She changed direction, headed for the courtside alley, and sat on the bench at the net, close enough that Viva would see her, far enough away that she was not intruding.

Viva was good. Gabriela watched her fluid lines and clean shots. Her thick plait bounced on her back, and even at this early hour, her clothes were wet with sweat. They clung to her lean figure. A frisson of warmth burned low in Gabriela's belly. She gave a mental shake. Viva was not a person to think about in that way. Better to focus on her offhand and aloof manner. Her rudeness.

Even in practice Viva gave her all. Her coach was hitting to her forehand, and Viva was returning so that the ball struck close to the lines. The coach mis-hit, and the ball went to her backhand. Rather than let it go, she ran for it and thumped a solid two-handed backhand return. The grunt of pain was unexpected.

Her coach let the ball pass by and came over to the net. "Take a break."

Viva's shoulders slumped for the barest second before she straightened and spun around on her heel. "I'm fine."

He drummed his racquet on the net cord. "Don't be a bloody idiot. You need to rehydrate anyway." He returned to the rear of the court and collected stray balls.

Viva turned back to the bench.

Gabriela stood; this was obviously not a good time. If she left now, she could avoid Viva seeing her. But Viva's stride carried her over to Gabriela.

"Hi." Her voice carried the breezy confidence it usually did. "I was expecting your call. I have your sports bag." Sweat dampened the strands of hair worked loose from her plait, and she wiped her wristband over her forehead.

"Thank you. I need to figure out how to get it from you."

"It's in my car right now." Viva glanced across at her coach, who lifted a hand in acknowledgement and left the court. "That appears to be the end of my session today. I can get it for you now."

"Thank you. I appreciate it."

Viva's forehead wrinkled. "You were playing just now?"

"Yes. I do know how to." She tried and failed to keep the sarcasm from her voice.

"Sorry. I didn't mean that. That *was* you hitting with Jorgen, then? I thought his opponent looked familiar. You're pretty good."

"Social tennis." She waved a hand in dismissal. "Is now a good time to get the bag? I will walk with you if so."

Viva studied Gabriela, her gaze sweeping from the top of her sweat-soaked hair to her well-worn tennis shoes. It was a leisurely assessment that paused and lingered. "I'm done here for the day. If you are too, it will be quicker to shower and then get the bag."

"Sure. I will meet you in the locker room." Gabriela turned and headed off without waiting for Viva's reply. Her pulse skipped in double time, and her feet kept pace. With luck, she would be in the shower before Viva arrived. Unselfconscious nudity was the norm in the officials' locker rooms at various tournaments. Skin was just skin. A body was just a body. Gabriela didn't have a problem with that, but suddenly, instantly, in the moments when Viva's gaze had passed over her body, Gabriela was unaccountably nervous. Not that Viva might see her naked—she had no false illusions about how she looked: neat, compact, fit, taut. No beauty. Nothing to make anyone look twice.

Except that Viva had.

———— ✧◇✧ ————

When Viva returned to the locker room, Gabriela wasn't in sight, but the shower was running in the end cubicle. She'd caught up with Deepak, told him she was going home for a while, and then would be at the physio in the afternoon.

Deepak's voice had been gentle. "Maybe you could call Dr Jacobwitz and arrange for the injection. If you want to have any hope of playing the Australian season, the sooner you get that done, the better."

She had nodded, a jerky up-and-down, and spun away to jog back to the locker room before he could see the tears forming. They fell in the shower, the hot water taking them away along with any other visible sign of her upset.

By the time she came out of the shower wrapped in a towel, Gabriela was dressed and sitting on a bench, lacing her shoes.

"Won't be long." Viva turned her back, dropped the towel, and reached into her locker for lotion.

When she turned back, Gabriela hadn't moved. Her gaze flicked away from Viva's body, and a rosy flush suffused her throat.

Viva's fingers clenched on the bottle, and a glob of lotion spurted from the top. She wiped it with her fingers, smoothing it on her thigh.

"I need to dry my hair." Gabriela rose and bolted to the far end of the room where the hairdryers were. The noise of the dryer, fluffing Gabriela's nearly dry hair made any further conversation impossible.

Viva's gaze lingered on the upright rigidity of Gabriela's back. She seemed uneasy, nervous in Viva's company. She couldn't blame Gabriela for that. Viva squirted more lotion and rubbed it on her arms. Shame twisted in her stomach. Her parents had brought her up to be fair. The Institute of Sport, too, put big emphasis on sportsmanship. Her actions towards Gabriela had been anything but fair. No wonder Gabriela was uncomfortable in her presence.

A memory surfaced of another locker room, over a year ago. Herself consoling Michi after a first-round loss, a match Michi had ultimately lost on a line call. There was no Hawk-Eye on the outside court, and Michi was convinced the call was wrong.

"You have to roll with it," Viva had said to her. "Accept it, move on."

Good advice. Except that she, Viva, seemed incapable of following it when *she* was on the end of the bad call. She dressed slowly. It was time for her to follow her own advice.

Viva's car was in the members' area, under the shade sails. She opened the boot and hauled out Gabriela's sports bag. "Where's your car?"

"I don't have one. I get a short-term rental when I want to explore a bit. Like when you rescued me."

Viva shifted the bag more fully to her left hand. "How are you getting home?"

"Train."

"You're staying in West End, right?" At Gabriela's nod, she continued, "My apartment's in South Bank. I can give you a lift."

Gabriela's face wiped clean of expression. "Thank you. But I will be fine."

Gabriela would rather lug a heavy bag to the train station than accept a lift. That same twist of shame pushed to the forefront of Viva's thoughts. She hadn't been fair, and she had been unpleasant. Well, she could try to remedy that right now.

Viva placed the bag on the ground between them. "Look, I owe you an apology. I haven't treated you so well. I was rude to you at my parents' place. You didn't deserve that. I've been having a bit of a difficult time lately, but that's no excuse to take it out on you." Her mouth quirked up at one corner. "Mum chewed me out for my lack of manners. I'm truly sorry for being a brat."

When Gabriela smiled, her face lost some of its stern lines and she became less the blank-faced official. "Apology accepted. And your parents are lovely."

"They liked you too." Viva snorted. "More than they've liked my last couple of girlfriends. Oh!" Warmth crept up her cheeks. "That didn't come out right. I didn't mean to imply anything."

Gabriela's smile was impish. "Parents never like partners. Not until the partner is for keeps."

Viva placed the bag back in the boot of her car. "Get in. It's crazy you taking the train when I'm going your way."

Gabriela slid into the passenger seat, and Viva got in and pulled away, joining the line of traffic heading towards the city. She accelerated to merge onto the freeway. Viva concentrated on the traffic, rather than on Gabriela's smooth, brown thighs underneath her denim shorts. The traffic was far less distracting.

"You must like it here as you spend all this time in Brisbane." Viva accelerated into the outside lane.

"Yes. It's nice to have a base, and Australia is so relaxed compared to other places."

"Spain's lovely too, though. The Madrid tournament is one of my favourites. The food!"

"There is that. When I visit my brother there, we usually manage one evening in the tapas bars. It's a highlight of my visit."

Viva rubbed her right wrist absently as she drove. Gabriela's family seemed so different from her own. She glanced across at her passenger.

"It's not fixed, is it? Your wrist." The words were quiet.

The sympathy in Gabriela's voice was her undoing, and she swallowed hard against the thickness in her throat. Everything she should be considering but couldn't bear to think about came rushing to the fore. Injections, surgery—or not. Resting the wrist. The Australian summer of tennis.

Retirement.

What would she do with her life if that was her only option? What *could* she do? Tennis was all she had known. It was all she loved. The chaotic thoughts of before deluged her.

"It's not perfect, no. But it will do." Her voice croaked.

She glanced at her watch as the traffic moved slowly towards the city. It was only ten in the morning, and the day stretched long and desolate in front of her. On a normal day, she'd rest up for a bit while watching replays of her opponents' matches, studying their strengths and weaknesses. Have a light lunch, then more training. A run, maybe weights. Or back to the courts for strength and agility exercises with her fitness trainer. Her wrist ached. Deepak was right; if she intended playing the Australian season, she needed to have that injection as soon as possible.

She glanced over at Gabriela, who was staring out at the traffic, seemingly absorbed by the ebb and flow.

"Would you like to have dinner with me this evening?" The words came from nowhere, surprising Viva when they fell in the air between them.

A tiny wrinkle appeared between Gabriela's eyes. "Why?"

"Why not? You're alone in a foreign city. I'm not doing anything tonight. I'd enjoy your company."

Gabriela studied her across the car. "You did not seem to enjoy it much in Waggs Pocket."

Viva lifted a shoulder. "You're right, and I'm truly sorry. I was very rude. I would very much like to take you out to dinner tonight—make it up to you in some small way."

"Players and officials can't date."

"Not a date. Just two acquaintances having dinner together."

"You are splitting hairs."

"We had dinner together in Waggs Pocket. I have dinner with people on the tour all the time. It's more pleasant than eating alone. That's all I'm suggesting."

"Waggs Pocket was a necessity, and you know it. We do not eat together when we are on the tour."

Viva shot a glance at Gabriela. "There's nearly a month until the season opening. No one will see us. I'm sure you'll be completely impartial if you umpire any of my matches."

Gabriela's frown grew more pronounced.

"It's one dinner. I'm not asking you to marry me." She lifted her chin. "If you don't want to, that's fine. It was just an idea."

Gabriela was silent, and her gaze followed the line of traffic. Then her hunched shoulders relaxed. "Thank you. I would like that." Her lips tilted up on one side, a curiously endearing expression. "You are right. It will be pleasant to share a meal with someone. What time?"

"Is six too early? I'm usually in bed by ten when I'm training."

"That's perfect. Where shall I meet you?" She pointed. "Turn left here."

"Do you know The Soul Bar on Broadbent Street?" At Gabriela's nod, she continued, "I'll meet you there."

"Next right please. This is my street."

Gabriela indicated an apartment block, and Viva stopped the car. "I'll see you later, then."

"I'm looking forward to it." A quick smile made her rather stern features come alive. "Thank you for the ride."

Chapter 8

WHEN GABRIELA ARRIVED, VIVA WAS waiting at the Soul Bar with a large glass of water in front of her. She stood, and Gabriela's glance was drawn to Viva's smooth cheek. What would it be like to press her lips to that tanned skin? She looked away. *This is not a date. This is two not-quite-friends having dinner. Nothing more.* She contented herself with a quick smile, sat, and picked up the drinks list. "What are you having?"

"Water." Viva picked up the glass and drained half of it. "I'll have a glass of wine with dinner."

Gabriela pushed the list across. "How about a mocktail? No alcohol."

"That's a good idea. Thanks." She glanced at the list and selected a lime-based drink.

Gabriela ordered the same and studied her companion across the table. With her thick chestnut hair hanging loose halfway down her back and wearing a sleeveless blouse and a short skirt rather than sportswear, Viva looked younger and more relaxed. She looked like someone Gabriela would date. *No.* She clasped her hands in front of her, primly, like a school marm. That thought had sprung, fully-formed, into her head, and it could leave just as quickly.

"What part of Spain are you from?" Viva studied her over the rim of her glass, her blue eyes intent.

"Extremadura. It's a dry inland area bordering Portugal. It reminds me a little of parts of Australia."

"I know it—well, parts of it—a little. I had a week off after playing Madrid a couple of years back. My girlfriend and I went road tripping. Had a great time." She grinned. "No one knew who we were, so we could be a bit more open than usual. I remember fat black pigs and almond groves."

The drinks arrived. Gabriela sipped hers and looked at Viva's arm where it lay on the table. How bad was the injury? The urge to take Viva's wrist in her hand and run her fingers over it was strong. Although was it to diagnose or caress? She couldn't tell. She clenched her fingers on the glass.

"This morning when I was hitting with Jorgen," she said. "he called you Queensland's golden girl."

Viva laughed. "That's what he calls every Queensland player, and there's been a few over the years. Do you hit with Jorgen often?"

"That was the first time, but we are playing again on Thursday."

"You must be good, then. Otherwise, he'd have thanked you and not suggested another time."

"Not really. But I enjoy playing to keep fit." She grinned. "Sitting in an umpire's chair isn't much of a work-out."

Viva's smile wiped from her face. She leant forward. "I have another apology to make. It seems I'm always apologising around you." She met Gabriela's eyes squarely. "The US Open. When you called me on a foot-fault. Twice."

Tension flooded Gabriela's body. Was Viva about to get angry about that once again? She shot her a glance.

Viva lowered her head and fiddled with the straw in her drink. "I blamed you for my loss. There on court, in my head. I blamed your bad call for losing the point, then the game that lost me the match. Of course, it wasn't your fault; it was entirely mine. Even if you had made a bad call, well, that's part of the game. Strong players are able to set it aside and find a way back." She shrugged. "I didn't do that. All I saw was my title defence going, and rather than accept I wasn't good enough, I blamed you."

Viva's slim fingers worried the edge of the menu, setting it square to the table edge, then turning it sideways once more. "See, with tennis usually there's no one else to blame. Sure, some players scream at the box, yell at their doubles partner, take issue with spectators or noises in the stadium, but really that's nothing to do with it. The match is won or lost by your strokes, your play, how fast, how agile, how mentally tough you are. But that match, there was someone else I could blame. So I did. Because then, I didn't *lose*; I was just unlucky."

"You're not the first person to do that." Gabriela touched the back of Viva's hand, stilling the nervous motion. "I have been insulted by players before—on court, off court. It's not nice, but you learn to ignore it."

"I'm sorry." Viva turned her hand over so that they were palm to palm and laced their fingers together.

The touch sent shivers along Gabriela's nerves from her fingers, up her arm. Feelings fluttered in her belly. Her breath hitched. *No.* Viva's clasp in public was unexpected. It was daring. It was wrong. But her own reaction, to allow the touch, to encourage it even, was more dangerous. Her fingers twitched, the need to withdraw from the touch warring with the simple pleasure of skin on skin. Gabriela stared at their hands. *Another few moments. Then I'll move.*

"I carried that grudge for a long time," Viva continued. "Until this morning, to be honest. But you don't deserve that. You were doing your job."

Viva's fingers gripped hers. They were cool and dry, despite the warm evening. To break the clasp now would be awkward; it would imply rejection of Viva's apology. A pulse beat strongly in Viva's throat, and Gabriela's gaze fastened upon it, that tiny movement, strong and regular against soft flesh. An image flashed in front of her eyes: herself, leaning over to place her lips upon that pulse. The thought was so instant, so real, that she pushed her free hand underneath her thigh to stop herself from reaching out to touch.

Where had that come from? She focussed instead on Viva's bent head, the part of her hair, the long tendrils that fell forward. That was no better—what would the mass of Viva's hair feel like entwined in her fist? Gabriela's fingers tingled, her pulse skittering in double time.

"If I hadn't bumped into you, I probably would still be carrying that grudge," Viva continued. She looked up again, catching Gabriela's gaze with her own. "You officials… You're so distant, remote. Players know your names and faces, but we don't know *you*. We might know the country you're from, but that's it. Do you have wives, husbands, children? Do you love tennis with a passion, or is it just a job? I understand the reasoning behind the divide, but that distance makes it easier to blame you."

The divide seemed smaller now. It had closed to a crack, the tiniest sliver of propriety between them. Viva's fingers still clasped Gabriela's hand. Her focus narrowed to the woman in front of her, Viva's oval face, with its high forehead, wide cheekbones, and the soft pink curve of her lips. *Oh God, her lips.*

"Officials are the faceless people." Gabriela's thumb twitched with the impulse to caress Viva's hand. With an effort, she stilled it.

"Yeah, that's part of it. I was playing doubles at Indian Wells a couple of years ago. My partner is Michi Cleaver."

"I know her. She is hard to miss, especially with that pink hair."

Viva grinned. "There is that. She's the most outgoing person on tour. Bouncy."

"That's an understatement."

"Anyway, it was match point against us. The opponents' ball landed on my side of the court. I had the shot, but Michi came barrelling over yelling 'mine'. I'm not sure why. She took the shot, it went long by a mile, and we lost. Did I blame her? No. Because she's my friend." Viva stared at their joined hands as if she had just realised they were still touching. She withdrew her fingers.

Gabriela's hand closed around the empty space where Viva's had been.

"I miss her. She'll be here in a couple of weeks, but in the meantime, she's home in Colorado with her coach."

"Who is also her husband." Gabriela grinned at Viva's surprised look. "Officials gossip too. When those two got together, we gave their relationship two years at the most. How long has it been now?"

"Nearly six."

"We were wrong."

"I'm glad you are. Michi's happy."

"Rumour has it you and she were dating a long time ago." The rumour was old, but Gabriela was curious as to the answer. Viva and Michi—did their friendship spring from a shared romantic history? If so, they had been discreet.

"Proves you don't know everything, then. Michi does like girls, but she and I never dated. We're just good friends." Viva pushed her empty glass into the centre of the table. "I made a reservation for us at Shank's Pony.

It's a restaurant that only serves food grown within a fifty-kilometre radius of here. Do you know it?"

"I have heard of it and intended going there at some point."

Viva stood and held out her hand. "Shall we?"

It was dangerous. It was wrong. But Gabriela placed her hand in Viva's and let her lead her onto the street.

The crazy impulse still surprised Viva. When she held her hand out for Gabriela to take, it hadn't been a planned move. It was something she did with many of her friends. She and Michi would often hold hands or link arms and wander around a city together. She didn't think anything of it. But it was different with Gabriela. Not an enemy anymore—if indeed she had ever been—but not quite a friend either. If indeed she would ever be.

Gabriela's palm was hot and dry against her own. The contact prickled with awkwardness, but it would be too pointed to drop her hand now. So they strolled along the street hand in hand.

Shank's Pony was only a short walk away. Viva let go of Gabriela's hand as they entered. They were shown to a table near the back, where there wasn't a view of the street, but it was how Viva liked it. Less chance of being hassled for autographs, less chance of reporters. It was unlikely unless there was a tournament on, but old habits died hard.

The fifty-kilometre radius for sourcing food included the ocean, so there was a lot of seafood on the menu. They agreed to share a seafood platter, a leafy green salad with goat cheese, and some sweet potato fries. Gabriela chose the wine, which was the only thing sourced from outside the area.

Thoughts churned through Viva's head that even the serene atmosphere of the restaurant and Gabriela's quiet company couldn't dispel. She rubbed her wrist absently.

Other people's words bubbled in her mind: Dr Singh, Deepak, her mother. The words churned together until she could no longer remember who had said what. Her mother had suggested Viva talk to someone about the choices she had in front of her. But there was no one. No one except Gabriela. Was she a person to trust? Instinct said yes, but Viva couldn't bring herself to start speaking. Her mind spun the conversations of the last few days like a centrifuge throwing out the extraneous waffle, until only the words of most importance were left.

Injury. Retirement. Future career.

"I've been told I should retire." Her words dropped into the silence between them, and she took a too-large gulp of her wine to quell the panic at what she'd just said.

Gabriela's expression didn't change, but she picked up Viva's right hand and ran her thumb lightly over Viva's wrist, tracing the pale scar. "Is this the reason?"

"Mainly. Okay, it's the only reason. It's not good. Tendons."

Gabriela nodded, as if she hadn't expected any different.

"It's always been my weak point. The surgery went well, considering. But it's flared up again."

Gabriela's fingers found an imperceptible point and pressed lightly.

Pain bloomed, but Viva stifled the gasp.

"More surgery is pointless. I'll need injections to keep playing, and there's only so much they can do."

Gabriela cupped Viva's hand in both of hers, cradling it as if it were something precious. "You will miss tennis." It wasn't a question, but a statement of fact.

"Yes." Viva's voice held the flatness of the outback. "I've been tennis; tennis has been me. I don't know if there's anything else."

Head cocked to one side, Gabriela said, "It is a short-lived profession. Unless you are Martina Navratilova. How she kept playing professionally into her fifties is beyond me."

"She's a legend. But I don't have a strong enough body for that."

"What will you do?"

It was hard to think while Gabriela cradled her hand so carefully. "Right now, I can't accept that this is the end of my tennis career. It's been my passion and joy for so long. I don't know if I can give it up."

"You could still be involved. Plenty of retired pros coach, commentate, work as player advisors."

"That might be worse. Being a part of the tour, but not playing."

"Do you have to stop playing completely?"

"No. There's exhibition matches. My wrist could take that; it's the stresses of the modern game that's killing it. I could try and drum up some more sponsorship for everyday items. Dishwashing liquid. Frozen dinners, that sort of thing."

"TV shopping channel presenter posing artfully with the fake gold chains."

Viva laughed. "I could do that." She removed her hand from Gabriela's clasp and struck a pose, batting her eyelashes in exaggerated fashion. Then she sobered and studied Gabriela. "Do you ever think about a life after tennis?"

"No. But an official's life doesn't usually end abruptly. Most officials simply get sick of the constant travel and want to settle down."

"No one travels with a family?"

"We don't earn enough to do that. Sad but true. But for me, right now, I'm still enjoying the life." She tilted her head and studied Viva. "If I make gold badge, there's no reason I can't keep this life for many years to come."

"Is that what you want? To stay with the tour?"

"Yes. Very much so. It does not bring the fame and fortune that you players have, but I love my career. I love being the glue that holds the tour together. Keeping players in order. It doesn't matter if it's a glamorous top-ten player or a junior outside the top two hundred, an official is impartial. I enforce fairness, and that really appeals to me." Her smile lit her face. "I studied Spanish literature in college; that does not lead to many good jobs. I had better stick with what I have!"

"A lot of players get sick of the constant travel. Do you ever feel like that?"

"No. Not yet, anyway. I enjoy seeing a new city or revisiting a favourite one. We umpires have more time available to us than players do, so there is time to explore. I like to take a walking tour. Sometimes, I will go with a friend to explore laneways and out-of-the-way local cafés."

"You probably know Brisbane better than I do."

"Maybe. I know Melbourne very well too, because the Australian Open is held there. There is plenty of time to explore."

"Tell me about a quiet café in Melbourne," Viva said. "I don't think there is any such thing. Everywhere is so busy."

Gabriela tilted her head. "Hm. There's a little coffee shop in the city, in a laneway near Spencer Street Station. It opens early, so a lot of the railway workers go there. They do hearty breakfasts, nothing trendy, just thick cut bacon and fried eggs. Or there's a little Greek café in Clifton Hill. Often I go there when I have been running along the river path. They do real Greek coffee."

"And baklava?" Viva grinned. "I adore baklava, all dripping with honey."

"Very good cakes. Now I am already looking forward to the Australian Open so that I can visit that café again."

"I'll have to see if I can find it when I'm next in Melbourne," Viva said.

"Don't tell anyone about it! I like that it is so quiet."

Viva sipped her wine and studied Gabriela. Gabriela looked somewhat older than she, maybe late thirties. Her shiny cap of short hair showed no grey and, while her olive skin boasted a few laughter lines and fine wrinkles, that was to be expected from someone who spent a lot of time outdoors. Viva touched the corner of her own eye, feeling the deep grooves from squinting into the sun. Gabriela had a stillness about her that few of the people Viva associated with possessed. For a second, she compared Gabriela to the effervescent Michi. It was like comparing a pool in the rainforest to a gurgling waterfall.

Michi would find a new doubles partner and move on with her tennis career.

But what would she do?

"When will you decide about retirement?" Gabriela sat back as the waiter approached. His description of the seafood on the platter overrode any possible reply.

When he had left, Viva loaded her plate with prawns, oysters, a Moreton Bay bug, and a pile of fries. Gabriela's question rolled around her head, but to answer it would force it to the forefront of her mind. Instead, she removed the flesh of the bug from the shell and broke it in half. "Have you tried these before? They're incredibly good. Poor man's crayfish."

Gabriela took the firm pale meat and squeezed lime juice over it. Strong white teeth flashed in her tan face as she bit. "This is amazing."

Viva slurped an oyster and chased it down with a mouthful of wine. A tiny part of her mind chastised herself for the wine. This was more than a glass a week. Thinking about retirement shouldn't mean the life of a lush.

They didn't talk much as they ate. But when the fries were gone, the salad eaten, they both reached for the final prawn at the same moment. Viva's fingers brushed Gabriela's, and she stilled. The quiver that settled in her belly had nothing to do with seafood. The buzz of the restaurant faded as if someone had hit the mute button. There was only Gabriela, her smooth skin, her dark eyes, the lift of her brow as she studied their fingers together.

Viva pulled back. "You have it."

Gabriela ripped the head off and shelled the prawn with deft movements. "We'll share." She bit off half and handed the remainder to Viva.

Their fingers brushed as Viva took the prawn. She shared food with Michi all the time; there was no reason for this to feel so intimate. But it did.

The food was gone. The wine was nearly gone. Viva twirled her glass in her fingers. The mellow buzz of the wine warmed her blood. Not enough to impair her judgement, not enough to affect her training tomorrow. Training. Was there any point? Deepak seemed to be waiting for her to make the retirement choice. Her doctors thought she was crazy, risking her future health by playing on. She should set the wheels in motion, contact her agent, schedule a press conference to make the announcement. Once done, she could breathe deeply and take some time to figure out what she was going to do with her life.

None of those things meant she needed to be on court hitting balls at six tomorrow morning.

"If I'm retiring, there's no reason I can't have more wine, stay out late. Party until dawn." But the words sounded hollow, the voicing of something she already knew she wouldn't do. It just wasn't her thing.

"Is that what you're suggesting for the rest of the evening?" Gabriela's voice held the amusement hers had lacked. "If so, you will have to find someone else for the party until dawn part. Now that I have got my bag back from you, I will go for a run early tomorrow. I have missed it."

A run. Something that had always been just a part of training, something to build her endurance and stamina, strengthen her quads. Something she couldn't do too much of, as a runner's physique wasn't a tennis player's.

"I should play hooky and come with you."

"If you want. I do ten kilometres in fifty minutes on these flat river paths. But why is it playing hooky if you are retiring?"

"Thinking of retiring. I haven't told anyone yet. Except Deepak and Mum." She met Gabriela's eyes. "And now you. Nobody has tried to talk me out of it."

"Do you want me to?"

"No. Yes." She pressed the heels of her palms into her eye sockets. "No."

"Final answer?"

"Final answer. I'll call my agent tomorrow, get things happening." Her gaze drifted away from the table, over to the far wall, away from Gabriela's concerned eyes. Retirement. She couldn't swim against the tide any longer. She closed her eyes. *What will I be when I'm no longer a professional tennis player?* She fought down the surge of panic, opened her eyes, and stretched her mouth into a smile, feeling as if her face would crack with the effort.

Gabriela was as still as stone, her face set in sombre lines. "That's it? You have just made your decision?"

Viva nodded. There was a heaviness in her chest, a great boulder of sadness. The end of an era. She met Gabriela's eyes. In contrast to her own subdued mood, Gabriela seemed barely contained in her skin. There was an air of anticipation surrounding her still figure. Viva studied her, the smooth skin, warm brown eyes, and her hand now resting on the table between them, over the halfway mark, past the boundary of personal space.

"Soon you will no longer be an active player." Gabriela's voice was low.

Viva shuddered as the meaning behind the words sank in.

The waiter approached them with a dessert menu.

"Does that mean there's room for dessert in your life?" Gabriela's voice was back to its usual mellow tone.

With an effort, she forced her attention to Gabriela's words. "Absolutely. Bring it on. Sugar. Wine. Late nights. I'll have to fill the spaces in my life somehow. Maybe I'll find a girlfriend who actually wants to marry me, settle down in the bush somewhere, and raise sheep. Or a baby. Maybe I'll go work in the pub." She passed the menu to Gabriela. "Surprise me with your sugar choices."

"You won't stay in the tennis world?"

"I did a bit of commentating when I was recovering from surgery. That was quite fun. I might explore that. I have an open offer from the tennis channel to commentate for the Australian tennis season." She propped her chin on her hand and watched as Gabriela called the waiter over and ordered dessert. Her gaze licked over Gabriela's torso, visible above the table top. She was a neat dresser, not a flashy one. Viva's eyes moved up. Small breasts, lightly muscled arms, a determined chin with a small, white scar on the bottom. Some childhood accident, no doubt. Her gaze shifted higher, over Gabriela's mouth. A firm, thin upper lip and a surprisingly full and lush lower one. Those lips were smiling.

Viva was sprung, caught in the act of checking out her dinner companion. Heat stole into her cheeks, and she lifted her chin, reaching for her water glass and taking a long drink. When she set it down again, her composure had returned, but any smart comeback had deserted her.

Gabriela leant forward, and those same arched lips that she'd been admiring said, "I have looked at you in that way as well. I'm just better at hiding it."

Oh. *When*? She'd been very discreet. An automatic denial rose in her throat, but she swallowed the word unsaid. Why not? Gabriela was attractive. They were both single. There was no reason not to look.

No reason except the obvious one: that players and officials shouldn't mix. And she was, at this point, a player.

This dinner, the two of them dining alone in intimate surroundings, already made a mockery of that. This was not, and had never been, the casual dinner that Gabriela had agreed to.

But it didn't matter anymore. Soon, she would be a retired player, not an active one. Not tomorrow, or the next day, but certainly before the start of the tennis season in the new year. And when that happened, there was no reason she couldn't be friends with Gabriela. No reason they couldn't date, if they wanted to.

She eyed her companion with a frank look. Starting at her head, down over the short cap of shining brown hair, the finely chiselled face with its almost haughty stare. Down her throat, into the vee of her blouse where there was only the promise of delights. Her appraisal ended at the table top.

"Seen enough?" Amusement shimmered in Gabriela's voice. "The look of revelation in your eyes means you have worked out something I thought of the first time I saw you grimacing in pain and clutching your wrist."

"What, that I'm a weakling?"

"Not that." Gabriela folded her arms across her chest.

Viva's gaze followed the movement, helplessly drawn to the push of small breasts against her shirt.

Gabriela's eyes grew sultry and heavy-lidded "I'm free and single. I can date anyone who isn't a professional tennis player. How about you?"

"Free as a bird. Of course, until I announce my retirement, I'm still a player."

"Not for much longer?" Gabriela leant forward, as if she could pull the words she obviously wanted to hear from Viva's lips.

"For a day or two more. It can't happen instantly. But the intent is there." The heaviness in her chest lessened.

"No vindictive exes?" Gabriela asked. "No groupies hanging around waiting their turn?"

"Not my thing."

"Then what sort of girl stands a chance with you?"

Viva sat back and picked up the wineglass. The promise of freedom beckoned. No constraints, no obligations. "Woman. Not a girl. That's number one." She bit her lip thinking. "Someone who is fit, looks after themselves. No ties. Someone who could jump on a plane at a moment's notice to join me at—" She stopped. There was no need to go anywhere at the last moment anymore. Any travel she now took could be planned in advance. A beach, a resort, a footloose backpacking lifestyle even. She could hike to Everest Base Camp without worrying she'd get altitude sickness and miss a tournament. She could go parachuting without worrying about injury. "A quiet person. Not a chatterer."

Gabriela smiled. "That is why you did not date your doubles partner, then."

"Maybe. Maybe a country girl, someone I could settle down with in a small town. Get a couple of horses. Make jam. Grow veggies." She lifted a shoulder. "It doesn't sound like I'm asking for much when I put it like that."

Gabriela's eyes were kind. "Yet if I was to bet on this, I would say you attract extravert party types, who think a tennis player's life is all designer gowns and red-carpet events, yes?"

Viva feigned outrage. "You've been spying on me!"

"I do not have to. I also would guess that you get an awful lot of men flirting with you. Ones who have no gaydar and do not read anything about you—or don't care."

"Them too. I've never hidden my sexuality although I don't draw attention to it either. But I'll sometimes get blokes trying to hit on me. Most have no clue I'm gay, but there's been a couple who want to 'save me' and a few who say I've just never met the right man, with a big enough dick."

Gabriela grimaced. "I would love to hear your put-down."

"Nothing too rude. I smile and say, 'I still haven't' and walk off."

Somewhere along the way the conversation had muted to something safe that she'd have with a friend. Did she want that? Was Gabriela backing away?

But then Gabriela reached over and picked up Viva's hand. She turned it so that it was palm up and uncurled her fingers, one by one. One tanned finger traced Viva's lifeline, then her heart line. The barely there touch that skated her palm made her shudder.

"I have accepted that my chances of finding a compatible partner are remote," Gabriela said. "Not unless I stop travelling on the tour. And that's not going to happen."

"Players sometimes date players. Or they take a partner on tour with them," Viva said. "Who do officials date?"

"Sometimes other officials. A few have a partner at home—the lower-ranked officials often only do part of the tour, say only the European leg—so it's easier on a relationship."

"Have you ever known an official to date a player?"

"No. Never. If anyone ever did, they kept it very secret."

"Do you date?" Viva propped her chin on her hand.

"In the past. Not for a long time. For all of the reasons I have just said." Gabriela hesitated. "Sometimes... Sometimes, I wonder if it is worth it. I am thirty-eight. Am I missing out on finding a partner because of my career? Occasionally, when I see couples or even a player and her entourage, I feel lonely. But I love my life. I hope maybe that I will find someone and we can make it work."

"Would you give up your career for love?"

Gabriela's smile was wry. "How can I know the answer until it comes up? Right now, I think not. Would you?"

"I've never considered it. I've never had to make the choice, but I think if I had, I would have chosen tennis. Now, though..."

"Now, you will choose love and plant that vegetable garden." Gabriela's eyes crinkled.

Would she? Would she really? Viva sighed, her thoughts skittering in her head. She pushed them away. She had made her decision. Second-guessing herself would do no good. She focussed again on Gabriela. "Who decides when you get your gold badge? Do you have to wait for someone to retire?"

"A panel sends you a letter each year giving your level. It depends on the tournaments you've worked, complaints against you. That sort of thing."

"But you're not at the end-of-year finals right now. Surely that would be as big an event for an official as it is for a player?"

The waiter arrived with their desserts and set them down with a smile.

Gabriela waited until he left before picking up her plate and slicing her lemon myrtle and ginger mousse into two. She slid half onto Viva's plate.

The delicate scent of lemon myrtle made Viva's mouth water. She scooped half of her own dessert—some sort of banana pudding—onto Gabriela's plate.

"The tour is too long." Gabriela continued their conversation as if there was nothing unusual about them sharing desserts like a long-married couple. "Early January to December. I have always taken the whole of December off. Usually a couple of weeks in the middle of the year too. Most officials take some extra time away." She took a bite of mousse. "This is delicious."

"Good choices."

"There is a lemon myrtle tree outside my apartment. I pick the leaves to make tea."

Viva was silent. Gabriela had mentioned that throwaway fact as if it was nothing. Viva had never made tea with lemon myrtle leaves—hadn't even known you could. Probably every Aussie knew that—everyone who hadn't spent two decades of their life on a tennis court, that is.

There was a whole world out there for her to explore. There was a whole new life for her. Starting now.

She refocussed on the woman on the other side of the table, watching as Gabriela's lips closed around a spoonful of mousse with the same precision and economy of movement that she used in the umpire's chair. What if they weren't two only-just friends sharing a meal? What if this was a date, a real date that might end with a kiss? Or more. The sort of date that could lead to breakfast the next morning, if she wanted it. If Gabriela did.

Oh yes, Viva wanted it.

Gabriela put her spoon down with a small sigh. "I'll have to run an extra couple of kilometres tomorrow." Her wide-eyed glance flashed across the table before she lowered her lashes. "Have you decided if you're going to join me?"

"Name your time, and I'll be there."

"Six?"

"That late?" Viva teased. "If we're having a late start, then we've time for coffee now."

Gabriela's smile spread like the sunrise. "I'd like that. There's a café around the corner that does a good cup, and there are comfortable couches. Shall we go there?"

"Why not."

Chapter 9

THE STREET WAS BUSY WHEN they left the restaurant. It was still before nine, but it was as packed as any Friday night.

"Maybe there was something happening by the river that's just finished." Viva looked in the direction people were coming from.

A group came towards them, taking up the entire footpath. She grabbed Gabriela's hand and pulled her to one side so they wouldn't get separated. Her fingers linked tightly with Gabriela's and settled into the clasp as if they were long-time lovers.

Gabriela's fingers were tense in her clasp, but after a moment they curled around Viva's hand.

The coffee shop was packed, with people standing, waiting for tables.

Butterflies somersaulted in Viva's stomach. "I live one block that way. We can have coffee at my place."

She'd taken a pace away before the tug on her hand stopped her.

Gabriela hadn't moved. She stood immobile on the pavement, and the streetlighting accentuated the worry in her dark eyes.

"Coffee." The word was clipped.

Viva frowned. "Isn't that what we were talking about?"

"Coffee or *coffee*?"

The butterflies lurched into a fast polka. Viva moved closer and freed her hand. She cradled Gabriela's face, carefully pushing back the short hair so that her fingers touched only skin. Her thumb stroked over Gabriela's lips in a slow pass.

Gabriela shivered, a frisson of movement. Her lips parted under the slow to and fro of Viva's thumb.

"Haven't we been moving towards *coffee* all evening?"

Gabriela's eyes were wide and dark. She straightened, lifting her chin. "In the restaurant, something changed. We flirted."

"Yes." Viva's fingers tingled with the need to touch Gabriela's lips again.

"It changed after you said one thing: that you were retiring. Before… anything else, I need you to tell me something."

Viva nodded. "Anything."

"Did you mean what you said about retiring?"

For a moment, Viva didn't understand the question. Then comprehension caught up in a rush. Did she mean it? Did she have a choice? The answer was there in the throb of her wrist, in the telling silences from her mother, from Deepak. She dragged in a breath, held it, and let it out in a long sigh. "I meant it. I'll make the calls tomorrow."

"When will you retire?"

"Immediately."

Gabriela nodded and half-turned away. "I normally would not ask. Asking implies a seriousness that is not yet warranted. But I am crossing a line for you. I am considering it *only* because you talked retirement, and then I can justify what we are doing." She was silent for a long moment. Then she said, "But I want this. So very, very much."

Viva hesitated. The next move had to be Gabriela's. Desire beat a low and urgent drum in her blood, but still she waited.

"Coffee," Gabriela whispered. "I would like to share *coffee* with you." She turned back to stand in front of Viva.

Viva splayed her fingers down Gabriela's neck, where the pulse beat fast and frantic. She leant closer, and her lips touched Gabriela's, pressing lightly, seeking, not demanding. For a moment they rested, lips touching, breaths mingling. The noise and laughter from the coffee shop faded to insignificance. There was only the two of them caught in the glare of the streetlights, a frozen pose as people flowed around them into the café.

Viva's breath caught painfully in her throat. *Please, kiss me back.* Her lips moved, supping, tiny nibbling kisses. Gabriela tasted of lemon myrtle and sugar, but her lips remained still. Disappointment churned in Viva's chest. Gabriela must have changed her mind. She withdrew, putting some air between her lips and Gabriela's.

But then Gabriela closed the gap once more, and suddenly she *was* kissing Viva back, and her hands rose to tangle in Viva's hair, pushing into the thick mass to hold her head steady so that there was firmness to the kiss.

Viva exhaled in a whoosh. Desire coiled sweet and hot in her belly, and colours blurred behind her closed eyes. The slow kiss of before evanesced into the white-hot haze of desire.

It was only when someone knocked into them with a muttered "sorry" that they broke apart.

Gabriela swallowed, and her lips formed words, but there was no sound. She swallowed again. She stood immobile, a picture of indecision in the busy street.

"We can wait. We don't have to do this." Viva touched Gabriela's hand, a light touch and retreat.

"I want this." Gabriela closed the gap between them once more. "Convince me there is no reason to wait. Convince me I'm not making a huge mistake. Kiss me again."

Viva curved an arm around Gabriela's waist and drew her closer. "I'd very much like to kiss you again. But only if you're sure."

This time, their lips met halfway, melded to a hot, wet kiss that flickered in a mantle of desire over Viva's skin until it was as if she were clothed in flame. She was intoxicated by Gabriela's lips more so than from the wine they'd shared earlier.

Gabriela was the first to break the kiss. For a moment, she stared into Viva's eyes with a fierce intensity, as if she were pulling the reassurance she obviously needed from Viva's mind. She traced a pathway down Viva's wrist and linked their fingers. "Take me home."

The walk was silent. Decision made, there was nothing to be said. Hands joined, they paced the quieter streets to Viva's apartment.

Viva led the way inside and turned on a floor lamp. It cast a soft pool of light in the otherwise dark room.

Viva turned to face her. "Wine?"

"No, thank you." Gabriela moved to the window where floor-to-ceiling glass looked over the Brisbane River to the city on the far side.

Viva moved to stand by her side. Their shoulders brushed. A ferry moved slowly through the inky water to a jetty. The tower blocks of the business district were walls of light, even late in the evening. From their position on the fifteenth floor, the dark humps of Mount Coot-tha were visible, speckled with lights against the sky.

"It's very different to Waggs Pocket." Gabriela's gaze never left the window.

"I don't spend enough time in either place. I've owned this for four years now, and I've probably spent less than six months in total here."

"That could change now. If you want it to."

"Yes." Viva looked out across the bright city. "It could."

Gabriela turned to face her, and her fingers rested on Viva's neck. Hot points of fire licked down to Viva's stomach. "You didn't bring me here to look at the view."

"No."

"You could show me your bedroom." Gabriela glanced about. "Or we could stay here."

"Here?"

"In front of the window. With the lights of the city below, spread out for us to enjoy."

"Someone might see us."

Gabriela chuckled. "Who? Unless they are in a helicopter."

"It's always possible." Viva moved to turn off the lamp. Now the only light was the diffused glow of the city coming through the tinted glass.

Gabriela took her hands and drew her closer.

Viva pulled the buttons of Gabriela's shirt open and eased the material aside until she could see her skin, burnished bronze in the light. Her fingertips brushed Gabriela's skin, shooting sparks of fire into her palms. She ached with the need to smooth her hands over more of Gabriela's body.

Gabriela kissed her, taking the lead. Now that the decision to do this had been made, it seemed she was an assertive lover. The leader. The official.

Viva sagged against her, helpless in the face of Gabriela's passion. Gabriela's kiss seared her lips, branding her, yet it was gentle. It moved around, sipping, lingering, or was simply the press of warm lips, the touch of tongue. An echo of the sweetness of dessert. The kiss was hot and persuasive, fanning the fires of arousal that coiled deep in Viva's belly. How deep could she fall into her without drowning? How long could she just keep kissing her? The wine they had drunk was surely responsible for some of her light-headedness, but not all.

They swayed together, the fusion of their mouths leading to the slow press of bodies. Gabriela's hands tangled in Viva's hair, drawing Viva even closer.

Viva's knees buckled as she responded to Gabriela's urging, her breath coming in short, fast pants. She broke the kiss long enough to draw a deep breath and looked down at Gabriela. Her heavy-lidded eyes were slumberous, and her lips curved in a slight smile.

"Enough?" Gabriela asked.

Viva couldn't answer. Enough? They were only just beginning. Heat and desire twisted deep in her belly, and she wanted nothing more than to sink to her knees in front of Gabriela, pull her clothes away, and explore her naked body. *Soon. Very soon.*

She moved back, pulled her top over her head, and unsnapped her bra. After returning to Gabriela, she reached behind her to remove her bra also.

City lights made mosaics on Gabriela's skin, urban colours—red, yellow, orange. On Gabriela's darker skin, they turned into the colours of flame.

Viva pressed her hand against Gabriela's small breasts, her fingers splaying over the warm flesh. A hard nipple peeked through. Viva bent to take it in her mouth, flicking the nub with her tongue until Gabriela moaned.

The sound sent a thrill through Viva, reverberating in her body.

She manoeuvred them so that Gabriela faced the window and she stood behind, the delicate curve of Gabriela's spine pressed against Viva's breasts. Gabriela's head rested back on Viva's shoulder. Viva inched her fingers slowly up Gabriela's body, skimmed her breasts, circled her nipples, then skated back to her waist, to where the tailored pants were fastened with a clasp. She ran one finger over Gabriela's belly, and Viva delighted in the shiver of skin, the desire evident in the harsh breathing loud in the quiet room. Even though the room was cool, she was melting, burning with the need to feel Gabriela's skin pressed full-body on her own.

Encircling Gabriela's waist, she fumbled with the clasp until Gabriela took pity on her and undid it herself.

She turned to face Viva, and the heat in the brown eyes caught Viva's breath in her throat. Without breaking contact, Gabriela lowered her pants and undies. When they fell at her feet, she kicked them aside.

Oh, God. Desire burned brighter, engulfing her. Viva's palms itched to explore every centimetre of that glorious bronze skin. Her heart sped up, thundering in an urgent pulse.

Naked, Gabriela cocked her head. "Are you just going to stand there?"

Was she? No. The urgency to complete filled her. She could push Gabriela back against the window, drop to her knees in front of her, place one of Gabriela's legs over her shoulder, and taste her, really taste her, without further ado or foreplay. She clenched her teeth, willing her imagination to subside. *Slow down. Give her time.* She closed her eyes, reeling her heated thoughts back to a calmer place.

"Do it." The words were low, throaty.

Viva's eyes snapped open. She needed to see if the desire in Gabriela's words was echoed in her face.

The sparkle in Gabriela's eyes reflected the thoughts in Viva's head. "Do what you're imagining. And then I'll do the same to you."

Viva's breath shuddered from her body, leaving her light-headed. Gabriela's words had conjured images, scenes of the two of them in an abandoned naked dance, their bodies joined.

She kissed her again, imprinting her mouth over Gabriela's. The other woman met her kiss for kiss, a give and take of lips and tongues.

Gabriela backed up until her spine rested against the glass door that led to the balcony.

Viva paused. Gabriela's lean lines beckoned. Her skin glowed warm in the low light; her slight curves and planes of muscle were sculptured by shadow.

"Beautiful," Viva whispered reverently.

She kissed her way along Gabriela's neck once more, down to where her breasts curved softly. A taste of each nipple and then she knelt as her fingers preceded her lips, feathering down over Gabriela's belly, flickering as lightly as flame, until her hands paused on Gabriela's hips.

For a moment she glanced up, along the length of Gabriela's body.

Her head was bent, her eyes intent on Viva.

"Open for me." Viva whispered the words.

Gabriela shifted position to a wide-legged stance.

Viva explored the satin length of Gabriela's inner thigh, seeking the delights between.

Gabriela's breath came in shallow pants, and she moved her legs even further apart, allowing access.

Viva's fingertips stroked, long and lingering, before she pushed one finger into the clasping, wet heat. She sucked in a breath. No matter how many times she did this, the intimacy, the trust, of the act always made her pause. The first time inside a woman was something to savour.

"More." The intensity of the word was echoed in Gabriela's glittering eyes. Her hand came down to clutch Viva's hair in a tight grip that pulled her scalp.

Viva leant forward, her nose bumping Gabriela's flat belly. The angle made it difficult, but she persisted and her tongue trailed a wet path up Gabriela's inner thigh to join her finger in the heat between Gabriela's legs. Her musky scent filled Viva's nose, and her own sex clenched in anticipation. She dragged her tongue through the dampness and circled Gabriela's clit. Her other hand reached around to cup Gabriela's backside.

Gabriela cried out, a long shuddering sigh, and her grip intensified on Viva's hair to the edge of pain. Her legs jolted into stiffness, and instantly her buttock was rigid under Viva's hand.

Viva circled again, mapping Gabriela's response, increasing her efforts. Gabriela's thighs squeezed closer as she drew nearer to her peak, but there was nowhere Viva would rather be than right there, her knees digging into the hard floor, her neck cricked from the angle, and the joy of giving pleasure to a woman. *Her* woman? Maybe.

Viva persisted, mapping the folds and crevices of Gabriela's sex with her fingers and tongue. Her pulse thundered, and she concentrated on learning the movements and pressures that Gabriela liked. When she cried out, and her sex fluttered around Viva's fingers in the shivers of orgasm, Viva stilled. The scent of arousal filled her nose.

Gabriela slumped, her thighs relaxing, and her grip on Viva's hair eased.

Viva straightened and stood on stiff legs. She stepped forward, and they embraced, lips meshing in a sticky kiss.

Gabriela's eyes were golden in the city lights. "Now you."

A low buzz of desire surged anew in Viva's belly, arrowing lower. "Oh yes," she breathed.

"But not here. Where's the bedroom?"

In answer, Viva took her hand, and they crossed the shadowy living area to the bedroom.

Gabriela glanced around as they entered, as if cataloguing the room, but then her gaze snapped back to Viva. Her heated glance travelled the length of Viva's body, lingering on the waistband of the skirt as if imagining what was underneath.

Gabriela approached and reached out to explore Viva's breasts, barely there feather touches that sent licks of flame across Viva's skin. Gabriela slid her fingers down, hooked them into the skirt's waistband, and tugged down the material, centimetre by centimetre, brushing over each newly exposed piece of skin with the same light touches. When the skirt reached Viva's hips, Gabriela bunched the material from the bottom, so that cool air brushed Viva's legs. With a final tug the skirt descended and pooled at Viva's feet.

The thrum of blood in her head was almost painful. She stepped out of her skirt and kicked it away.

Gabriela trailed her fingers along the line where tanned skin turned to pale, the line where Viva's tennis dress stopped. She traced around the leg of her undies, running once over the juncture of her thighs to map the other side. Her fingers hooked in the elastic and pulled them down.

Viva's legs went weak. That slow-moving finger, the promises it elicited. Impatient, she reached for Gabriela's hand and drew her down onto the king bed.

Gabriela's gaze was intense, and Viva shivered under the heat and hunger in her look. Then Gabriela did more than look.

Viva gasped, a soft sound of anticipation as Gabriela touched her, exploring Viva's centre. Her fingers stroked seeking the patterns of movement and places she liked. Viva moaned her pleasure, and Gabriela increased her pace. *How does she know, so exactly?* Viva gasped again as the pressure sparked an instant pleasure, a pin-point of intensity that was so much greater than the diffuse pleasure of before. When Viva closed her eyes, stars swirled in a fast dance behind her eyelids.

Gabriela pushed a finger up inside, curling her way to the secret places, and Viva's head spun in a frantic whirl from the pleasure.

The soft waves of feeling were swallowed up before she could voice them. She was caught up in the inwards spiralling of her body, sweetly increasing, pulling her ever higher along the upwards surging, until her whole world was centred between her legs. When she came, her universe exploded into a starburst of white.

Slowly, Gabriela withdrew her fingers and moved up to lie alongside.

Viva turned to face her, and again they kissed. After all they had just done, every inch of skin explored and touched, Gabriela's kiss still burned sweet between them. Their skins were damp with sweat.

Viva left the bed and returned with two glasses of water. She wrapped a thigh over Gabriela's and nuzzled her neck.

"Still want to go for that run in the morning?" Viva was already sinking into sleep, the boneless realisation of the sated.

"Maybe not tomorrow." Gabriela stroked Viva's hair away from her face. "Another day."

Chapter 10

THE PERSISTENT NOISE OF AN unfamiliar alarm woke Gabriela.

Beside her, Viva stirred and raised up on one arm. Her hair was a snarl of tawny colour. She silenced the alarm and fell back onto the bed.

The blinds were raised, and the low light of dawn and the muted sounds of traffic told Gabriela that it was still early. She stretched, luxuriating in the soft sheets.

"You look like you're enjoying that." The husky voice was close to her ear.

She turned her head. Viva was close enough that she could see the flecks in her blue eyes and the way her lashes tilted up at the corners. "I am. This bed is very comfortable."

"Is that all I've got that's great?" Viva's eyes crinkled as she smiled.

"Lovely hair." Gabriela reached out to wind strands of it around her fingers. "Kissable lips." She moved in for a soft kiss. "Beautiful breasts." She touched a nipple with her free hand. It puckered instantly under her touch. "And a killer first serve."

Viva's smile froze. "Not for much longer." The words were flat.

Gabriela closed her eyes in mortification. "I'm so sorry. That was incredibly thoughtless of me."

"It's okay. I'll have to get used to comments like that. I may as well hear them from someone who means well." Her legs twitched, and the sensual mood of the morning fled. "I have to get going."

The heaviness of disappointment settled in Gabriela's belly. "I hope you have time for coffee." The words, supposed to sound light-hearted, came out hurt and accusatory.

"Of course." Viva's smile stopped short of her eyes. She bent to kiss Gabriela. "But I need to get to the courts."

Was she being bundled out of the door? Gabriela forced a smile. "I thought you weren't going?"

"I should have called Deepak last night. He's expecting me." Her gaze slid over Gabriela, and her face softened. "Hey, it's okay. I'm still retiring. But I can't just not turn up."

"Of course." Gabriela bit her lip. It made sense—indeed, to do otherwise was inexcusable. Viva still had a team of people supporting her. She could not just cut them off.

Viva sat up and swung her legs to the floor. "How do you like your coffee?"

"Strong with just a little milk. No sugar."

"I'll rustle up some breakfast. You'll find clean towels under the vanity if you want a shower." She was all brisk and business.

"Thank you. I will wait until I get home. I do not have clean clothes."

Viva's state-of-the art coffee machine sat in solitary splendour on the pristine countertop and was obviously well used in contrast to the blinding white benches and stainless-steel splashbacks that surrounded it.

Viva ground enough coffee beans for two mugs and popped frozen bread into the toaster. She handed a mug to Gabriela. "Want to sit on the balcony?"

The hum of early-morning traffic drifted up as they sipped their coffee and munched toast and Vegemite. Gabriela tried to focus on the view of the city, the heat already shimmering the air to a haze, but her glance kept sliding to the woman beside her.

Viva, too, was staring at the city, but her hunched shoulders pulled a shell around her. "I'm sorry. I'm a bit distracted." She pushed her hair behind her ears and reached out a hand across the gap between their chairs.

Gabriela took it, stroking a thumb over the back of Viva's fingers. "Would you like to meet for coffee later?"

"I'd like that." Viva tightened her grip. "Very much. But I don't know what time I'll be finished with…everything. Can I call you?"

Gabriela nodded. "I hope it goes okay."

"Yeah. Me too." She drained the last of her coffee. "I'm going to have a quick shower."

The words conjured the image of Viva's long body, wreathed in steam, an alluring vision behind the frosted glass of the shower.

Viva smiled. "I know what you're thinking. I'm thinking it too—but not this morning." She bounded out of her chair, the strange lethargy of earlier evaporating in an instant. She bent and pressed a kiss to Gabriela's cheek, then disappeared.

Gabriela washed and dried the coffee cups and was wiping the sparkling countertop when Viva returned. She wore shorts and a singlet, her hair tied back in the long, thick plait she favoured for tennis.

"Do you want a lift home?" she asked.

Gabriela summoned a smile. "I will walk. Make up a little for the run I skipped."

In the foyer, Gabriela caught Viva around the waist. "Call me." Her lips sought Viva's, and the kiss scorched in its intensity.

With a nod, Viva was gone.

When Viva arrived, Deepak was already there, chatting with the club coach. He finished the conversation and turned to her. "We're on court five."

The court was at the rear of the complex, where commuter trains rattled past every few minutes. Viva sat on the bench and pulled out her water bottle. Now that the moment had come, she didn't know how to start. She tested the racquet strings and bent to tighten her laces.

Deepak watched in silence. "You have something to say?"

"Am I that obvious?"

"I think after six years of working together, I know you well. Talk."

"I've decided. I'll retire, effective immediately. I wanted to tell you first." They were only words. They should not have the power to rip her world from under her, but they did.

He reached for her hands, turned them palm up, closed one into a fist, and pressed it to her breast. "That decision is right for you? You feel it in here?" He pushed her fist firmer against her heart.

"Not yet. But it will be. And I don't have a choice."

"I will miss you, Viva. Working with you has been a great pleasure."

"Even when I'm being a prima donna?"

"Even then."

It took two tries to get the words out past the thickness in her throat. "You're the best, Deepak. You made me what I am. I wouldn't have that US Open title if not for you."

"Don't underestimate yourself." He lowered her hand, squeezed it, and released. "You'll call Shirley? As your agent, she should know immediately."

"Yes. Later today. Tomorrow maybe. There's no rush. As long as I announce it before the Brisbane International, that will be fine." She forced her mouth into a smile. "Maybe I'll get some pre-Christmas sponsorship first."

"Not much of that around right now. What there is goes to that glamorous American."

"You'll be coaching her and more like her if you join with your friend in his Florida academy."

"I'll have some good Australian swearwords to teach them thanks to you."

She bounced her racquet on her knee. "I haven't decided if I want to continue with doubles for a while. Maybe that would only prolong the agony. Maybe in a while I can play the exhibition match circuit."

He nodded. "I understand. I think I'll go to Florida over Christmas. Take some time off."

"Go whenever you want. I won't hold you to anything."

"Thank you. Now what do you want to do today? For now, I'm still your coach. We can work on your oh-so-terrible footwork, which you will need to improve if you're playing exhibition matches, or we can go and have breakfast. Something unhealthy with sausages to celebrate your new freedom."

Freedom. An image of Gabriela as she had looked naked in her bed earlier sprang into her mind. The lightness in her chest surprised her. Maybe it would be all right. "Let's do both. We play one set. All out. No coaching. May the best person win. And then I'll take you to breakfast at that five-star place on the river. We'll have sausages *and* bacon. Got to get you used to the huge American breakfasts again!"

It was late afternoon before Viva called Gabriela.

"It's done," she said without preamble. "I told Deepak. Released him from his contract, effective immediately."

"How do you feel?" Gabriela's voice was careful, as if she expected Viva to shout and scream.

"I'm okay." Viva tested the words on her tongue. *Okay.* Was she? The tearing feeling of loss that had nearly crippled her earlier had faded, muted to a dull ache in her chest. "I'm more than okay, actually. I cried a little, then I played a set against Deepak, beat him 6-2, and then we went for breakfast. I'm not sure I can eat anything else today after that."

"I was going to ask you out for dinner." Laughter resonated in Gabriela's voice.

"I couldn't. How about a walk along the river, then tapas on South Bank? You can eat as much as you want, and I can watch you."

"Only if I can watch you as well."

"Nothing to see. I'll be sipping water after the wine last night." Viva perched on one of the bar stools at the kitchen counter.

"I'm sure I will find something to look at. How does five suit you?"

"That's good. How about we meet at the Ferris wheel?"

"That will be easy to find. I will see you then. Viva?"

"Yes?"

A hitch in breath came down the line. "I'm looking forward to it."

"Me too."

Viva set the phone down on the counter and stared at it. There were other calls she should make: Shirley, of course, and her fitness trainer. Personal calls too—her family. Michi as well. But those people knew what tennis meant to her. The thought of the silences on the line, the well-meaning platitudes... Those she couldn't handle. Not yet, anyway. No. She was an officially retired professional tennis player. She could sit at a South Bank café and have coffee. With a double shot. She could do anything she wanted.

Except continue her career. Viva shut down that line of thought, grabbed her purse, and headed out the door. She would have cake with that coffee.

Viva was ready early, so she strolled the long way to where she was meeting Gabriela, pausing to listen to a busker and to watch children splashing in the water at Streets Beach. By the time she reached the Ferris wheel, she was already damp with sweat, and her hair curled madly in the humidity.

Gabriela was waiting, and when she saw Viva, she walked straight up to her and into her arms. There were a few curious stares.

Viva drew Gabriela closer into her embrace and bent to kiss her properly. The echo of desire from the night before kindled anew low in her belly.

Gabriela linked her arm through Viva's. "Haven't these people seen two women kissing before?"

"I doubt it's that. Remember I'm a Queenslander. They're probably wondering where they've seen me before. People usually only recognise me in tennis gear, but I get a few puzzled stares sometimes."

Without debate, they started along the river, through the crowds that thronged South Bank. Once they could walk comfortably next to each other, they ambled along, with other people out for an early evening stroll. They stopped to watch a man learning to tightrope-walk, his wire only a metre above the ground strung between two of the sturdy pieces of public fitness equipment. He was persistent, despite only managing to get less than halfway along the wire each time.

"That's me now." Viva watched as he wobbled and slipped once again. "I expect I'll try and fail at a few things now."

"What will you do first?"

She considered. "I think I'll go home for a bit. Being at Waggs Pocket always relaxes me."

"Despite having to serve beer to a crowd of rowdy pensioners?"

"Even then. Even when it's just Max rambling on about his cattle. Maybe I will go and work there." She grinned. "It would put Jack's nose out of joint. He's been the de facto heir to the pub for a long time now." It would be a way of winding down, a time to consider exactly what she did want to do. Her family wouldn't pressure her; they'd give her a bar towel and tell her to go and pour beer, but they wouldn't push her into answers or decisions.

"It is beautiful there," Gabriela said. "Lovely in a sparse sort of way."

"Wait until the rains come. It greens up in a week. Fat cows, long grass, lots of weeds. Flooded roads. You can sit in the pub and watch the mould grow." Viva grimaced. "I better not time my trip home in the wet, or Mum will have me in the bathroom on mould patrol before I can say 'bleach'." They parted around a man with a dog on a long lead.

"I'm going to Fraser Island for a few days," Gabriela said. "I'm going to walk on the beach, maybe do some surf fishing. Swim in the clear freshwater lake I have heard about."

"We holidayed there as kids most years. We camped on the beach. Once, Jack left the lid off the tucker box, and the dingoes stole all our food." She looked across at Gabriela. "Where did you holiday when you were young?"

Gabriela's gaze followed a ferry out on the river. "We seldom went anywhere. There was never much money. But once we went to Portugal and once to Barcelona. It seemed such a huge city to us country kids."

"Where are your family now?"

"I'm the youngest of three—the afterthought by nine years. My parents are both dead. My brother lives in Madrid with his third wife. My sister lives in Sweden. We're in contact on and off. You are lucky to be close to your family."

"I am. Although there's times I'd like to give Jack a swift kick in the knackers. He can be very irritating. When I was a kid, he pushed me in the creek more times than I can remember. Once, he stole my diary and gave theatrical readings from it to his friends. I hated him when we were younger. I got him back once with a trip-wire where I knew he'd catch it on his motorbike in the paddock. He came flying off and broke his arm. I got into such trouble for that from Mum, but all Dad said was lucky it wasn't his neck. Jack and I get on fine now, though."

"I never had that sort of relationship with my brother. Hugo was the studious sort. He still is—he's a civil engineer and builds bridges."

He didn't seem to build many bridges with his sister. Gabriela's words were offhand. How would it feel to be so devoid of connections? Viva pondered. Sure, she travelled the world often alone, but her family were there for her, if she needed them. Silent, loving support.

"Are they there for you if you need them?"

Gabriela's white teeth flashed briefly. "In a way. Hugo wired me some money and bought me an air ticket to Spain once, when my credit cards were stolen. Carla, my sister, is there if I really need to talk, but I seldom do. I have friends on tour. And I'm self-sufficient, most of the time anyway."

Viva shortened her stride to match Gabriela's. Self-sufficient described Gabriela very well. But everybody needed somebody at some time or another. Maybe, they could be there for each other occasionally. *Maybe.*

Gabriela looked at her watch. "Do you want to turn back? You may not be hungry, but I am."

"Sure."

They turned around and retraced their steps. The day was cooling into evening, and the temperature was pleasant. They walked closer, hands brushing every so often. The third time it happened, Viva caught Gabriela's fingers with her own and secured them in a clasp. Hand in hand, they strolled back to South Bank.

Chapter 11

THE TAPAS BAR WAS ONLY half full. Viva led the way to a table near the back. "It's not like a real Spanish tapas place, but it's good all the same."

Gabriela picked up the menu. "Are you hungry now?"

"A little." Viva rested her chin on her hand and studied her companion. "You order what you want, and I'll eat a few mouthfuls. I'll eat anything except octopus. The suckers make me squirm."

Gabriela seemed to be ordering for a long time, finishing with a request for a dry rosé wine. "Sure you only want water?"

"Yes, thank you."

The waiter brought out the tiny plates a couple at a time, with enough break between servings that they weren't rushed. Each plate held two morsels. Viva found she ate more than she expected as the conversation flowed.

Then there was only a small, solitary plate between them. Viva reached with a fork to spear the titbit and raised it to her lips. "I didn't think I was hungry. This was delicious." She glanced up.

Gabriela's gaze was fixed on her lips, on the forkful of food still hovering ready to be tasted.

A frisson of desire spiralled into Viva's belly. There was heat and yearning in Gabriela's eyes and memories of the previous night in her quirky smile.

Last night. Viva's breath hitched, and she put her fork down. Gabriela's hands on Viva's body. Her mouth, her lips. Oh God, her lips. She leant forward, caught in the intensity of Gabriela's gaze.

"You are remembering it too." Gabriela's voice was low, husky. "Last night."

Her throat closed, and she could only nod.

"I remember the taste of your lips." Gabriela's glance flicked to the remaining tapa, untouched on the plate between them. "I remember how you sounded when you came." She touched Viva's hand. "What do you want?"

Viva could barely force the words past the lump in her throat. "I want you."

"How do you want me?"

"Spread wide on my bed so that I can taste you. Your hands in my hair."

"Music between us."

"Come home with me?"

Gabriela nodded. She picked up Viva's water glass and took a long draught. Then she held out her hand. "Shall we?"

It took only a couple of minutes to sort out the bill, but the wait seemed interminable. Despite the early hour, South Bank was busy as they wove their way through the parklands to Viva's apartment.

Once inside, Viva turned to her, excitement and desire coursing in twin channels through her blood. She kissed Gabriela, a long, slow kiss, languid and sensual rather than heated and urgent. Her blood pulsed with a drumbeat of desire, and her thoughts were full of the woman in front of her. The kiss bound them together, as if they were tangled in fine skeins, Viva's hands on Gabriela's shoulders, Gabriela's palms smoothing the skin under Viva's loose top.

They eased apart, and a slow smile passed between them before Viva once again drew her close to continue the connection.

They moved to the bedroom, and Viva watched as Gabriela shed her clothes with economical movements. When she was naked, she moved to Viva, and her fingers brushed Viva's skin as she helped her undress, caressing each exposed piece of skin with her fingertips.

Finally, Viva slid between Gabriela's parted thighs, and her tongue touched the magic and mystery there. Gabriela's sharp indrawn breath was her reward.

Gabriela woke first, not in a sleepy, slow surfacing but in the instant jolt of wakefulness. Daylight filtered in. Careful not to disturb Viva, she left the bed and went for a pee. Her legs twitched restlessly. A run. That was what she wanted. It was the perfect morning for a run along the river. She found her phone and looked at the time. It was just after five. If she left now, she could go to her own apartment, find her running gear, and still have an hour's exercise before the day grew uncomfortably hot.

Viva rolled onto her back, her mass of hair in a snarl on the pillow, her hand palm up, fingers loosely curled. She hadn't woken.

Gabriela couldn't just leave.

She sat on the edge of the bed and stroked Viva's hair from her face. She bent and placed a kiss on her forehead.

Viva's eyes flew open. Instantly, she was alert. "Hey." She sat up and took in Gabriela's place on the edge of the bed. "Are you sneaking away?"

"Stark naked?" She kissed Viva's lips. "I was thinking of going for a run. Want to come? I'll need to go home for my clothes, though."

"That sounds great." Viva bounded out of bed, a whirlwind of movement, as she grabbed clothes and shoes and shovelled her hair into a messy ponytail. "Give me two minutes." She disappeared into the bathroom.

It was only a few minutes' walk to Gabriela's apartment. She led the way into the living area, conscious that Viva was looking around at the bland decor and practical furniture. It was a small space, barely more than a studio.

"It reminds me of being on the tour." Viva went over to the kitchen. "Short-term rentals. But apartments like this were always so much nicer than a hotel room." She opened a cupboard, found a glass, and filled it with water. "It means you can cook. Or someone can cook for you."

"You only made toast the other day," Gabriela teased. "So do not pretend you cook."

"I don't much. But I can."

Gabriela shed her clothes and rummaged in the drawer for running gear. Even from behind, she sensed Viva staring at her naked back. She turned, and Viva's gaze snapped to her bare breasts.

Viva smiled sheepishly. "Caught in the act. If you really want to go for a run rather than seeing how your bed compares to mine, you better get dressed."

Warmth pulsed through Gabriela's body, and her nipples tingled in anticipation. Did she really want to run? When the alternative was so very tempting? But a morning run could always be followed by equally sweaty, more carnal pleasures. "A run first. Then maybe..."

Viva crossed the room and pressed her hot palms against Gabriela's upper arms. She bent to kiss Gabriela's neck. "I'll hold you to that."

"I will look forward to it." Gabriela turned away from the desire in Viva's eyes before she changed her mind about the run. She pulled a sports bra over her head and found shorts and a singlet. "Ready."

They set off along the river path at an easy warm-up pace. Gabriela's breath came in steady pants, her even footfalls already finding the rhythm of the run. By her side, Viva looked very comfortable, running lightly and easily. Gabriela increased her pace, her arms swinging in time with her stride, her mouth stretching into a grin with the joy of movement. They parted around a man with a dog, and the labrador seemed to answer her grin.

It was good to run with someone who could match her pace so easily. Who didn't try to talk, who seemed to enjoy the fluidity of movement as much as she. Viva's stride was longer, but they were able to stay side by side, without the effort it often took when she ran with someone new. Running, it seemed, was another area where they were compatible.

"How far do you want to go?" Viva asked, after they had been running for thirty minutes.

"Had enough already?"

"Hardly. But I'm thinking of coffee and eggs Benedict. There's a café on top of the cliffs overlooking the city that's calling my name."

Gabriela eased her pace. "That is the second-best reason I can think of to turn around."

"And the best?"

"My bed versus yours. The official comparison." She slowed to a halt.

Viva stopped too, reached out, and squeezed Gabriela's fingers. "Do you know how utterly tempting you are?"

The touch—hot and damp with sweat—still sent a pulse of desire into Gabriela's belly. Maybe they could skip breakfast. But then her stomach growled. There was always later for lovemaking.

They circled around and started back at an easier pace.

The cliff-top café was busy, but there was a vacant table with a view of the city. Viva had finished her first coffee before Gabriela had had so much as a sip of hers.

"Good thing caffeine isn't a banned substance," she teased, as Viva ordered a second one.

"I only have a single one when…" Viva stopped. "I used to only have one when I was training. Now, I can caffeinate myself into orbit if I want."

When the food was eaten, Viva pushed away her plate with a sigh. "I'm going to settle into an easier life no bother." She stirred a third coffee. "I'm not looking forward to telling my agent I'm retiring, though. I have to do that today."

"I thought you'd already done that." Gabriela's voice sharpened, and she struggled to keep the edge out of it. Worry pricked at her that Viva hadn't made the call.

"No. I talked to Deepak and my fitness trainer. Not my agent. Nor my parents, not officially, although I hinted to Mum. I'll go home to Waggs Pocket on the weekend and tell them then. They'll be fine. Delighted probably as they'll see more of me. But Shirley, my agent, will be put out. I make her a lot of money. I won't be making nearly as much once I'm retired."

Gabriela glanced around the café, half-expecting a journalist to pop up from the next table with a camera. "You didn't tell me you hadn't done it."

"It doesn't make that much difference." Viva touched the back of Gabriela's hand as it lay on the table. "No tennis happens now. I'll be retired before the season starts in January." Her mouth twisted. "Although I'm making the assumption you want to continue seeing me."

Gabriela closed her eyes. To Viva it must be simple; she was retiring, so there was no problem. But a niggle of worry still churned in Gabriela's stomach. The code of conduct for officials was rigid. She pushed down the unease. "I do want to keep seeing you," she said. "Very much."

"I'll talk to Shirley today. I promise. She'll arrange a press conference."

She nodded. It would be okay. Once Viva was no longer an active player, it would be fine. They would be free to be whatever they wanted to be. It was too early to think past a few dates, but what they had already done together was enough to compromise her standing with the International

99

Tennis Federation if anyone were to find out. She looked around the café again, suddenly as jumpy as a rookie official umpiring her first match.

The open-air space was packed with couples intent on each other, office workers reading the paper over a coffee, and a table of rowdy young tourists who looked as if they had yet to make it back to their hostel after a night out. No one was paying Gabriela and Viva any attention.

With an effort, she focussed back on Viva, on the damp tendrils of hair that had escaped from her ponytail, the curve of her arm, the way her top teeth bit her lower lip when she concentrated. The desire, tamped down from the morning, surged again.

It would be all right.

Chapter 12

"SHIRLEY, IT'S VIVA JONES."

"Viva, darling. I've been expecting your call."

Viva put her phone on speaker, went over to the fridge, and pulled out the makings of a sandwich. "It hasn't been that long since I called you. A couple of weeks maybe."

"An eternity. But I spoke to Deepak yesterday, and he mentioned in passing that you were retiring. Don't blame him—the poor man thought you had already told me."

So Deepak had talked with Shirley. The noose of retirement pulled tighter. Her pang of hunger faded, and she left the sandwich ingredients on the counter and went to sit on the couch overlooking the wide window. Yes, she was retiring. But, *hell and damnation*, it would be good to feel as if the choice was *hers* and not made for her by well-meaning others.

"I was going to call you, Shirley. I've been busy."

"He said it's your wrist. How bad is it?"

Viva sighed. "Bad enough. I could play another few months, no more than that." She studied her wrist. So deceptively small, so amazingly strong—when it was healthy. Now, though…

"Deepak said you're pulling the pin now. You're not going to play the Australian season. Is that right?"

"Yeah. I'd only be torturing myself. Why put myself through it?"

"Is that the only reason?" Shirley's voice sharpened.

"Yes." Gabriela's finely chiselled face floated behind her eyelids, and she pushed the thought aside. This was not about Gabriela. This was about her health.

"And what are your future plans?"

"I'll remain connected to the game, of course. I plan on taking up the tennis channel's offer to commentate for the Australian tennis season. Brisbane, Sydney, and then the Australian Open. If that works well, we'll continue the relationship. I'm hoping too you'll still be able to find me some sponsors. I could advertise frozen food with the best of them." The words felt hollow. Posing in front of a camera with a cardboard dinner in her hand had no appeal. Not compared to the adrenaline of match play, the thrill of victory.

"You could. You can. But I have a better offer for you. Although you'll have to change your plans temporarily."

Viva frowned. "What do you mean?"

"I approached Tennis Australia after speaking to Deepak. Don't be mad at me, Viva darling, but we have a proposition for you. Aussie grand slam winners are few and far between. Tennis Australia want to give you a send-off."

"You make me sound like the space shuttle." She rested the phone on her knee. Tennis players generally didn't get send-offs. They faded away slowly in a mishmash of injuries and first-round losses. Interest piqued, she leant forward, staring at the phone, as if she could drag Shirley's words out faster.

"Like the space shuttle, we have to make sure you come safely back to earth, but with a nice landing pad of cold, hard cash for you. Right now, you're marketable, Viva. Next year, you'll be just another commentator in a polo shirt."

"There's something in this for you too, no doubt."

"Of course. That's why I'm in the business."

"So what are you talking about? A round of press conferences, maybe a couple of charity dinners? A final exhibition match? Then I disappear into the sunset and go and pour beer in my parents' pub?" That would be a decent send-off. A recognition of her career and achievements. Something to look back on in the years to come when she had faded from the public eye. Her interest bubbled up. She picked up the phone from her knee, stood, and paced over to the window.

"A little bit more than that. As I said, right now you're hot news. Or you could be. It's a shame you disappeared from the tour these last few months—"

"I didn't disappear. I was injured." Shirley knew that; her blasé approach twisted a knife in Viva's guts. Shirley made it sound as if she'd been partying in the Mediterranean.

"I know, darling. I didn't mean it like that. But you haven't the high profile you had when you won the US Open. If you were fit, you'd still be right up there, in the marketable tennis stars' top ten. You're lucky you have the looks. With them and your outspokenness on LGBT+ issues, you're still in demand."

"Of course. It's all about the looks, isn't it?" She tried to keep the bitterness out of her voice. Years of top-level tennis and it came down to whether she looked good in a short skirt.

"Not all, but it helps." Shirley paused. "The Brisbane International starts in a few weeks."

Viva supressed a sigh. "I do know."

"Then Sydney, followed by the Australian Open."

"I know the schedule, Shirley. You don't need to rub it in."

"I do, darling. That's my point. Tennis Australia want you to announce your upcoming retirement now, but it will only take effect after you get knocked out of the Australian Open. They want you to play Brisbane, Sydney, and the Open and then quit. You can still commentate after you've been knocked out of each tournament. How deep do you think you could go? Quarters maybe?"

"I was aiming for that," she said automatically. "But Shirley, I'd be going against my doctor's advice to play." The leap of interest subsided somewhat. She'd be risking her health for a final few matches. But the spotlight would be on her and her tennis career. Recognition of her contribution to Australian tennis. What if she agreed? She bit her lip, and the longing to be once more on a court, fighting for a match point, rose up, overwhelming her with its intensity. What if she did make the quarters? An epic match as her final competitive game. She would be bound to lose at some point—she wasn't in any shape to make the final—but if she went down fighting in her home grand slam… She closed her eyes, visualising the crowd on its feet, the cheers, the applause, and the foot stamping. That was the way to exit a career. That was how she would be remembered.

"You said you could play another few months." Shirley's cajoling tone brought her back to the present.

"Possibly. If I had cortisone and analgesic injections."

"Would you consider that?"

"I did initially. But since I made the decision to retire, I haven't done anything about it. I don't need the injections for everyday life. Even exhibition matches, coaching, that sort of thing, with a light playing schedule and sufficient rest periods, I should be fine." The tiny seedling of hope unfurled a little more. Could she do this? A few more matches. It would give her time to come to terms with retirement, she reasoned, time to adjust to the withdrawal.

"That's good." There was a silence down the line. Viva pictured Shirley scribbling *Exhibition Matches!!* and underlining it three times on her yellow legal pad.

"So what do you think?" Shirley's voice came back on the line. "It's not just tennis. You'd play the three tournaments and commentate. If you played doubles with Michi, that would be a sweetener. The two of you look so good together."

"We *play* well together." She kept her voice even. Shirley's emphasis on Viva's looks had always irked her. Usually, she ignored it, and the woman did have good taste. She always managed to procure her a gorgeous frock for awards nights and galas.

"Yes, of course you do." Sweetness crept into Shirley's voice. Her persuasive tone. "There'd be a TV crew following you around for a bit. They also want to make a one-hour TV special. They'd film you playing, practicing, at the players' parties, and also at your parents' pub, being a normal girl. That sort of thing. Talk to your family and friends. *Australian Story* are interested as well. Your matches would get the centre court prime time slots, of course. Good exposure."

Viva bit her lip. This was more than she could have hoped for. This would be an unbelievable end to her career. The words "I'll do it" sat thickly on her tongue, waiting to be said. She swallowed, unable to speak for a moment.

"With all of that, I should be able to get you another sponsor. You've already got clothing, shoes, and racquet sponsorship. What about make-up?"

Viva still couldn't speak.

"Okay, no make-up." Shirley must have taken her hesitation as doubt. "You're not really the sort for that. How about cars? Are you still driving that nondescript little hatchback?"

She found her voice. "It's a VW, and I love it."

"Good. I'll approach them first. And then, at the end of the Aussie tennis season, you can sweep into the commentary box for your new career."

Viva rolled her eyes. Shirley was very good at her job. Frighteningly efficient, with a manner like polished concrete: smooth, shiny, surprisingly beautiful, and very unyielding. That attitude worked great when persuading a recalcitrant sponsor to come on board, but when it was turned on her, Viva felt like a butterfly on a pin. "Slow down, Shirl. I haven't said I'll do it. I need to talk to Deepak. He's probably flying to Florida as we speak."

"He's not, darling. He's in that funny little motel he likes near the tennis centre, waiting for your call."

"I need to talk to my parents and my doctor." *Gabriela.* What would she think? Viva had been so adamant she was retiring, and now... She didn't know. She stared out at the wide window, and her mind filled with the image of Gabriela as she had been, naked in front of this window, the lights of the city washing over her skin. *Gabriela.* The word stung. If she did this farewell tour, what would it mean for them?

"Well, talk quick. Wheels need to start turning."

"I don't know if I *can* do this." Viva stood and moved back to the counter, where the mental picture of Gabriela was not as strong. The sandwich ingredients sat neglected. She pulled out a slice of bread and started buttering it. The automatic movement of her fingers calmed her.

"Is it the wrist?" Shirley's voice softened.

For a second, she was tempted to say there was no way she wanted to risk her wrist. That was probably the only thing that would get Shirley off her back.

"That's part of it. But not all of it. I've psyched myself into wanting to retire. I don't know if I can revisit the argument."

"Think of the money. It would be what, one month out of your life, and you'd be boosting your coffers considerably."

"Yours too."

"Of course, darling. That's what I do. This sort of deal is what you pay me for."

She put the knife down. It wasn't about the money. Shirley, though, wouldn't see that. Shirley was a pragmatist, and, to her, money was the final clincher.

"Don't you want to know how much the offer is?" Shirley asked.

"Not really. If I do this, Shirl, *if* I accept, it will be because after nearly twenty years of tennis being my life, I want the recognition of my career. I have enough money."

"There's no such thing as 'enough'. Wait until you've been divorced three times before you say that again."

Viva chuckled. The money wouldn't sway her; it wasn't the make or break Shirley seemed to think it was. This was about the intangible things. One final hurrah. A chance, maybe, to tell her story to a TV audience. Maybe it would inspire some other kid to keep practicing, slog through the drills, in the hope that one day she, too, would win a grand slam.

"Tell me how much, then. You know you're dying to." She broke the cold chicken into pieces, added lettuce and mayonnaise.

Shirley named a figure. It was huge. It was more than she'd earned in the last six months of tournaments. It was enough to buy her parents' pub. Enough to make her comfortable, even if she never worked again. Viva closed her eyes. She'd accepted retirement. Needed it for her body. And the last few days, the idea had worked its way into her mind so that she was resigned to the idea, optimistic about a new life of opportunity even. But this… She swallowed down her excitement. Maybe she'd give her parents the money, let them have an easier life. There were no dollar signs in her head; there were butterflies in her stomach at the thought of playing on centre court once more. The Australian tennis season, her home state tournament. Excitement leapt as the vision of a cheering centre court crowd filled her head. To play again. *To win again.* To feel the racquet in her hand, the focus, the concentration, to win a match. She could do it. One final go-round. One final hurrah. Her wrist would hold out. The injections would see to that. Three more tournaments.

"Would I have to reach a certain round? What if I get injured?"

"No. You get as far as you get. If you need to withdraw from a match to protect your wrist, then that's what you do. No one will say you gave less than your best."

"I have always given my best. I've played through injury before." She struggled to keep the hurt from her voice. How could Shirley even intimate otherwise?

"I know that. But this is different. Obviously, Tennis Australia want you to get as far as you can. There's a bonus if you make a quarterfinal, bigger if you get to the semis or the final. But not at the expense of your health."

She perched on a stool, anticipation leaping in her chest. Something like this didn't come along often. Sure, it was a marketing ploy, another push for ratings in the sport, but it was also a shout-out to her career as a player. It would feel good, better than good, to end on a high note like that.

It would be incredible.

Her wrist would be okay. Dr Singh hadn't said she couldn't play, just that she couldn't expect to go deep in any draw. Deepak would be happy—it would give his tennis academy a boost. Her parents would be delighted—a television crew in the pub would be great exposure for them. Jack would be his most outrageous—he would love it too.

What about Gabriela? She was the only person who wouldn't be thrilled. She'd told Gabriela she was retiring. What would it mean for them? Viva's mind ticked through the possibilities. They'd had two dates and two nights together. That wasn't a commitment. Although, the tiny voice whispered, Gabriela had only agreed to those dates because she thought there was no conflict of interest.

A couple of nights did not make a relationship, despite what they both so obviously wanted. She couldn't put her feelings—maybe even Gabriela's feelings—above the culmination of her entire career. Gabriela would have to understand. And in six weeks, the Australian Open would be over, and then she would be totally free. She and Gabriela could see what they were to each other, free to pursue a relationship without impinging on the officials' code of conduct.

"I'll do it."

"Of course." There was no surprise in Shirley's voice. She probably thought the dollars had reeled Viva in.

"I'll have to see my doctor for the cortisone injections as soon as I can."

"You handle that; I'll handle the contract."

"Thank you, Shirley, for arranging this."

"My pleasure, darling. But the appreciation from you is nice."

Viva hung up, her head buzzing. She took the sandwich outside onto the balcony. There was less than a month until the Brisbane Open. Butterflies danced in her stomach, and she took a huge bite of sandwich to subdue them. Back on the courts again, if only for a few weeks. A golden send-off. It was perfect. She finished her lunch and went back inside to look up Dr Jacobwitz's number. She was in luck. Upon hearing the urgency, his secretary checked with the doctor and said if she could be at the clinic by five, she could have the first injection done today.

Her next call was to Deepak.

"This is what you want?" His voice came down the line. "Of course I'll work with you for the extra weeks, my friend. I would be insulted if you hadn't asked me. You rest the wrist after the injection and let me know when you're back in Brisbane. We'll have a lot of work to do. Where will you be?"

"I'll go home to Waggs Pocket."

"There's no reason you can't do cardio. Run, cycle. If you can get to a gym a couple of times in that week, work on your core."

"I will."

"And do the footwork exercises. You'll need them. Good footwork will get you into position and make it easier on your wrist. I'll see you in a week. Take care, Viva."

"I will. Thanks, Deepak."

She ended the call and dropped the mobile on the table. The plan was in motion.

Chapter 13

"So, TELL ME AGAIN WHAT we have to do." Viva's mum glanced across at her husband. "The film crew will come to the pub?"

"Yes, that's what Shirley said. They'll take footage around Waggs Pocket, including me pouring beer, chatting with locals, going for a run in the bush, that sort of thing. But they want all of you to be involved too. A few 'informal' chats that will actually be fairly scripted."

Jack grinned. "Can I tell them about the motorbike-and-trip-wire incident?"

"Not that." Viva glared. "If you do, I'll tell them you read my diaries. That will lose you all cred."

"Maybe I could round up my friends for a repeat performance." He put his hand on his heart and parroted, "I realised when I was thirteen that marriage to a man was not for me. For I was different. Special in ways I can barely articulate, even to you, dear diary."

"Shut up, Jack. Any time now is fine. In fact, you're always asking if you can use my apartment in Brisbane. How about going tomorrow? Stay all week."

"And miss the excitement? No way."

"You will behave, Jack. For Viva's sake." Her mum softened her steely tone with a smile.

"Okay." Jack threw up his hands. "I'll do whatever you want. I'll sing your praises to the rafters, say I couldn't have a better sister. On one condition."

"Which is?"

"You introduce me to Jelena Kovic."

"Jelena?" Viva shrugged. "If you want. Just an introduction, though. No more. After that it's up to you."

"Deal."

"Who's Jelena Kovic?" her mum asked.

"Up-and-coming Serbian player," Viva replied.

"Very hot," Jack added.

"Very gay." Viva smiled sweetly.

"Really?" Jack's face fell, then he rallied. "I still want to meet her. Even if I'm not her type—"

"Trust me, you're definitely not."

"—she seems like a lot of fun. Intelligent. I bet she'd be great for a friendly night out."

"There's hope for you yet. I'm proud of you, brother."

"There's still one thing about all of this that I don't quite understand." Her dad's interjection was quiet, but every head turned towards him. "Why now, Viva? Why do the TV song and dance now and not when you won the US Open or the end-of-year championship? Why not when you won three of the four doubles grand slams in the same year?"

"I'm sure it's a recognition of a long career." Her mum's voice was soft.

"It's a bit more than that. I haven't told you officially, but I mentioned the possibility to Mum. I'm sure you've guessed, though: I was going to retire before the start of the Australian season." She held up her wrist, the words she should say stuck in her throat.

Even Jack was silent.

Her dad's gaze drilled into her. She'd never been able to put one over him. "You said *was*, Viva. I don't think that was a slip of the tongue."

"I've agreed to play two tournaments and the Australian Open. They're giving me a send-off. Hence this TV special, prime-time matches and the like. Then after the Open, I'll do some commentating and see what else I want to do with my life. Maybe I'll come and work here. Or write my memoirs." She kept her gaze on her dad, as a myriad of expressions crossed his face: sympathy, sorrow, a flicker of a glance at his wife's stoic face. *Relief.*

"I won't lie to you. I was worried. Your wrist was obviously not back to normal, even after the surgery. And these medical appointments in

Brisbane you've been so closed-mouthed about… Well, there was obviously something going on."

She nodded, still staring at her father. "I'm sorry I didn't tell you. I sort of said it to Mum—"

"She never breathed a word. Anything you or Jack say to either of us in confidence stays that way. We don't want you to feel you can't talk to us."

"Never that." She reached out a hand, and her father took it, cradling her injured wrist as if it were precious. "I just hope I find something to fill the gap. I'm not sure who I am if I'm not a tennis player. I might still be able to play doubles. I'm not sure if I can give up everything, just like that. I haven't decided yet."

"Whatever you do, you won't sit around, will you, love?" Her dad smiled across the table. "Learn to cook, and there's a job here as chef for you anytime you want it."

"You can't do worse than Dad," Jack said. "Do you know he put battered deep-fried lasagne on the menu last week? The only person who ate it was Max. And us, but we had no choice."

She forced a watery grin. Her family: down-to-earth, loving, slightly bonkers. And very definitely there for her.

"How long are you staying here?" her mum asked.

"A week. Then it's back to Brisbane to prepare for the tournament, but I'll be back for Christmas."

"Of course you will, darl. Aren't you always? I'm so glad the first tournament of the year is the local Brisbane one. It makes it easy for us to go."

"Do you mind if I invite Michi for Christmas? She's flying into Brisbane on the twenty-third, but her husband can't come until later. She'll be on her own otherwise."

"Of course not. We love having your friends, and Michi fits in so well."

"Invite Jelena Kovic as well," Jack said.

"What about that lovely girl, Gabriela?" Her dad's gaze was steady. "Isn't she by herself as well?"

Would she want to come? It was one thing to invite a good friend like Michi, but inviting Gabriela might make it into something it wasn't. Not yet, anyway. She hadn't talked to Gabriela since she had made the decision to postpone retirement—maybe Gabriela would want to stay away. Maybe she would feel she *had* to stay away. "I'm not sure what she's doing over Christmas." The urge to see Gabriela again swamped her. And she had to explain. To let her know of her change of plans. "I was thinking of inviting her up for a couple of days this week, though. She missed seeing a lot of the area last time when her car broke down."

"I thought you were enemies? Ow!" Jack's exclamation stopped the conversation, and he glared at his mother. "Why did you kick me? Viva said they weren't girlfriends."

"Don't make things hard for your sister." Her mum stood. Conversation over. "Invite Gabriela, Viva."

Viva nodded. She would call her soon. Whether Gabriela came... Well, that remained to be seen.

———— ⬦ ————

The TV crew arrived early the next morning to take some footage of Waggs Pocket before concentrating on the pub. They filmed Viva's parents serving meals, Jack distributing plates of happy-hour nibbles to a packed bar, and Viva pouring beer. The town had turned out in force for the promise of being on TV, and a few of the locals were interviewed. Viva didn't like to think too hard about what they might have said.

When the crew finally left at dusk to head for a modern motel in Dalby, Viva worked the bar for a couple more hours, ate a late dinner, and went to sit by herself on the balcony with a cup of tea. The last time she'd sat here, Gabriela had been with her, eating rare steak and drinking red wine. Gabriela. Her mind skittered around the edges of what she had to say to her. She had to tell her she wasn't retiring just yet. It was only fair that she not delay any longer. She picked up her phone and pressed the call button.

"Hi," she said, when Gabriela answered. "It's Viva."

"*Hola,*" Gabriela's richly accented tones came down the line. "Are you in Brisbane?"

"No, Waggs Pocket. On the balcony. It's quiet. Max wants to know if you're coming back, Jack's still being a dickhead, and my parents send their best to you."

"Please send my regards to them as well."

"How was Fraser Island?"

"Fantastic." Gabriela's voice bubbled. "I swam in Lake McKenzie, spent a day surf fishing, and took a four-wheel-drive tour around the island. The seafood was fantastic. The local prawns were amazing. I would have called you, but the mobile phone reception is very bad there."

"Are you back in Brisbane now?"

"Yes. I got back last night. I need to catch up on sleep before I decide where to go next."

"I wondered if you'd like to come here for a bit? There's good bushwalking in the Bunya Mountains and a few places to explore."

The silence trickled down the line, long enough that Viva started to worry. "Don't feel obliged." She kept her tone offhand.

"It is not that. I would like to come. I am just looking at the calendar. I have been invited to visit one of the Barrier Reef islands by a couple I met on Fraser Island. I thought I would go. They say the scuba diving is far better there than it is on the reef further north."

"That sounds great."

"Would it be too rude if I came on Thursday and stayed two nights?"

"No! I'd love to see you anytime."

"Do I need to book a room?" A chuckle sounded in Gabriela's voice. "Will the Harley Davidson Club or the Vintage Wheelbarrow Club be staying?"

"There's no car clubs coming." Viva's conscience twinged. Gabriela was doubtless assuming she would sleep in Viva's room. Now was the time to mention she wasn't retiring just yet. But the thought of saying it over the phone seemed callous. There would be time when Gabriela arrived. Now that the TV crews had gone, Waggs Pocket was back to being a sleepy, tiny town. No one would see them together.

"I'm looking forward to seeing you again, Viva." Gabriela's voice was low.

"Me too." She gripped the phone as a wave of longing flooded her. It had only been a few days, but the memory of Gabriela—her compact, fit body, her easy way of talking—overwhelmed her. It would be good to sit with her on a quiet balcony and look over the street to the hills beyond, lit by a starry night. Good to hike with her in the mountains, show her the quaint little towns.

"I will bring my running gear. I would like to go for a run along those long, dusty roads of yours."

"We'll go at dawn and look for kangaroos." She had to tell her about the change of plans. It wasn't fair not to. No matter that it was over the phone, she couldn't let Gabriela assume nothing had changed. "Gabriela, I—"

"Viva!" Jack's shout came up the stairs. "Can you mind the bar for a few minutes? I've got to move kegs in the cellar. Now if you can."

"Just a moment," she yelled back. Then to Gabriela, "I have to go." Telling her would have to wait.

"I heard. I think all of Brisbane did. Send my best to Jack."

"He doesn't deserve your best, but I'll do that anyway."

"Go. I will see you in a couple of days."

Viva hung up and went bounding downstairs to find Jack.

"You look happy." He pushed his floppy hair out of his eyes. "Girlfriend decided not to dump you?"

"Very funny. At least I can get a girlfriend if I want one."

"Only because you're famous. Once I'm on television, the women will be falling all over me."

She looked pointedly around the bar. The only woman under thirty was Molly, who was chatting animatedly with her husband. "I'll step aside so I don't get crushed in the stampede."

"Just you wait. I'll come to the Brisbane International, and they'll be lining up. Jelena Kovic will be at the head of the queue."

"Don't hold your breath." She nodded to Molly and went to get her another glass of wine.

Jack returned a few minutes later, bringing with him some leftover pizza slices.

Viva finished serving a customer and returned to where Jack leant against the fridge, munching pizza. "What would you say if I told you I wanted to spend more time here once I've retired?"

"I'd say about bloody time. Thought you were getting too good for all of this."

"So you don't mind? You don't think I'm muscling in on your territory? The pub's always been Mum, Dad, and you. I just come and go occasionally, do the celebrity barmaid gig for a couple of hours." She tilted her head and

114

eyed him, watching for his reaction. She never knew with Jack; his jokey manner hid all sorts of things.

"Nah." He balled up the tinfoil from the plate of pizza and aimed at the bin. He missed. "The pub's mine. Or it will be, one day. You know that, right?"

She didn't, and the knowledge gave her a momentary pang, a twinge of sadness that maybe she wasn't loved as much as joker Jack. She swallowed, and when she could speak, she said, "I didn't know. But it's fair. You were here when I wasn't."

Jack came around to stand in front of her. His face wore an uncharacteristic sombre expression. "You're always welcome here, sis." He took her hands and clenched his fingers tight around hers. "Always. I mean it."

"Hey!" The shout came from the bar. "Less of the soppy stuff. There's people dying of thirst out here."

"Aw, shut it, Thommo. You can wait while I hug my big sister." He gathered Viva in his arms, pressing his cheek against hers for a second before releasing her and spinning around. A ruddy blush crept up from his T-shirt.

Viva went to pour Thommo a beer and glanced around the bar. The paint from Jack's last decorating attempt was peeling in places, and there was a water stain above the door. The furniture had a shabby look. It was like every other country pub in Queensland struggling to keep a community together and to keep the local feel. She could make a difference here, with her money, and some work and elbow grease, even if she wasn't here full-time.

"I've been away too long," she said out loud.

"That you have, lovely," Thommo said as he took the pot. "But you've had reason. We gunna see you win Brisbane this summer?"

"Not likely. I'm old and slow compared to—"

"Jelena Kovic." Jack came up to stand next to Viva. "She's my tip this year, Thommo. Don't waste your money on old Viva here."

"I don't know who that Jelena person is." Molly leant across. "My money will be on Viva, same as always."

"Thanks, Molly." Viva flashed her a big smile. "You get more wine for the vote of confidence." She tipped the rest of the bottle into Molly's glass.

"Hey, that's my inheritance you're frittering!" Jack nudged her in the ribs.

"For that, I'll have a glass of your best red."

Jack came up and gave her a huge smacker on the cheek. "For you, dear sister, only the best. And I didn't breathe a word to the TV crew about that whole trip-wire thing."

"Was that supposed to be a secret?" Molly's eyes opened wide. "Because I may or may not have mentioned it to that nice presenter."

Jack sniggered, and Viva glared. "No wonder Jack didn't mention it. He didn't need to."

"I wouldn't worry too much." Molly patted Viva's wrist. "The presenter was more interested in the details of your last crazy girlfriend than he was in Jack's busted arm."

It was late by the time Viva made it up to bed. Was this what life would be like after the Australian Open, a crazy whirl of family and small-town friends? That didn't seem so bad. What would Gabriela have made of this evening? Viva turned restlessly onto her other side. Jack's interruption meant that she hadn't told Gabriela that her retirement was postponed.

Guilt nagged her. That was something she should have done, not only as a lover and friend, but as a professional courtesy. Gabriela was conscientious. Would this delay have any bearing on their fledgling relationship? If what they had could be called a relationship. Viva gripped the sheet and pulled it up over her shoulders. Hopefully not. After all, she was still retiring.

Chapter 14

Gabriela pulled her rental car into the area behind the pub and killed the engine. It was later than she'd expected. Roadworks on the highway out of Brisbane had delayed her, and then she'd been distracted by a country market in one of the small towns she'd passed through.

She exited the car and made her way in through the rear door of the bar. It was quiet. Max sat on a stool in the corner, and Jack was behind the bar. Rather than be caught by Max, she took a seat on the far side.

Jack came over. "Hello again. Can I get you something, or do you just want my annoying sister?"

"Just your annoying sister, please." Her lips twitched. Good-natured sibling insults had never been a part of her family, but they seemed to the be currency of language in Viva's.

Jack nodded towards the door to the kitchen. "Last I saw, she was trying to talk Dad into letting her do the meals tonight. That will probably change now that you're here."

She smiled her thanks and went through to the kitchen.

Lindy and Ethan were sitting at the table, heads together, studying papers, but her gaze went to Viva, who strode from oven to workbench, a deep dish of something in her hands.

Gabriela stopped at the door, unwilling to interrupt.

But Viva turned and saw her hovering there. A wide smile flashed across her face, and she set the dish down carefully before coming over to Gabriela. Her hug was hard and tight, a brief press and release.

"I'm so glad you came," she said.

Lindy also smiled. "Come in, darl. Sit down. Kettle's on, or do you want something stronger?"

"Tea would be nice, if it's not too much trouble."

"Viva. Get on to it." Ethan snapped his fingers, but his smile gave away the joke. "That daughter of mine needs to learn to move quicker."

"Nothing wrong with my footwork," Viva grumbled, but she flicked the kettle on and grabbed mugs from a shelf.

Lindy gathered the papers and pushed them to one side. "Good drive?"

"Too nice. It's peaceful out here. I stopped for the market at Rosella Creek." She pulled a jar of mango jam from her bag and handed it to Lindy. "This looked too good to pass on."

"Thank you. It looks delicious."

Viva brought mugs of tea over to the table. "I'm rescinding my offer to cook tonight. Something better has come along."

"No surprise there. You enjoy the time together," Ethan said. "But sit for a minute first, Gabriela, and tell us how you're enjoying Brisbane."

Gabriela sat and cupped her hands around the mug of tea. "I enjoy it a lot. After all my time there, I feel as if it's a home away from home. But every year I go somewhere different too. I have just spent a few days on Fraser Island, and last year, I spent a bit of time on the Sunshine Coast. I learnt to surf."

"You'll be able to do that soon, Viva." Ethan's smile at his daughter was affectionate. "When you're retired and don't have to worry about injury."

"I intend to." Viva pulled the tea bag from her mug and set it aside. "There're lots of things I intend to do."

Curiosity piqued, Gabriela studied her. "Let me guess. Write your memoirs?"

"Too obvious."

"What, no kiss and tell?" Gabriela winked.

"No." A slant-eyed glance at Ethan and Lindy. "I have nothing to share about that."

"We'll let that pass." Lindy patted Viva's hand.

"What, then?" Gabriela asked. "Take up macramé? Learn a language?"

"The second actually." Viva's smile was infectious, and Gabriela's lips stretched automatically in response. "I know a few polite words and how to say 'She was the better player today, congratulations' in several European languages, but I'd like to become more fluent. I was thinking of either French or Spanish."

"Spanish is easier. And I could teach you a bit. If you want."

"*Sí. Me gustaría eso.*"

Her accent was terrible, but Gabriela smiled. Viva wanted to learn Spanish—Gabriela's own native tongue. Was that part of the reason Viva picked that language? An image flashed in her mind of the two of them, in a café in Spain maybe, and Viva testing her new skills on the wait staff.

Jack stuck his head around the door. "Is anyone cooking tonight? There's been two food orders on the counter for the last few minutes."

Ethan rose. "Guess it's me, seeing as our substitute cook has decided she's having the night off."

Gabriela rose too. "I am interrupting. Let me get out of your way."

"Go." Lindy drained her mug of tea so fast she must surely have burned her mouth. "We'll be fine here."

"Are you parked out the back?" Viva too had finished her tea. It would seem the entire family had asbestos mouths.

Gabriela nodded, and they went out to the car park. Once away from any curious eyes in the pub, Gabriela tugged Viva behind the mango tree, positioning her so that her back rested against the wide trunk. She trailed her fingers down Viva's cheek and felt her smile grow. "I'm glad I came."

Viva's eyes were serious. "Not as glad as I am to see you. You must believe that." Her hand captured Gabriela's fingers and held them to her chest.

Gabriela touched Viva's lips with her own.

Viva hesitated, a swift indrawn breath that ended on a soft sigh as she leant into the kiss.

Gabriela sank into the touch, the sweet taste of Viva, and a kiss that was already becoming a special kind of familiar.

Viva stepped back. "Let's get your bag."

"Leave it for the moment." Gabriela took her hand, linking their fingers together. The heat of Viva's palm reminded her of the magic in her hands. "I've been cooped up in that car for hours. Can we walk for a bit?"

"Sure. I'll show you the creek path. I've been running there most mornings. I thought maybe we could run there tomorrow—if you want to."

The gravel path led through the camping area, scattered with caravans and trailers, and over the footbridge that connected the two sides of the town. Gabriela's fingers curled around Viva's, joining them even more tightly. The sun was low, a red haze in the sky, and somewhere in the bush a kookaburra cackled its maniacal laugh. They walked in silence for twenty minutes before turning back to where the lights of the pub shone through the gum trees.

Through the window, she could see Ethan and Lindy busy in the kitchen.

"We should put our dinner order in," Viva said. "Before the only thing left is deep-fried lasagne." She led the way through the back door to the kitchen hatch, where she handed Gabriela a menu.

"Roast chicken, please." Gabriela set the menu down.

"Want to eat upstairs on the balcony?"

"Yes, that would be good."

Viva poured two glasses of red wine and led the way to the balcony. Once Gabriela sat, she raised her glass. "To us, to summer, and to the Australian tennis season."

They clinked glasses and drank.

"I've missed you." Viva set her glass down on the old wooden table. "I've been busy: with Deepak, with all sorts of crazy happenings since we were last together, but despite the busy times, I wished you were here." She fiddled with her fork. "Is that weird?"

Gabriela's skin prickled, a frisson of desire. "No. I missed you too. I loved Fraser Island, but I wanted you there to share it."

"Things have changed for me in the last few days." Viva's expression changed. The playful, open expression now had a serious cast.

Gabriela pushed aside the moment of unease. "What has happened? Has Jack thrown you out of the family business?"

Viva's gaze flickered between her glass and Gabriela's face. "There's no easy way to say this. Tennis Australia made me an offer, and I accepted. I'll play three tournaments over summer, and then I'll retire after the Australian Open. There's a lot of exposure. It's a golden send-off into retirement. It's a huge honour." Her fingers sought Gabriela's and squeezed. "I'm still retiring; it's just a little later than I originally planned."

The hot clasp of Viva's fingers was stifling. For a moment, she couldn't take in the words. *Not retiring.* How could that be? Viva had set the wheels in motion. She frowned. *Not retiring.* She swallowed. A miasma of emotion surged to the front. "You're playing on?" Her voice croaked. "You're still an active player?" The white haze of anger expanded in her chest. "How nice. For you, anyway. Not so good for me. Conflict of interest." She spat the words. "Remember that discussion, Viva? Player and officials cannot date." She surged to her feet, the glass of wine shaking precariously. "I cannot be here."

Viva bit her lip. "I'm sorry. I thought it would be better to tell you in person than over the phone. It's only three tournaments. After that, I may only play a few doubles matches."

"If they want exposure for you, you must be playing the bigger tournaments. I'm sure they're not packing you off to Hobart where there's barely any TV coverage." Gabriela turned away and stared out into the evening. Her stomach turned over, and she was glad she hadn't started eating.

"Yes, Brisbane, Sydney, and then the Australian Open."

"The same tournaments that I'm officiating at." She couldn't keep the bitterness from her voice. "I wonder did you listen to me at all." She swung around again.

Viva hunched wide-eyed at the table, her face pale. "I did." She reached out a hand. It hovered in the air.

Gabriela stared at it, and her fingers clenched into a fist.

Viva's hand lowered to the table.

"If you listened, then why are you still not taking in what I say? Now you say you will keep playing doubles. You never even mentioned that. That does not sound like retirement to me."

"I didn't think it would matter that much." Viva was pale, her eyes wide and shell-shocked. "You're a high-ranked official; you don't umpire many doubles matches. I just can't give up tennis entirely. It's everything to me. My wrist could cope with a few doubles matches. I thought that would be okay…for us."

Gabriela smashed her fist onto the table, hard enough that Viva's wine slopped over the rim of the glass. "It may be okay for you. To me, it *matters*. You're a player; I'm an official. We cannot have a relationship."

"Not now maybe. I thought if we eased off now and waited until I've retired from singles. The end of January, after the Australian Open. Six weeks. Then it'd be all right."

"Too many people already know: your family, your coach, probably your agent. Any number of people who saw us having dinner in Brisbane. Maybe they do not know me, do not even recognise you, but you can bet your ass they will remember when your face is plastered over the news on your farewell tour. Your *singles* farewell tour." She heaved a breath and sat once more. "I was wrong to go out with you the first time. It was wrong that we slept together, and there is no excuse for why we kept seeing each other. I take the blame for that first date. But Viva," she leant forward so that their faces were close together, "I told you what my career means to me. I wouldn't have slept with you if you hadn't assured me you were retiring. Not next month, but the next *day.*"

Across the table, Viva's face was white under her tan and still. She was listening now. Too little too late. Her lips parted. "Gabriela, I'm—"

"Do not speak to me. Do not apologise. I cannot decide if you are deceitful or just thoughtless. Your career may be as good as over; mine is not. If word of this gets back to the International Tennis Federation, I can forget about reaching gold badge. I'll be lucky to get any high-level matches at all. My best chance is to disclose our relationship to the ITF and try to explain." Anger and misery warred in her chest. Viva had been magnificent. A woman she could really have fallen for. *Have already fallen for*, a small voice whispered. But not at the expense of her career, if indeed it was still salvageable.

Viva seemed to shrink into herself, her shoulders hunching, her face a closed wall of disquiet. "It's only three tournaments," she whispered. "Surely, we can just stay out of each other's way during that time? Then we can—"

"What? Carry on as if nothing had happened? Maybe you can do that; I can't."

"I can't stop it now." Viva pushed shaking fingers into her hair. "I'm committed. They've commenced filming a TV special on me. I'll be commentating. My matches will be centre court, prime time. It's the end of an era for me. I have to do this."

"At my expense? I'm sure the money you'll get for this will keep you warm at night. I'm sure you're laughing at me, worried about a career that nets me a tiny fraction of your earnings."

"I'm not laughing. That's the last thing I'd do. I know how important your career is to you." Her expression was anguished. "I'll go to the ITF on your behalf. Explain. Ask that they not allocate you to any of my matches. I'll be lucky to get through the early rounds."

"Stay out of my career. You will make it worse." Gabriela clenched her fingers on the glass and drained the contents in two swallows. "You have done enough damage."

"I'm sorry. I'm so very sorry."

Gabriela stood. "Hang on to that thought. I hope it keeps you satisfied at night. Thank you for the wine." She spun on her heel and turned to the door.

"Where are you going?"

"First to see if Ethan and Lindy have a room for the night. I do not see a car club, so I am sure they have. Then I will ask for dinner to be served in my room. Tomorrow morning, I will be gone."

"You can—"

Her laugh was curt, and she swung back to face Viva. "What, stay in your room? I don't think so. Goodbye, Viva."

Viva looked beaten. But she swallowed and stood, uncurling her long body so that she stood tall and proud. "As you will. Goodbye, Gabriela. I will treasure the time we shared."

Gabriela met her gaze. Viva's blue eyes were unblinking, a sadness already hiding in the depths.

"As will I." Gabriela steeled herself against the rush of sadness that threatened to overwhelm her, and her eyes burned with unshed tears. *It is over.*

Resolve alone carried her away from Viva, down the creaky wooden stairs to the kitchen to find Ethan and Lindy.

"I'm hearing all sorts of rumours about you." Michi's face filled the screen, her hair—still pink—in a messy pile on the top of her head. She wore a bra with stars on one breast and stripes on the other.

"Is it legal to desecrate the flag like that?" Viva adjusted the laptop so that Michi would be able to see her better over the Skype connection.

Michi glanced down at her chest. "I like to think I'm enhancing it." She leant forward so that her face filled the screen. "Stop changing the subject. I want to know about the rumours."

"Since when have you paid attention to them? If you believed the rumours from ten years ago, you and I'd be married."

"Wasn't legal back then." Michi grinned and sat back.

"No one I want to marry."

"Oh? That's one of the rumours I've heard lately. But it's the other one I want to talk about. Retirement. Sound familiar?"

"It does. Where did you hear that?"

"Brett heard that Deepak was moving to Florida early next year. Does that mean what I think it means?"

Viva sighed. "It does."

"Your wrist?"

"Yeah. I've tried, Michi. It's never going to be strong enough to play consistently at high level."

The ebullient Michi was uncharacteristically silent. "I'm sorry."

"I still intend to play doubles—if you'll still have me as your partner. I'll understand if you wave bye-bye and skip off into the sunset with Paige as your partner."

"She's good. Really good. Better backhand than you."

"Glad you're going to miss me."

"I'd trade her perfect backhand swing for your two-handed grunt anytime. Of course you're still my doubles partner!"

Viva managed a weak smile. "That's the best thing I've heard for a while. I don't know how long I'll be able to keep playing. Even doubles might be too much."

"I'll have you as long as you're available." Michi winked. "When are you going to announce your retirement?"

Viva sat back in her chair. "At the start of the Brisbane International. Tennis Australia cut me a sweet deal. I'll be tennis history after the Australian Open."

"Now that's settled," Michi's grin crinkled her eyes, "what's this I hear about you with a girlfriend?"

"Who told you that?" *Shit, shit, shit.* Viva exhaled in a long, shaky breath as her pulse pounded in her ears. Michi wasn't one to spread gossip unless there was something behind it. Who had mentioned seeing her and Gabriela? She bit her lip as she tried to work out who it could be.

"I'll tell you once you've told me if it's true or not."

"The rumour mill's false on that one."

"Then why did you blink fast just then, as if you had something in your eye?"

"Because I did have something in my eye."

"Bullshit." Michi snorted inelegantly. "Shall I save you this evasive dance? Rumour has it you're dating an official. Gonna tell me what's going on?"

"Nothing. Absolutely nothing." *Not now.* "Now you have to tell me where you heard it."

"Alina Pashin. I didn't listen, because you know how she likes to make trouble, but then I heard it again from someone else."

"Who?" Viva expelled her breath shakily. It was a worry that Michi had heard rumours over in the States. And Alina was about as bad as it could get. The ITF would have wind of it now—Alina would have made sure they knew, even if they hadn't heard it any other way. Then what would that mean for Gabriela, for her career?

"One of the club coaches. But I don't think she really knew anything. She was pumping me for information."

"What did Alina say?" Anxiety swelled in her chest. Alina, of all people. Why couldn't it have been Paige, who would probably have shrugged and figured it wasn't her business? But no, it was Alina. Someone who seemed to have it in for Viva and would delight in bringing her down. But this wasn't just about her. It was about Gabriela.

"Ha! It's true, then. You wouldn't give a rat's patootie what Alina said otherwise."

"Are you going to crow about being right, or are you going to tell me?"

Michi was silent for a second. "Alina's a bitch. You remember that, right?"

Viva grimaced. "I'm hardly likely to forget. She said to me after I won the US Open, 'You got lucky once and won a grand slam, but you're not that good a player.' That was so charming of her."

"Hold on to the fact you dislike her. I spent a couple of days in Florida, at Delacourt Tennis Academy. That's where Alina trains."

Viva nodded.

"I had the pleasure—not—of hitting with her. She makes even a friendly hit a slugfest." Michi scowled. "I made her pissy because I refused to run for her shots if it was likely I wouldn't reach them. Anyway, at the net at the end, she said, all offhand, 'I hear your little doubles partner is dating an official. Guess she has to win somehow.' And then she swished away like she was on the red carpet."

Viva swallowed hard, worry jumping in her throat in jagged stabs of anxiety. "Shit. So much for thinking no one would find out. And how does *Alina* know?" She dropped her head into her hands.

"The rumour mill, but I have no idea how she found out. She keeps herself so aloof." Michi leant forward again, her face wiped clean of expression. "Viva, an official? What the *hell* were you thinking?"

"I *know*, Michi. Believe me, it's come up. It's also why I am not dating anyone at the moment. Although I wish I was. I really wish it."

Michi touched the screen, as if she could touch Viva's hand. "What happened?"

"The rumours are about Gabriela Mendaro. We met by chance. She spends every December in Queensland. It was a bit of a rocky start, as I recognised her as the lineswoman who called me for two foot-faults in the US Open."

"And you crashed out of the Open after losing that match." Michi whistled. "I'm surprised you didn't slaughter her."

"We got past it. I like her. She's good to talk to, warm, understands our lifestyle of course. And she's simply gorgeous."

"I wondered when you'd get around to mentioning that." Her head tilted quizzically. "Reckon Alina's attracted to women?"

Viva considered. "I used to wonder, but then she turned so unfriendly I stopped caring. She's dating one of the male players."

"Bisexuality. It's real, remember?" She pointed to herself. "And Alina wouldn't be the first player to date a guy to deflect rumours. She's not important, though, Gabriela is. So, what happened?"

"Gabriela's car broke down near Waggs Pocket. I gave her a lift to Brisbane, and she left a bag in my car. We went out for dinner, it turned into overnight and then grew from there. I liked her, Michi. Really liked her. She was hesitant about spending time with me because of the whole player-official thing. Her career is important to her—of course it is. But I told her I was retiring." Her laugh was hollow. "Then I talked to Shirley. You can guess the rest."

"Gabriela wasn't happy, and that was the end of what had barely started. Am I right?" The naked sympathy in Michi's face made Viva swallow hard.

She nodded. "Pretty much. I've gained the sort of send-off from the sport that every player dreams of, but I've lost the promise of... Well, I don't know what to call it at the moment. It was too early for it to be anything more than potential."

Michi was silent. "In your heart, do you think it could have been more?"

"Maybe. Yes. I think so. I'll never know now. Gabriela stormed off. I don't blame her. I was a bit caught up in my own life, and I disregarded her feelings on all of this. She's too honest, too straightforward for subterfuge." She bit her lip. "If Alina knows, though, that's about as bad as it can get. She won't keep it to herself."

"If it's over, does it matter?"

"It does to Gabriela. She's worried the ITF will penalise her. If they do, it's all my fault." Viva pushed her fingers into her hair. "I don't want that for her. Her career could be destroyed because of me." She paused. Gabriela was the one who would pay the price. *It's all so fucking unfair.* Guilt and misery welled in her chest, and she couldn't speak. She took a quick breath. Another, willing away the sadness. "Anyway, I'm hitting again as of yesterday. Can't let my doubles partner down."

"That won't happen. Hey! Does this mean I'll be getting centre court time because I'm playing with you?"

"I guess. They're giving me prime-time slots for my matches."

"Great. I'll wear a really risqué outfit. Want me to keep the pink hair? It will show up really well against the blue courts in Oz."

"Absolutely. I love the pink."

"I'll be over soon enough. A couple of days before Christmas."

"My parents asked if you want to spend Christmas with us at the pub. Nothing special. Family time. Mum and I will be cooking, so the food should be okay."

"I'd love that. Please thank them for me. It will be so much nicer to spend the day with you rather than on my own in some hotel."

"There's a tennis court an hour away if we want to hit, but it's a cracked concrete court, nothing fancy."

"I remember. And I love running the river path."

Unbidden, the memory surfaced of her and Gabriela strolling that same trail. That was the last time she'd seen her, before she'd stormed off back to Brisbane. Viva pushed the thought from her head. What was important now was tennis.

She ended the conversation with Michi and wandered downstairs. It was early. Her dad was preparing breakfast, and her mum was outside, putting out minced meat for the wild magpies.

Viva perched on a stool and watched her dad work. "Michi's coming for Christmas."

"Good. Nice girl, Michi. Think she'd do a turn in the bar? We could advertise it as doubles night. You and Michi behind the bar and two-for-one drinks."

"She'd be up for that. Make it trivia night too. She's a whiz at that."

Her dad cracked eggs into a bowl. "How's the wrist holding up?" He turned, wooden spoon in hand, and regarded her. "Truthful answer, Viva. None of your half-truths or positive evasions."

She smiled at his perceptiveness. "It's holding up fine. So far, so good."

"Any word from Gabriela?"

"No." She slid from the stool. "Want me to do the toast?"

"Sure," he said after a moment. "It's just you and me. Your mum's not eating brekkie, and Jack's still in bed."

When the eggs were ready, her dad slid them onto plates. "Have you given any thought to life after January?"

"Of course. If my commentating during the Australian season goes well, maybe I'll get work over the American and European seasons. I thought I'd sell the Brisbane apartment—I hope to make Waggs Pocket my base a bit more. I'll be travelling a lot less than I was."

"Your room is always available. You know that."

She stretched out a hand, tears unaccountably pricking at the corner of her eyes. "Thank you. I do know. But I'm going to look for a small block.

Build something airy and light, with a view of the ranges. If you hear of a couple of acres that fit that description, you might let me know."

"I will." Her father cut his toast into squares and forked some eggs on top. "It makes my heart glad, Viva, that you still want to live near us."

Her fork paused in the air. "Why wouldn't I?"

"You were so young when you left home. And when you came back, you were changed. More worldly. It was inevitable, I suppose, but you were only fourteen and you were travelling the world by yourself."

"Yeah. Just me and a couple of dozen people from Tennis Australia."

"You know what I mean. We missed out on your teenage years—"

"The tantrums, the sulks, the angst and dramatics."

"Except there weren't many of them, were there? You were so controlled. You went away a mess of nerves and emotion, and you came back with a composure and focus way beyond your years."

"Meditation. Seriously, try it sometime."

He ignored her. "Viva, I worry sometimes that you traded your childhood for tennis."

His words brought up a flickering cinemascope of images: herself, battling through pain and injury, the bone-deep weariness that no child should have to feel. The dormitory-like atmosphere she lived in. Being so self-sufficient so young. She'd missed her parents at first, had hated the noise and bustle of the city after the quiet open spaces of Waggs Pocket. It had been a forced maturity. But weighed against that was the passion that had driven her, the rewards, both material and otherwise, that stemmed from being so good at something she loved. It had defined her life. It had been her life.

And now it was nearly gone.

Her dad regarded her steadily. His breakfast cooled in front of him. "What will replace that passion for you now, Viva? I'm not sure that a quiet life in Waggs Pocket and occasional commentating will be enough for you."

"What would you wish for me?"

"Something to make your heart sing again. *Someone* to make your heart sing. A woman to love, who loves you just as deeply."

"I've had girlfriends. But it's difficult to sustain a relationship on the tour."

"I know. We've met some of them."

"Please don't mention Chitra."

"I wasn't going to. But since you have, it was obvious she loved you very deeply, in her own way." He took a mouthful of tea. "I think Chitra gave more to you than you gave back to her."

"I was at the peak of my career. She only played doubles."

"*Only*. That's exactly what I mean. Chitra may have *only* played doubles, but those matches were as important to her as any grand slam was to you."

"What are you saying?"

He took another swallow of tea as if it were liquid courage. "Nothing you can't already work out for yourself. Just that a lesser amount of skill, of luck, of circumstance, doesn't make another person's dreams any less important. A different goal is not a lesser one. Chitra wants to win a doubles grand slam. I hope she does."

"I wish her luck."

"I know you do." His eyes were steady on her face as he said, "I guess I'm saying that supporting another person in their dream can be as rewarding as chasing your own. If it's the right person. Especially as you've realised yours."

She pondered his words. "I hope I'm not that selfish that I wouldn't do that for someone."

"The right someone, Viva. And they have to want it for themselves. Don't force someone into what you wish for them."

"You're a wise man, Dad. What about your dreams? Did you realise them?" With a lurch, she realised she didn't know. Was her father's dream a bush pub, a wife, and two grown-up children still hanging around?

"Lindy was always my dream. That and life in a small community. So yes, I'm still living it. You and Jack were the icing on the cake. And Viva, talking of Jack… You know the pub is his baby, don't you? He jokes around, he's flippant, but this is his life. I think you can complement it, but I'm asking you not to usurp it."

"I know. I won't."

An outer door banged. "Lindy will be here in a minute." Her dad stood. "I wish you all the luck in the world in your final season of professional tennis. But remember, Viva, it's not everything." He collected their breakfast plates and put them in the dishwasher. "What time are you leaving for Brisbane?"

"Later this morning. I'll be back with Michi for Christmas, but we'll be gone again the day after."

"I understand. I love you, darling. You've always been such a pride and joy to us."

She walked into his wide embrace and laid her head on his shoulder as she used to do as a little girl. "Love you too, Dad."

Chapter 15

The email still wasn't perfect. Gabriela flexed her shoulders, stiff from hunching over the keyboard. How many times in a career did an official have to write an email like this? She wished the flippant approach would work: *Dear ITF, I've been having hot sex with a player. Sorry about that. But it's all over now. Carry on!*

No, this email needed a combination of diplomacy, acknowledgement of her error, apology, and sincere assertion that it would make no difference for the three tournaments that Viva was playing and she was umpiring.

Then she would have to wait and see what difference it made to her career in the long run. And what if Viva did continue playing doubles? What then? Her mind glanced away from that.

The facts. She had to concentrate on the facts, not the emotion. Not on Viva and her long athlete's body and the way she felt under her hands. Not on how well they ran together, the things they had in common. Not even on her delightfully normal family and the quirky bush community of Waggs Pocket. Certainly not on the noises Viva made in the back of her throat as she came or the wicked look of anticipation on her face as she parted Gabriela's thighs and moved between.

No. Better to remember that Viva had let her down. Maybe she never had any intention of retiring immediately; she had certainly changed her tune fast enough once big dollars and time in the spotlight were on the table. Whatever the reason, the loser wasn't Viva with her mega-dollar enticement and promise of a future as a commentator. No, the loser was Gabriela, scrabbling to salvage her career.

She wrote fast, trying to convey the perfect mix of formality and appeal.

The player, Genevieve Jones, assured me she would be retiring as an active player prior to the Brisbane International. However, she has now delayed retirement from the singles tour until after the Australian Open. Our relationship has now ended. I assure you that this previous association will in no way impact upon my commitment to be a fair and impartial official.

She stood, stretched, and paced over to the window. Brisbane buzzed outside the window. Was Viva back in town, or was she still in Waggs Pocket? Was she hitting again? And if so, how was her wrist holding up?

Gabriela had played a couple of sets with Jorgen the other day. He hadn't mentioned Viva, and neither had she, although the question had burned on her tongue. Gabriela made a coffee in the tiny kitchen and returned to her email. Once it was sent, she would reward herself with a walk along the river, maybe a coffee and a slice of citrus tart in one of the waterfront cafés.

She read the email over a final time. Her finger hovered over *Send*. She clicked. It was done.

The walls of her tiny apartment closed in, and the memory of Viva was in every corner. It would be Christmas soon. If Viva had gone through with her retirement, maybe they would have spent it together. Maybe at Waggs Pocket in the company of her family. Maybe they would have gone out to dinner in Brisbane, uncaring of who might see them. She would never know what might have been now.

Gabriela grabbed her purse, found her keys, and left, out in the bright sunshine.

———◆———

"I love this tournament." Michi bounced along at Viva's side as the tournament director led them into Brisbane's Queen Street Mall. "Even the draw is an event. Aussies love tennis, and I love how Aussies love tennis!" She waved at a cluster of teenage girls holding oversized tennis balls and pens in the hope of an autograph. "And thanks to you, Queensland's golden girl, I get to do part of the draw."

"Just don't draw me against Alina in the first round," Viva said out of the side of her mouth as she, too, waved to the crowd pressing against the barricades.

Angus, the player representing the men's side of the tournament, grinned. "I did this last year and went up against Roger Federer in the first round. I lost, 6-0, 6-1. Not my finest hour."

"Or even finest forty-five minutes," Michi quipped.

They reached the stage and posed for photos with the sponsors and tournament directors. The draw itself took only a few minutes.

"I drew you a qualifier." Michi grinned at Viva. "You got lucky. She'll be so tired after playing three qualifying rounds in this heat that you'll stomp all over her."

Viva smiled in return, but her thoughts pushed past the draw to the announcement she had to make at the end. Her fingers pressed her wrist in an automatic gesture. It felt fine. The steroids and painkilling injections had worked their magic. She glanced at the journalists and bank of cameras. They had been tipped off for an announcement following the draw, and social media had already speculated as to what it could be. For the most part, the rumours were accurate. Shirley and Deepak waited unobtrusively in the crowd. Once the announcement was made, all three of them were lined up to give interviews for the rest of the day.

Viva sighed. After today, she would be Genevieve Jones: nearly retired tennis professional.

Gabriela waited in the officials' lounge for her match to start. The preceding match had dragged on to a slow third set. She glanced at the TV monitor showing the progress. 4-3 in the third. Hopefully, it would wrap up soon. The smell of coffee wafted over from the café area, and she thought longingly of a cup. But it didn't do to drink too much ahead of a match. Toilet breaks were awkward things when you were in the umpire's chair.

A burst of applause sounded, and she glanced at the screen again. 5-3. Surely now the match would wrap up soon. She stood and stretched.

Arno, one of the other officials, came over, coffee in hand. He pointed to the monitor. "Interminable match. Bet you're glad you didn't get that one."

She nodded. "I hope mine goes quicker. But with two qualifiers playing each other, you just never know."

"I hear the American youngster, Nicholas Simmons, is tipped to win over the Belgium kid." Arno set down his cup and reached for the sugar packets. "But watch Nicholas. He's at the uppity stage where he thinks he knows it all. Likes to argue line calls, and there's no Hawk-Eye on the outside courts here."

"Thanks for the heads-up. I will be extra vigilant."

"You always are." Arno grinned. He tilted his head towards the screen. "Match point. You could be up now."

She turned in time to see an ace fly down the T. "Looks like I am. See you around, Arno."

"I hope your match is quick. I'm after you on that court." He paused, and his gaze flickered her way quizzically. "I was a little surprised that you got the two qualifiers and I got the seeded players' match. I'm still only bronze badge—I would have thought it would be the other way around."

"Maybe they think it's time you had some better matches." She bent to pick up her bag and water bottle. "Don't overthink it. Just enjoy the experience."

She strode off before he could reply. So other officials had noticed the matches she had been given too. Qualifiers and unseeded players for the first round and nothing past the quarterfinals. It was hard to maintain a nonchalant attitude when she was seething inside. Damn Viva and her selfishness. Damn her for her naive assumption that it would all be corrected with one apologetic email. She wasn't the one being penalised for this.

There had been no official reply to her email; there didn't need to be. The matches allocated to her said it all.

<hr />

"I give you Queensland's own Genevieve Jones, ladies and gentlemen." The commentator led the applause as Viva made her way to the centre of the court for the post-match chat.

"Congratulations, Viva. I thought Ellen was going to take you to a third set for a while there, but you came through. A tough match for your opening round here in Brisbane." The commentator directed the mic towards her.

"Thanks, Andrew. Yes, it was a tough start. Ellen is always a tricky opponent, and she played well today. I think we'll be seeing more of her in the future."

"How did your wrist hold up?"

"Good. No problems there. I'll be ready for Paige in a couple of days."

"Paige will be a difficult one for you." Andrew turned so that the camera caught his best angle.

"Yes, she's beaten me the last couple of times, but I'm ready for her. I'm looking forward to it." She smiled and shifted her racquet bag to the other shoulder.

"I'll let you go now. Genevieve Jones, ladies and gentlemen."

Viva lifted her hand in acknowledgement and headed for the exit, giving a particular wave to the group from the Stockyard Social Club. She paused to sign a few autographs, then left centre court.

One down. Who knew how many to go.

Once she'd showered and the post-match press conference was completed, she met Deepak as arranged in the players' lounge.

"That was harder than it should have been, despite what you told Andrew," he said. "Ellen was metres behind the baseline. You should have sent more serves wide to take advantage of that."

She nodded and took a sip of her sports drink.

"Remember that when you play Paige. She doesn't have good movement. She's also carrying a bit of extra weight after the break and has dropped a bit of fitness. You make her run in this humidity, and she'll feel it." He glanced at his watch. "It's time for our stroll around the outside courts for the TV crew. The Aussie kid, Kimberley, is fighting hard on an outside court. She'll probably go down, but if you can talk her up, Tennis Australia will like that. And Michi is a set and a break up. We'll go there first so you can cheer her on."

Viva nodded, and with the camera trailing behind, they set off on their walk.

Michi's match finished as they got there with Michi as the victor, and Viva applauded loudly. "Glad you didn't wear yourself out for our doubles tomorrow," she called, and got a grin and thumbs-up in response.

The courtside crowds started to disperse, and the next court over came into view. Two men slogged it out in the full sun.

"15-0."

The accented tones came clearly to her, and her step hitched. The catch in her chest caught her unawares.

Gabriela's neat figure perched on the umpire's chair as she made a note on the scoring tablet. Her short cap of hair shone like burnished mahogany in the bright light.

Cameras forgotten, Viva stopped, her gaze drinking in the neat blue polo shirt and green shorts of Gabriela's umpire's uniform. Gabriela was intent on the match as she waited for the server.

Beside her, Deepak cleared his throat discreetly. "Two qualifiers. I think we'll be seeing more of Nicholas Simmons in the future."

She stared at him, grateful for his comments. She had no idea who the two players were. The twinkle in Deepak's eye said that he was aware of her distraction, as well as the likely reason for it.

"Nicholas trains at DeSantis Academy in Florida," he continued.

"An excellent place," she responded. "Many top players have come from there."

He nodded and led the way to where young Kimberley was fighting to stay in her match.

Viva focussed again on the job. It was inevitable she would see Gabriela here. She would have to get used to seeing the woman who had taken such a hold of her life in such a short time. She would have to learn not to let her interest show. For Gabriela's sake.

"No!" Michi's shout of dismay echoed as her return went long. On the other side of the court, their opponents whooped and hugged.

Viva turned to Michi. "It happens." She hugged Michi around her shoulders, pretending to bounce her racquet off Michi's pink head.

Together they walked to the net and exchanged brief hugs and congratulations with their opponents.

It wasn't a bad loss; she and Michi had fallen easily into their partnership once more but were outplayed by their second-ranked opponents.

"Keep smiling," Michi muttered, as they packed their sports bags. "There are about a bazillion cameras focussed on you."

"This month yes; next month, I'm history." She straightened and waved to the crowd, and she and Michi exited.

The corridors surrounding centre court were busy with players, officials, and event management staff going about their business.

"I need water, a shower, and food in that order." Michi grimaced and glanced down at her damp top, pulling it away from her skin. With her head down, she nearly walked straight into a player coming the other direction.

Viva grabbed Michi's arm and pulled her to one side as Alina swept past. She wore a jacket, even though the day was hot, and her customary headphones. She didn't acknowledge them.

Michi watched her pass. "There goes the next Australian Open champion, if the word on the street is correct."

"Since when have you listened to the word on the street? Besides, according to the Aussie press, *I'm* the next Aussie Open champion."

"Ha!" Michi glanced around to make sure no one was in earshot. "Even you don't believe that."

"I don't." Viva smiled ruefully. "Much as I would love it, my chances are Buckley's and none. Alina will win or Angie. Maybe you, if you stop fooling around with your husband and eat your greens!"

"What do you know about the fooling around?"

"The spare bedroom in my apartment adjoins my room. I hear you both—"

Michi's eyes opened wide. "Nothing to hear. No sex until after the tournament. Then there's a slim window of opportunity until the next one starts."

"I was about to say I hear you *laughing*." Viva dug her elbow into Michi's side and smirked. "What did you think I was going to say?"

"Never mind." Michi shut her mouth with a snap.

They turned a corner, and Viva's laughter dried.

Gabriela walked towards them, her leather umpire's bag hanging from her shoulder. She walked purposefully, eyes front, the walk of someone who had to be somewhere.

Viva's steps slowed. It was a chance meeting, Gabriela could hardly cut her dead in a crowded corridor. Maybe this was a chance to show she could be polite and friendly and no more.

"Come on, draggy ass." Michi grabbed her arm. "Oh." She took a discreet step away and pretended an interest in the photos of past tournament winners on the wall.

Viva halted. Gabriela was in front of her, about to walk past. Her tongue stuck to the roof of her mouth, and she couldn't think of a thing to say. The corridor wasn't that wide, and Gabriela slowed.

"Hi, Gabriela." It was a desperate croak. "How have you been?"

Gabriela nodded, a curt acknowledgement, and her pace increased. In a second, she had passed by, leaving Viva staring at her upright back and squared shoulders.

"Come on. People are staring." Michi ambled back, outwardly casual. "Where do you want to eat tonight?" she asked loudly. "That Italian place again for some carb loading?"

Viva stretched her mouth into a grin that felt like a grimace. "Sure. I'll need that before tomorrow's match." She bent to fiddle with her shoelace so that no one could see the hurt on her face.

When she straightened, her smile felt more natural, and she squeezed Michi's arm. "Let's get showered and out of here. I'm starving!"

Gabriela sucked in a breath and rested against the wall. It was inevitable, of course, that she run into Viva around the tournament. Before they had become involved, the curt nod would have sufficed. Now it pulled her apart. Her feet twitched with the need to follow Viva down the corridor, pull her to one side, and tell her... Tell her what? There was nothing she could say that would make any difference. She was already umpiring low-level matches. Any lower and she'd be on the junior circuit.

Viva was the one who had misled her. Viva was the one who'd brought this smear on Gabriela's head. That, if nothing else, should have made it easy to forget her. Gabriela pushed away from the wall and clutched her satchel more firmly. It was time to move on, refocus on that elusive gold badge.

Chapter 16

"15-40." THE UMPIRE'S CALM TONES cut through Viva's tension. Two match points to her opponent.

She turned the balls over in her hand as she walked to the service line. She twitched the toe of her shoe into place, a couple of centimetres behind the line, and waited for the crowd to settle.

It was the first evening match, and centre court was full. Her player's box contained not only her parents, but also a few of the stalwarts from the Stockyard Social Club, their red T-shirts a blaze of colour in the otherwise staid attire.

Viva's concentration narrowed to the ball in her hand. Two bounces and she rocked back on her heel, the ball thrown high and true into the air. Her swing was good, and the racquet connected, smashing the ball over the net. It grazed the line and spun wide. *Ace.* She whirled around with a jubilant fist pump. She could do this.

"30-40."

The roar of the crowd thundered with the excitement of a possible comeback.

Viva wiped her damp hands on the towel and threw it back to the ballkid. Still a match point to Paige. She focussed on the strings of her racquet to steady her mind, then returned to the service line. *This point matters. Only this one.*

On the other side of the net, Paige crouched, waiting.

"C'mon, Viva!" The yell from the crowd broke her concentration, and she waited until the umpire had called for quiet.

Heart pounding, Viva took a deep breath, tossed the ball, and struck. The serve was good, but not good enough, and Paige's return went deep on Viva's backhand side. She struck it back, and for agonising moments they rallied back and forth. Then Paige took advantage of a short ball, sprinting for the return, and her forehand drive clipped the line.

"Game, set, and match, Westermeier!"

The tournament was over, at least for her. For a second, Viva bowed her head and closed her eyes in defeat as disappointment overwhelmed her. Then pasting a smile on her face, she jogged to the net to congratulate Paige and shake the umpire's hand.

Deepak waited for her as she came through the tunnel from centre court. "Not a bad effort. She kept sending balls to your backhand side. How's the wrist holding up?"

She flexed, winching as the movement brought pain. "A bit sore. Not too bad."

"Make sure you see the physio before you head away tonight."

"I will. After the press conference and an interview with a tennis blogger."

"Before that." Deepak was firm. "Now you're eliminated, you'll be commentating, no doubt. Let me know when you have your schedule. We need to keep you fit for Sydney next week."

"Slavedriver." She punched him affectionately in the biceps. "I pity the students in that fancy Florida academy when you get there."

"They'll listen to me. Unlike you, sometimes." His grin took the sting from his words. He sobered and grasped her shoulders, waiting until she looked him in the eye. "Give it to me straight up. How's the wrist? Don't say 'fine'."

"It hurts when I hit a slice backhand or hit a ball at full stretch. Other than that, it's holding up well."

His nod was short. "Good. Let's hope it stays that way."

Viva slung the racquet bag over her shoulder and headed for the locker room. If she hurried, she could get through her list of commitments and maybe catch the end of Michi's match.

It was deep into the third set when she slid into Michi's player's box, next to Brett.

He nodded at her before focussing back on his wife. The score was even, with no break of serve. Viva's gaze ranged around the court, at the ballkids setting up balls, the players waiting for time to be called, and then at the umpire, high above the court in her chair. *Oh, this is not fair.*

The umpire was side on and just in front of where she sat, but it was obviously Gabriela. Her slender fingers tapped on the scoring tablet, and she leant forward to call time.

"4-5, Cleaver to serve."

While Viva shot a glance at Michi, it was Gabriela who held her attention. Viva exhaled slowly so that she didn't disturb Brett. Michi's serve went long, but Viva barely noticed. She was intent on Gabriela's profile, the curve of brown calf, and the way her white shoes were drawn neatly together on the step.

How had she ever thought it would be easy to avoid Gabriela? A tournament was a small place. Every corridor or alley between courts, every cafeteria, and every common space in the tennis centre was somewhere she might bump into Gabriela. And each meeting was a jolt to the senses, a reminder of what she'd had—and lost.

The audience burst into applause and yells of encouragement.

Viva dragged her thoughts back and looked at the scoreboard. Michi had held. It was now 5-5. She added her voice to the cheers.

"Quiet, please." Gabriela's calm tones cut through the cacophony.

The first two points went to Michi's opponent, but a lucky drop shot put Michi on the board. She bounced lightly on her toes at the back of the court, moving forward to take the serve on the rise. It was a good serve, but Michi's return was better and she smashed it home.

Viva nodded to herself. 30-30. "C'mon, Michi."

Beside her, Brett glanced her way. "She's got this," he muttered. "Inez is tired."

It was the work of a minute for Michi to put away her opponent's next serve to take the game to go 6-5 ahead.

Viva gripped her thumbs, willing her friend to hold her cool. A line of red T-shirts across the court caught her eye. As one, members of the

Stockyard Social Club leant forward and banged on the railings, cheering for Michi.

The final game went by in a blink. Michi served two aces and skipped around the court, chasing down her opponent's shots. She ended the match with a lob over Inez's head. The Argentinian could only watch in disbelief as the ball dropped abruptly and clipped the line. Game, set, and match to Michi.

Michi tossed her racquet, caught it expertly in one hand, and dropped an elaborate curtsy to the crowd, who roared their approval. A long hug for Inez at the net and then she jogged over to shake Gabriela's hand and blow kisses to Brett, Viva, and the Stockyard Social Club. Then she was gone, pushing through the crowds back to the locker room.

"She's doing well." Brett turned to Viva. "Don't tell her I said this, but I think she's got a chance of getting to the semis—if not here, then in Sydney."

Viva angled her body towards him, as much to avoid seeing Gabriela descend from the umpire's chair and leave the court. As much to avoid seeing her tanned legs, the muscles of her thighs. As much to avoid remembering exactly how those legs had felt underneath her fingers. "I won't tell her. But I think she'll have worked it out for herself. She's got a great sense of her game."

"And now that the number one seed lost earlier today, she's in with a chance. Michi plays Signe next, and she's beaten her the last three times they've played."

"If she makes the semis, the champagne is on me."

Brett stood. "I'm away to catch up with her. I'll see you at your apartment later."

———◇✕◇———

Maybe it would be all right.

Gabriela glanced around centre court, at the familiar blue playing surface, the crowd of spectators filling the stadium, clutching food and drink. At the last minute, her match had been switched, and she now had a quarterfinal on the main arena to umpire. Maybe her banishment to the outside courts was over.

The evening match promised to be an exciting one. The number two seed, Alina Pashin, was playing the surprise quarterfinalist, Michi Cleaver. Alina was tipped to win, but Michi was a crowd favourite here. The Aussie crowd loved her pink hair and exuberant personality, as well as her agile and attacking style of play. It probably also helped that she played doubles with Viva.

Was Viva in Michi's player's box, watching the match? Gabriela didn't let herself glance around to check. Really, what difference did it make? Viva was *then*, a moment out of time in her life, and this was *now*, and it was her life. Her career.

Gabriela descended from the chair for the coin toss, which Michi won and elected to serve. Was Viva here, cheering on her friend? Her fingers twitched, and the desire to know got the better of her. She glanced to her left, where the players' boxes were. There was Brett Cleaver, and, surprisingly, a row of red T-shirts from the Stockyard Social Club, including Viva's brother, Jack. But no Viva.

She snapped her gaze to the front. What did it matter that Viva wasn't there? It didn't, not to her. The sooner she stopped thinking about her, the better.

Michi was playing well, but Alina was simply too good. Viva leant forward in the commentary box, her eyes on the game. Andrew, the regular commentator, was easy to get along with and, being an ex-player himself, knew his stuff.

"You know Michi's game as well as anyone," Andrew said, "playing doubles together as you do. What does she need to do to win this?"

"Michi is a superb serve-and-volley player, old school if you like, in the mould of Martina Navratilova. She's very quick—"

"Small and nimble," Andrew said.

"—with excellent anticipation. Watch her racquet head as she approaches the net. She doesn't telegraph her shots."

Michi played a crafty drop shot that Alina, from her position just outside the baseline, was unable to reach.

"Excellent shot!" Viva said.

"Good tactics," Andrew said at the same time.

They looked at each other and grinned.

Despite the drop shot, Michi lost the match. Once they were off air, Andrew removed his microphone and headset. "Same time, same place tomorrow for the semifinals. You did well today, Viva."

"Thanks." She smiled at him. "You made it easy. And you covered my bloopers."

"Only two. Not bad for a rookie."

"Thanks. I'll be off. I have a best friend to console about her loss."

Michi and Brett returned to the apartment a couple of hours after the match. Considering she had lost, Michi seemed quite upbeat. She and Brett sat on the high stools at the breakfast bar, watching as Viva pulled cheese, dip, and veggie sticks from the fridge.

"I nearly had her." Michi's irrepressible personality had already bounced back. "If I hadn't dropped serve at the start of the second set, if only Hawk-Eye had given me the call on her serve, I could have taken it to three sets."

"I thought the ball was out." Brett laid a comforting hand on Michi's knee. "It was only in by the tiniest of margins."

"The umpire called it well. Hawk-Eye supported it." Michi shrugged. "Them's the breaks."

Gabriela had indeed called it well. Viva turned from the fridge, a bottle of wine in her hand. "A glass to celebrate you reaching the quarters?"

Michi covered Brett's hand with her own. "If my coach says I can."

"You've earned it. A glass tonight, then tomorrow it's back to training."

"Want to hit tomorrow?" Michi asked Viva.

"Sure, if it's early. I'm meeting Deepak at eight."

"Seven, then."

Viva twisted the cap on the wine, poured three glasses, and pushed the cheese board nearer the others. "I'm commentating for both semifinals later. Is it wrong of me to hope that Alina loses?"

"Human, not wrong. She's never been that pleasant to you. To anyone, actually. She's always by herself in the locker room. Sticks to her own clique."

"Unfortunately, I think she'll win. Her opponent's the only qualifier left in the draw. Alina will mince her up and spit her out."

"Make sure that's not part of your commentary." Brett reached for a carrot stick and heaped it with dip.

"It won't be."

"Do you know who the chair umpire is?" Michi asked.

"No. But I know who it's not, and that's the main thing." She glanced at Brett. He was studying the cheese board as if it was the strangest food he'd ever seen. Brett was okay; she trusted him. "I don't suppose you've heard why Gabriela isn't umpiring for the semifinals? I would have expected someone of her level to at least be there for one semi."

"I haven't heard anything," Michi said. Beside her, Brett gave up the pretence of staring at the cheese and shook his head.

"She said…before she dumped me, that she'd be penalised for our relationship. I thought she'd get a slap on the wrist, maybe a fine; I didn't think it would be this bad for her." She bit her lip. "I don't know what I can do."

"Probably nothing. If you try to interfere, you may make it worse for her. The ITF may see you butting in as some sort of cover-up."

"The lady doth protest too much," Brett added.

"But I can't just do nothing. I'm barely a player these days. Two more tournaments and then I'm gone from the singles tour. And I'm unlikely to make it past the first round the way I'm playing right now." She reached for a carrot stick. "It doesn't seem fair on her."

"Imagine if more players and officials had relationships," Brett said quietly. "Right now, it's only you and Gabriela—that they know of."

"And that's not a relationship now." Viva sipped her wine.

"If there were more player-official relationships, it would be a scheduling nightmare." Brett glanced at Michi, as if seeking her approval for his words. "Did you notice Gabriela only had matches on the other side of the draw to you? That's not so hard to accommodate, but what if there were other relationships to take into account? They could hardly say it's okay for you two and then squash down other people's relationships."

"It's a workplace relationship. They're allowed practically anywhere else." She banged her glass down on the counter and glared at the drops of red wine on her pristine countertop.

"It's not the same." Michi's words were quiet. "Imagine the potential for match fixing."

The breath whooshed out of Viva, and she sighed in defeat. "I know. I really do know all of that. Of course it makes sense. It's just… Well, I miss her."

"Oh, honey-bun." Michi scooted around the bench and took Viva in her arms, hugging her hard. "Maybe when you're retired, it can be different."

"I said that. She blew me off."

"She was angry, upset. She probably felt betrayed. People say all sorts of things they don't mean at times like that."

"I'll be playing doubles anyway. With you. So, in that way, I'll still be a player."

"But not every tournament."

"No. Just a few."

"Maybe." Michi's arms dropped away, and she poured more wine into Viva's glass. "Don't argue," she said when Viva opened her mouth to protest. "You have at least four days before your next match. Two glasses won't kill you."

"I could text her." Her phone sat on the countertop, shiny and tempting, like chocolate before bedtime.

"And what could you possibly say at this point that could make it better?"

"Sorry? I miss you? I want you?"

Brett cleared his throat. "I think I'll go and change before we go out to eat."

"Poor boy." Michi's fond glance took in his departing back. "We've made him uncomfortable."

Viva wrinkled her nose. "What, by talking about lust between women?"

"Hardly. He's well aware I've been there, done that, and got the pink T-shirt. No, I think he's being tactful, in case you want to talk to me by myself. Do you?"

"I don't know what I want, Mich. Well, I do—I want Gabriela. But she doesn't want me, and really, what else could she do? Look how she's been sidelined because of me so far. I haven't been good for her." The phone sat at the edge of her vision. She reached for it.

"Put the phone down and no one will get hurt."

Viva laughed and laid the phone back down. "Maybe I need to find someone else. A date. A one-night stand."

"Is that what you want, because if you do, I know someone who would love to go out with you."

"No." She cut a slice of cheese and paired it with a cracker. "Another time, maybe."

Michi took the titbit from her fingers. "Mine, I think. You know blue cheese is my favourite. You're not interested in who wants to date you?"

"Honestly? Not really. Not now. The only woman I want to date is off limits."

"Okay. My lips are sealed. But if you're pining that badly, I don't think you should walk away from Gabriela. Oh, you can't really do anything now, but after the Australian Open, maybe. If you're serious, show her you are. You go, girl."

The phone kept tugging her vision, but she resisted. "Enough about me. Go and rescue Brett from the bedroom, and we'll go out to dinner. After all, we have to celebrate Michi Cleaver, Brisbane International quarterfinalist and, if my calculation is correct, the new world number thirty-five!"

It had been easy when the three of them were laughing over dinner, dropping sushi from their chopsticks into the soy sauce and then eating with their fingers. Easy to play the light-hearted tennis star when she and Michi were recognised and approached for autographs. Easy to relax in an open-air café by the river and gaze up at the Southern Cross and the swathe of stars that shone through, even with city lights. It had been easy to forget about Gabriela then.

But back in her apartment, alone in her bed, in the slight haze of three glasses of wine, Viva remembered.

Gabriela's way of tilting her head as she listened. Her full-throated laugh, her smooth skin, darker from the sun on her arms and legs, the rest of her a pale olive. Her keen interest in trying new things. The way she listened so intently, with her complete attention. Her total immersion in what they did to each other in bed. The noise she made as she came.

Viva rolled onto her stomach and pressed her head to the pillow. The bed was huge and she was lonely.

Moving to the edge, she picked up her phone and opened a text message. She shouldn't do this. Gabriela had made it clear she couldn't have anything more to do with her.

I miss you, she texted. *Can we meet for coffee sometime? Anywhere you want. I would like to explain.* Clutching the phone to her chest, she rolled onto her back. Explain what? What could she say that hadn't already been said? The city lights of Brisbane traffic made wild patterns on the ceiling. *I'm sorry.* She threw the phone down on the bed. She shouldn't send the text. But, she argued to herself, how could a text make things worse than they already were? If Gabriela did not answer, she would not text again.

She picked up the phone again and pressed *Send* before she could talk herself out of it.

Alina won her semifinal easily and would play the number four seed in the final. Viva dropped her headset down with a sigh and grinned at Andrew. "That's me done until tomorrow."

"Doing anything exciting with the rest of your day?"

"Not really. Meeting my brother for lunch."

Jack was waiting in the players' café when she entered. She kissed his cheek and sat down, staring out across the mostly empty courts. At this stage, the day before finals, most players had already moved on to their next tournament.

"About time you got here," Jack grumbled.

"You know the match has not long ended. After all, you were watching it—thanks to your kind sister, who got you the tickets."

"It was a good match." Jack brightened. "But what took you so long to come from the commentary box to here?"

"I stopped to see if a friend wanted to join us for lunch."

"Another of your weird friends?"

"She's as normal as they come in the tennis world. She should be here—Ah! Here she is. Hi, Jelena."

Jelena Kovic slid gracefully into the vacant seat. "Viva, how is life treating you? I heard your commentary on the semifinal. It must have seared your tongue being so complimentary about Alina's game."

"Not really. Her game is good. Jelena, I'd like you to meet my brother, Jack."

"Nice to meet you, Jack. I have heard a bit about you." She held out her hand, which Jack took in a bemused fashion.

"If it's from my wicked sister, it's not true."

Jelena's eyes opened wide. "So, you are not a nice, hardworking guy who is fun to hang out with?" She turned to Viva. "Do you have another brother?"

"Nope. Just this idiot."

"Well, thanks, sis. That's my good impression shot down in flames before I've started."

"Not necessarily." Viva turned to Jelena. "It struck me that Jack could be the solution to your current need. If you're happy to have lunch with him, I'll leave the two of you alone. He has my recommendation for what it's worth, but if you're not comfortable, then no pressure."

At Jelena's nod, she stood and bent to kiss her cheek. "See you later, then." She stepped around the table to hug Jack.

"What's going on?" he whispered.

"Nothing. I'm just making good on a promise."

"To me or to Jelena?" he grumbled but sat back down.

As Viva left, she heard Jelena say, "So, Jack, you are in the Matrix. Red pill or blue pill?"

Chapter 17

"HAVE YOU SEEN THE DRAW?" Michi's voice hummed down the line. "I bet you haven't. I'll wait while you look."

Viva brought up the Sydney tournament website. "From your voice, you've got a good draw."

"Yes, the first match at least. You never know, though. Check yours."

Viva scrolled down the draw. "You got a qualifier in the first round."

"Yup. I have a good feeling about this tournament."

"Oh *no*." Viva's wail came from deep within. "The world hates me. Alina Pashin. Of all the people to get in the first round."

"That's not the way to look at it. Just because she beat you the last time you played—"

"And the time before and the time before that, practically back to the dawn of time."

"Time for a change, then." Michi's voice was bright and airy.

"All very well for you to say. I have an interview for *Play Tennis* magazine this morning. How am I supposed to be positive about my chances with this draw?"

"Fake it 'til you make it, girlfriend."

"Neither of us has a match tomorrow. Want to practice away from the tournament courts? I'm fed up with the press."

"Sure. You got anywhere in mind?"

"There's decent tennis club at Coogee. I'll see if I can get us a court. Afterwards, there's a bonus cliff-top walk as a cool-down."

"Striding over cliffs doesn't sound like a cool-down."

"You don't know the winds around here. I'll book the court and let Deepak know. We may as well do the full training session there."

———— ✦ ————

The next morning, she met Michi at the Coogee courts. Deepak arrived shortly after and claimed Viva to go through a set of drills and footwork exercises, followed by work on her serve.

They sat in the shade together, waiting for Michi and Brett to finish a similar coaching session.

"Michi has made the leap to the next level." Deepak nodded to where Michi was smashing back lobs that Brett sent her way. "That moment where it all clicks and comes together. Confidence soars. She probably feels invincible right now."

"That was how it was for me, right before I won the US Open." That had been one of the best days of her life.

Deepak's shrewd gaze assessed her. "You could still win a doubles trophy. But not singles, Viva. The game is too hard, too fast."

"I know." She sighed. "I'll have to live vicariously through Michi's success."

"It will come to her, that one." He stood. "Now, when you hit with her, I want you to come in as much as you can. You'll need to do that against Alina, or she'll just hammer you off the court. Michi's game isn't as powerful as Alina's, but use this practice to reinforce your game plan."

"Okay. Thanks."

"I'll watch. I'll call you later."

Impulsively, she hugged him. "Thank you, Deepak. You really are the best."

He hugged her back, one-armed. "Remember, serve and volley. Channel Martina Navratilova."

"I wish." Viva sighed and then jogged out to where Michi waited.

She and Michi rallied back and forth for a few minutes, easing into each other's game.

Michi stepped up the level and sliced a wicked angle to Viva's backhand.

Viva grunted as she lunged for it but couldn't return the ball. "Nice shot. But you're supposed to take it easy on me."

"That's not what Deepak said." Michi collected balls and returned to the service line. "Prepare to receive, Jones."

Without the height advantage of other players, Michi nevertheless had a pop on her serve and a high-bouncing kick that sent the ball spinning high out of reach.

"Do that again," Viva said. She settled into a receiver's crouch, trying to read Michi's body language. This time, she was able to drive the return back down the line.

As she went out to the side to collect balls, the game two courts over caught her attention. Two women rallied with the effortless ease of a pendulum, obviously trying to keep the ball in play rather than win any serious point. The woman facing Viva was older, with the weathered skin of an avid outdoorswoman. But it was the other woman who held her attention. Viva's steps slowed. She knew that economical movement, the contained, controlled strokes, and tidy play. Her gaze followed Gabriela's quick steps around the court, her precision-perfect swing as she returned the ball. Backhand, forehand, a step to each side in succession, the balls looping over the net, heavy topspin making them drop down at the opponent's feet.

Her throat tightened, and she blinked furiously. *Dear God, why do I miss her so much?*

"Hey." Michi jogged up. "Change ends. Before your eyes fall out," she added in softer tones.

Viva turned back to her own court. "Was I that obvious?"

"To me, yes. Deepak too." Michi jerked a thumb to where Deepak sat with a frown on his face, watching them. "Probably not to anyone else."

"I wonder who she's playing with?" Jealousy twisted like a poker.

Michi shot a glance to the other court. "I've seen her before somewhere. An official probably." She cleared her throat. "So, shall we play a set? Loser buys dinner tonight."

"I should just hand over my credit card to you now." Viva forced her feet to carry her to the other end of the court. "The way you're playing, I haven't a hope."

"What? Queensland's golden girl throwing in the towel just like that?" She snorted. "Shall I call Alina and tell her she only needs to show up to beat you?"

Concentration. Focus. Key attributes of any successful player. Deepak's words ran through her head. His fierce glare from the sidelines was reinforcement. She squared her shoulders. She could beat Alina. And if she did, she could probably go deep in the draw. She'd made her choice; now it was up to her to make something of this farewell tour. And beating Michi in a practice set would be a start.

She grinned at Michi. "I take it back. You'll be buying me dinner tonight."

"What does one wear to a players' party anyway?" Jack's voice echoed down the line. "Is it jeans or a penguin suit?"

"Like you even own a dinner suit," Viva teased. "You're going to be in the spotlight, so try and look nice. Trendy even. Good jeans and an open-neck shirt should do it. Did Jelena tell you what she's wearing?"

"She said a turquoise dress."

"Keep that in mind when you pick your shirt, then. You have to pose for a photo together when you arrive, so you don't want to clash with her."

"Okay. What about shoes?"

She sighed impatiently. "Did you bring a choice?"

"No. Only my charcoal loafers, but I've still got time to go and buy something."

"My tight-arse brother spend money?"

"Viva, cut it out. This is important. Did Jelena tell you why she needs a male date tonight? I can't let her down."

Viva sobered. "She did. And while I don't agree with it, her sponsor has her over a barrel. You're a good man, Jack, going along with this."

He snorted. "The sportswear company has lost this customer over their stance. In this day and age, telling Jelena that they'll cease their sponsorship if she's seen with a same-sex partner is bloody ridiculous."

"Like you ever wore their tennis shirts in the first place! But thank you. I appreciate the support, and I know Jelena does. She only has one sponsor. If she loses them, she would barely be able to support herself on the tour."

"One day, she'll be top ten. Then I hope she tells them where to go."

"I hope so too."

"I like Jelena, I really do. I know you think I've got some creepy ulterior motive, but it's not like that. Sure, if she were straight and unattached, I'd try and date her for real, but I genuinely *like* her. She's great fun to be with. We hung out together in Brisbane that night, after you introduced us. Mainly to see if we felt comfortable enough to carry off the pretence, but we had a lot of fun. She introduced me to her girlfriend. Marissa's less enthused with the whole idea, but she realises Jelena has to do this—at least for now."

"I'll look forward to seeing you at the party."

"Who are you going with?"

"Michi. Brett has had enough players' parties to last a lifetime. He plans a *Game of Thrones* marathon in their hotel room."

"I wonder if he wants company later?"

"Nope. Michi will be back then, and you'd be the third wheel."

"Then I'll just have to go on the town with my dear sister."

"Don't force yourself. Besides, I'll be tucked up in bed by nine."

"Then I hope you'll hang out with Jelena and me at the party. It will add an authentic touch to our supposed budding romance."

"Don't push it."

"So, do you think I'll get away with black jeans, loafers, and a silver-grey shirt?"

The sincerity in his voice touched her. "You'll look as good as you're going to get."

Gabriela checked her email, looking for her match allocations for the Sydney tournament. Qualifiers, a few minor seeds in the first round, but at least she had been given a semifinal as chair umpire. She bit her lip. Was the ITF still penalising her?

Her gaze marched down the list of familiar players in the draw. She told herself she wasn't looking for anyone in particular, just generally to see which matches could be difficult from an official's point of view, but as her glance jumped and skittered from name to name, she gave up the pretence. Whom had Viva drawn? Was it an easy draw, a young and nervous qualifier, a veteran nearing the end of her career, or had she the misfortune of drawing a seeded player?

She found Viva's name in the final quarter of the draw. Gabriela frowned: it could hardly be worse. Alina Pashin was a tough opponent at any time and in this tournament was the number two seed.

Gabriela made herself continue to the end of the draw. Viva was not her business. If she lost in the first round, well, she simply hadn't played well enough. That was all it was; no more, no less. But as she closed the email, a sliver of the disappointment that Viva was surely feeling lodged in her chest. It would be a difficult farewell tour if she was eliminated in the first round. And it wouldn't bode well for her chances in the grand slam event later in the month—Viva's final tournament as a professional singles player.

Ha. Gabriela huffed a breath. Unless some other offer came thudding in to tempt Viva to remain on the tour for longer. Not for the first time, her conversation with Viva slid into her mind. Had she been fair, walking out on Viva as she did? Each time, the answer was the same: she could not honestly have done any different, not if she wanted to keep her career. But could she have been more understanding? Viva and she… Well, they had been lovers, possibly girlfriends. If not then, well, they had been on the way to such a relationship. Viva had said they could put the relationship on hold until after the Australian Open. One month. That was not long in the grand scheme of things.

Gabriela stared at her phone without really seeing the names lined up on the screen. Had she been too hasty? It was an amazing send-off for Viva, a fitting end to her long career. Who was she to demand that Viva turn it down?

But Viva could have told her earlier. Discussed it. Mentioned it before Gabriela had driven three hours to Waggs Pocket to see her again. That was thoughtless at best, deliberately deceptive at worst.

Her fingers tightened on the phone, and she switched to her text messages. Viva's message leapt from the screen. *I miss you.* The words were burned into her mind. Not for the first time, her finger hovered over the *Reply* button. She missed Viva too. More than she thought she would when she'd walked out on her. The longing for what they'd had gripped her at the oddest moments.

She'd seen Viva and Michi on the court the day before, and it had taken all her willpower to keep focussed on her game with Irene.

Viva missed her. What would it cost her to say the same in reply? To extend a hand, fingers outstretched for Viva to grasp. Would it be so bad to meet for coffee? Sydney was a huge metropolis. They could surely find some out-of-the-way coffee shop where they could meet for thirty minutes. She could say to Viva that she missed her too. To see if there was a way past this for them, not now, but later, when Viva had retired. She stared at the phone. She could at least reply to Viva's message.

The chair opposite creaked as Irene dropped heavily into it. The Italian official stuck both elbows on the table and leant in. "Gabriela, I am so very unlucky. I have the opening match on centre court, as chair umpire for the match between that little *stronzino* Nicholas Simmons and Roger Federer. Nicholas *hates* me, ever since I defaulted him from a match in Madrid last year. Roger, of course, will be the perfect gentleman, but even he is not enough to make up for the pain of Nicholas."

Gabriela pushed her phone into her pocket. "Nicholas is a total bastard with everyone. I'm sure it's not personal."

Irene's weathered face creased into a delighted grin. "So you say. I, on the other hand, prefer to assume it *is* personal, and therefore I do not feel bad if I have to issue him a warning or a code violation."

"The chair umpire is totally impartial." It was impossible for her not to smile back at Irene's infectious grin.

"*Sí*, I am." Irene opened her eyes wide in pretend horror. "You know that. An official has to be. But that doesn't mean I do not do a little happy dance inside as I issue that code violation."

Gabriela's shoulders tightened. It was that easy to caution a player, make a call against them. Irene made no secret of her contempt for Nicholas Simmons, but no one called her integrity into question over it.

Irene flung an arm out. "Now. You are staying at the same hotel as me, so how about we escape this miserable canteen food and find ourselves a cosy restaurant for the evening. One with good Italian wine—"

"Spanish wine."

"Maybe. Or we will compromise as we always do with Australian wine, and you can tell me all about your life since I last saw you."

"Not much has happened since our game yesterday. I had seafood for dinner, I watched some bad television."

"I know all about your quiet life. Instead, you can tell me why you became oh-so-distracted and let me win three games in a row after we were stared at by Genevieve Jones. Is she still angry with you about that foot-fault in the US Open?" Irene tilted her head, and her shrewd, bright gaze fixed itself on Gabriela's face.

She forced herself to shrug. "I didn't see her," she lied.

"If you say so. But *I* saw, and I don't tend to notice when I'm being stared at by a beautiful woman. Now, if it had been her handsome coach, that would be different."

"Down, girl. Keep your cougar tendencies under control."

"So, we've established you didn't notice the very beautiful Genevieve Jones staring at you, and I'm sure you're going to say you haven't heard the rumours about you and her."

"I've heard them." Gabriela's easy smile and relaxed demeanour put a frown of doubt on Irene's forehead. Her hand clenched under the table so hard that her nails scored her palm. Would she ever get away from this gossip? And if Irene had heard it, the ITF would surely have too. Thank heavens she hadn't replied to Viva's text. The moment of insanity, when she'd nearly agreed to meet, evaporated under Irene's stare.

"And?"

"When have you listened to gossip, my friend?"

"All the time." Irene's eyes twinkled. "It is the lifeblood of the tour: who has hooked up with who, who is in the closet, who has been dumped by their sponsor, who is only playing tennis as a stepping stone to other things. Like that oh-so-gay Polish player who was dumped by his sponsor but got a movie deal so he does not care. Compared to him, my friend, the gossip about you and a certain Aussie player is small potatoes."

Irene's voice had risen in volume, and Gabriela glanced around cautiously. "Ssh."

"So, it is true?"

"I would tell you to be quiet whether it is or isn't. I do not like being talked about." No one was paying them any attention. She breathed a little easier.

"Then let us go and find a wine bar where we can talk."

"Why not?" Gabriela stood. "I am done. I was just checking the draw."

"Which match have you got first?"

"Show Court One. Two well-behaved veteran women from peaceful countries that are not at loggerheads. I believe I will have an easier time of it than you, my friend. Now, lead me to this wine you have promised."

Chapter 18

VIVA STARED FIXEDLY AHEAD AT the change of ends, eyes locked on an insect that had landed on court. Absently, she towelled the handle of her racquet and wiped her damp palms. She'd never had an easy time playing Alina, but this match was about as bad as it could get. Alina's freight train serve and punishing groundstrokes had kept Viva pinned at the baseline, unable to get the chink she needed to move forward. Alina ran her ragged, side to side like an erratic pendulum, and Viva was unable to find her game.

When the umpire called time, she stalked to the baseline to serve. *This point matters. Only this one.* If she held serve now, if she broke back in the next game, if she— She drew a veil down over her chaotic thoughts. *This point matters.* The mantra worked; her pulse steadied, and her mind focussed.

Her first serve barely cleared the net, but it skimmed the surface low and flat. Her first ace of the match. *Yes! This is where it changes.*

Her serve wasn't as strong on the next point, but it was enough. Alina's racquet tipped the ball and sent it wild, high into the air before it landed in the crowd.

30-0. The crowd, maybe sensing a home player comeback, yelled their appreciation.

I can win this. This point matters. Only this one. Viva bounced lightly on her toes as she waited for the crowd to calm.

Alina returned Viva's next serve with laser-like precision, drilling the ball past her as she approached the net.

Viva lunged for it and missed. The ball shot past her, and she could only watch as it clipped the line. 30-15.

She stalked back to the service line, tucked a sweaty tendril of hair behind her ear, and prepared to serve. *This point matters.* If she could get 40-15, she still had the edge. She rotated her shoulders and served, hard and flat down the T.

Alina's anticipation was perfect, and she was in position to return equally hard. The rally continued.

Viva didn't count strokes, simply focussed on the fluorescent ball as it rocketed towards her each time. Her breath came in hard pants, and the force of Alina's strokes jarred her forearm.

Then Alina hit to her backhand side.

Viva ran for it, her backhand swing ready. *Wrong, all wrong.* Even before her racquet connected with the ball, she knew it was a bad shot. Her wrist was bent back at an unnatural angle, and she couldn't get the power she needed to drive the ball hard. She hit it as best she could, grunting as the pain seared her wrist and then travelled up her arm. She faltered, the mist of pain in front of her eyes turning to a red haze. *No!* She gritted her teeth, willing the wave of agony to recede.

Her shot hit the net cord and dribbled over to the far side. Alina sprinted for it but couldn't get close. 40-15.

Viva closed her eyes. *My wrist is fine. It's good.* Still the pain pulsed. If she could win the next point, there was a two-minute change of ends and she could call for a medical timeout. She flicked a glance at Alina, summoning a cool disinterest. Alina had to have noticed what had happened. There was no way she'd missed it.

One more serve. Then she could ice her wrist and call for the physio.

Her serve wasn't the strongest, but it had a kick, spinning wide and bouncing high over Alina's head. Game.

Thank God. She returned to her chair, signalling to the umpire that she needed the physio. He jogged out on court a minute later and removed the icepack she'd wrapped around her wrist.

"The tendon needs to settle," he said to her. "It's pulled and inflamed. Do you want to play on?" His tone was neutral.

She nodded, a quick up-and-down jerk. Giving up was unthinkable, and she'd played through worse. "Can you strap it again?"

"Yes." The physio pulled tape from his bag. "It will be sore, but you should be okay if it's a quick match. See your own physio immediately, though."

"I understand."

He strapped her wrist with quick, efficient strokes.

She moved it cautiously, testing the range of motion. "Thanks. It's good." She took a final mouthful of sports drink and jogged out to continue.

Alina's first serve came straight to Viva's backhand. The next two points were the same.

Viva managed to return the third, and the jolt of pain nearly made her drop the racquet. Her game plan was in tatters, and a jittery panic swamped her.

The next serve came straight to her backhand again, and Viva's muscles tensed in anticipation of pain. She took the shot, and the pain was there, like an old enemy, hiding in plain sight. The ball went into the net. A love game to Alina, who went on to take the first set.

Viva called for her coach during the break, and while Deepak's calm voice steadied her, she'd been unable to implement any of his suggestions or her game plan.

Her opponent was just too good.

Viva rose and stalked back to the baseline, prepared for another humiliation on the receiving end of Alina's serve. Her wrist twinged as she gripped her racquet with both hands, but the sharp pain was just another thing to think about later.

Alina's serve thundered across the net, and Viva blocked it, trying to at least get the ball into play.

Three points later and she was staring in the face of another love game. A point later and Alina had the game.

Viva grimaced. This was humiliation, pure and simple, a ruthless dismantling of her game. *I am better than this.* But hot on the heels of that thought was the knowledge that yes, she was better—but not today. Not today when she had an injury that, by rights, should see her retire from the match. *I will not withdraw.* She would not give Alina the satisfaction. She daren't look at Jack in her player's box, at Deepak, no doubt with his arms folded and a frown on his face. *Just get through this. Make it as good as it can be.*

Summoning her mental strength, she wrapped the pain in its own compartment, pushed it down and away. It would not be a part of her. Her serve was good, and Alina barely managed a return. Viva ran to take the shot on her forehand. *Yes!* The shot was good, a cross-court drop shot that Alina couldn't get to.

"C'mon, Viva!" The shout, over the roar of the crowd, was Michi's voice.

Viva flashed a glance and saw Michi had joined Jack and Deepak. Her pink hair stood out like a beacon as she leant forward and beat on the sideboards.

But no support in the world could get her through the match. Alina's barrage to Viva's backhand didn't let up. Viva fought. She ran down every ball and played the angles and lines to make Alina run. But every backhand sent a fiery stab into her wrist. Thirty minutes later, she was staring down the court. Match point to Alina. Her wrist throbbed raw pain. Her supporters were quiet. *This point matters. Only this one.* The mantra buoyed her, but as Alina's serve flew past, Viva knew it was not enough.

Her tournament was over; she was dismissed in the first round.

Somehow, she managed a smile and a congratulatory comment to Alina at the net. Somehow, she lifted a hand in salute to the crowd and left through the tunnel back to the locker room. She slumped to the bench and put her head in her hands.

What a bloody mess. Her performance today wasn't worthy of the champion's send-off that Tennis Australia was giving her. She'd tried, fought every point; no one could accuse her of throwing the match. When it came down to it, she just wasn't good enough. Tennis Australia would probably pull the plug after this and quietly drop her.

She levered herself to her feet, grabbed her bag from the locker, and headed for the shower. In the cubicle, she rested her hands against the wall. Tears welled. She was a failure, a fraud for thinking she deserved this send-off. There was now only the Australian Open—the grand slam event—to prove herself, and after the drubbing from Alina, she would be lucky to get past the first round.

No. Viva straightened. That was the thinking of a loser. She flexed her wrist cautiously. Maybe the physio could work a miracle. She had lost not because she had lost the will to win, but because her body had let her down. She dashed away the tears and tipped her head back, letting the water stream over her face.

She wasn't done yet. There was the Australian Open still to prove herself.

She was combing her wet hair in front of the mirror when Alina's reflection appeared in the glass behind her. She was still in her tennis clothes, the euphoria of her win lighting her face. Alina dumped her bag on the bench and pulled out her towel and toiletries.

"Bad luck." The insincere words echoed in the tiled room. "Of course, I was always going to win."

Viva's fingers tightened on the comb. "You played well."

Alina's face wore a smugness that grated. "You've picked a good time to retire. Home ground send-off and of course things would only get harder now that you're as old as you are."

"That doesn't seem to bother Serena Williams."

"She's exceptional." Alina's words held a dismissive quality, designed to wound. "And, of course, now that your secret relationship is out in the open, you've lost that advantage. No more line calls going your way."

Viva resumed combing her hair, tugging the wide-toothed comb through her unruly hair with more force. The comb snagged on a tangle. "I don't know what you're talking about."

Alina moved closer so that her cool, beautiful face loomed large in the mirror. "Your girlfriend."

"I don't have a girlfriend."

"Oh? That's not what the gossip says. Even the ITF must be listening, as your girlfriend has been umpiring some very low-grade matches lately."

Viva pasted a smile on her face. It stretched her cheeks and felt as fake as a political campaign promise, but it was there. "You should spend more time working on your drop shots and less time gossiping about things that don't concern you. You missed three in our match."

Alina took a step back. "I need to shower. I have a winner's press conference in twenty minutes. Good luck in the doubles."

She sauntered away, over to her locker, and undressed, leaving her sweaty clothes scattered over the floor.

Viva glanced after her, then she stepped over Alina's discarded clothes and went to meet her physio.

Gabriela changed back into her civvies in the officials' locker room. Her head ached from a long day in the sunlight. The match she was umpiring had gone for over three hours, and although the shade parasol over the umpire's chair kept off most direct sunlight, it had still been hotter than Hades on the court. She sipped from her water bottle, contemplating her evening. She could see if Irene wanted to join her for dinner, or she could return to her hotel and soothe her aching head in the curtained dimness of her hotel room. She sighed. The vivacious Irene could wait for another night. Right now, all she wanted was to stroll back to her hotel to stretch her legs after the hours in the umpire's chair, flop on the bed, order room service, and catch up with the matches she had missed.

Decision made, she left the grounds and took the long way to the hotel. It was around six, and the day's matches had finished, and the evening ones were yet to start. Gabriela ordered her meal, then sat on the bed and flicked to the tennis channel, calling up the match options on the remote.

She paused briefly at the match she'd umpired. They were replaying a Hawk-Eye challenge. A linesman had called a ball out, and Gabriela had overruled the call, saying it was in. The other player then challenged the overrule. On the TV, she saw herself leaning down from the chair to talk to the second player. He was gesticulating fiercely, and while the coverage didn't relay what he said, Gabriela remembered his voice, rising in annoyance as he told her exactly why the ball was out. Then as the replay came on the stadium screen, he turned to watch it, shrugging as he was proven wrong. He was a gentleman, though. With a nod to Gabriela and a quiet "*Pardonnez-moi, madam*" he resumed play.

Gabriela sighed in satisfaction. A call that was correct, an orderly court, well-behaved players, and an enthusiastic and appreciative crowd—they were the components of an umpire's dream. Her dream, part of a career she loved. She took a mouthful of water. After all these years, it was pretty special to still love one's job. It had the trappings of a glamourous career without the fame and glitz. World travel, hotels and eating out, a variety of countries to explore.

She took a final look at herself on the TV, head turning back and forth as she watched the match. Pride shot through her. Her career.

She went back to the guide and selected another match to watch as she ate. A woman's match that promised exciting tennis and explosive personalities.

Room service arrived, and she went to the door to collect her meal. When she sat back down, the TV had switched to showing a press conference. Her heart turned a slow somersault. Viva sat in front of the press. Her hair was damp and curled loosely on her shoulders, and her right wrist was heavily strapped.

Gabriela turned up the volume.

"Yes, absolutely, my wrist injury played a part in my loss today, but it wasn't the only thing. Alina played well. She deserved to win."

The same sportsmanlike phrases that every losing player said after a match, whether they meant them or not.

"My wrist is strained. It's not a recurrence of my previous injury," Viva continued. "I'm having treatment—a painkilling injection, physio, anti-inflammatories—and will rest it over the next couple of days. I fully expect to play my doubles match on Thursday and, of course, the Australian Open next week." She smiled. "And I fully expect to go deeper in the draw there than I've done here."

The TV reverted back to the match in progress. Gabriela ate her burger without really tasting it. How much of Viva's answer was real? No player would ever give away the extent of her injury; to do so would give an advantage to her opponent.

She set the burger down and wished for a glass of wine. Maybe that would take the edge away from her longing to see Viva again. Right now, she missed her so acutely it was a physical pain. Gabriela pushed the sandwich away and took out her phone. She found Viva's text and stared at it. It would be very wrong to meet her for coffee. The risk of being seen was very real, even in an out-of-the-way place. If that got back to the ITF, it would negate everything she had assured them. But, the other side of her argued, it was only coffee. Two friends, meeting for coffee. Friends everywhere met; why shouldn't she?

She closed her eyes, conjuring Viva's face behind closed eyelids. She could wait until after the Australian Open and then see Viva. Or she could meet her sooner. Viva's wrist injury—how bad was it really? How was Viva coping? The longing intensified, along with the urgent need to find out what, if anything, was still possible between them.

Gabriela put down her phone. Nothing had really changed—she was fooling herself. She switched the TV channel to a cop drama and picked up the burger again.

———— ⋅◇⋅ ————

From her position in the chair, Gabriela could see not only the match she was umpiring, but also the one on the next court. Her match took all of her concentration during play, but during the two-minute change of ends, she had a tiny window of time to look around her. The match on the next court drew her gaze.

Viva and Michi conferred behind raised hands, and then with a leap in her stride, Viva ran back to crouch near the net, while Michi returned to the service line.

The two of them had settled into their game and seemed about to cruise to an easy victory. There was heavy strapping on Viva's wrist, and she was positioned on the forehand side of the court. It seemed physio and a painkilling injection had allowed Viva to continue in the doubles. From where Gabriela sat, Viva was all hard lines of muscle and angles, not a hint of softness about her. Even her wild hair was tightly contained in a thick plait that hung down to well below her shoulder blades. As she leapt for a volley, her muscles stood out in fine definition.

Gabriela kept her expression blank, but her breath seemed stolen by the sight. Her fingers tingled with the memory of how Viva's muscles had felt under her palms—the softness of skin contrasting with the firm underlay. Her legs turned from a deep tan to pale cream at the point where the hem of her skirt came. Likewise, her back bore a geometric pattern of tanned skin where there was an oval cut-out in the shirt she habitually wore.

She bit her lip. It would take time to be able to look at Viva without remembering how it had been.

Her tablet beeped once, and she glanced down. "Time."

The players returned to the match, and Gabriela's focus shifted back to the match in front of her, the movement of the ball, the spectators, the officials, the ballkids, and all the myriad of things under her command in a tennis match.

Michi moved restlessly around the locker room, tension shimmering in her body as she paced. "Tell me again."

Viva leant against the locker and repeated her words of a moment ago. "Her footwork is terrible, and she hates coming forward. Move her side to side, and then hit a short ball to bring her to the net. She can't volley worth a cracker, and her reaction times at the net are slow."

Michi nodded. "You're saying exactly what Brett said."

"She's bad at drop shots, and she also isn't good at taking shots on the run. She's got fantastic anticipation, though, so it's hard to put one past her."

"Anything else?"

"Win this against Alina and you're into your first tour final."

"I know *that*. I can hardly forget." She grinned. "If I win the final, I'm getting an Australian tattoo. Maybe a cute koala on my shoulder."

"Make sure it's not your serving arm. The Australian Open starts two days after the final here."

"I'll probably have a lot of time to get it done after I'm dumped out early from the Open."

An official stuck her head around the door. "Five minutes, Michi."

"I better go. Good luck." Viva hugged Michi and left, up to the player's box where Brett waited.

She glanced over at the commentary box, where Andrew and another regular commentator sat. She would be there later, for the second semifinal. But in the meantime, she was able to give Michi her full attention.

At first, it seemed that Alina would romp home, but gradually, Michi eased into the match, a cross-court slice here, a volley there. And she chased down Alina's shots, returning them with a wily approach that seemed to fluster the normally cool player. When Michi broke serve with a crafty drop shot, the crowd exploded with cheers. From there, it seemed easy, and in only eighty minutes, Michi made her first tour final.

Alina's congratulations at the net were perfunctory, but Michi didn't seem to notice. She hugged Alina and went on a leaping, prancing circuit of the court that had the crowd applauding her joy.

The second semifinal was even shorter. In the commentary box, Viva struggled to find any positive thing to say. It was an uneven, error-prone match that was tedious to watch. But Viva's gaze kept straying to the chair, where Gabriela sat high above play, calling the score in a calm voice. Did Gabriela's presence mean that the ITF had accepted her explanation and were done penalising her? Viva fingered the phone that sat heavy in her pocket. Gabriela hadn't answered her text. Had she really expected her to?

Down on court, the players sat at the change of ends. Gabriela's chiselled profile was intent on the tablet in front of her. As Viva watched, she raised her head and stared straight at the commentary box. Was Gabriela watching her? Viva didn't know; the sunlight could be at an angle where it reflected off the glass of the commentary box. Gabriela could merely be irritated at the light in her eyes and probably had no idea who was behind the glass. But as Gabriela continued to stare, it seemed she knew very well that Viva was there. A tiny half smile played on her lips, and her head tilted to one side. Was it in question? Was it an invitation?

Viva snorted. More likely she was calculating first service percentages.

The favourite thrashed a lower-ranked player in a mere fifty-five minutes.

"See you tomorrow." Andrew turned to her as, duties at an end, she stood.

"I'm looking forward to it."

"No doubt you want Michi to win. I thought you and she had a shot at the doubles title. You had bad luck in the quarterfinals."

She shrugged. "It happens. And to be honest, being out of the doubles allowed Michi to concentrate on singles, and look where that has got her."

Matt nodded. "I think she's got a very good chance tomorrow."

Viva left the stadium to return to her hotel. After throwing herself onto the bed, she pulled her mobile from her pocket. There were two text messages. Her heart rate sped up. Maybe it was Gabriela. Maybe she was agreeing to coffee. Maybe she wanted to see her again.

The first message was from Jack, saying he and Jelena were having a "date" that night in Chinatown, if she wanted to swing by. The second was from Gabriela.

Coffee. Just coffee. I'm leaving for Melbourne tonight. Maybe when you get there, we can go someplace quiet.

Viva started at her phone, anticipation already coursing through her blood. Soon she would sit across a table from Gabriela. The days before then seemed unbearably long. Viva fumbled the letters, a typo in every word as she replied.

I'd like that very much. Will be in Melb on Sunday.

She set the phone down on the bed and had a quick shower. The bubbling anticipation in her chest was not because Michi might win tomorrow, nor was it that she was commentating at the final of a high-profile event. It was because she would be seeing Gabriela—really seeing her, face to face, across a café table—very soon.

———◦◦◦◦———

Michi won the final in straight sets in a decisive match that had her in control from the first ball. As her opponent's shot went long on match point, Michi dropped to her knees on the court, her hands pressed to her cheeks, eyes wide. Then she rose to her feet to hug her opponent, who seemed on the edge of tears.

"A great victory for Michi Cleaver," Andrew said. "Viva, how do you rate her chances in the Australian Open next week?"

"I see her going deep in the draw, but I don't think she'll win the trophy. Not this year anyway."

"And we'll be seeing you too at the Australian Open. Your final tournament before you retire from singles. Do you have any expectations as to how you'll go?"

"I'd like to see the draw before I answer that."

"Wise answer. We'll be seeing more of Viva during the two weeks of the Open—both on court and here in the commentary box."

Next week. Her final singles tournament and one of the biggest events of the year. Even as she nodded and smiled at Andrew, determination was gripping her. She would make this tournament one to remember.

Chapter 19

Viva hadn't said what time she would arrive on Sunday. Gabriela woke early and prowled her hotel room before settling for a coffee on the tiny balcony overlooking Melbourne. Twelve storeys below, traffic moved sluggishly through the city. The caffeine coursed through her system, and her mind spun in wild circles. When her knee started jiggling, she jumped to her feet. A run would settle her.

She crossed the Yarra River to the Botanical Gardens, where a popular path for runners led around the outside. A couple of circuits of The Tan was just what she needed. But for once, the rhythmic beat of her shoes on the path failed to clear her head. Where was Viva? Would she call her? Would she answer if Viva did? She accelerated to pass a group of slower runners jogging in a pack and then slowed again.

She shouldn't answer her phone. She shouldn't meet Viva, even for coffee. It was career suicide if anyone were to see them together. She should turn her phone off so that the temptation wasn't there.

But oh, how she wanted to see Viva again.

Her phone rang around eleven. Gabriela stared at Viva's name on the screen. Her heart pounded. Two rings. Her finger hesitated over the button. She should reject the call, forget Viva. Move on with her life. She closed her eyes. She couldn't. It was a visceral thing, an urgent drumbeat in her heart. Whatever the risk, she wanted to see Viva face to face, just one more time. She pressed the button to accept the call. "Hi."

"Hi, this is Viva." The line fell silent, as if Viva had exhausted all her courage with the one sentence.

"Are you in Melbourne?" Gabriela cursed her inanity. Of course she was.

"Yeah. I've just checked into the hotel."

There was silence again.

Gabriela bit her lip. She had agreed to meet for coffee. Why was it now so hard to form the words?

The sound of Viva clearing her throat came down the line. Maybe it was hard for her too.

"So," Viva said. "Coffee. Just coffee."

"That is all it can be. A few minutes, nothing more. I would like to know how you are doing." It was concern about Viva's injury, she told herself. Nothing more.

"And I you." Viva paused. "I have time today or very early tomorrow morning if either of those times suits you. My first match isn't until Tuesday."

"Today is good for me. I am chair umpire for two matches tomorrow."

"Where would you like to meet?"

"Do you mind going somewhere away from the city?"

"That's fine."

"Do you know Clifton Hill? It's a suburb about twenty minutes away by tram."

"Yes. I sometimes go there. There's a nice café by the river."

Viva's voice was husky, a little breathless, as if she'd finished a work-out. It reminded Gabriela of her voice at other, more intimate moments. Desire unfurled a tiny shoot, and she quashed it, focussing her mind. Coffee. It was just coffee.

"That will be busy. There is a little café, The Athenian. It is a local one in a residential area. Very quiet. It is run by a Greek couple, and they do not seem to take much notice of their customers. It is on the corner of Studley and Yarrawonga streets." Gabriela waited.

"I think you mentioned it once before. I'll find it."

"There are booths at the rear that are quiet. That is where I usually sit."

"What time? I can leave anytime now." After a beat, Viva added, "If that's what you want."

"I can be there in an hour."

"I'll see you soon. And Gabriela?"

She waited.

"Thank you."

———————— ✦ ————————

When Gabriela arrived, Viva was already waiting. The café was as quiet as ever, and Viva was the only customer. She sat in one of the booths at the rear, idly stirring a tiny cup of something. Gabriela placed her order and came to join her.

Her first thought was that Viva looked well. She wore a soft lilac T-shirt, and her wayward hair was loose down her back. A large pair of sunglasses sat on the table in front of her. Her face was relaxed, lacking the pinch of pain that had dominated the last time she'd seen her.

"Hey." She sat down opposite Viva.

"Hey yourself." Viva leant forward, as if she were about to kiss Gabriela.

Gabriela bit her lip. How she wanted that kiss. But she couldn't. Her upper body leant away, a tiny motion.

Viva paused and sat back in her seat. "How's things?"

"Good. It is nice to be back in Melbourne." When had their conversation become so inane? "I heard your commentary on some of the Sydney matches. You are doing well. You have got a nice blend of knowledge and informality."

"Thanks." Viva fiddled with the sunglasses that lay on the table between them. "Andrew keeps asking me for gossip about the players, but I won't do that unless it's already common knowledge."

"Like the fact that your brother is dating Jelena Kovic? Allegedly."

"I haven't mentioned that." Viva studied Gabriela, as if making up her mind about something. She lowered her voice. "You know that Jelena—"

"Is gay. Yes. I imagine Jack is helping out one of his sister's friends for some reason."

"Something like that. I wish Jelena didn't have to fabricate this story, but I understand her reasons. That doesn't mean I'm going to talk about it as if their engagement is going to be announced any day now."

"I guess you have been reading the tabloids."

Viva grimaced. "Unfortunately, they're kind of hard to avoid. If it's not a story about the young romance of the year between Jack and Jelena, it's a story about me and retirement. One paper says I'm going to marry Deepak and open a tennis academy."

"Tell them it's Michi who married her coach."

"Another says I'm pregnant."

"Of course. What other reason could there *possibly* be?"

"Then, of course, there's the rumour that I'm going to move to the States so I can marry my girlfriend to gain US citizenship. Were all of these journalists comatose during the press conference when I announced my retirement? I distinctly remember saying I was retiring due to my wrist not being able to keep up with the demands of the modern game."

Gabriela tilted her head and regarded Viva. "So, you are still retiring?"

"Yes. Of course."

Of course hadn't meant much in the past. Gabriela let it slide. This meeting was too precious to waste in recriminations.

Viva broke off as the café owner brought Gabriela's coffee and a square of honey-soaked baklava.

"Thank you," Gabriela murmured.

A brief half smile flickered across the owner's face, and then she returned to the counter without another word.

Viva lifted her head and looked Gabriela full in the face as she resumed the conversation. "I said I would retire after the Open. And I haven't forgotten I told you I'd be retiring before the Australian tennis season, and I reneged on that promise. I want to apologise." She sighed, a waft of breath. "I seem to spend a lot of time apologising to you."

Gabriela waited. Viva seemed to be picking her words with difficulty, dragging them up from a place deep inside.

"When I got the offer to keep playing until after the Australian Open, I thought of lots of things, but mainly it seemed an acknowledgement of my career that few athletes are lucky enough to get. But I was too focussed on what the offer meant to me, and I blew aside what it would mean to us. To you."

"There wasn't an 'us' then." Gabriela's fingers inched closer to where Viva still fiddled with the sunglasses.

"No? I think there was. Not a forever and always necessarily, but there was the possibility of something meaningful between us." Her mouth quirked down. "Maybe you don't think so."

"I don't know what to think," Gabriela said truthfully. "I was enjoying what we had, and then it all changed. Then there was too much uncertainty and evasion between us. At least, that's what it seemed like to me."

"Evasion. I guess that's what it was. It all came up so quickly, and I focussed on that. I thought it wouldn't matter much, that it wouldn't change things between us. I thought a month wouldn't matter."

"You thought wrong." Gabriela's words were ashes in her mouth. Viva still didn't get it. "To you, it's a month. To me, it' s possibly my career. I know you're the high-flyer and I'm an expendable official, but I've worked hard to get where I am. It's my life."

"I know that now, and I should have known that then." Her shoulders moved in a tiny movement that could have been negation or simply a shrug. "Self-absorbed tennis player. It's not like I've never had any dealings with the media. I know what they're like. Once they get stuck on an idea, as long as people are clicking on the stories, buying the magazine, then they'll milk it for all its worth."

"Like Jelena and Jack."

"Exactly. That won't be dropped anytime soon. So, for me to think we could just ease back for a month, be discreet about our relationship without anyone finding out was naive at best, selfish, and incredibly thoughtless to you. Even my change of plan put a huge burden on your career. I didn't realise how much." She took a sip of the dark coffee and stirred the tiny cup with the spoon. "I'm guessing you don't remember when I came out to the press? There's no reason you should. I was seventeen, in my first year of professional tennis, and someone took a photo of me walking hand in hand with my girlfriend. We were in Canberra, not even on the tour, and I was practically a nobody then. The next day, the press were at my apartment, wanting statements, going through the mail, bribing our rental agent to tell them what names were on the lease."

"I do remember it, actually. I remember thinking that if the press paid half as much attention to a player's game as they did to her looks or her private life, then sports reporting would be a better place."

"The stupid thing was I wasn't in the closet at all. Never had been. I've always been open about my sexuality—but equally, it's no one's business except my own. A straight player doesn't have to hold a press conference to announce she's heterosexual."

"But you did hold a conference." The memory of that conference returned. Viva, so cool, so confident. "Yes, I'm gay," she'd said, "and that has no bearing on my tennis." And she'd changed the subject to talk of her first season on the tour.

"I thought it would get them off my back. Instead, it made them worse. Headlines like *Loved-Up Genevieve Jones*. So, for me to think that you and I could hide a relationship was foolish—even to think we could put it on hold for a month. It would be bound to come out. It was outed to a small degree, although I think that's just within close tennis circles."

"I think so too. Maybe a leak from the ITF. I had to tell them, of course. I couldn't risk otherwise."

A small wrinkle creased between Viva's eyebrows. "I'm sorry. That must be why you've had lesser matches, outside courts."

Viva *had* noticed. "Yes." Gabriela swallowed.

"Then it seemed to improve. I saw you umpire a semifinal in Sydney."

"I was happy to get that. But I was lucky—Irene was to do it, but she got an upset stomach. I was available."

"Alina Pashin also gloated about it."

Gabriela stared down into her coffee. She shouldn't be surprised, gossip being what it was on the tour, but it still made her stomach lurch in dismay. "How did she find out?"

"I've no idea. Her tentacles must stretch far." Viva fell silent, and her intense gaze rested on Gabriela's face, studying each of her features in turn until Gabriela broke the stare and glanced away, over to where the owner served a customer, cutting honey cake into squares and placing it in a small box with great care.

"I missed you, Viva." The words welled in her throat, dragged from within. "I didn't expect to. What's a couple of nights together? What's a few days, dinner, sex? Nothing much, in this day and age. I thought I'd move on and forget you."

"But you didn't." It wasn't a question. Viva's hand stole across the table, her fingers stretched out towards Gabriela's wrist. There were scant centimetres between them.

Gabriela looked down at those long, strong fingers with the short, blunt-cut nails. Viva's index finger twitched, but her hand remained still, as if she couldn't make the final move to bridge the distance.

She cleared her throat. "When's your first match?" She knew of course. She'd scanned the draw, looking for G. Jones (Aus).

"Tuesday." Viva smiled. "I told you that only this morning—you must be distracted. I got lucky this time, and I'm playing a qualifier. Hopefully, I can at least make the second round before my arse gets kicked six ways to Sunday. Court allocations aren't out yet, but I've been told unofficially they're putting me on Rod Laver Arena. I guess they want the cameras there for what might be my final competitive match."

"I'm chair umpire for two matches tomorrow."

Viva nodded and withdrew her hand, picking up her cup. "Good matches?"

"Not bad. Men's singles—that could be fiery. And Paige's opening match against a qualifier."

Viva took a sip of her coffee.

"How is your family?"

"Good. Mum and Dad sent you their best. I said it was unlikely I'd be able to pass it along, but here we are."

"Here we are." Gabriela echoed the words, and this time it was her hand that moved into the no-man's land of Formica table between them.

"Why did you agree to meet me? What changed your mind?" Viva's expression had a wistful, eager look, a strange and vulnerable mix in someone so confident.

Gabriela concentrated on Viva's short nails again. It was easier than looking at her face. "I saw your loss to Alina. Your wrist looked bad. I wondered how you were."

Viva's mouth twisted. "A medical update? Is that all you wanted?"

"Honestly? I wanted to see you. I can't get you out of my head, and I didn't think much past that. I wanted to see if there was still *something* between us. Potential, yes?"

"And is there?" Viva's voice was hesitant.

Gabriela's fingers twitched with the need to close the gap between them. "It is still there, I think. I… I still want you." She took a deep breath. "But nothing has changed, Viva. I don't think it can right now. I am being penalised; I can't afford to lose more standing. Everything I have worked for."

"After this tournament?"

"I do not know. I cannot think about that now. I am taking a huge chance just meeting you here." She glanced around the café. Two women gossiped by the door, and the owner wiped the counter with a cloth, methodically in circles. A snatch of song in a foreign language echoed from the rear yard, but otherwise the café was quiet. It was probably the emptiest café in Melbourne on a Sunday morning in summer. She met Viva's eyes. "When it came to it, I just couldn't stay away from you."

"It won't matter then. Afterwards." Viva's words held a strained quality, as if she had rehearsed them in her head.

"It is not up to me. It is nothing you can influence. I simply have to wait and see." Gabriela picked up the fork and used it to divide the flaky pastry. "You want half?"

Viva barely glanced at it. "Will you think about it? Please?"

The baklava was cloying sweet in her mouth, and she took a gulp of coffee to ease it past the lump in her throat. "I will think about it."

Viva's fingers combed through her hair, tugging at a knot. Her face twisted. Abruptly, she stood. "I'm sorry. I shouldn't have asked you to meet. You're risking so much for me, and that's not fair on you. I don't know what I hoped for. I just wanted to see you, too. To remember how it was." She pushed her hands into the pockets of her shorts. "I guess I'll see you around."

"Wait." Gabriela stood, too and, leaving the coffee and cake unfinished on the table, she moved to Viva's side. "I'll walk with you."

Viva nodded. "If you want to, I'd like that."

The sunlight made Gabriela blink after the dimness of the café. She turned along the residential street, where the heat made the trees droop over front yard fences. They paced along, side by side, without speaking. The buzz of traffic from Hoddle Street grew louder, and a tram rattled past.

They crossed over a cobblestone laneway that ran behind the rows of neat Victorian workers' cottages. A loquat tree with dark green leaves hung low. They were nearly at the busier street, with cars and people, where someone might recognise Viva. The laneway was narrow, secluded, hidden from prying eyes. The thought that leapt into her mind was stupid; it was something she should not do, but Gabriela swallowed, reached for Viva's hand, and tugged her into the laneway and under the tree. Even though the leaves were dense, there was only patchy shade up close to the fence. Gabriela leant against the fence and settled her hands on Viva's hips, urging her closer.

Viva's eyes burned with an intense fire. "This isn't wise."

"No."

Viva didn't move, but the sudden tension in her body, taut and quivering under Gabriela's hands, gave her away. Desire, tamped, banked, but not extinguished. It leapt anew in Gabriela's belly, a kindling fire of warmth and desire. The laneway was quiet.

It was now or never.

It should be never.

With a small sigh, Gabriela urged Viva closer and raised her hand to cup the taller woman's neck.

Viva's lips opened on a word. It may have been "can't", but the thrum in Gabriela's head drowned out any sound.

"We can," she said, instead. "If you want this. Only here, only now."

In answer, Viva dropped her head and claimed Gabriela's lips. There was bitterness on her breath, strong coffee maybe, but as their lips moved together, Gabriela tasted only joy and need and the rightness of the moment. The kiss was hot, drugging and sweet, and it echoed of need and tenderness.

So much tenderness. Viva's hands stroked up Gabriela's bare arms and curved around her neck with the lightest of touches.

Gabriela arched up, into the kiss, against Viva's chest, pouring all the words she couldn't say, all the feelings she couldn't let free into the meeting of lips.

And then Viva broke the kiss and stepped back a pace. "This is all we can have, isn't it?" Her voice was hoarse, husky with need and underlying sadness.

Gabriela shook her head, a slow one-two. "Nothing has changed. I still cannot." She hunched her shoulders. "I'm sorry. This was a tease."

"I'm not sorry." A touch on the cheek. "I'll remember this."

And then Viva was gone, pushing past the green leaves back out to the real world of sunlight and people who might know them.

Gabriela waited for enough time to let Viva walk away, and then she, too, exited the laneway, turning in the other direction, towards the Yarra River. She would walk back. After all, what else was there for her in this day?

<hr />

Viva threw the paper on the table, stood, and moved to the balcony of her hotel room. *The Wildcard Wonder* screamed the headline. "Genevieve Jones may have made an undignified exit from the Sydney tournament, but those in the know have tipped her as a long shot for the Australian Open title."

If only they knew. Viva gripped the rail and let her head drop. Her wrist throbbed with the familiar bone-deep ache. Her first match was tomorrow, and her best hope of playing through was painkillers, ice packs, and the tightest physio strapping she could bear. She'd said in the press conference in Sydney that her wrist was fine, but that was a fabrication. She was barely holding on.

She gripped her injured wrist with her other hand, willing the tendons to become less inflamed, for them to knit firmly and strongly. Her wrist pulsed pain against her fingers.

She went back inside to where the TV was tuned to the tennis. The channel was showing highlights of the opening day: Alina Pashin grinning as she raised her hands above her head in triumph. Michi's grimace of concentration as she slammed a backhand winner to clinch her first-round match. The defeated slump of a veteran player as she lost to an up-and-coming young player whom, in days gone by, she would have wiped from the court in under an hour. And the joy of a teenage qualifier as, against all odds, she made it to the second round.

Viva picked up the icepack she'd discarded earlier and once more wrapped it around her wrist. Deepak had cut short her session that morning, telling her sternly to rest the wrist and study her first-round opponent's qualifying matches. She had no commentating duties until she was knocked out of the tournament, so once her cardio and strength training were done, she had little to do.

The qualifier she was to play had a solid, obvious game. If Viva's wrist held up, it should be a straightforward match for her. The TV switched to a men's match. The power game held her interest for a while, but then she turned it off and went out to the balcony again.

Her phone beeped in her pocket, and she pulled it out, heart racing. She hadn't heard from Gabriela since their coffee date the day before—but why would she? Gabriela had made her position very clear. Until Gabriela had kissed her.

The text was from Jack. *Back in Waggs Pocket missing my lovely girlfriend Jelena.*

Viva smiled. The media were still making much of the supposed relationship between the pair. If she were a betting woman, she expected she would see her brother in Melbourne before the week was out—courtesy of Jelena's agent.

She switched to a news channel, and it was talking about the Australian Open and the favourites for the title.

"Alina Pashin would have to be considered the number one pick in the women's draw." The commentator, an Australian ex-player, said, over a pastiche of some of Alina's winning shots, "With Serena Williams out this year, Alina has to be the best bet."

"Who else?" the sidekick asked.

"Michi Cleaver is hot off her Sydney win, and while she could be a semifinalist, I don't see her going all the way."

"Any prospect of an Aussie winner?"

"Genevieve Jones is our best hope. She won the US Open a couple of years back, but she's yet to find that winning form since. While I'd love to see an Aussie girl hoist the trophy, you'd have to say Viva is a long shot at best."

She didn't need an expert to tell her that. Viva took a deep draught of water and changed channels.

She fired off a text to Michi: *Hey, hotstuff, Oz TV just talked you up.* She called up another blank text and typed in Gabriela's name. Viva stared at it for a moment before deleting the text and throwing the phone back on the couch.

Chapter 20

VIVA BARELY BROKE A SWEAT to win her first-round match.

"Good game." Deepak grunted in satisfaction. "She was an easy opponent, but you played it perfectly. Rest up tonight, and then tomorrow we'll work on your court angles. How's the wrist?"

"Not too bad." It wasn't quite true, the dull throb was only partially masked by painkillers, but she would cope.

"You're playing Anke, a true backboard," Deepak continued. "She'll run down anything you send her way for as long as it takes for you to make a mistake. You'll need to mix it up."

Viva nodded. She would rest—eventually—but first she had an interview with a women's magazine and a guest spot on a radio station picking her three all-time favourite songs.

Much later, she returned to the hotel, ordered room service, and settled in front of the TV. If only the public could see her now. So much for a tennis player's glamorous life—she lay on the couch in her underwear, eating sushi with her fingers and drinking from a litre bottle of water.

As she flicked channels, she saw that the program about her life and career was airing. She smiled wryly. Apparently, the programming gods didn't have as much confidence as Deepak that she'd survive the next round. They'd done it well, she conceded. Interviews with her family—even Jack was charming, and the story about the motorbike and the trip-wire didn't make an appearance. Waggs Pocket and the pub got several mentions, and there was a couple of minutes footage of her and Michi behind the bar serving drinks for the pub's doubles night.

For the umpteenth time, Viva watched the final point in her US Open win. Forehand, cross-court backhand, half-volley winner and the Viva of two years ago dropped her racquet to the court and fell to her knees, hands pressed to her mouth. Genevieve Jones, grand slam champion.

Her phone pinged with a text, but she ignored it, transfixed by her younger self on the screen. Echoes of that elation tingled in her fingers. It had been the best of times. The program moved to a clip of her discussing the charities she supported and then, inevitably, her being a role model as an out lesbian in the mainly closeted world of professional sport.

"I've never seen myself as a role model," the on-screen Viva said. "I am who I am, and hiding my sexuality never once crossed my mind."

"Do you think that holds true for the younger players as well?" the interviewer asked.

"For many it does. But there are still countries that make it difficult or impossible for the LGBT+ community. No one should make that decision for another person."

Viva crossed her legs on the couch and swallowed a piece of sushi. Was Jelena watching this? She picked up her phone, expecting another text from Jack, but Gabriela's name flashed up. Viva wiped her fingers on the napkin, as if smeary fingers would make the text impossible to read.

Saw you on TV. You and Waggs Pocket looking good.

She hit *Reply.*

Not looking good right now. Eating sushi on couch in my undies.

She hit *Send* and waited. A minute passed, and she set the phone down on the coffee table. There was no reason Gabriela would reply. She picked up the last piece of nigiri sushi from the tray and wiped it in the wasabi. The pungent horseradish made her eyes water.

On the TV, her mother was showing the cameras through her office, where Viva's trophies going all the way back to her tennis club days took up most of one wall.

Her phone pinged, and she snatched it from the table.

I wish I was there too. Even though your undies are probably total coverage tennis shorts.

Viva glanced down at herself. Grannie knickers were de facto wear on court under a short tennis skirt. Off court was different. As Gabriela already knew only too well. She stood and went to the bathroom where the mirror showed clearly what she was wearing: turquoise and purple striped chain-store bikinis. A couple of dollars a pair. Her skin was white around the underwear; further down her thighs the all-year tan of a tennis player started. She snapped a photo of herself in the mirror, waist-down, nothing identifying, and sent it off before she could talk herself out of it.

She settled back on the couch, staring absently at the TV, where she and Michi were playing doubles. The camera cut to Michi outside the pub, pink hair blowing in the wind. Michi could have been talking about good farming practices for all Viva took notice. She stared at the phone in her hand, and when it pinged, she had the text open before the sound had died away.

Just as I remember.

Viva dropped her head into her hands. She and Gabriela were the past. She heaved a shuddering sigh, and the phone pinged again.

I miss this. I miss you.

Her fingers trembled as she hit *Reply.*

I miss you too. I wish I could come to your room. Even as she hit *Send,* she knew she'd gone too far. She sent another text.

I know I can't. I just want to be with you so badly.

Would Gabriela respond?

The minutes ticked past, and the TV program ended on a montage of her career highlights. Viva barely glanced at it. Her parents would have recorded it; she could watch later. Right now, the silent phone in her hand was all that mattered. But even as she stared at it, she knew Gabriela would not respond.

Michi's volley spun hard and true and landed between their opponents. Both players flailed for it and missed as the shot thudded into the backboard.

"Yes!" Viva flung her racquet in the air and ran to hug Michi, spinning her around. "Third round, partner!"

After a final fist bump, they jogged to the net to hug their opponents and shake the chair umpire's hand before moving to the centre for the on-court interview.

"I won't keep you," the interviewer said, "but this is big congratulations for you. Just one question—Viva, how are you going to pull up after this match? You're playing your second-round singles match later tonight on Rod Laver Arena. Anke's a tough opponent. Are you going to have the legs to run her down?"

"I guess I'll find out later." Viva slung the towel around her neck. "I'm going to have an ice bath, see the physio, and rest up. We're last up on Rod Laver Arena, so Roger Federer, if you're listening, take all the time you want to defeat your opponent."

The commentator smiled and turned to Michi. "You're already in the third round after your win yesterday. How far do you think you can go in this draw?"

"I have no idea. Does anyone? As far as I can."

"Thank you both. And good luck in your next matches—both singles and doubles."

Whoever said a tennis player's life was glamorous had obviously never had an ice bath. However many Viva took, the shock as she lowered herself into the icy water always hit her like a fist to the chest. But for muscle recovery it was still the best, so into the freezing water she went. She ducked her right wrist so that it could get the benefit as well.

Deepak appeared as she started to shiver. "Two more minutes, then see the physio." He crouched at the edge of the bath. "You should be fine against Anke this evening. Stick to your game plan. Think angles. Try to keep the match short. You'll need your energy for the third-round match. As of five minutes ago, Alina Pashin is into the third round and is your next opponent—if you get past Anke."

Viva groaned and sank lower in the water. "Great. Maybe I'll just drown myself right now. It will be less painful."

Deepak smiled slightly. "It's a good thing I know you're joking."

"Don't bet the house on that," she called to Deepak's retreating back.

Maybe the tennis gods had been listening or just Roger Federer, but he took five sets and four hours to get past his lower-ranked opponent. By the time Viva and Anke stepped out onto Rod Laver Arena, it was already past eleven at night. But the Australian Open was known for the night matches taking as long as needed to finish under lights. For the caffeinated tennis fan, a seat at the evening session could go until three in the morning.

As she bounced the ball to serve first in the match, Viva willed energy into her legs. She felt sluggish, her legs heavy and slow to react.

Across the net, Anke bounced lightly on her toes, blonde ponytail swinging.

Viva tossed the ball, swung, and the ball thundered across the net down the T.

But Anke was there, with her customary anticipation and light-footedness, pushing the ball back into play. Eleven strokes later, Anke had drawn first blood on the opening point.

Viva swallowed and concentrated on the ball, the toss, the stroke. She hung on doggedly, and after two hours found herself staring down Anke on the far side of the net. Match point to Viva on Anke's serve. Match point to take her to a third-round encounter with Alina.

Across the net, the Swede bounced lightly, looking as fresh as she had two hours ago when she bounded onto the court like an eager Labrador puppy.

A twinge shot across Viva's wrist, and she ignored it, concentrating on the ball. She rocked in her stance, ready for Anke's serve. She was just so tired. She pushed the thought aside. *This point matters. Only this one.*

Anke netted it.

Viva wiped her palm on the side of her tennis skirt and moved forward a metre inside the baseline, sending a signal to her opponent that she was ready to pounce on the weaker second serve.

The serve was a high bouncer, and Viva drove it back into the middle of the court. For several strokes, they rallied, and then Viva saw an opening. One wickedly angled slice that scraped the net and shot out to the side and the match was over. Relief swamped her. Viva was into the third round.

Gabriela heaved a sigh. It was nearly two in the morning, and she had a match at eleven that would need her awake and alert, not doped with fatigue. When she'd sat to watch the live TV from Rod Laver Arena, she'd told herself she'd watch the opening two games, no more.

But she'd stayed. The camera had focussed on Viva's face, concentration etched in her brow, her eyes keen and sharp, and Gabriela had been lost. Each close-up of her face brought back memories of that same face immersed in lovemaking; each wipe of sweat from her forehead reminded her of licking other, more pleasurable, tastes from Viva's skin. Whenever the camera zoomed in on Viva's long, slender fingers with their neatly trimmed short nails, Gabriela remembered the patterns those fingers had drawn on her skin, the skill with which they had coaxed pleasure from her body.

With Viva's final fist pump of victory, Gabriela rose, picked up her phone, and walked over to the window. She found Viva's last text. What would it hurt? It was a simple congratulatory text to a friend. That was all it was. *Congratulations! Good luck in the third round.* She hit *Send* and returned to the bed, throwing the phone down on the pillow. On the TV, Viva smiled at the on-court interviewer and congratulated Anke on a good game.

"Your next opponent is Alina Pashin," the interviewer said. "Any thoughts on that match-up?"

"She's got a big lead on me in our previous match-ups." Viva pushed her hair behind her ears. "An enormous lead to be honest. Still, I have to beat her sometime, and it might as well be tomorrow. Actually, it can only be tomorrow." She grinned.

Gabriela's own lips stretched into a smile as well. How like Viva to use self-deprecating humour. She must know Alina would be the favourite in that match.

The interviewer waited until the laughter from the crowd had died down, then said, "Still planning on retiring? Third round of a grand slam isn't too shabby."

Viva held up her wrist. "Yes. I don't have much choice."

Gabriela turned off the TV and got ready for bed with robotic movement. She heaved a sigh. The room seemed empty, devoid of character, of life. It was just another bland hotel room: clean, tidy, pleasing, but ultimately just a shell. For a second, she thought of calling Irene, simply to hear a friendly voice, but she resisted. Irene, too, had an early match. Friends didn't call friends when they had to get up early for work.

———————◆◇◆◇◆————————

I have her.

The power of victory surged in Viva's blood, bringing her nerve endings alive, her mind sharp and focussed. The invincible feeling she'd had in the first set, as if she could do nothing wrong, as if Alina were her puppet, pulled hither and thither by the power of Viva's racquet, surged up in her again. The dismal failure of the second set, which she'd lost 6-1, was gone. That was in the past. What mattered was the here and now.

The score stood at 4-4, third set. Alina was serving, and it was 40-0. But the score didn't matter. This point did. If she won this point, she could win the next and the next, put the game to deuce, then two points to win the game. Viva focussed on Alina as she methodically bounced the ball. The crowd didn't matter, not even Deepak, Michi, Brett, and Jack sitting together in her player's box. This point was what counted.

Until Alina let loose an express train of a serve, a thundering bullet that swept over the net, hit the court, and spun off to one side at a dizzying 153 kilometres per hour. Viva didn't even get near it.

"Game Pashin. Miss Pashin leads five games to four."

Viva strode to her chair and drank, a mix of water and sports drink. A bite of banana, a bite of energy bar. Her sweat-drenched hair clung damply to her neck, and her dress was wringing wet. The on-court temperature was over forty degrees Celsius.

Viva stared into the middle distance, eyes focussed on a spot on the court surface. The ballkid behind her held an umbrella for shade, but even so, the heat was intense.

I can take her. I'm used to this heat. Pretend this is Waggs Pocket, where this heat is nothing. Nothing.

When the umpire called time, Viva sprang to her feet and jogged down to the service line. She was in position, bouncing lightly on her toes, as Alina walked with her customary calm to the receiver's position. A flick of her eyes to ascertain Alina was ready and Viva swung, hitting the ball cleanly down the T. It wasn't the bullet that Alina's had been, but it was good enough. Ace.

Viva nudged her toe behind the service line and focussed on the balls in her hand. Her serve sent the ball spinning over the net.

Alina slammed it back. Game on.

She held serve to level the match once more.

This game. This is the game to break her. She flicked a glance at Alina on the far side of the net. Was she tired? Flagging? It was hard to stick to her game plan of mixing it up, making Alina run side to side in the face of the stronger woman's relentless barrage, but if there was a time in the match to try harder, it was now.

Alina's serve thundered down, and Viva blocked it with just enough force that it bounced over the net. She came in towards the net and was ready when Alina sent a blistering shot to the body. Her half-volley put the ball out of Alina's reach. 0-15.

The second point turned into a gruelling rally. Eleven shots, back and forth. Viva stopped thinking; her mind was a blur of instinct as she drilled the ball side to side. And then Alina's shot hit the net cord and dropped back on her side. 0-30.

Then Alina double-faulted to make it 0-40.

Hope leapt in Viva's belly. Three break points. If she could convert just one of them, she would serve for the match. The wall came up in her mind. *This point matters. Only this one.*

Alina served an ace. 15-40.

Two break points left. The rally was long, and this time it was Alina who controlled it. Viva's breath heaved as she battled to return the balls. Then Alina hit a long drive down the line to her backhand.

Viva lunged for it but could only tip it with the racquet frame. The force of the ball sent a shock wave through the racquet to her wrist, which was already bent at an awkward angle. As pain streaked up her forearm, she gasped and dropped the racquet. She pressed her injured wrist against her body for a second, then straightened. The cool glance she shot to Alina took all of her fortitude. Then she bent, picked up her racquet, and returned to the baseline. 30-40.

She swallowed against the rush of saliva in her mouth. There was no way Alina would have not noticed. She would exploit it to her full advantage. The grey mist of pain surged again, and she pushed it back. Not now.

Alina's serve went to Viva's backhand. She slammed it back and blinked away the wave of red in front of her eyes. Alina's return again went to the backhand. Viva gritted her teeth and hit, but the ball went into the net. Deuce.

Viva was almost glad when Alina's serve was an ace as it meant she didn't have to hit it. She blinked away the haze that threatened her vision. *Hold on.*

The next serve would have blistered paint. She didn't have a chance. Game Alina.

She called for the physio at the change of ends, taking advantage of a medical timeout for him to restrap her wrist. She flexed it experimentally, senses alert for the twinge of pain. It would have to do. If she didn't win her service game, the match was lost, and she would have played her final game of professional singles.

She shot a glance at her box. Deepak sat in his customary pose, leaning back, arms folded, no expression on his face. Next to him, Michi leant forward, her pink hair loose.

Viva rose and walked to the service line. A piercing wolf-whistle rang out, and Viva glanced across in time to see Michi lower her two fingers from her mouth and high-five Jack, who sat next to her. Her brother and her best friend. And her parents had promised to fly down from Queensland if she made it to the fourth round.

Viva squared her shoulders and prepared to serve.

Viva waited, her heart in her mouth, staring at the screen that showed the Hawk-Eye replay. If her shot had clipped the line, she was into the fourth round. If it was out, the score was deuce, and they would battle on. As the screen showed the ball's arc slowly moving towards the line, the crowd gave their customary slow clap.

Viva stared unblinking, and then as the screen zoomed in and she saw that the ball had clipped the line by no more than a millimetre, she sank to her knees.

"Game, set, and match Miss Jones," the chair umpire intoned.

Viva took a second, then rose to her feet and jogged to the net for the customary handshake and hug. One glance at Alina's stormy face told her this would be brusque and brief. She held a hand out to Alina. "Well played. I thought you had me there."

Alina didn't reply, and her fingertips brushed Viva's palm before withdrawing. No hug, no double cheek kiss. No exchange of words as was customary in a close-fought match. Alina shook the chair umpire's hand, gathered her things, and marched off court, ignoring the hopeful autograph hunters clustered around the exit.

Fourth round. She was through. Viva waved and tossed her wristbands and a towel into the crowd. *Fourth round.* Her eyes closed momentarily as the buzz settled into a warm glow.

Chapter 21

"HAVE YOU SEEN THE PAPERS?" Irene jogged up alongside as Gabriela entered the official's locker room.

Gabriela shrugged. "No. Has some politician been caught coming out of a strip club, or has Kim Kardashian got a new dog for her handbag?"

"Tsk. You know me better than that." Irene grabbed Gabriela's arm and pulled her to one of the benches. "Page five."

Gabriela opened the paper. She didn't have to look far. The photo was blurry, as if taken from a distance or the photographer had moved, but it was clearly Gabriela. And it was clearly Viva. The two of them, leaning forward, intent on conversation. They were sitting in the booth at the little Greek café in Clifton Hill—the one she'd suggested as it was quiet and out of the way and no one would know them.

Genevieve Jones and Her Secret Lover! the headline screamed.

"What the fuck!" Gabriela flung the paper down. "Who prints this crap!"

Irene regarded her steadily. "When you swear like that, my friend, that means there must be something to it. Otherwise, you would have laughed and ignored it."

"Two people having coffee. That's what the photo is." Her hands clenched into fists on her thighs. *Coffee. And more.*

"Two people who stare into each other's eyes and whose body language screams sexual tension. Whether it's unresolved sexual tension is the issue."

"We both work on the tour. Okay, we were meeting for coffee which we shouldn't have done, but it was *coffee*. Not an orgy. We picked that café as it is tiny and unfashionable. Who the hell took the photo?"

Irene shrugged. "It does not say."

Gabriela picked up the paper and scanned the columns. *"¡Dios mío!* I'm named. 'Alluring Spanish official Gabriela Mendaro may be the real reason that Aussie tennis great Genevieve Jones has announced her retirement. This love match—'" Gabriela snorted "'—is forbidden under player-official fraternisation rules. Maybe Genevieve will be moving to Spain with her lover.'" She threw the paper down again. "I may as well take the next flight out of Australia as I doubt I'll be umpiring any more matches."

"Not Viva Jones's anyway."

"I haven't been. I already had to tell them that… Oh, never mind." She pressed the heels of her hands into her eye sockets.

Irene clasped her fingers around Gabriela's wrists and lowered them. "It will blow over. Viva's retiring, is she not? They will have nothing on you, then."

"It's the perception that I don't adhere to the rules. More than a perception—this makes it clear I haven't. You know how difficult it is to move up the accreditation ladder. Well, this means I've slid down. I'll be lucky to retain my silver badge, let alone anything higher." She heaved a sigh. "I need a drink."

Irene's eyes were kind. "If you are saying that, Viva must be important to you, my friend. I wish you every happiness." She stood. "But in the meantime, I have a match to umpire. Call me later if you want to talk." With a final pat to the shoulder, Irene left.

The worst thing was having to be polite to the press—including the very newspaper that had leaked the photo. Viva smiled sweetly and refrained from ripping the microphone from the reporter's hand and grinding it under her heel. "Yes, I've seen the photo. I don't know what the big deal is. That's a coffee shop. We were having coffee."

"If it was so innocent, why pick somewhere so out of the way?"

Viva regarded him steadily. "Don't you ever leave the office for a change of scenery?"

Someone tittered, and this time her smile reached her eyes.

"Is she your girlfriend?" the reporter persisted.

Viva shrugged. "No. Is she yours?" She directed her attention to a journalist at the front whom she knew to be a serious sports reporter. "Ken, you have a question?"

"How do you rate your chances against Hitomi Matsuda in the fourth round?"

"Hitomi's a tenacious player who's had a lot of success this year. She'll be hard to beat."

Once the press had departed, she went back to the hotel. Deepak had told her to rest up. She lay on the bed and pressed the buttons on the remote. Nothing held her interest. Her phone was heavy in her hand. She brought up Gabriela's congratulatory text from the other night. The TV blared some soap opera, and she muted it. Was Gabriela okay? How was she taking the media hounding? Had she been taken to task for fraternising with a player?

Viva bit her lip and hit *Reply*. *R U OK? Press are hounding.* She hit *Send*. Would Gabriela even see it? She didn't know if she was working.

The phone rang, and her heart leapt in anticipation, but the caller ID showed it was her mother.

"Darl, we're here. Now, can we have dinner with you tonight?" Her mother's voice came down the line.

She sank lower on the mattress. "That would be lovely. As long as I'm home and in bed by nine. I'm the first match tomorrow."

"Of course. You pick the restaurant—wherever suits you. Your father and I are staying on the north side of the city—the same hotel as Jack. Most of the closer places are booked out."

"How about sushi? There's a good place near you."

"That would be lovely. Mainly, we want to see you."

"I'll text you the details. Thanks for coming down. Will Jack be coming out for dinner with us?"

"He said he would."

"Then I'll see you later. Six thirty?"

Viva ended the call, and the phone rang again.

"Darling, you are on fire!" Shirley's voice hummed with satisfaction.

As well it might, Viva thought wryly. She was certainly getting her money's worth from Viva right now.

"Fourth round! You'll make the quarterfinals, won't you?"

"If I could predict that with any certainty, I'd be rich."

"You *are* rich, darling. Don't forget this contract that I set up for you. Which you are executing wonderfully. The press is all over you. A secret lover *and* the fourth round."

Viva took a calming breath. "Consider reversing the order of those phrases, Shirley. I'm a tennis player. And I don't have a lover, secret or otherwise."

"You might want to reconsider that. You're getting good headlines with that angle."

"She's a friend." Was that even true anymore?

"With benefits?"

"Drop it, will you?"

A beat, then Shirley answered, "Sure. I was actually calling about a potential new sponsorship deal I have lined up for you. Right up your alley. It would've been a better match if you'd a girlfriend, but—"

"Shirley, I said drop it."

"Okay, okay. It's jewellery. Unfussy jewellery for the active woman. Because sporty does not equal unfeminine."

Viva studied her fingernails. "I'm not really the sort for bling."

"I think you'll like this. Take a look at their range and let me know. It's a good deal. Now, this evening, what are your dinner plans?"

"Are you asking me out? Why, Shirley, I never knew you cared."

"You're not my type, darling. I like them a little more hirsute than you. I ask because I heard your parents were in town. I'll ensure there's a photographer at the restaurant for just a couple of casual shots."

"I really don't think my parents would like that."

"I'll send him early so that you're left in peace afterwards. After all, if you're knocked out tomorrow, it'll be all over."

"And you just told me I was sure to win tomorrow."

"I'm an optimist. But you'll win, won't you? That little Japanese girl can't hold a candle to you."

"Don't rule Hitomi out. I'm certainly not."

"Tell me which restaurant, and then I'll leave you in peace."

"Rose Sushi on Brunswick Street. No later than seven please. I'd like to enjoy my dinner."

"Thank you. I'll see you tomorrow. We've a corporate box. It'd be good if you could swing by to say hello after the match."

"I'll see what I can do. It would be brief, five minutes, no more."

"Good enough. Well, all the luck in the world tomorrow and we'll see you in the quarters."

"Let's hope so." Viva threw the phone down. She was too restless to read or do anything that qualified as "resting up" in Deepak's vocabulary. Instead she swung her legs off the bed. A gentle run. No more than five kilometres max, maybe a circuit of The Tan. That would suffice.

It was hot in the middle of the day, with few people out. She ran at a steady pace, letting the run clear the mishmash of thoughts in her head. But as she slowed at the end of the circuit, getting ready to walk back to the hotel, one thought popped into her head: Who had leaked the photo of her and Gabriela to the press? Was it a random stranger, or was it someone out to make waves?

———— ✦ ————

Viva draped a towel over her legs and sipped from her sports drink. She jiggled her legs to keep her muscles warm. Hitomi's medical timeout was taking a while—and it was the second one of the match. She'd had a long slog of a match the day before on an outside court where temperatures had reached forty degrees Celsius. Hitomi was a tough veteran player, but even the toughest could be felled by Australia's punishing heat. It seemed she was cramping badly, barely able to move, let alone run and stretch for the shots.

Viva had taken the first set 6-1 and was now 4-0 up in the second. She switched to her water bottle, took a sip, and then left the chair for a slow jog up the court and back.

A burst of applause signalled that Hitomi was back. The Japanese woman looked drawn, and her face was pinched, but she nodded at Viva and took her place at the service line.

But Hitomi was barely able to hang on. As she hobbled from side to side, letting balls pass her without even trying to return them unless they were close to her, it was obvious she was in severe pain. Viva took the next two games without dropping a point to win the match.

At the net, Hitomi hugged her. "I did not wish to retire from this match. This is your final tournament, yes? It would have taken the credit you are due had I retired. This way, you have won your way through to the next round."

Viva hugged her back hard. Hitomi's gesture touched her; it was a sign of respect from the older player, one that came at some cost to her. "Thank you. It's always an honour to play you."

Hitomi received a standing ovation as she left the court.

Andrew waited for Viva for the on-court interview. "What a legend," he said. "Hitomi Matsuda is one of the greats of tennis. Do you know this is her twentieth year on the tour?"

The crowd roared their approval.

"So, Viva," Andrew continued. "You're in the quarterfinals. Tell me honestly, on the back of that Sydney first-round loss—"

Viva covered her eyes in mock despair.

"—did you think you had a chance to make it this far?"

"I knew I had a chance. Every player does. You have to believe in yourself. That said, it hasn't been an easy road here."

"Your next opponent is Paige Westermeier. Any thoughts on that match-up?" Andrew tilted the microphone in Viva's direction.

"Paige and I have a pretty even head-to-head. I'll just have to do my best and hope I come out on top."

"Thank you. Genevieve Jones, ladies and gentlemen."

With a wave to the crowd and a particular wave to her parents siting with Deepak in her player's box, Viva left the arena.

"Darling, well done!" Shirley's plummy tones came clearly over the phone. "I knew you'd make the quarterfinals. Now all you have to do is beat Paige and you're in the semis. What are your chances, do you think?"

Viva slung a towel around her neck, glad of the distraction from her work-out. The gym was quiet, with only a few people running on treadmills or working out, but she took the phone to a quiet corner. The plate glass window overlooked train tracks, and a commuter train rattled its way past. "Your guess is as good as mine. You never know with Paige."

"She's the girl who knocked you out of the US Open two years ago, isn't she?" Shirley's voice sharpened. "Think we could promote it as a grudge match?"

"No way. Paige is a friend; she doesn't deserve negative publicity."

"A pity." Shirley's sigh was long. "I have one other thing to ask you, Viva."

"Only one?" Viva propped her butt against a rowing machine. "You usually have a list."

"It's about the commentating. Now, I know the deal was that you would commentate after you got knocked out of the Open, but here we are at the quarterfinal stage and you're still going. Tennis Australia have asked if you could commentate on one of the other quarterfinals. It's great publicity."

"For them or for me?"

"Both, darling. Try to see it that way. I thought you could commentate on Michi's match. It's the day after yours; that should give you enough time to recover."

"I'll do it." Shirley was right; if she wanted exposure as a commentator, she'd need to get more involved.

"Good girl." Shirley didn't sound surprised. "Now, don't forget you're on breakfast TV tomorrow, before your match in the evening."

"I haven't forgotten. Thanks, Shirley. I know how hard you've worked to set all this up."

"Appreciation is a wonderful thing, darling. Thank you for your kind words."

Viva hung up and pocketed her phone. Her work-out was over. Time for physio.

Chapter 22

GABRIELA WOKE LATER THAN USUAL. Her match the previous evening had dragged on, and it had been past midnight before she got to bed. She made a coffee and checked her email, scanning her inbox in dread of a message from the ITF, another slap on the wrist—or worse—because of the photo of her and Viva.

Nothing. Was that good or bad?

She turned on the TV as she dressed. The breakfast program was on, the host standing outside the Melbourne tennis centre. Gabriela found her Fitbit and stuffed her room key into her waist belt. A run would take her mind away from worry about her career. She was turning to leave when the breakfast host cut to the studio. Viva sat in one of the interview chairs, smiling slightly towards the camera.

Gabriela hesitated, then, closing her eyes at her own weakness, she raised the volume and sat on the bed.

"—I am very pleased to make the quarterfinal. Tennis is an unpredictable sport." Viva held up her wrist, which was heavily taped. "It's hard on the body, especially the hard and fast game played today."

"I enjoyed your commentary from the Sydney and Brisbane tournaments," the host said. "Will you be doing any commentating for the remainder of the Open?"

"That's the idea. Tomorrow, I'm commentating on the quarterfinal match between my doubles partner, Michi Cleaver, and Maria Lucashenko."

Her smile reached her eyes. "A commentator is unbiased, of course, and Maria is a fine player, but I admit to hoping this is Michi's year."

"Will you be continuing your doubles partnership?"

"There will need to be a break while I have treatment on my wrist," Viva said, "but I hope to be playing again by the time the US season rolls around."

The commentator's eyes were sympathetic. "You've just said how hard tennis is on the body. At thirty-two, did you ever think of quitting completely?"

Viva paused. "Yes. When I first decided to retire, I thought a clean break was the way to go. But it didn't take me long to realise I couldn't walk away completely. Quite simply, I love tennis too much. The thought of not competing, of not being a part of the life on tour was not something I could consider. Not yet, anyway. Tennis isn't just my career; it's my passion."

There was a burst of applause from the studio audience.

Gabriela pressed her lips together. There were Viva's intentions, clearly spelt out. Did the ITF know this? Would Viva's lack of singles play be enough for them? Her stomach felt leaden and the thought of breakfast off-putting. She sipped her coffee.

"There are some very good up-and-coming players at the moment," the commentator said. "Apart from Michi, do you have anyone you'll be watching out for?"

"Jelena Kovic is high on my list," Viva said. "She's playing her first quarterfinal of a major event tomorrow. I doubt it will be her last. Jelena is—"

The host held up a hand. "I think you should say these words to Jelena herself. Ladies and gentlemen, Australian Open quarterfinalist Jelena Kovic and her partner, Jack Jones."

The camera caught Viva's stunned expression, but she regrouped and stood, hugged Jelena, and pretended to pummel her brother.

After the pleasantries, the interviewer leant forward in her chair. "Jelena, when we contacted you to come on this program, you agreed on the proviso that Jack came with you. Does this mean you have an announcement?"

Gabriela snorted softly. The interviewer's arch smile made it obvious what she expected that announcement to be.

Jelena's smile was strained, but she leant closer to Jack and took his hand.

Alarm bells rang in Gabriela's head. *What is going on?*

"Life is hard on the tour for an up-and-coming player," Jelena said. "You have to play a lot of smaller tournaments where a first-round loss might only get you a couple of hundred dollars. Even a later stage is often only a few thousand. If you're a top-ten player, life is very different, and one day I hope that will be me. But right now, it's tough for me to pay my way to the next tournament, pay expenses, my coach, physio, even racquets and tennis shoes. Players rely on sponsorship." Her chest heaved, and she continued with a seeming effort.

"Until today, I had one sponsor. They provided my clothing, gave me money in exchange for using my face to advertise their products. I did a few appearances. I'm not well known, so that sponsorship was important to me. So, when they said 'jump', my response was always 'how high?' At the start of the year my sponsor said if I was publicly linked with my girlfriend, they would withdraw their sponsorship."

The camera cut to the interviewer. Her brow wrinkled, and her gaze flicked over Jelena's and Jack's linked hands. "Girlfriend? As in—?"

"Girlfriend. My partner. I couldn't afford to lose my only sponsor. Jack is my friend, my very good, supportive friend, and he agreed to help me out and pretend to be my boyfriend. But I'm here today to say enough is enough. I will not live a lie. I will not encourage the idea that being a lesbian is something to be hidden. I will not support the message that this sends to young people."

"Why did you pick today?" the interviewer asked.

Jelena reached out her free hand to Viva, who took it and held it. The camera cut to a close-up of Jelena's fingers trembling in Viva's grasp. "Viva is an inspiration to me. Not only as a player—a strong, fearless player with a tennis career I hope to one day emulate, but she's also an inspiration in her private life. She's never hidden her sexuality. She's never—that I know of—come out on breakfast television, but then she's never needed to. She's a lesbian, but it's as much a part of her as her smile, her gestures, the way she dominates a tennis court. And while she understood my need for the deception, I know she wishes it hadn't been necessary."

The camera cut to Viva. Expressions flickered across her face, a montage of empathy, surprise, and pleasure.

Jelena smiled ruefully. "I won't deny that getting through to the quarterfinals of a grand slam and the prize money I'll get from that—even if I advance no further—made a difference to the timing of this. It does. A huge one. It will give me enough of a financial base to cope with the loss of my only sponsor. I am sure there will be some people watching this who will say that I should never have gone along with the deception in the first place. To them, I say try not to judge me too harshly. I knew it was wrong, but I could not have stayed on the tour if I'd lost that sponsor—until now."

"Does your sponsor know yet?" The interviewer's eyes were as soft as Gabriela had ever seen from a hard-bitten reporter.

"Yes." Jelena's lips twisted. "As of this morning, I have no sponsors. After this interview, I'm off to a chain store to buy myself some tennis clothing. I thought that might happen, but it was still something I had to do—be true to myself."

A hush fell over the studio.

Gabriela twisted her fingers in her lap. Brave Jelena, cutting herself loose like this.

"Jack, what do you have to say?" the interviewer asked.

He glanced down and gently released his fingers from Jelena's clasp to hug her briefly about the shoulders. "Jelena is a fantastic player. If she doesn't win this year, I'm sure we'll see her hoisting the trophy in years to come. On a personal level, she's been a terrific friend, and it's been great hanging out with her and her girlfriend. With Viva soon to retire, I throw all my support behind Jelena." He directed his words at the camera. "And if there's any potential sponsors listening, well, I say get in touch with Jelena now."

Viva cleared her throat. "I echo everything these two have said. I'm honoured that I was a role model for Jelena, and I applaud her for standing proud. It's not an easy time for her do this. Most players would be focussed inward, on their next match, but Jelena's stand now is good for LGBT+ people everywhere. Especially in sport. We won't be hidden."

The hush from the audience broke as first a handful, then what seemed like the entire studio broke into loud applause.

Viva stood and urged Jelena up, and the two hugged tightly.

Gabriela swung her legs onto the bed, her run forgotten. It seemed Viva was still Australia's golden girl. There'd been no mention of the photo of the two of them in that interview. No snide comments, no finger pointing. What did Australia care if Viva had a girlfriend who was an official? No, they would probably smile, wish her happiness, and go on their way, unknowing of the complexities and conflicts such a relationship might bring.

Her, though… Her laptop sat on the desk. Every time she opened her email, her heart was in her throat as she scanned the senders for anything from the ITF. A warning, a breach of the code of conduct. So far nothing, but the waiting was almost worse.

———— ✦✧✦ ————

Paige was already on court when Viva entered Rod Laver Arena. The noise of the crowd swelled around her as she walked to her chair and set down her bags. Quarterfinalist. She heaved a breath. She'd been in this position before of course, but this time was different. This time was the last time. Maybe even her last match.

Paige was at the net with the umpire ready for the coin toss, and Viva went across to join them. Paige, bouncing from foot to foot, blonde ponytail swinging, won the toss and elected to serve.

Viva's match plan was to attack from the first point and not allow Paige any inroad into the match. By keeping her on the back foot, she hoped to take the lead and stay there, hopefully wrapping the match up in two sets. She flexed her wrist, testing the hold of the strapping. She'd taken the allowed limit of painkillers before the match. With luck, it would be enough to get her through.

Maybe Paige was intimidated by the patriotic crowd, but her game was tentative from the start. Her returns played it safe, landing well inside the lines. Viva made the most of it, aggressively attacking Paige's weaker shots and running around balls on her backhand side to take them with her stronger forehand. It took fifteen minutes for Viva to gain an early break of serve and go to a 3-0 lead.

As she sat at the change of ends, Viva glanced over at her player's box. It was full. Deepak was there, of course, plus her fitness coach. Next to him were her parents and Jack. And behind them, a row of the red T-shirts of the Stockyard Social Club stood out vividly. She hadn't known they would be there. She recognised Max and other stalwart supporters who had been there for her over the years.

Viva switched her concentration back to the court. She would make it memorable for them.

When the umpire called time, she leapt to her feet and jogged back out to serve.

Viva won the first set 6-3 and held serve to take the first game of the second set.

At the far end of the court, Paige lined up to serve. The ball whistled over the net, grazed the line, and thudded into the backboard. Ace.

It was as if the ace was a wake-up call. Paige's body language now reflected an aggression that had been missing in the first set. Her shots sizzled, bouncing true off her racquet.

The match had turned. Viva hung on doggedly, chasing down balls, slamming them back. As fit as she was, her legs ached with the effort of quick sprints and stops; her ankles protested at the abrupt changes of direction.

When Paige broke back, Viva gritted her teeth. She was wrung out, her clothes wet with sweat, clinging to her in the heat and humidity. She flexed her wrist. The tape was holding, but the painkillers were wearing off. Her wrist ached. She pressed gingerly at the base of her thumb, and pain stabbed deep into the joint. Her muscles were like lead, weighing her to the ground.

Paige held serve to go 4-3 up.

Viva bounced the ball, preparing to serve. The crowd was noisy, and the yells of "C'mon Aussie, c'mon" were persistent enough that the umpire had to call for calm. Viva waited, outwardly composed, until the arena was quiet. She took a breath. *This point matters.* Her mantra focussed her, and she tossed the ball, smashing it over the net for an ace.

She could do this. Her concentration narrowed to the ball in her hand, the rasp of her breath, her grip on the racquet. This may be her final singles match, but by all that she had in her, she would go down fighting. Her pulse thundered.

Her serve was good, but Paige was in position and slammed it back. Every angle she tried, Paige was there, her speed getting her to the ball, her strength getting the ball back.

Viva hung on. Her tennis wasn't pretty; it was desperate and determined, shots made by instinct rather than learnt patterns, but they did the job. She took the game with an ace.

Paige's arm went up in challenge.

Viva watched the Hawk-Eye replay, the ball's trajectory as it approached the line, then the close-up. The ball was in by no more than a millimetre. 4-4.

I can do this. Viva crouched on the base line, waiting for Paige to serve. *I can break her.* Certainty swelled in her chest, the confidence of knowing when an opponent was on a downslide. The incorrect challenge had rattled Paige, and the momentum had swung again into Viva's favour. *I will get this.* The certainty lifted her game. Adrenaline forced her muscles to respond, and the roar of the home crowd cheering her on pushed her, point by point, closer to victory.

Until she held match point. Butterflies somersaulted in her belly, and her shoulders tensed in anticipation. Deliberately she relaxed them. *It's only a point. It matters.* Her mouth was dry. If she won this point, she was into the semifinal. Her, Viva Jones, written off by tennis experts and doctors as a has-been. She would show them.

Across the net, Paige moved from foot to foot.

Viva tossed the ball, swung, and the racquet connected. *Bad serve.* She knew it as the racquet connected. The ball dropped down into the net. Second serve.

Still the chance. Viva took her time, deep breaths forcing the butterflies into submission. She didn't look at her player's box; she only cared for this ball, this serve, this point. Her second serve was more careful, a safer shot to get the ball into play.

Paige returned it, driving it hard over the net, and for a few strokes they rallied back and forth.

Viva's breath rasped in her ears, along with the bounce of the ball on each shot. *Another shot. Another.* There was only the ball, flying over the net, only her tortured breath in her ears, only Paige on the other side of the net.

Paige mis-hit, and her return went into the net.

Viva dropped her racquet, euphoria coursing through her. She *had* won. She *had* shown them all she wasn't past it. She was not a tennis has-been. Not yet.

She jogged to the net to kiss Paige on both cheeks.

She was into the semifinals.

Viva had heard that Robin Willis was a chauvinist who disliked sharing the commentary box, especially with a female player. He was from an era where women's sport had been relegated to the dead TV hours—if it was shown at all—and he refused to accept that women's tennis was as popular—or more so—than the men's game.

Viva entered the commentary box before the quarterfinal to find Robin intent on his headphones and controls. When her cheerful "Hello, what a great day for tennis" went unanswered, she concentrated on her own board, making sure all was as it should be.

Finally, Robin turned to her with a half nod that might have been a greeting. "Try and keep your comments succinct. Leave the analysis to me."

Viva's nails dug into her palm. "I'll chip in when needed. I have a good insight on their games."

Robin grunted. "A player's perspective isn't necessarily insight."

"I think it is," Viva said in saccharine tones. "Obviously, the tennis channel agrees as they hired me. Would you prefer I talk about their dresses?"

Robin's lips thinned, and he grunted an unintelligible reply. Then they were on air, and Robin switched to the smooth commentator, welcoming the viewers to Rod Laver Arena for the third women's quarterfinal match.

"I'm here with Genny Jones," he said. "Genny announced she would retire after the Australian Open, and she now joins us in the commentary box. Welcome, Genny."

"Thank you, Robin. However, as many viewers know, you're welcome to shorten my name, but I prefer Viva."

"Of course." The look he shot her was pure venom. "Today's quarterfinal match-up is between Michi Cleaver of the United States and Maria Lucashenko of Ukraine. Cleaver is fresh off her first tour win in

Sydney, and while Lucashenko is yet to claim her maiden title, she's one of the hungry young players sniffing at the heels of the top ten."

Robin continued, barely drawing breath. Viva pasted a half smile on her face and waited. She might have been a novice in the commentary box, but this sort of monopoly was designed to put her in her place. She summoned the outwardly calm exterior that had served her so well on the court over the years.

Robin droned on, and Viva switched her gaze to the players. Michi looked eager, her tension and energy barely contained in her petite body. Maria, on the other hand, was the epitome of the cool Eastern European player. She was renowned for her lack of emotion on court, hitting every ball with cool precision from the baseline.

Then the chair umpire called the two-minute warning, and Viva froze. *Gabriela.* She sat in the chair, tapping on the tablet the umpires used. The excitement of being in the commentary box was rapidly fading. Robin was a dick, and Gabriela was in the chair. Viva shot a glance at Robin and found he was staring at her, a calculating expression on his face. *He knows.* Despite his professed scorn of the gossip and social aspects of tennis, he had obviously heard the gossip about the two of them—and from his expression, he intended to use it to his advantage.

"Viva," he turned to her for the first time on air, "you know Cleaver's game a bit; what can we expect to see from her in this match?"

"I know her game better than anyone," Viva replied. "We continue to be doubles partners. You can expect Michi to play aggressively, to come to the net at every opportunity. What she lacks in height, she makes up for in speed and agility."

"Yes, her husband has been a beneficial influence on her."

"Her *coach*," Viva corrected. "Michi is married to her coach, but it's his coaching abilities that have improved her game."

Viva hoped that the coverage had switched to the court and was not on Robin's face. His look of spite told her she was in for an uncomfortable time.

Maria took the first set after a tie breaker.

"A good solid set from Lucashenko," Robin pronounced. "Cleaver, on the other hand, is looking shaky, and her challenge on set point was unnecessary."

"I beg to differ." Viva nodded in the direction of the screen mounted above the court, which was showing a replay of the final point. "Michi's shot landed close to the baseline so near to Maria's feet it was hard to see. It would have been difficult for the line umpire to get a clear view, too. So Michi's challenge made sense."

"Cleaver didn't look too happy with the result. I guess the question is will she hold composure enough to put up a fight in the second set."

"She's strong mentally. If I was a betting woman, I'd be putting my money on Michi for the second set. Maria played well in that first set, but she's a player who likes an even rhythm of play. Michi mixes up her shots and pace enough that Maria is not getting that rhythm."

Robin blinked. "That tactic is used by some of the best male players. I doubt that Cleaver has the game or the strength to pull it off."

"She has." Viva's reply was clipped. "It's the tactic that won her the Sydney tournament ten days ago."

Robin leant back in his chair. "I miss the women's game of old. The days when women were women, and it was a graceful sport, a delight to the eye. Cleaver is pleasant to look at, granted, but the women's game is losing crowd appeal now that the players are so masculine-looking."

Does he realise what a chauvinist he is? Viva stared, open-mouthed, for a second. "The women's game is exactly where it should be," she managed in civil tones. She clenched on the pen in her hand so hard that the plastic bent.

Robin leered, showing large white teeth. "Of course, I was joking."

Viva inclined her head but did not reply. The silence stretched, an awkward silence that was only broken by Gabriela calling time.

Michi won the match in three hard-fought sets. Her racquet fell to the ground, and she pressed her hand to her mouth, disbelief written in every line of her body.

"Michi is through to her first grand slam semifinal, with a very well-deserved win." Viva fought to keep her voice neutral, but the delight vibrated in her words. "She will play Meghan Olsen, the number three seed in the semifinal. Next up is the last women's quarterfinal: Jelena Kovic of Serbia against Oksana Lebedeva of Russia." Viva turned to Robin so that, as senior commentator, he could give the wrap-up of the match.

He did so, with barely a glance in her direction. Once they were off air, he stood and squeezed past her to leave the commentary box without a word.

For a second, Viva watched his wrinkled trousers depart, then shrugged. She'd made an enemy there. If her future commentating career depended on his assessment, she was out of a job.

Jelena won her quarterfinal, beating Oksana Lebedeva. Jelena was now Viva's opponent for the semifinals.

Shirley called the second Jelena won her match. "This couldn't be more perfect! You're Jelena's idol, you're friends, she dated your brother."

"Fake-dated."

"Same-same where the press is concerned. You're the most newsworthy player in the Open at the moment."

"Roger Federer might not agree."

"Roger doesn't have your glamour, darling."

Viva could almost hear Shirley's brain ticking. No doubt she was trying to work out the best publicity angle. But it would be good to play against Jelena. Despite their friendship, they'd only played against each other twice, and Viva had won both times. But that had been a long time ago, and Jelena was a very different player now.

She ended the call with Shirley and flopped on the bed. Tomorrow morning, she'd meet with Deepak, and they'd go over Jelena's game, fingering the weaknesses. But for now, she had nothing to do, nowhere to go, no place to be.

She rolled over and stared up at the ceiling. Jelena's huge gamble with her career seemed to have paid off. Jack mentioned that the same day the breakfast program aired, Jelena had gained two new sponsors—more than enough to make up for the one she'd lost. She and Marissa were now seen openly together, and the papers were full of photos of the two of them holding hands, having coffee together, and kissing. Jelena's happiness was a palpable thing.

Jelena hadn't wanted to live a lie. She'd put Marissa over her tennis future. Viva rested her head on her arm. Jelena had put love first. How bold and brave was that move. She could have found herself with no sponsors, struggling to fund her career. That sort of pressure took its toll on a player's game. It was yet another reason why it was so hard for the lesser-ranked players to break into the elite.

Viva crossed her legs at the ankle and stared up at the ceiling light. Since she'd mainly dated other players or people on the tour who were either openly out or didn't care if they were outed, she'd never had to make that decision.

Until now.

Would she give up her career for Gabriela if it came to it? Viva frowned. She shouldn't have to; whatever happened in her next match, she would be retired by the end of the week. From singles anyway. And doubles? Surely it shouldn't matter. Umpires for doubles matches were the lower-ranked officials. The chances of having Gabriela umpire one of her matches was exceedingly slim.

But what if the ITF didn't see it that way? What if it came down to her doubles career or Gabriela? What then? Could she do as Jelena had done and put love first? The chance of love, she amended.

She gripped her bad wrist with her other hand. It was holding up surprisingly well, way better than her doctors had led her to believe. Yes, there was pain, but she was used to it. Any professional athlete was. But the pain wasn't as bad as before. She could keep playing doubles. Her pulse quickened. Yes, she could still be a part of this life, an active part, not just a passive commentator. She could still experience the adrenaline of match play, the thrill of victory. Still lift a major trophy if she was lucky.

Could she give that up for love?

Chapter 23

MICHI LOST HER SEMIFINAL. VIVA'S match followed on, so she saw Michi's final netted shot and heard her anguished cry over the TV monitors. On-screen, Meghan threw her racquet in the air and ran to her player's box to hug everyone in it.

Viva left the locker room and went out into the corridor for a final warm-up. Jelena was already there, intent on her own preparation. They nodded at each other, then returned to their own space, their own routine and mental exercises.

Viva knew she was in trouble from the first point in the first game, when Jelena's serve thundered down the T and her legs just wouldn't get her there in time. She spun on her heel and moved to the other side of the base line. She got a racquet to the next serve, but the ball hit the frame and shot high in the air.

"30-0," the chair umpire called.

Viva bounced lightly on her toes, encouraging her sluggish muscles to react. The serve touched the outside line, and she managed to get it back, but Jelena came in on the short ball and slammed it down for a winner. In only a couple of minutes, Jelena had won the first game to love.

As Viva changed ends, she glanced at her player's box. Her parents applauded politely, and Deepak sat with his customary stony face, arms folded over his chest. Jack waved a sign: *C'mon, Jelena!*

She snorted softly. Jack had said he'd throw his support behind Jelena. She couldn't fault him for that.

Viva held her first service game—barely. When she looked over at her box again, Jack waved a different sign: *Viva Jones—Champion!*

She hung on grimly. Her legs were heavy, as if glued to the court, and her footwork was terrible. Panic swelled. She pushed an imaginary wisp of hair from her face and fought for mental fortitude. This was not how it would be. She would not lose her final match like this, playing like an amateur and missing easy shots. There was a way through this, and she would find it. She set her jaw and swept the next point with a precision-perfect shot that clipped the line.

The home crowd applauded wildly, trying, it seemed, to spur her on with their enthusiasm.

Gradually, her muscles responded, her mind honed to a sharper point, and the balls that flew off her racquet started landing where she wanted. With the rise in her game, the enthusiasm of the home crowd fired up even more. Her parents started yelling encouragement, and Jack waved both of his signs at the same time.

But as good as Viva became, Jelena was better. The youngster had found an extra level in her game, and her deadly accuracy and incredible angles found the mark.

Viva's injured wrist bloomed with pain; the constant dull ache she'd grown accustomed to became a twisting knife of agony. The first set went to Jelena. Viva closed her eyes momentarily. Jelena was the future of the game, and she was… She lifted her chin. *No.* She was not past it. She could still win this. Summoning a look of cool collectedness, she went back out for the start of the second set.

Focus. Her mind honed to a point where all that mattered was each individual shot. Her tired muscles and throbbing wrist receded. It was only the here and now.

Somehow, Viva scraped a break in the second set, but two games later her foot landed awkwardly as she ran for one of Jelena's drop shots, and she crashed to the court.

She sat for a moment, head drooping, feeling her ankle with cautious fingers and catching her breath. The ankle seemed fine, but she now had to cope with an aching hip from hitting the hard court as well as a wrist that seemed strung with tendons of fire.

When she levered herself to her feet, the crowd's applause surrounded her. She bent to pick up her racquet and smiled a thanks at Jelena, who stood at the net, a concerned expression on her face. Viva acknowledged the applause of the crowd and jogged slowly back to the baseline.

"You okay?" the chair umpire asked.

She nodded and settled into the receiver's crouch. *This might be my final singles match.* She focussed on Jelena's swing, the racquet coming up, the explosion of the ball over the net. *Make it good.* She was in place; her return was deep. *Make it memorable.* Her point.

But despite everything she flung at it, three games later, she was staring down the barrel of two match points to Jelena.

Viva closed her eyes for a second, wrapped the weak ankle and painful hip in mental cottonwool, and pushed them into a corner of her mind. Her wrist was harder to dismiss, but she managed it. *Make it memorable.* Everything she had went into the serve. Her heart and mind, the culmination of her long career, the power and gratitude of every point, every game, every set, and every match she'd won in her life. The serve was an ace. She'd known it would be.

She dropped to a crouch on the service line. One point saved. One to go. She needed one more perfect serve. *This point matters. Only this one.*

Viva's serve was good, but not good enough. Jelena returned, and for a minute they rallied back and forth. Jelena's strokes were almost tentative, and Viva pushed forward, taking advantage of the more inexperienced player's match point nerves. Heart pounding in time with the throb in her wrist, Viva saw the opportunity and advanced. Her drive felt good coming off the racquet, low and hard. In horror, she saw the ball tip the net cord, balance precariously for a moment before falling to the court on Viva's side of the net.

The crowd groaned with one voice.

She had lost. She bit her lip. Disappointment crashed through her, and suddenly, the aches she had pushed aside surged anew as the adrenaline of the match receded. She walked to the net to congratulate Jelena.

Jelena's smile beamed like a beacon, and her eyes sparkled. She dropped her racquet and drew Viva into a hug. "I'm sorry it had to be you," Jelena said into her ear.

Viva clasped Jelena's damp back and hugged her hard. "You were the better player. Keep going; you deserve the trophy."

"Your final match?" Jelena asked, although she surely must have known.

Viva nodded, stupid tears pricking at the back of her eyes.

"Don't leave the court. Wait for me."

They shook the chair umpire's hand, and Viva packed up her bag, taking the towel from her chair and pushing it into a corner of her bag. A souvenir from her last match. Standing, she waved to the crowd and took a long, slow look around Rod Laver Arena. The blue surface, the ballkids standing to attention, the linesmen and women, and of course the crowd, on their feet, cheers and applause lifting up into the air.

Jelena came towards her. "We'll go together."

"No," Viva said. "The loser leaves first. This is your moment. Your first semifinal win. You'll need to do an on-court interview."

In answer, Jelena slung an arm around Viva's waist. "Walk with me."

Viva put her own arm around Jelena, and the two of them walked slowly towards the entrance, surrounded by the roar of the crowd.

Viva glanced to her player's box. Deepak, her parents, and Jack were on their feet. Her mum had tears streaming down her cheeks. She caught Deepak's eye, and he smiled back at her and gave her a deep, formal bow.

With her arm around Jelena, Viva left the arena.

Chapter 24

THE TOURNAMENT MIGHT BE OVER for her, indeed her singles career was now officially past, but she still had to commentate on the final. Her new career.

That morning, Viva met Michi in the locker room. Michi had just emerged from the shower after her work-out. Now, in the second week of the Open, the locker rooms were quiet. There was only one other shower still running. Viva sat on the bench while Michi towelled dry.

"I thought Brett would take it easy on me today," she grumbled. "He made me do ladder drills and sprints for *hours*. Then I had a hit with him. It's not the same as hitting with you. I miss you on the other side of the net."

Viva looked down at her hands. When would she next grip a racquet in competitive play? Months maybe? "I miss you too. But I must rest my wrist for longer. I hope to be back playing doubles with you in time for Indian Wells in March."

Michi froze, her towel dropping to the floor. Uncaring of her nakedness, she hugged Viva. "I'm so sorry. So, so sorry. That was an asinine comment."

Michi's damp hair ticked Viva's nose, and she hugged her friend back before moving away. "Don't worry about it. You're not the only one who says things like that. My parents do it too."

"But I should know better. I know what tennis means to you. And I can find another hitting partner. It's not all about me." Her mouth twisted wryly. "Even though it's easy to think that it is sometimes."

Viva bent to pick up the discarded towel and handed it to Michi who wrapped it around herself once more. The second shower had stopped, and the tiled room echoed their words. "We do think we're the centre of the universe, don't we? We have coaches, trainers, physios, fitness professionals. Luxury hotel rooms, red carpets, upgrades to first class." She closed her eyes momentarily. *She* didn't have that anymore. "Well, you do. But I'll miss hitting with you more than I'll miss the glamour events." She turned away so that Michi wouldn't see her sadness. How long before she got used to being a has-been?

"I'm *me*. I'm not a tennis star." Michi's voice was low. "If I ever get obnoxious, please tell me. If I ever say I don't want to hit with a player ranked one hundred and something, because they're not good enough for me, tell me I'm being an ass. I don't want to be one of those snobs of the top ten, sashaying past, nose in the air, talking to no one."

"You'll make top ten, I'm sure of that, but there's not much fear of you becoming too superior."

"It happens to others. Exhibit A: Alina Pashin."

"You're no Alina."

A shower door at the far end opened, and Alina stepped out, wrapped in a towel. "Michi most definitely is not me. She doesn't play well enough." She regarded them coolly across the locker room.

"I'm sorry you heard that." Viva managed a rueful smile.

"You're mistaken if you believe I care what you think. You're both irrelevant as far as I'm concerned."

"Liar." Michi's voice was as cold as a Russian winter. "You obviously cared that Viva beat you. Why else would you want revenge?" Michi stuck her hands on her hips. The towel dropped to the floor again, leaving her naked, but she didn't even blink.

"I have no idea what you're talking about. Jones was no threat to me when she was playing. Retired, she's a nobody."

"Then why did you go to the trouble of having her followed? Why did you get that photo of her and Gabriela and sell it to the papers?"

"Gabriela?" Alina's smooth brow creased. "Oh, the official. Do you *honestly* think I'd go to that trouble?"

"Someone did." Michi was short. "And it's the sort of thing you'd do."

Viva's glance flickered over to Alina. She looked calm, composed; certainly, she didn't have the guilty expression of someone who had done exactly what Michi was accusing her of. But then Alina wore the same stony face when she was down three match points.

"Well, obviously, Jones has more enemies than she knows. It wasn't me." Alina unwrapped the towel from around her body and began to dry her hair.

Michi stalked over so that she could stare Alina in the face. "Why should we believe you?"

Alina shrugged. "I don't care whether you do or not. But for what it's worth, I know how hard it is to find happiness with someone on the tour. If two people have found each other, why would I sabotage that?"

"Because you couldn't stand being beaten by Viva. Because you were worried Viva would have an unfair advantage in competition."

"What competition? Everyone knows she's retired from singles. And I don't bother with doubles. Look at the stats. Viva's beaten me twice. I've lost count of the number of times I've beaten her—and that was when she wasn't carrying an injury."

"Then maybe you're yet another homophobic person who thinks there are too many lesbians on the tour." Michi turned away in disdain.

"Is that what you think?" Alina's words were so quiet Viva had to strain to hear them. "It's still tough for lesbians. Look at Jelena and the deception she had to play to keep her sponsorship. If you think I'm homophobic, you're very much mistaken." She heaved a breath. "My country's government is pretty bad. They still harass gay people, but there are other governments that are worse. Much worse. Why would I deny someone their pleasure, just because I can't have the same thing?"

With shaking fingers, she wrapped the towel into a turban around her head. "Excuse me." She pushed between Michi and Viva to return to the main locker room.

Michi frowned. "Did she just say she was gay?" She stared after Alina's upright back.

"I think so." Viva, too, focussed on the lanky player, who faced away from them, rummaging in her locker. *Alina is gay?* How did she feel, not being able to live her life? Not even having the chance to choose love. At least Viva had the chance to do that.

Viva followed her into the main locker area and placed a hand on her arm.

Alina's head jerked up, her posture instantly becoming tight.

"Thanks, Alina."

Viva turned and left.

───────────◈───────────

The women's final was a stinking hot day. Temperatures soared to over forty degrees Celsius, and one of the TV channels filmed an egg sizzling away on the surface of an outside court. Even though the commentary box was air-conditioned, Viva sweated in the muggy heat.

She hadn't checked who the chair umpire was, but she knew it wouldn't be Gabriela. Viva watched as the umpire came down for the coin toss and for a photo with the players. Would this be Gabriela one day? Officiating at one of the world's most prestigious tennis matches.

Jelena and Meghan started to warm up, and Viva glanced around the court, at the ballkids distributing balls, the crowd still filtering in, at the lineswomen and men in their green and gold uniforms and wide-brimmed hats.

Her gaze ran around the court, and she froze. Sitting on a chair at one of the service lines, knees and feet neatly aligned, dark green trousers neatly pressed, was Gabriela. Her short cap of hair was barely visible underneath her hat. Not the umpire for this match, but a lowly linesperson.

Is this how it will be? Major tournaments, bumping into each other, doubles matches, seeing Gabriela from the commentary box. Funny how for years, she'd barely noticed Gabriela. She'd been just another official, earnest and silent, sitting like a statue in the chair or watching the line.

With an effort, Viva dragged her gaze away and shot a glance at her co-commentator. She needn't have worried that he'd seen her staring.

Robin was expounding at length on the players and their paths to the final. At least he'd got her name right this time, but beyond an initial mention, he was doing a good job of pretending he was the only person in the box.

The score was tied at 5-5 in the first set when Meghan served. The service action was smooth; the ball thundered over the net.

"Foot-fault." Gabriela raised her hand.

"The linesperson has called a foot-fault. Second serve," Robin said.

Meghan took her time selecting a ball and returning to the service line. On court, Gabriela sat with her hands in her lap. As Meghan bounced the ball, preparing to serve, Gabriela leant forward again, eyes intent on the line. The serve had barely left Meghan's racquet when she signalled again. "Foot-fault."

The crowd murmured, and Meghan dropped her racquet and jogged over to the chair umpire, gesticulating fiercely. There was a short conversation, then Meghan returned to the service line.

"Call stands. 30-40," the chair umpire said.

Robin shot Viva a look of pure malice. "Seems like a trigger-happy linesperson."

"It's hard to see from this angle, but it looked like a foot-fault to me." Viva glanced at Gabriela quickly so that Robin didn't notice her interest.

Gabriela sat calmly, eyes to the front, no expression on her face, seemingly oblivious to the murmuring of the crowd.

"I would have thought you'd side with the player," Robin said. "After all, it was a foot-fault call like this one that stopped your US title defence. If I remember rightly, you didn't take that well. You had a few choice words for that linesperson." He peered through the commentary box window. "In fact, isn't that the same official?"

As if on cue, the overhead cameras in the arena cut to Gabriela.

"It was the same line official," Viva said. "And she was doing her job back then, just as she's doing it now."

Play resumed on court, Meghan smashing two aces to give herself a game point.

"Let's look at the replay on that foot-fault."

Viva gave a half smile. Robin was obviously trying to rile her.

In silence, they watched the replay zoom in on Meghan's feet. Back and forward it went, focussed on the close-up of Meghan's pink shoe going back and forward over the line. An obvious foot-fault.

"A good call from the linesperson," Viva said.

"It was close. I think the linesperson was a little too tough, though. On such an important point."

"Which is exactly when she should be tough." Viva leant back in her chair.

On court, Meghan won the game, and the players sat down at the change of ends.

"Calls like this slow the game. Make it less appealing for spectators. And no one likes to see women behaving badly."

Viva's fist clenched on her thigh, hard enough that there would be nail marks. "Women?" she said, thankful that her voice remained even. "Or sportspersons?"

Robin's eyes narrowed. "Sportspersons," he conceded. "Slip of the tongue."

"In the heat of the moment, when a call goes against you, it's too easy to let that frustration boil over into bad language or a physical moment of release. That doesn't mean we should condone it, but it's somewhat understandable." She gestured at the court, to where Meghan sat at the change of ends, eyes focussed on some distant point. Only her jiggling knee gave a hint to her inner turbulence. "Meghan handled this well, considering."

"Yes," Robin said with some reluctance. "She did. I imagine this is something you might be expected to feel strongly about. I recollect you were less than happy when the call came against you in the US Open." Barely concealed glee infused his voice. "Tell me, does a player hold grudges? Do they remember the umpire and make life difficult for them?"

"Some obviously do. I admit I found that particular call hard to let go. But not any longer."

"Obviously." Robin's snigger left her in no doubt that he'd been reading the gossip columns.

Would she get off on a murder charge if the whole thing was captured on live TV? Surely Robin wasn't vindictive enough to bring that up now. He would know exactly what that would do to Gabriela. Inside, Viva seethed, but she arched an eyebrow and kept the same cool, half-amused smile on her face that she used when asked a difficult question in a press conference.

"Quite," Robin said when the silence had stretched long enough that it was dead air. "After all, we are all professionals in our way."

"Exactly my point."

⟶⟵◇⟶⟵

Jelena held her cool, and in a bit over two hours she smashed down the final winner to claim the title. Tears pricked the back of Gabriela's eyes. Jelena's battle had resonated through the tennis world, and it seemed she had a lot of support. Gabriela watched as Jelena ran to her player's box and embraced her girlfriend. It was long and tight, and when she moved away, the tears on her face were plainly visible. She hugged the rest of her team, along with Jack, who was beaming from ear to ear at her victory.

Gabriela lined up with the rest of the officials as the trophy was presented. Jelena walked a victory lap of the arena, the huge trophy clasped in her arms, before returning to shake the hand of every official, tournament sponsors, and marketing people. Her face was alive with joy, and she kept glancing at the trophy as if she couldn't quite believe it was hers.

No wonder Viva doesn't want to give this up entirely. Gabriela looked down at her toes. Viva had been in this position before; she'd hoisted the US Open trophy aloft, kissed it for the barrage of camera flashes, reaped the rewards of being a sports celebrity.

How could Viva possibly walk away from the chance to live that again?

Chapter 25

THE AUSSIE PRESS SEIZED ON the foot-fault as the reason for Meghan's shock loss in the final, comparing it to Viva's loss in the US Open.

Gabriela threw down the paper, glad there was only the hotel receptionist in the lobby to witness her anger. Was there nothing she could do to take the attention away from herself and from her and Viva as a potential couple? *Robbed!* screamed one particularly dramatic—and inaccurate—tabloid headline, which talked at length about Meghan's loss. Gabriela snorted. While Viva's foot-fault had played no small part in her loss, Meghan's had had zero impact. Meghan had won the first set, the one with the foot-fault, and had lost the next two.

But the damage was done. Gabriela's name was in the headlines once more, coupled with Viva's. A second paper had even dragged up the photo of the two of them at the Clifton Hill café. Gabriela studied it again. Who had taken the photo?

But whatever tennis gods were conspiring against her, the end result was the same. She and Viva were still linked in the eyes of the tennis federation, and this would call into question her impartiality, especially given that the photo had been taken before Viva retired, negating Gabriela's assurance that any relationship was over.

Over. It had such a final ring to it. Over before it had really begun. Gabriela folded the paper and shoved it in the hotel waste bin, not caring that they were courtesy papers for the use of all guests.

Gabriela turned on her heel and strode towards the lift. A run would clear her head. A brisk few kilometres along the river path would drive officialdom, the all-too-claustrophobic tennis world, and Viva from her head.

A few minutes later, clad in her running kit, she jogged along the path that ran alongside the Yarra River. Her footfalls thudded rhythmically as she dodged between strolling couples and dogs on overlong leads. Gum trees drooped in the heat. Gabriela crossed over a bridge to run along the greener parkland side, where there was more birdsong than traffic noise. She crossed the river again to the trendy suburb of Abbotsford, thinking she might stop for a cold drink at the café there, but when she jogged up to the door, it was closed. She returned to the river path, passing alongside the imposing old convent building to Dights Falls, where a few kayakers surfed the man-made rapids.

Gabriela stopped to slurp water from a drinking fountain. Her breath came in short pants, and her legs were heavy in the heat. She glanced at her watch. No wonder she was tired—she'd shaved nearly two minutes off her usual time for the distance. Glancing up the road from the falls, she saw she'd reached Clifton Hill. The backstreet café was a short distance away. She hadn't been there since the time with Viva, shying instinctively away from the place that had brought her trouble. But that damage was already done. Slowing her pace, she walked the short distance to the café.

It was as quiet as ever, the long, narrow space dimly lit. Gabriela ordered an iced tea and, because she wouldn't be back again until next year, a piece of the sticky baklava. The same woman nodded at her unsmiling, and Gabriela went to sit in the cooler area at the back. The same booth where she'd met with Viva.

The café owner brought her order and set it down.

"Thank you," Gabriela said.

The café owner hesitated. "I was hoping you would return. You and your friend, the tennis player."

"It's just me this time."

"The photo of the two of you in the paper." The woman twisted her hands together. "We didn't take that. Not me nor my husband. We didn't know who you were—we don't watch tennis."

Gabriela glanced up. The woman's normally expressionless face was agitated. "That's okay. It doesn't matter anymore."

"A customer came in when you were here. She saw your friend and asked me if she was the famous tennis player. I shrugged and told her I didn't know. She seemed quite excited about it. She said your friend likes women and maybe you were her girlfriend. She took a picture with her phone when she was at the counter." She spread her hands wide. "I'm sorry if it made it difficult for you and your friend."

"It's all right. Really. It wasn't your fault." She paused. "What did the customer look like?" Was it anyone she knew, someone out to make trouble for her?

The owner shrugged. "An older woman. Dark hair. She lives near here, I think. I've seen her several times."

Unlikely to be anyone connected to the tennis world, then. Just a random stranger getting their celebrity shot.

"And things are okay with your friend?"

"I'm not sure she's my friend anymore. It's not that easy on the tennis circuit." Sadness gripped her chest. Saying it out loud made it so much more final.

"You find a good woman and settle down. Buy a café. Have beautiful babies." The conviction in her voice was strong.

Gabriela met her eyes and gave her a genuine smile. "I might just do that. I'm sorry, I don't know your name. I'm—"

"Gabriela, yes, I know. Now I do, anyhow. I'm Cristina, and I'm happy to meet you. And if you want a good woman to settle down with, my niece is a good hardworking girl. Beautiful too. She will inherit this café one day. You think about that, eh?" Cristina turned. "Your drink and baklava today is on me. Good luck, Gabriela." She walked away, her stout, black-clad shape moving slowly to the front of the shop.

Gabriela sucked down her drink. She was glad it wasn't Cristina or her husband who'd sold the photo—but who would have blamed them if it had been? Celebrities were considered public property, and while she was a nobody, Viva was still a *somebody* and probably would be for some time.

What if she let Viva into her life, the ITF be damned? Whichever way she looked at it, wasn't she just trading one happiness for another? Gold badge umpire or a girlfriend she might love? Coffee or tea. You couldn't mix them together; you had to have one or the other, or it just didn't work. Viva or gold. Gold or Viva.

She nibbled the baklava, the honey taste bursting on her tongue. The ITF generally sent out emails after the Australian Open, confirming an official's level of accreditation. Last year, she'd waited impatiently, convinced that it would be her year and she'd make gold. Every ping of the email had her scrambling for the phone in case the email was from the ITF. When the email had come reconfirming her silver level, the disappointment had been intense. Next year, gold, she'd sworn to herself. The pinnacle. That would not happen now; she was sure of it.

So what if she rang Viva, said yes, yes, a hundred times yes, let's see what we can be? Would it really matter in the longer scheme of things? The scenarios flickered through her head in a kaleidoscope of possibilities. Her and Viva, catching up over coffee, drinks, dinner in hotel bars around the world. Time in Australia, maybe with Viva's welcoming family, maybe by themselves. Maybe they'd buy a house together, maybe some land. Horses, chickens. She rested back against the cracked vinyl of the booth. Her as a silver badge umpire, never making gold. That was where the scenario stuttered and failed. As long as Viva was playing doubles, gold badge was unlikely. Indeed, it would lead to a string of lower-level matches, reduced income, a massive setback in her career.

She'd come too far in her career to walk away now.

———◦◦◦———

The contract was a dream. A guaranteed minimum of ten tournaments a year, including three during the Australian season, plus two of the three remaining grand slams. The option to select the tournaments she covered so that she could do a few close together over the American hardcourt season or the European clay court season. A clause giving precedence to her doubles matches if they clashed with commentating duties.

Viva signed with a flourish and grinned at her parents across the dining table. "Don't worry. You'll be rid of me soon enough. Another two weeks and I'll be off to Qatar for my first commentating gig under this contract."

Her mum poured boiling water over tea bags and brought the mugs over to the table. "Don't stay away too long. You didn't retire to keep seeing the inside of hotel rooms."

"I won't. I'll be home for much of the year. I'll look out for that house and land I keep talking about. Maybe a dog."

"Hold off on the dog. We'll care for any babies you or Jack might have in the future, but not a dog."

"I'd prefer to have a partner before considering babies. A dog I could manage alone."

"Dog?" Jack wandered past to find a mug for himself. "I'd look after a dog for you. Especially if it was big and tough. Pit bulls are great."

"Because you're such a marshmallow you need a scary dog," Viva teased.

"That wouldn't go down well in a pub." Their dad frowned at his son. "I don't want to be sued. If you're getting a dog, Viva, make it something friendly and unthreatening."

"Don't worry. I need somewhere to live first. Maybe someone to love."

"There's a woman out there somewhere for you." Her mum reached out and clasped Viva's hand. "A sweet girl who'll love you for who you are."

"Self-absorbed, rich, and temperamental." Jack's grin took the sting from his words.

"I would have said warm, generous, and outgoing," their mother said. "Jack, pass the bickies while you're there."

Jack passed the biscuit tin to their mother. "Viva has good friends, I'll give her that. Talking of friends, I'm thinking of going to California to catch up with Jelena and Marissa before Indian Wells. Go to Vegas. Ride a Harley Davidson through the desert."

"You're a bit young for a mid-life crisis." Viva picked an Anzac biscuit from the tin.

"I'm a bit old to have stayed in Waggs Pocket for most of my life," Jack countered. "Now that you're going to be around more, I'd like to see some of the world before I settle down, grow a beard, and become the revered publican of the Stockyard Hotel."

"You can join me any place I'm commentating," Viva said. "I'll pay for your hotel room. You're on your own for the bar tab, though."

"I'll take you up on that. Are you doing the French Open? I've always wanted to go to Paris."

"I'll let you know."

Their mum dunked a biscuit in her tea. "What happened to that lovely girl, Gabriela? Did you patch up your differences?"

"We did. But we're not dating, if that's what you're wondering."

Something in her expression must have warned Lindy off the subject, as she didn't reply.

Not dating. Such short words to hide a wealth of heartbreak. They skimmed over the surface of career obligations and regulations and reduced it to a simple negative. Viva sipped her tea, uncaring that it scalded her mouth. Maybe Jack had the right idea. Friends stayed around, lovers not so much.

Chapter 26

GABRIELA'S EMAIL PINGED, AND SHE glanced at the laptop, open on the hotel room desk. Maybe this was the Airbnb confirmation she'd been waiting on. With a week to kill before the next tournament in Malaysia, she'd been looking at accommodation in southern Thailand.

It was the Airbnb. They apologised and said a family emergency meant they could no longer take bookings for that week.

Gabriela exhaled in a long sigh. Maybe she should book the flight anyway; there was no shortage of places to stay in Phuket, but the thought of being forced to stay in a resort hotel put her off. She'd had enough of fancy hotels through her work; pleasure meant a quiet stay with a local host.

She replied to the host anyway, thanking them for their response, and clicked out of her email program. As she clicked *close*, an email flashed past her eyes. Her fingers froze on the keyboard. Had that been from the ITF? Heart pounding, she fumbled to reopen her email. The program seemed to take an eternity, but eventually, it stuttered into life. She clicked on the message.

Dear Ms Mendaro. Her eyes scanned past the opening pleasantries, the notification of new office holders, a link to a website about FAST4, the abbreviated tennis game, designed to entice more viewers. Her fingers tightened on the mouse. Would they ever get to the point, or was this email purely a general update?

Finally, down at the bottom, as if it were the most unimportant part of the email, she found what she was looking for.

After due consideration, the ITF has determined your level for the next twelve months will be silver badge. Thank you for your dedication over the past years.

Silver. Gabriela sat back in the chair and closed her eyes. Although it wasn't unexpected, a rock of disappointment lodged in her belly. Silver was good; silver was still high on the ladder. But it wasn't gold. She re-read the email in case she'd missed anything. No reason was given, but there never was. She rose from the chair and went over to the window. Was it only because of her relationship with Viva? She pressed her fingers to her forehead as if she could pry the reason from her mind. It could be anything. Gold badge was notoriously hard to reach—indeed, there were only a couple of dozen gold level umpires in the world, and very few of them were women. But before Viva had upset her chances, she'd been so sure that this year she'd be joining that elite level.

It could be simply that the ITF felt there were enough gold badge umpires. Or maybe someone else had received the accreditation. There were many hungry silver level people like Gabriela. Irene for instance. But of all the silver badge umpires, Gabriela was the most senior.

The photo of her and Viva wouldn't have helped. Even though she had disclosed the relationship to the ITF, had accepted without complaint the restrictions she'd been given, even though she'd tried to do the right thing, the ITF may have viewed that photo unfavourably. Maybe they'd considered the relationship wasn't over. There were so many possible reasons.

Gabriela went back to her laptop. She had a week before she had to be in Malaysia, and if she wasn't going to Phuket, she needed to find somewhere else.

What if she stayed here? Not Melbourne, but outside the city? She could take a tour of rural Victoria and fly from Melbourne to Kuala Lumpur. She checked the flights—they were available and not too expensive.

Her finger hovered over the button. She should book the flight, but her finger refused to move. Inertia stole over her. The solitary trip around Victoria that had sounded so tempting only moments ago now seemed long and empty. A procession of small towns, tables for one, no one to turn to and exclaim about the scenery. The laptop flicked over to the screensaver as she pondered. Two weeks of crowds and company in Melbourne with scarcely a moment for solitude would normally have made her crave silence and a space to be alone. But the reluctance to commit to this was visceral.

Would Irene be up for the trip? But then she remembered Irene was working that week, one of the smaller tournaments somewhere in Asia.

Gabriela opened Skype. She needed to get over this introspection, shake the mist out of her head. Maybe her sister would be around to chat with, but Carla was offline.

Gabriela stared at her screen. Who was she fooling? She didn't just want company; it was a particular player's company she wanted. She wanted what she'd denied herself for these last weeks as she hung on to the prospect of gold badge. But gold badge was not happening. Not this year anyway.

She went back to the flight site. A single flight, from Brisbane to Kuala Lumpur. There was one available on the date she needed, and it was cheap. And there was a flight tomorrow on a budget carrier from Melbourne to Brisbane.

Was Viva even in Brisbane, at the apartment she owned? Viva could be anywhere, although Gabriela's gut said she'd be in Queensland. At home, basking in the pleasure of being in one place. If not Brisbane, then Waggs Pocket.

The email from the ITF resounded in her head. Was she hanging herself out to dry by attempting to see Viva again? Maybe, though, she had nothing to lose. She wouldn't even get a shot at gold badge for another year, and in the meantime, maybe there was other happiness for her to take. She could take a week, a single quiet week of what her heart was calling for, before returning to the tour. If Viva had moved on and wanted nothing to do with her, well, then she'd spend the time elsewhere in Queensland. Maybe enjoy some of the beaches.

She picked up her phone. Now that her mind was made up, the sensible thing would be to call Viva, but she hesitated. Their last conversation had ended on a sad note, and there was no guarantee this one would end any better. There were still the same blocks in place for anything long term: she still couldn't have any sort of relationship with Viva. Her career was still at stake. This was a short-term, off-the-radar catch-up. Maybe it would be a friendly drink and a winding-up of what they had shared. The finality of friendship.

She would go to Queensland. If Viva was there, well, so be it.

———◆◇◆———

It was the end of the long summer holidays, and there were long lines at the check-in desks and baggage drops at Melbourne Airport. Gabriela was early, and rather than fight the crowds in the food court, she headed for the airline priority lounge, one of the perks of being such a frequent flyer. Inside was an oasis of calm after the craziness of the departure area. She helped herself to coffee and a plate of fruit from the buffet and found a table. She'd just opened her ereader and settled into a spooky thriller when a discreet cough sounded next to her.

"Gabriela?"

She looked up and immediately rearranged her face into lines of polite welcome. George Kostantis was one of the bigwigs in the ITF. It was a surprise he had even recognised her, let alone said hello.

"George, how nice to see you."

He hovered, coffee in hand. "Do you mind if I join you?"

She swallowed her surprise. "Of course not. I am just killing time before my flight to… My flight." She bit down on too much information.

He nodded. "A week off before Malaysia. Anything exciting planned?"

She stirred her coffee. "Not really. Just a bit of touring, maybe catch up with a friend."

"Yes. You have to take your chances when you can when you travel so much. I'm going to the States. Meetings." He took off his glasses and rubbed his eyes. "I'm glad I bumped into you, though. It gives us a chance to talk a little, off the record."

Gabriela set the spoon down carefully. "Oh?" Nerves fluttered in her stomach. This was a new thing to her. She'd never been friendly with any of the ITF officials—indeed, she wasn't aware that anyone was. They were the upper echelon of officialdom: remote, shadowy figures who made occasional TV appearances when there was some scandal or change to the game and who sent *the* anticipated email once a year. The rest of the time, any contact with the ITF was done through the workforce of administrative personnel.

"You've opted out of a few tournaments lately. The end-of-year WTA finals, this current week. Are you cutting back on your schedule for some reason?"

"No." She kept her face impassive although questions churned inside. "I have skipped the WTA finals for a few years now. That close to the end of the season, I need the break. As for this week, it is a small tournament, and I knew Irene was working it. I was not aware it was a problem."

"It's not. Curiosity, that's all. I wondered if you were setting your sights elsewhere. Coaching, maybe a position with a national tennis body."

"No. I love being an official. This is my career for the foreseeable future."

His direct gaze skewered her, and she resisted the urge to shuffle in her seat.

"So, when you received the email saying you were to remain as a silver badge umpire, you were disappointed."

It wasn't a question. Gabriela swallowed hard through a suddenly dry throat. Was this leading up to something big, something unwanted? She took a sip of coffee to buy time. "Yes, I was somewhat. I have been a silver badge for a few years now. I realise the importance of gold badge and the relatively few officials who attain it, but I thought I was in with a good chance. Did anyone reach gold this year?"

"No. No one." George replaced his glasses. "Surprised?"

"Yes. A little." The comment was as noncommittal as she could make it.

George leant forward, his hands flat on the table between them. "I pushed for you. You're next in line. But the committee wouldn't recommend it. I think you know why." He glanced at his watch and took a hasty swallow of coffee. "I'm going to have to sprint to the gate in a minute, so now isn't the time for prevarication."

"Because of Genevieve Jones." There it was. All of her fears confirmed.

"Yes, because of Viva. You know the rules, Gabriela, I'm not going to repeat them to you. The committee was appreciative that you disclosed the relationship before the Brisbane International, along with the fact that it had ended. But then there was that picture in the paper."

"I told you the truth. The relationship has ended. That picture was just coffee." She pushed the image of a hot and dusty back lane and Viva's heated kiss from her mind.

"I believe you. The press can be relentless. The scandals we've had to dampen over the years... But the fact remains that Viva, while retired from singles, is still an active player. She's indicated her intention to play doubles with Michi Cleaver. They're entered for Indian Wells, if I remember correctly."

"I get it. As long as Viva's still an active player in any capacity, as long as there's even the *perception* of a relationship between us, even though it's ended, then no gold badge for me."

"That's it, I'm afraid. I wish that wasn't the case, at least as far as you are concerned. I have no doubts about your integrity, Gabriela. None whatsoever. But we can't make an exception for you and not set a precedent." He pushed his coffee cup aside and stood. "I have to run. I'm happy I caught you. I wanted to set things straight. Right now, even though the relationship is over, the fact that there was one in the first place is an issue. When Viva retires from doubles, then there isn't any problem that any of us can see to raising you to gold."

Gabriela rose too and shook his hand. "Thank you, George. I appreciate your candour." She watched him hurry from the lounge.

The plate of fruit that had seemed so appealing now turned acid in her stomach. Any remaining thought that maybe she could try a relationship with Viva was shot to smithereens. Viva could potentially have a long doubles career if she was careful with her wrist. As long as Viva remained active, Gabriela would not reach gold.

But the damage was already done. How much worse would it be if she and Viva were open about their relationship? George hadn't spelt that out. But she knew, without needing to be told. If she were open about her relationship with Viva, not only would she not make gold, but she would also find herself sidelined. Fewer matches, especially prestigious ones, and even when Viva retired from doubles, if that was years down the track, then despite what George had said, it would be difficult for her to advance. By then she would have a record of umpiring low-level matches. It would be nearly impossible.

Gabriela pulled out her boarding pass for the flight to Brisbane. Was there any point in even going now?

She went to pour another cup of coffee. Indecision swirled around her head. She closed her eyes, tried to filter the thoughts, remove the anger and doubt and injustice that was clogging her mind.

She would take the week. Go to Queensland, hopefully spend the week with Viva. One week. That was what she would allow herself. She wouldn't tell the ITF. After that, she would put Viva from her head, fly off to Malaysia, and hope the ITF would eventually be persuaded that the relationship was truly over.

She pulled her phone from her pocket. Now that the decision was made, there was no time to waste in hoping Viva would be there. She dialled the number.

"Hi, Gabriela." The wariness in Viva's voice tore at her. "How are you?"

"I miss you." The words surged up from within, forcing their way out of her throat without any preliminaries.

A long sigh. "I miss you too. So much."

"I am about to board a plane to Brisbane. I have a week before I have to be in Malaysia. Can I see you?"

The silence grew over the line, enough that worry clawed its way up. Maybe Viva had found someone else. Someone less complicated.

"I'd like that. I'm in Waggs Pocket. I can't come to Brisbane, not for a few days anyway—I've promised to work in the pub."

"I will come to Waggs Pocket. If that is okay with you."

Another sigh, but shorter, more a gust of relief. "Are you sure? What about your level? What if the press find us?"

"In Waggs Pocket? It is unlikely. I will hire a car and be there by dusk."

"Gabriela, what is this? Is this a visit to say goodbye?"

How could she answer that? "I have a week. Can you handle that? If not, tell me, and I will stay away."

"A week," Viva echoed. "I guess I'll take what you're offering." A pause. "I'll reserve a guest room for you."

"Not unless you prefer that."

"No. Definitely not."

"Then I'll see you later. I'm looking forward to it."

"Me too." The words gusted down the line. "Me too."

Chapter 27

THE DRIVE FROM BRISBANE WAS longer than Gabriela remembered, and the dusty road where she had broken down those weeks ago was drier, more parched, the gum trees grey and drooping. She patted the dash of the rental car as she passed the spot where the previous one had died. "Keep going, little car," she murmured.

The car surged on, and soon she was swooping down the road into the valley towards Waggs Pocket.

The pub was as she remembered it. She glanced up at the balcony where she'd had dinner with Viva, where she'd tried to sleep while being eaten alive by mosquitoes. Hopefully, tonight would be different. For a second, she was light-headed with anticipation.

She left her bag in the car and pushed the door into the bar open, hoping to see Viva.

Jack was behind the counter. "G'day, Gabriela. It's good to see you again." His cheerful grin reassured her somewhat. "Viva's out in the kitchen, attempting to cook. Go and find her before we're all poisoned."

Her feet remembered the way over the worn boards to the kitchen, and she pushed through the swing doors.

Viva had her back to the door. She was bent over a bench, which was covered with salad ingredients. She turned at the sound of footsteps and waited.

"Hi." The urge to wrap her arms around Viva's waist, to raise her lips for Viva's kiss was strong, but she held back. For a moment, they simply stared at each other, the tension strung so fine, Gabriela fancied she could see it shimmer in the air.

"This is silly." Viva took a step forward. "You've come all this way. You're staying a week, and I'm afraid to greet you properly."

Gabriela closed her eyes in relief, and when she opened them, Viva was nearer, close enough that Gabriela could see tendrils of her hair sticking to her forehead in the heat, the warmth of her blue eyes. Then Viva was in her embrace, Viva's arms wrapped around her shoulders, her own wrapped tightly around Viva's narrow waist. The anxiety of the last few days dissipated, and her body softened against Viva's. For several moments, they simply held each other in silence. Then Gabriela stretched up, Viva bent her head, and they were kissing, really kissing. There was no tentative peck, no easing into it. The kiss was lips and tongues, heat and need, a duel of mouths that gave and took all in one frantic dance.

When they moved apart, Gabriela's heart pounded as if she'd played a three-set match.

"We've a week." Viva cupped Gabriela's cheek with her palm.

Gabriela leant in to the tender touch. Her pulse juddered with anticipation.

Viva stepped back and gestured to the salad. "I'm so very glad you're here, don't think otherwise, but it's not the best timing. My parents are in Adelaide. They went a few days ago, and they're not back for another three days. It's the first decent break they've had in a long, long time. I said I'd help Jack with the pub. So I will have time to spend with you, but I'm rather tied here, at least for the first few days."

"That's okay. I do not want to go anywhere; I just want to spend the time with you. I can be chief bottle-washer to your chief cook."

"You can be chief cook if you want. You can't be worse than Dad." Viva resumed chopping tomatoes. "Pub menus are basic. Mostly, you take food from the freezer and throw it in the deep-fryer. Add a bit of salad garnish on the side. Heap up the hot chips, and no one ever complains."

"I can help with that." Gabriela reached for the menu that sat on the counter and ran her eye down the list. "What is the daily special?"

"Generally whatever Dad concocts. There isn't one today. Unless you're feeling inspired."

Gabriela opened the fridge, noting the trays of eggs, ham steaks, and a bag of mushrooms. A pile of red and green capsicum was jumbled on the bottom shelf. "Are you using the capsicum for anything?"

"No. They're locally grown. One of the customers brought them in. I have no idea what to do with them."

"Then make room for me at that bench. The daily special is *huevos flamencos.*"

————— ◦◇◦ —————

The kitchen was hot and steamy, and even the air conditioning was struggling. Viva pushed a wisp of hair away from her face with the back of her hand and stole a glance at Gabriela. She was chopping the capsicum with a speed and dexterity that was humbling. Diced onions, sliced mushrooms, and cubes of ham and potato were piled next to her. Viva had no idea what Gabriela intended to do with them, but already it looked way more interesting than the normal fare the pub served up.

And working side by side with Gabriela was a special pleasure. Sliding past her to reach the fridge allowed a brief kiss on the nape of her neck. Filling a glass of water was an excuse to slowly run her fingers down Gabriela's spine. And when Gabriela turned around to face her as Viva slipped past in the confines of the walk-in refrigerator, they shared a full-body hug that was not so much about warmth as it was about the joyousness of the reunion.

Reunion. Not just of their friendship, but tonight they would be lovers once more. Viva was sure of that. Butterflies danced in her stomach in anticipation that no amount of chilled water could douse.

A week. She pushed that aside. A week could be a long time. No doubt they would talk, but not yet. *Please, not yet.*

By the time six rolled around, Gabriela had assembled her recipe in some large ramekin dishes that had sat forgotten on a high shelf. She'd simmered the diced ingredients in some of the bulk pasta sauce from the larder, spiced with a touch of chilli and pepper. Gabriela showed Viva how to break a raw egg on the top, sprinkle the dish with sherry pilfered from the bar, and then bake it in the oven until the egg was set. A sprinkle of chives from the garden and the *huevos flamencos*—Eggs Flamenco—was ready.

They took a break outside before the dinner rush and sat on the back steps with a cool drink of soda and lime.

"You must bring your luggage in." Viva gestured to Gabriela's rental car, baking in the sun.

"Mmm." Gabriela looked over the dusty car park. "I know where your room is."

Viva moved closer on the step and placed an arm around Gabriela's shoulders. "You do. And tonight, you'll stay in it. Not like last time."

"I am sure I still have mosquito bites from then."

"No mozzies. But I can't guarantee you'll be cool."

Gabriela turned into her embrace. "I hope not. I would like it to be as hot as hell."

And then they were kissing again, and the heat unfurled in Viva's belly, and the need to take Gabriela's hand and lead her upstairs grew to a compulsion.

A discreet cough interrupted them. "No fraternising amongst the hired help." Jack grinned down at them from the kitchen window. "First dinner orders are in, and Max wants to know what *who-eevies flaming-costs* is. I told him it's ham and eggs. Is that right?"

"Sort of." Gabriela rose. "I will go and explain."

The special of the day sold out in the first hour. The only person who complained was Jack, when told that there was none left for him and he'd have to eat steak and chips.

The evening was one long torment. Viva watched Gabriela move around the kitchen with the same precision and economy of movement that she brought to her work. Viva longed to curve a hand around the back of Gabriela's neck and draw her close for a kiss or smooth a palm down over a buttock, reaching down to trace the hem of her shorts.

There was a brief and glorious moment when Viva pressed against Gabriela's back, her hands slipping around, up over her ribcage to cup her breasts. Viva closed her eyes and concentrated on how Gabriela's nipples peaked under her fingers, on Gabriela's rapid breathing and how it hitched when Viva touched Gabriela's nipple over her singlet.

"The chips are burning!" Gabriela darted away to pull them from the deep-fryer. They were crunchy brown, too burned to serve to customers.

Gabriela piled them into a bowl, and Viva grabbed two glasses of red wine from the bar, and they ate and drank as they continued working.

Viva added a scoop of ice-cream to a dessert.

On the other side of the kitchen, Gabriela stacked plates into the dishwasher.

Ice-cream forgotten, Viva's gaze lingered on Gabriela's lean, brown arms and the slight hint of breast visible through the armhole of her singlet.

Gabriela concentrated on her task with the same intensity she gave to a match point. Her short hair was flattened by the heat and humidity of the kitchen, and her shoulders were shiny with sweat.

Viva glanced at the clock. Meals were finished; this was the last dessert order. *Soon.* Soon she would be able to leave the bar to Jack, and she and Gabriela could retire for the evening. Such a tame way of describing what was going to happen between them. Viva grinned, suddenly glad that her parents were away.

Gabriela slammed the dishwasher closed and turned it on. She straightened, and her gaze locked with Viva's. The promise of what was to come shimmered in her eyes.

"I'll deliver this, and then we're done." Viva picked up the final dessert and took it out to the bar.

When she returned, the kitchen was in darkness. Gabriela stood in the doorway. She grasped Viva's hand and pulled her close. Her body was warm against Viva's, her singlet damp from the hot evening.

Viva ran her hands up Gabriela's arms, to cradle her face between her palms. The kiss stole her breath, filled her head with the buzz of static so that her entire world was Gabriela and how she made her feel.

When she could breathe again, she linked her fingers with Gabriela's, and together they ascended the wide staircase and walked down the darkened corridor to Viva's room. The air conditioning made the room cool. Outside, the purple haze of evening moved slowly to the blackness of night. Viva drew the curtains across the glass door to the balcony. It made the room feel smaller, more intimate. There was only the slow turn of the ceiling fan, the quiet hum of the air conditioner. The wood-panelled walls absorbed the quiet sounds.

It was as though she were underwater, so heavy and dense was the air between them. Viva turned on the bedside light so that the room was pools of light and shadow. With this night in mind, she'd changed the sheets, and they were crisp and white in the muted light.

"Do you want a shower?" she asked.

Gabriela nodded. "Please. It was a hot day and a hotter evening." Her smile broke over her face. "And I do not mean the heat of those commercial ovens."

Viva threw her a towel. "Hold on to that heat a while longer. The showers are shared with guests."

It was hard for Viva to concentrate knowing that Gabriela was naked in the next cubicle. As she soaped herself, the image of Gabriela's hands running over her own compact body, then sluicing the soap from her skin made Viva hurry her own shower. She dropped the soap and then fumbled the shower control, accidentally turning it to cold, before she finally finished.

With a glance at the next cubicle, she wrapped herself in the towel and went back to her room. She frowned. Something was different. Her glance fell on an ice bucket on the bedside table, the neck of a bottle of sparkling wine sticking over the top. Two champagne flutes rested next to the bucket. It had to have been Jack's doing. She would thank him later.

The door opened, and Gabriela came in, wrapped in a towel. Her olive skin glowed warm in the light.

Tears sprang into Viva's eyes. This moment, this woman. Their time. *How long have we got?* She pushed the thought aside. This was for them and was not to be wasted on talk. That would come later. For now, their lips and bodies would say anything that had to be said.

Her fingers clenched on the towel, holding it closed above her breasts. She took a step forward, bare feet soundless on the rug.

Gabriela echoed her movement, and then they were face to face.

"Please drop the towel. Let me see you," Gabriela said, her voice husky and threaded with need.

Viva raised her chin, her heart beating as if it were match point, and her fingers loosened on the material so that it fell to the floor.

Gabriela followed suit and kicked both towels away to the side of the room. She fluttered her fingers over the distance between them to trace up Viva's arm in the lightest of touches. Her face was intent as she outlined

Viva's collarbones and mapped a path down between her breasts before skimming underneath, over her ribs, and up the outer edge of Viva's breast.

Viva's breath caught as Gabriela flicked her a wicked glance before again focussing her gaze down to where her fingers moved in the slowest of concentric circles, around Viva's breast, closer and closer to her nipple. It was the lightest of touches, almost lazy in its approach, advancing so slowly that every centimetre sent widening ripples of desire along Viva's skin. The tingles coalesced until her body was one heated pathway of flame. When Gabriela's fingers finally passed over Viva's nipple, the magic her touch elicited was so great that Viva's knees shook. She stiffened. *Please don't stop.*

She glanced at Gabriela's bent head. Her gaze was fixed on Viva's breasts, on the slow movement of her own fingers. As if sensing Viva's look, Gabriela raised her eyes, and their glances met.

"I love your body," Gabriela said, her voice low. "I love the strength in your muscles, your flexibility. I love the power, the way you walk, graceful and upright, but coiled like a big cat about to spring. I love your war wounds." Her fingers moved to Viva's wrist, and she raised it and traced the fading scar with her fingertips. "I love your skin." She pressed her lips to Viva's neck.

When she straightened, Viva too leant forward, and then they were kissing again. Gabriela's kisses were agile, somewhat restrained, like the woman herself. But then Gabriela's lips opened under Viva's, and the kiss moved to a new dimension, one of open mouths and the soft, slow, slide of tongues.

Somewhere outside, a shout of laughter from the bar downstairs drifted up, but Viva barely heard it. Being here, in her room, together in their own cocoon, was what was important.

"I love your body too," she said. "I love the stillness you project when you're in the umpire's chair. The concentration, the calmness. And I love how you take such joy in movement. How light-footed you are when you run."

Gabriela was heavy-lidded, her eyes slumberous as she looked up at Viva from under her thick lashes. "I think my body would move better in a horizontal position right now."

Viva's heart hammered in her chest. *Oh yes.* She drew Gabriela down onto the crisp, white sheet and aligned her body next to her. She slid her palm down Gabriela's shoulder, along her arm to her breast, mimicking Gabriela's movement of earlier.

Gabriela lifted her leg and rested her thigh over Viva's hip.

The slide of her skin was a sensual torment. The movement drew Viva's gaze downwards, to between Gabriela's legs, to the dips and curves of her body, to where her sex was hidden in the shadows thrown by the bedside light. She shuffled down, her lips unerringly finding Gabriela's nipple, and she took the hard nubbin between her lips, swirling her tongue, opening her mouth over the small breast.

A pulse throbbed between her own legs, but Viva ignored it.

Gabriela's hands tangled in Viva's hair, taking her long plait and winding it around her fist. When she tugged down, the meaning was clear.

Viva moved down, her lips gliding over Gabriela's belly, rigid with need. She rested her head on Gabriela's thigh, and her nose nudged the soft mound in front of her. The sharp scent of arousal and the damp curls told their own story. Viva parted Gabriela's sex with her fingers, and her tongue darted to taste.

Gabriela's grip tightened in Viva's hair, tugging the roots to the edge of pain.

Viva winced and withdrew. What was wrong?

Gabriela released her grip on Viva's hair. "Please don't stop. Sorry. I didn't mean to hurt you."

Did the words mean more than just the grip on her hair? It was Viva who'd done the hurting. Both of them, circling each other, trying to balance love and conflicting careers. Sadness crept like a grey blanket over Viva, but she pushed it aside. Not now.

Gabriela's palm curved around the back of Viva's head. "Please..."

The angle was difficult, but it was what Gabriela wanted. Viva tilted her head and parted her lover's sex with careful fingers. Her tongue followed, and she circled Gabriela's clit, pressure on one side, a flicker over the tip, then the flat of her tongue on the other side. Circles, more circles, led on by Gabriela's cues, the clench and release of her fingers on Viva's hair, the tilt of her hips, the firmness of her belly.

And then Gabriela's thighs tightened around her, making it hard to continue, but the clench of her belly under Viva's hand, the long, low keen of pleasure urged her on as her body arched in orgasm.

"*Mi corazón.*" Gabriela's whispered endearment fell softly on Viva's ears.

My heart. Viva rested her head on Gabriela's thigh, while Gabriela's fingers smoothed the dishevelled plait she'd been tugging so hard on earlier.

Viva's heartbeat slowed, soothed by Gabriela's fingers. The night wasn't over, but there was no rush. No rush for Gabriela to work her own magic on Viva's body, to bring her to the same shattering climax that had wracked her. For the moment, she was happy to lie in the dim room, her heartbeat slowing from its frenetic race, the softness of Gabriela's skin under her cheek.

Later, she lay, eyes wide open, staring at the ceiling. The bar was quiet; it must be very late. Viva turned her head to see Gabriela. She lay on her side facing Viva, body relaxed in sleep. Her hand rested palm up on the pillow, fingers loosely curled. She looked utterly at peace, so different from the tension that had shimmered in her body when she arrived.

One week, Gabriela had said. They had one week. *Why?* What had changed to give them the week—and only that time, no more? At the time, Viva had grabbed at the offering. But she wanted more. So much more. Gabriela must be taking a huge chance to be here at all. And she was doing it to be with Viva.

She'd told herself she wouldn't push Gabriela, wouldn't demand answers or reasons. She would simply take what was offered and be grateful. But she wasn't sure she could keep to that anymore. The uncertainty ate at her, whittled away at her happiness until she could barely think of anything else.

If it came to it, her own career or Gabriela, what would she do? Careful not to wake Gabriela, she rose, wrapped herself in the discarded towel, and went out onto the balcony. Waggs Pocket was peaceful. There were no lights in the few houses, no traffic or people on the street. Somewhere, a frog chorus trilled, and a hare ran across the quiet road. Viva sat on the balcony couch and propped her feet on the table.

If it came to it, could she stop all competitive tennis? No doubles, no exhibition matches? Her shoulders hunched at the thought, and she instinctively rejected it. It would remove her from life as she had known it for the past twenty years.

Twenty years. Wasn't that time for a change?

Her thoughts skittered to Jelena. She hadn't seen Jelena since the final, but her face and Marissa's were still in the news, the poster children for love. Jelena had it all.

Why couldn't she?

But Jelena had gambled a lot for that love. *Because it was worth it.*

Viva sighed. *Love.* Was that what this was? Even if it destroyed their week together, she would talk to Gabriela tomorrow.

Despite the pleasures of the night-time hours, Gabriela woke early. Cracks of daylight seeped through the blinds, and magpies warbled their liquid song. Gabriela rose quietly from the bed and found a towel to cover herself before she padded barefoot down the corridor to the bathroom.

When she returned, Viva was awake. The sight of her long, lean body stretched out on the bed, arms behind her head, legs crossed at the ankles, brought back memories of the night before. Of her mouth travelling new and exciting patterns along that body. Of the taste and feel of Viva under her lips and tongue.

Gabriela dropped the towel and lay on the bed next to her, resting her head on Viva's shoulder. Her cheek rose and fell with Viva's breathing.

"Is it unromantic to say that I'm starving?" Viva's words vibrated through Gabriela's skin.

"No. I'm imagining bacon." She raised up to see Viva's face. "Well, I'm also imagining you and the things we'll do again in this bed. But breakfast is slightly winning."

"Coffee."

"I would like scrambled eggs and a pile of toast with that bacon."

Viva's lips caressed her hair, and her fingers ran down Gabriela's arm.

Thoughts of breakfast receded.

Viva reached for her phone. "It's nearly seven. How about a run before breakfast?"

The path along the creek was quiet. They passed two dogs out exploring by themselves and disturbed a pair of wallabies grazing on the greener grass by the water, but otherwise there was nothing. They ran side by side, keeping a gentle pace that still saw the kilometres flash past underneath their feet. The soft thud of their shoes on the gravel path and the rasp of synchronized breathing was the only sound.

The run ended with a race to the back door of the pub. Viva touched first and bent double, trying to catch her breath.

Gabriela grinned at her. "That was close. You're losing fitness fast if I could nearly catch you."

Viva raised her head. "Not too fast, I hope. Michi and I are playing doubles in a few weeks in Indian Wells. That should be time enough for my wrist to recover from the Open."

Doubles. Some of the light went out of the morning. Gabriela turned away. "Is that coffee I can smell?"

It was. Jack sat at the kitchen table, a mug of coffee in front of him. "The lovebirds awaken." He grinned and ducked as Viva aimed a pretend slap at his head.

Gabriela spied the commercial coffee machine in the corner. By the time Viva had joined her, she'd figured it out, and the second mug was brewing.

"If my brother loved me," Viva said loudly, "he'd offer to cook bacon, scrambled eggs, and a toast mountain. With Vegemite."

"If my sister loved me," Jack retorted, "she'd make her own breakfast, knowing that her brother had had a late night working the bar by himself while she was getting loved up with her girlfriend."

Girlfriend. Gabriela's hands stilled on the mug. Is that what they were? How could they be, when they now had only six more days together? It wasn't enough. Last night had shown that, binding them closer. In the background, Viva and Jack's banter raged on, their voices rising and falling with their good-natured insults. Six days.

She pushed the thought away. She and Viva needed to talk, but if talking and the setting of boundaries destroyed what they'd found again, then Gabriela could wait.

As if sensing her stare, Viva turned. "Jack's just offered to make us breakfast." She grinned. "So, let's sit outside, out of his way, while he does it."

"I did not offer—" Jack rolled his eyes. "Okay, I get it. Off you go, sister dear. I'll call you when breakfast is ready."

Viva picked up one of the mugs and added milk. "Let's go before he changes his mind."

"You're cleaning up," Jack shouted after them. "Frying pans and everything. Greasy and disgusting."

They found a bench in the shade overlooking the camping area. There were few vans. Most had probably moved on to the coast, where there was at least the chance of a cooling sea breeze.

"I love it here." Viva tipped her head back. The gum leaves above created patterns of light and shade on her face. "I'm looking for a block of land where I can build a house. Not too much to look after, as I'll still be away a fair bit."

"Around here?" Gabriela sipped her coffee and pushed down the envy that Viva's words had brought. What a beautiful place to live, to come home to, as Viva intended doing.

"Ideally. Within the town or at least close outside. Close enough that I can help in the pub if needed. Not next door that they call me in every five minutes."

"How much land?"

"Maybe a couple of acres. Enough that I can have chickens, maybe a horse. Space and privacy. But I don't want to spend all my spare time going around on a ride-on mower or mending fences. That narrows it down a bit. Blocks around here are either huge, or they're house lots in town." Her face was wistful as she gazed out over the dry ground. "It will be nice not to be travelling fifty weeks of every year."

"That's why I stop in Queensland every year. I need the longer break." Would she continue to come to Brisbane? Or would it be awkward after she and Viva had gone their separate ways? But Brisbane was a big city, and if Viva was based in Waggs Pocket, well, their paths would not intersect too often.

"I'm supposed to be looking at a property later today," Viva said. "It's three acres, with a creek frontage, on the edge of Waggs Pocket. It's part of Max's land. If I like it, he's offered to subdivide the block from his land for me, and I'll build a house. It's by itself, no neighbours. I think it might work." She peeped at Gabriela from under her lashes. "Want to come?"

Gabriela worried a pebble with the toe of her running shoe. In other circumstances, they could be looking at that land together, working out the best aspect for a house, the best view, the angle of the northerly sun. "Sure." She sipped her cooling coffee.

"Breakfast!" Jack's yell from the back door drowned out any reply Viva might have made. "If you don't come now, Mumbles gets your bacon."

He pointed to a small terrier wagging its tail on the kitchen steps.

"Mumbles is the neighbour's dog." Viva grinned. "He's a bacon thief. We better go before he steals it."

The morning disappeared with kitchen clean-up, and then they worked together to prepare and cook the lunchtime meals. It was quiet, with the only meal orders being from three road-crew workers repairing the bridge over Waggs Creek.

Once the kitchen was ready for the dinner service, Viva hung her apron on the back of the door and turned to Gabriela. "Still want to look at that land?"

It was only a fifteen-minute walk, but in the heat of the day, Gabriela's shirt was damp before they had walked more than a couple of hundred metres. The land was on a back road that meandered around the edge of town. It was a gently sloping paddock that ended at the creek.

Viva stood by the road, hands on hips, and turned in a slow circle.

"Pretty spectacular view." She turned to the north, where the Bunya Mountains rose up, visible in the vee of the valley. The bunya pines that gave the mountains their name were scattered over the block in twos and threes.

Gabriela moved further from the road, to where a rise provided an even better view. A cluster of gum trees gave sparse shade, and a kookaburra perched on a branch, staring at the ground in search of its next meal.

Viva joined her on the rise. "This would make an awesome house site. I'd have a big veranda looking north up the valley."

The kookaburra darted to the ground and rose again, a skinny snake struggling in its beak.

"It would be a lovely place to live." Gabriela's words sounded stilted in her ears. She could picture the house in her mind: something airy and modern, with huge verandas on three sides to take in the view.

"Do you want to walk down to the creek?" Viva asked.

"Sure."

"Watch out for snakes!" Viva led the way through the dry grass to where the creek cut a winding path.

"We ran along here earlier." Gabriela turned full circle. "You will be able to leave your house and be on the path in a couple of minutes. It is beautiful."

When she turned again, Viva was behind her. The sun caught the wisps of hair escaping her plait, turning them golden. Her shoulders were burnished brown by the sun.

"You're beautiful." Viva caught Gabriela around the waist, stepping close so she could hug her.

Gabriela sighed and let the moment drift into something more, into a kiss that was as soft and sweet and loving as any she'd had.

Viva moved away and turned to the sun once more. "If Max will subdivide, I think I'll buy this. It's perfect."

"It is." She looked around her once more, daring to dream that she and Viva would live here together. A life for the two of them, blending travel with a home that they would build together.

She snorted softly. *Dream on.* Her chance meeting with George had proved that.

"Gabriela." Viva's voice was tentative, unlike her normal assured manner. "Can we talk? I need to know why you're here, what it means. You said we'd a week. I've tried not to press you, but it's eating me up inside. Please, can you let me know what's behind this? Something must have changed, or you wouldn't be here. I've been hoping…"

Gabriela turned to stare at the view down the valley. It was easier than looking at Viva's face. Her mouth twisted as she realised that she and Viva had been in this exact same situation before. But then, Viva had been the one holding the knowledge that would break them apart. Now it was her turn.

"I have been given my ranking for the next year. I am remaining on silver." She focussed on a herd of cattle huddled together in the sparse shade of a gum tree. "It is not unexpected."

"Did anyone make gold?"

"Apparently not."

"But they didn't demote you. You should make the level next year." Viva's tone sparkled with optimism.

"No one gets demoted. It doesn't work like that."

"Then isn't it just a case of waiting until next year? Now that I've retired from singles, once the publicity dies down again, will it be okay?" Viva moved in front of her and took both her hands. "You've done the right thing all along. You disclosed our relationship. You can't be blamed for the photo in the papers."

"Not for the photo, but in the eyes of the ITF, it still casts doubt on my integrity. It was a random customer in the café who took it. Someone who recognised you." She pulled her hands from Viva's and folded her arms across her chest. "I bumped into one of the ITF decision makers at Melbourne Airport. He told me, off the record, that as long as you are still an active player on the tour, even in doubles, then I cannot be seen to associate with you in any way. It calls my professionalism into question. I am leaving for Malaysia at the end of the week. You are playing Indian Wells in March—and I will be umpiring." She tightened her arms around her body, as if they were a physical defence. "So, one week it is."

A myriad of expressions flitted across Viva's face, ending in confusion and sadness. "You seldom officiate doubles matches. They're done by the lower-ranked officials. It's only the semis and finals."

"That doesn't matter. I could still run into you at that level. There's not many high-level officials allocated to doubles."

"Could you just not work the doubles in tournaments I'm playing? I won't be playing many—my wrist won't allow it. Maybe half a dozen tournaments a year." Her voice held a tinge of desperation.

"You do not get it, do you? I am not sure you ever have." Gabriela turned away, directed her words to the creek at the bottom of the rise. "You are still an active player. *Potentially* you could play most doubles tournaments on the tour. Fifty weeks a year if you wished. Maybe you will come out of retirement even. You would not be the first player to do so. The way they see it, as long as you are an active player in any capacity, I cannot associate with you. Not if I want the gold badge."

"I thought…" Viva's forehead creased. "I thought we were doing the right thing. I thought if you just avoided the doubles matches in tournaments that I'm playing, it would be okay."

"I hoped for that too. But at some level, I always knew I was fooling myself. An official who cannot take any match, cannot at least potentially work every tournament, is not flexible, at least in the eyes of the ITF. Even if I completely avoided every tournament you are playing, not only would I be cutting my income, but the ITF would put that mark against me." Gabriela spun back to face her. "The chances of my making gold would be even more reduced."

Viva was silent. When she spoke, her voice was thick, as if with unshed tears. "I wondered if it would come to this. Last night, I asked myself what I'd do if this happened."

Gabriela nodded, too afraid of her own voice breaking if she said anything more.

"What if I retire from doubles? Back out of all the tournaments I've entered?"

"Then there would be no problem. But if you came out of retirement—"

"That won't happen."

"But if you did, it would go against me again. But if you are not on the tour as a player, then there is no conflict of interest."

"That's what I thought before. That if I retired from singles, we could make it work." Viva's voice held an edge of misery. "Would the ITF object to you being with me and me being friends with Michi? Would even that level of association be suspect?"

"As long as *I* was not friends with her, it would be okay."

Viva paced away so that she could see further down the valley. "I brought you here because I wanted to see if you liked it too. If you could ever see yourself living here. Not all the time, not at first, but in between tour commitments. A week here, a week there. The long break at the end of the year. I thought maybe, just maybe, we could make it work. You, here. Us, together on the tour when I'm commentating."

Gabriela bit her lip. Longing rose in her throat, thick and intense, so much longing she couldn't swallow it away. Viva's words were everything she would have hoped for—before. Before it all fell apart.

"Is that what you want, Gabriela? Would you take that, if you could? Or is this just a week of sex before you go back on the tour?"

She glanced sideways at Viva, who was facing her, her thick plait over one shoulder, twisted in her fist.

"Yes. I would take that, if I could. In the past, I'd hoped..."

"You're sure?"

Gabriela nodded. "I thought we had something, you and me. Something between us to build a relationship on. I am not sure it was ever just about sex. There was always the potential for more." She shrugged. "I cannot put a name on it. I cannot say I love you or that I would have been with you forever or that I would have married you. But maybe we could have been all of those things to each other."

"I saw all of those." Viva's voice was barely above a whisper. "I'd dreamt of us together. I at least wanted to try." She flung out an arm, encompassing the land where they stood. "Would you want to live here? Or would you want to be in Spain?"

"Spain is beautiful. But I've always thought of living in Australia someday."

Viva fished her phone out of her pocket. "If I retire from doubles, would you at least give us a chance? This must be a final answer, Gabriela. I'm asking you now, very seriously. Would you be with me?"

"I would be with you." She said the words steadily, with certainty that came from the heart.

Viva glanced at the phone. "There's good mobile reception here. Always a consideration when deciding where to build a house." She scrolled through her address book and connected a call.

Gabriela took a pace away to give her privacy. She had no idea what Viva was doing, but the sincerity in her eyes had unfurled a new tendril of hope.

"Michi?" Viva's voice came clearly across the space between them. "How's it going in Japan?" She closed the distance again and pressed a button on the phone.

"Good." Michi's reply came loudly across the speaker. "I'm in the quarterfinals. And guess who I'm playing. Alina Pashin. I'm almost tempted to let her win after that last conversation with her. Almost."

"You won't."

"No, of course not. Where are you?"

"Waggs Pocket. Looking at a block of land."

"Ohhh, you're serious about the Australian dream, then."

"I am. I'm here with Gabriela."

"Gabriela?" Michi's voice rose. "So, you're back together?"

"You're on speakerphone, Michi. But yes, we might be back together. And that's why I'm calling."

"You're pregnant." Amusement hummed in Michi's tone.

"Don't be daft." A sideways glance at Gabriela. "Not yet, anyway. I'm calling about something more immediate. I'm retiring from doubles. Effective immediately."

Viva was retiring. Gabriela stared at her speechless. The landscape swirled about her for a moment, as her world tilted on its axis.

"Is it your wrist?" Michi asked.

"No, I have a heart complaint. One that won't let me play any sort of tennis on the tour."

"Your heart?" The anxiety in Michi's voice came through clearly. "Viva, are you okay? Have you seen a specialist?"

"I'm seeing her right now. The only person who can cure me. I'm not sick, but I must retire completely so that I can be with Gabriela. I'm sorry to do this to you, but it means I'm pulling out of Indian Wells and every tournament after that."

She meant it. Gabriela clenched her hand to stop her fingers from trembling.

"Don't be sorry," Michi said. "That's the best reason ever."

"It'll be official. I won't play again on the tour. No coming-out-of-retirement comeback tour for me."

"A good idea. Leave that to aging rock stars."

"What will you do about doubles? Will you be able to find a partner at short notice?"

"Don't worry about that. I partnered with Paige when you were injured. I know she'd like that to continue."

"I'll cheer you on from the commentary box." Viva took Gabriela's hand, sliding her fingers underneath Gabriela's clenched ones. "I have to go, Michi. I have other calls to make, and then I have to convince Gabriela once and for all to be my girlfriend."

"Don't waste another minute! We'll catch up soon. Bye!"

Viva slipped her phone back in her pocket. "One call down, five to go."

"You're serious about this?" Gabriela fought to keep her voice even. Her mind turned over Viva's words, wondering if she was misunderstanding their meaning. "You're really closing the door on tennis—for me. You could have many years more of doubles. Look at Martina Navratilova. She won doubles grand slams when she was in her forties."

"I'm no Martina. Maybe I'd play for years. Maybe not. But even if I could play for another twenty years, that'd mean I'd lose you. Or you'd lose your chance of gold badge." She smiled. "It's not worth it, Gabriela. I don't want that. I want you. If you'll have me." Her voice shook.

There was no mistake. Gabriela sucked a quick breath, and the joy expanded in her chest, pulsing through her body. She tightened her grip on Viva's fingers. "I do. So very much. If you're sure."

"Never more so." Viva moved closer, the sun behind her turning the loose strands of her hair to a burnished gold. She cupped the back of Gabriela's head with her free hand and urged her closer.

Gabriela leant in, and their lips met. It was gentle; it was a promise. It was passion.

They broke apart, and Viva said, "I have other calls to make." She scrolled through the phone contacts again and pressed a number. "Hi, Deepak, it's Viva..."

By the time they returned to the pub, there was only one call to make. Viva had contacted Deepak and the rest of her team, Shirley, and Tennis Australia. The only remaining call was the most important one of all: to the International Tennis Federation. Viva looked up the number for their headquarters in the UK.

"Lucky the time difference is in my favour." Viva stared down at her phone, at the numbers illuminated on the screen. She pressed the call button and put the call on speaker.

Gabriela waited for the call to pick up. It was truly happening. Every one of Viva's calls made it more of a certainty. She searched Viva's face for any sign of regret, but there was only firm resolve.

At first, no one at the ITF seemed to know who had to take the call. "You don't have to call us to retire," one assistant said. "An email is fine, as a courtesy."

"I'm aware of that," replied Viva, "but on this occasion, it's necessary."

"Ask for George Kostantis," Gabriela whispered. "He's the person I bumped into at the airport. He'll talk to you."

"One moment," the assistant said when Viva asked for George. "I'll see if he's available." The phone clicked over to the hold music.

Finally, George came on the line.

"Mr Kostantis, this is Genevieve Jones calling."

"How can I assist, Ms Jones?"

"I'm calling to advise I have retired from professional tennis, effective immediately. Singles *and* doubles. I've notified my agent, my coach, and my doubles partner. I'm aware of the formalities, but I'd like it on record immediately. My agent is in the process of arranging a press conference."

"I see. Can I ask the reason for this? In particular, why you felt the need to call?"

"The wrist injury that forced my retirement from singles is one reason. The other, though, is to avoid a conflict of interest for my partner."

Partner. The intensity in Viva's eyes showed her commitment.

Gabriela bit her lip. She shouldn't be surprised that Viva didn't do things by halves. Her single-mindedness, though, was heartening. Viva was doing this for her.

"Oh?" George's voice held no trace of surprise.

"As of now, my partner is Gabriela Mendaro. She continues to officiate at matches. I don't want there to be any difficulties for her because of our relationship. Hence, I'd like it on record that I am no longer an active player in any capacity."

"I see. Thank you for letting us know. And Ms Jones, please send my best wishes to Gabriela."

"I will indeed. I'll confirm this in writing later today."

She ended the call and turned to Gabriela. "It's done. It feels good. *Very* good." She moved over to the balcony railing and gripped it with both hands. "Celebratory good. We might have to see what Jack has in the way of bubbles."

"We didn't drink the bottle he left last night," Gabriela said.

"Let's swap it for a cold one. We should celebrate the end of my career and the start of something new for us."

Us. The word sat delicately in Gabriela's mind. She rested her hand over Viva's where it clenched the railing. "Us. I never thought this would be possible."

Viva turned towards Gabriela. Her face was lit with a smile, her warmth and enthusiasm displayed on her face. "I hoped. So much." She lifted their joined hands and brought them to her lips in an old-fashioned gesture. "I'm yours."

Joy at Viva's words suffused her nerve endings. She drew Viva towards her and slipped her arms around her waist, and they came together in a tight embrace. Gabriela sighed and laid her head on Viva's shoulder, letting the rightness of the moment steal through her.

Finally.

Shirley had pulled some strings and managed to secure some premier sporting journalists to attend the press conference, and the room was packed. It seemed word had leaked of Viva's complete retirement, but not the reason for it.

Viva sat alone at the table, facing a bank of cameras and microphones, as she had done so many times in her career.

"Thank you for coming," she began. Her voice shook slightly as she read her prepared speech about retirement, and then she opened the floor to questions. She pointed to Gavin, from the Melbourne paper, whom she knew was factual, rather than sensationalist.

"Viva, we already knew your singles career was over, so why formally end the doubles as well? It's not a usual step. Is it due to injury?"

Viva shot a glance at Gabriela, waiting to one side with Shirley, and she smiled her reassurance. "No," she said. "It's for a more important reason than injury. It's to protect the career of someone I care deeply about."

There was a second of silence, then a cacophony of calling.

"Gavin, you have more to ask?" Viva said.

"Is this the woman you were linked with during the Australian Open?" He consulted a tablet. "The official, Gabriela Mendaro?"

"It is, yes." Viva clasped her hands on the table and leant forward. "My private life is, as much as I can keep it, private. However, this is important not just to me, but also to Gabriela. My career is over; Gabriela's is still to peak. For that reason, I state for the record that Gabriela and I were not in a relationship during the Open." Gabriela's gaze from the wings of the stage warmed her, waves of love and reassurance flowing towards her. She took a sip of water to ease the lump in her throat.

"She hopes to make gold badge?" a journalist from a New Zealand paper asked.

"Indeed. And that cannot happen if we have a relationship and I'm playing doubles. As Gabriela is important to me—she's my partner—there really was no decision to be made." She smiled around the room. "I'm leaving for love, ladies and gentlemen. I think you'll find the headline is easy."

"Is Gabriela here?" someone called. "Can we have a picture?"

Viva shrugged. "That's not up to me." Her eyebrow arched in question at Gabriela.

Shirley whispered something in her ear and gave her a nudge.

Gabriela's nervous gaze met Viva's, and then she walked across the stage.

Viva rose to meet her and wrapped an arm around her waist. Together, they turned to face the flashing cameras.

"Please, not too long," Gabriela whispered. "I am not used to this attention."

Viva pulled her closer, her encircling arm protective.

For a minute longer, they posed, ignoring the calls for them to kiss, and then with a wave, they left the conference.

Shirley met them. "That was perfect." She oozed satisfaction. "Gabriela, dear, you're a natural in the spotlight. I wonder if I can find an advertising deal for the two of you together."

"Please do not," Gabriela said. "I would rather stay in the background."

"Okay. Sports memoirs are selling well, and I don't believe there's any written by tennis officials. The stories you must have!" Shirley brightened. Her phone rang, and she waved at them as she disappeared down the corridor, phone pressed to her ear.

"Was that terrible?" Viva squeezed Gabriela's fingers.

"Not too bad. But I mean it. Don't let Shirley come up with any advertising deals featuring us as a cutesy lesbian couple."

"I won't. I promise." She glanced around. "Let's leave."

———◆◇◆———

Back at her Brisbane apartment, Viva poured two glasses of wine and turned on the TV. The news was on. They sat together on the couch, sipping wine and discussing where to go for dinner. For, as Viva said, they needed to celebrate their first official date as a couple.

The news showed a snippet of the press conference. Viva tipped her head to one side and watched as Gabriela joined her on the stage. "You're very photogenic. Maybe Shirley's idea is a good one."

"No way." Gabriela drew her legs up underneath her. "Make me do that, and you'll find out exactly how unphotogenic I can be." She scrunched her face up into an exaggerated leer.

Viva rested against the back of the couch, her fingers idly caressing Gabriela's bare thigh. The ordinariness of the situation stole over her. This was life from now on. She was a part-time tennis commentator, sometimes barmaid, sometimes pub cook. She was a supportive girlfriend, a partner, a lover.

It sounded good.

Chapter 28

THE WEEK THAT GABRIELA WAS in Malaysia dragged. Viva struck a deal with Max to buy the land and researched architects online, but she didn't want to make any decision without Gabriela. Although they would, by necessity, spend many weeks apart, she hoped that it would feel like Gabriela's home too.

Viva was to commentate at the Qatar Open the following week. Her flight from Australia arrived a couple of hours after Gabriela's flight from Kuala Lumpur. The taxi ride to the hotel through the modern city was fast. Viva propped her chin on her hand and stared out at the clean streets of Doha, barely seeing the waterfront, the swirl of people going about their business. Gabriela. The name reverberated in her mind, a drumbeat of need.

The hotel used by the tour was one of the modern tower blocks by the water. The room was in Gabriela's name. Conscious of local laws that meant homosexuality was still illegal, Viva checked in, asking for the room she was sharing with her colleague. The process seemed to take an eternity, but finally, she slipped her key card in the door and dragged her case into the room.

Gabriela stood by the window, looking out at the heat haze.

The door clicked shut behind Viva, locking out any prying eyes. She dropped the case with a thud.

Gabriela turned from the window, and they moved towards each other. Gabriela's arms went around Viva's waist, Viva's around Gabriela's shoulders, and they hugged, their bodies pressed close.

Viva's breath stirred Gabriela's hair. "I've missed you. Was it only a week? It seemed longer." She shifted so that she could see Gabriela's face.

"Eight days. In that time, I have umpired seven matches and eaten too many noodles."

"I've bought land, told my parents the reason I'm retiring from doubles, and turned down a contract for us to advertise an overly sweet breakfast cereal together."

Gabriela's eyes crinkled with her smile. "I'm glad you did all of that, although I'm particularly glad about the last one."

"We were to be having breakfast together, calling each other 'honey' and 'sugar', and then it cuts to the cereal, which is called honey sugar snaps or something. Shirley was most disappointed I refused to consider it." She cupped Gabriela's cheek, smiling as she leant in to the touch. "I don't want to talk about Shirley or unhealthy cereals." She pressed her lips against the soft down of Gabriela's cheek. "I don't want to talk at all."

"Oh?" There was a lazy smile in Gabriela's voice. "You want to go out to eat and pretend we're only colleagues? This is the Middle East, after all."

"I was thinking room service. Close the curtains, shut out the world."

Gabriela's smile was beautiful. The way her mouth curved up, one side higher than the other, was mesmerising. Viva focussed on those lips. The memory of those lips on hers, on her breast, on her thigh, and other places in between, obliterated the thought of food. Food could wait. Gabriela could not. She leant in so that her lips hovered a centimetre from Gabriela's, her breath coming in small puffs.

"Do you have to be anywhere this evening?" Viva asked. "I don't. I'm not commentating until tomorrow afternoon."

"I have a most important engagement right here with you."

And then Gabriela closed the distance between their lips, pressing hers firmly over Viva's, her insistent tongue pushing into Viva's mouth. For a while they kissed, and the world closed in for Viva until there was only this room, this woman, these lips, that kiss. It grew in intensity, Viva's lips taking and demanding, Gabriela's giving back and asking for more, a clash of lips and tongues that was oh so satisfying and not nearly enough.

Finally, Gabriela drew back, and without breaking eye contact, she unsnapped the buttons of her white shirt and pulled it away from her chest with a neat economy of movement. Her bra followed, then her pants. She stepped out of her undies, and, naked, closed the gap once more.

"Have you forgotten how to undress?" Amusement threaded her tone.

Viva hauled her T-shirt ungracefully over her head and fumbled at the closure of her pants, clumsy in her haste. She caught her toe in her undies as she shucked them and nearly tripped.

"Your footwork needs attention, Ms Jones." Gabriela's voice hummed. "Other parts of your game also look like they need more care."

"I'll need extra coaching. Know anyone who can assist?"

"I'm sure I can help. We'll start working on your stamina immediately." Placing her palms on Viva's chest, she urged her backwards until the bed caught her behind the knees and she tumbled onto it.

Gabriela straddled her, her strong thighs gripping either side of Viva's hips, her sex hot and damp on Viva's leg. She leant forward, and her mouth hovered over Viva's.

Viva's breath hitched in anticipation of the kiss, and she raised her legs, tipping Gabriela forward so that Viva could clasp her shoulders and pull her down.

Gabriela's tongue darted out to moisten her lips, and Viva's gaze fixed on the small movement. The urge to pull Gabriela even closer to kiss her again was strong, but the delightful torment made her resist.

Gabriela's fingers found the end of Viva's plait and unwound the elastic holding it in place. "You don't need this now. I love to see your hair so wild and untamed."

"It's easier when I'm travelling."

"Sí, por supuesto. But you're not on a plane now. I like to feel it on my skin." She worked the plait loose.

And then Gabriela's breath was warm on her cheek, and her mouth slid over Viva's again, taking her in a kiss that was warm and sweet, heavy with lust.

This is how it will be now, Viva thought, her mind already cloudy with desire. *We will always have this between us.*

She arched her back and let Gabriela move down, along her body, until her nipples were bathed in the damp heat of Gabriela's mouth. And lower still, her thighs parting to accommodate Gabriela's lips and tongue and then fingers, bringing Viva to a shuddering crescendo.

Later, they picked one of the queen beds to sleep in and lay naked on the sheets under the air conditioning. The TV was on, and a reporter was discussing the upcoming tournament.

Gabriela turned to Viva. "Do you want to watch this?"

"Not really."

Gabriela clicked the TV off and found Viva's hand, threading her fingers through her own. Their future had to be mapped, small decisions made, a way forward for them.

"I'm having dinner with Michi and Brett one night while we're here in Doha," Viva said. "You're invited, of course, but—"

"I will stay here," Gabriela said. "Have an early night. I would love to get to know your friends better, but I cannot while Michi is still on the tour."

"I understand. I thought you'd say that, but I didn't want you to feel excluded."

Gabriela pressed a kiss to Viva's shoulder, tracing a triangle of freckles with her tongue. "Tell me about the house instead."

"There's not much to tell right now. I've looked at a few architects' websites, but I thought you might like to help me select." Viva's voice was hesitant, as if she expected the offer to be knocked back.

"We will look at them together. Maybe without me, you will pick something ugly, with small windows and dark furnishings." She pushed up onto her elbow and smiled into Viva's face.

"No, no. It has to be light and bright, with high ceilings and big doors and windows to see the view."

"A big, firm bed."

"Oh yes. I want to make love to you in morning sunlight, with the windows open to the outside." Viva's wave encompassed the room, the curtains closed tight against the bright daylight.

"I just want to make love with you." Something clenched tight around her heart. Happiness. Contentment. She traced Viva's lower lip with her finger.

Viva kissed the finger as it passed along her lip. "A tennis court, of course. Even though it won't get much use, I don't think I could live somewhere that didn't have one."

"We can play together. Although I won't be a match for you."

Viva's eyes glistened, the emotion welling up in her face. "You will always be a match for me. *Always.*"

Epilogue

Two years later

"There's something so special about coming home." Gabriela dropped her bag inside the door and looked around at their home. The space always had the power to make her relax and unwind, stresses and worries left at the door. "Two weeks in Melbourne is wonderful, but I love coming back here to some peace and quiet."

Viva followed her in, her own bag hitting the wooden floor with a thump. "You won't think it's peaceful when my parents and Jack arrive. Which will be in about ten minutes if the Waggs Pocket grapevine does its stuff. Somebody will have seen us drive through town and told them."

Gabriela went around the living area, raising the blinds to let the late evening light into the room. The house was everything they had hoped for and more. A modern space with high ceilings that was basically one enormous room. The kitchen was open-plan, the sleeping area half-hidden from the main room by a bank of bookcases. Only the guest bedroom and the bathrooms were totally private. A wide deck surrounded the house on three sides, so no matter the time of year, there was always sun or shade to be had.

Viva stuck her hands on her hips and surveyed outside through the window. "I hope Jack remembered to water the garden this time."

Gabriela came up behind her and slipped her arms around Viva's waist. "Is it terrible to say that I do not really care if he forgot? The kangaroos eat all the vegetables anyway."

"There is that." Viva turned and wrapped her arms around Gabriela's shoulders. "Have I said how much I love coming home with you?"

"Not since two days ago, when you came back to our hotel at three in the morning after celebrating Michi's Australian Open win."

"That was pretty spectacular." Viva pressed a kiss to the top of Gabriela's head. "I wish you could have joined us to celebrate, though."

"Maybe one day. When Michi is no longer an active player, she and I can become friends. In the meantime, I will play by the rules."

"Don't expect Michi to retire anytime soon. That's only her first grand slam title. She's hungry for more."

"She may not get them. Some of the greatest players only ever won one grand slam." Gabriela smiled up at Viva. "Genevieve Jones, one of Australia's greatest players, only ever won a single US Open title, but her place in the history books is assured." Her tone parroted the diction and delivery of a newsreader.

"Thank you. A ringing endorsement from one of Spain's top-level officials. Soon, if the rumours are true, Spain's only gold badge official."

"Do not celebrate that one yet. After all, the rumours said the same last year. But let us not talk about that. I would rather put our lips to other uses."

Viva's slow smile crinkled the corner of her eyes. "Now you're talking."

Their kiss was broken when a scrape on the deck outside announced the arrival of Viva's parents, welcoming them home. Then a little later, Jack got a break from the bar to come over. By the time he went, the light had left the sky and there was only the hot summer night, the constant whirr of crickets, and the occasional call of a frog from the creek. The Southern Cross hung low in the sky, and moonlight bathed the deck in a silvery glow.

Gabriela sipped the last of her wine. "I love you, you know."

Viva reached out a hand across the gap between their chairs. "And I you."

"Shall we go to bed?"

"I should check my email first." Gabriela stood, pulled out her laptop, and set it in the corner that she and Viva used as an office. Once the laptop had booted, she scrolled through her inbox. An email jumped out at her, and she stiffened, licking suddenly dry lips. "Viva, can you come here?"

Viva came over, a glass of water in her hand. "What's the matter?"

Gabriela pointed. "That email. It's from George Kostantis at the ITF. Maybe it's my ranking for the year."

Viva pulled up a chair and sat. "It's due. It always comes immediately after the Australian Open."

"I know." She glanced at Viva. "I'm nervous."

"Don't be." Viva squeezed her hand. "The worst that can happen is you remain on silver level for another year."

Taking a deep breath to steady the butterflies in her stomach, Gabriela opened the email.

Dear Ms Mendaro, I am pleased to inform you that the ITF has amended your level, effective immediately, and made the decision to promote you to gold badge chair umpire. Congratulations.

There was more, but Gabriela's eyes blurred with moisture. Gold badge. She'd made it. Her hand shook in Viva's clasp. Gold badge. "I've done it."

Tears shone in Viva's eyes, and a smile split her face. "That's the best new year present we could have gotten."

"Second best." Gabriela couldn't clearly see Viva's face through the tears in her eyes, but her grip on Viva's hand was firm and sure. "The best is right here. You, me, together."

And then Viva's kiss sealed them together once more.

About Cheyenne Blue

Cheyenne Blue is the author of the "Girl Meets Girl" series, four standalone stories with interconnecting characters. *Never-Tied Nora, Not-So-Straight Sue, Fenced-In Felix,* and *Almost-Married Moni* are also available from Ylva Publishing. Her short fiction has been included in over ninety erotic anthologies since 2000, including *Best Lesbian Erotica; Best Women's Erotica; All You Can Eat: A Buffet of Lesbian Romance & Erotica; Sweat; Bossy;* and *Wild Girls, Wild Nights.* She is the editor of *Forbidden Fruit: stories of unwise lesbian desire,* a 2015 finalist for both the Lambda Literary Award and Golden Crown Literary Award, and of *First: Sensual Lesbian Stories of New Beginnings.*

Her collected lesbian short fiction is published as *Blue Woman Stories,* volumes 1-3, with more to come. Under her own name she has written travel books and articles and edited anthologies of local writing in Ireland. She has lived in the U.K., Ireland, the United States, and Switzerland, but now writes, runs, makes bread and cheese, and drinks wine by the beach in Queensland, Australia.

CONNECT WITH CHEYENNE
Website: www.cheyenneblue.com
Facebook: www.facebook.com/CheyenneBlueAuthor
Twitter: twitter.com/Iamcheyenneblue
Instagram: www.instagram.com/cheyenneblueauthor/

Other books from
Ylva Publishing

www.ylva-publishing.com

Not-Go-Straight Sue
(Girl Meets Girl Series – Book 2)

Cheyenne Blue

ISBN: 978-3-95533-597-7
Length: 287 pages (86,600 words)

Lawyer Sue Brent has buried her queerness deep within, until a disastrous date forces her to confront the truth. She returns to her native Australia and an outback law practice. When Sue's friend, Moni, arrives to work as an outback doctor, Sue sees a new path to happiness with her. But Sue's first love, Denise, appears begging a favor, and Sue and Moni's burgeoning relationship is put to the test.

The Get Piece

Catherine Lane

ISBN: 978-3-95533-376-8
Length: 284 pages (64,000 words)

Amy gets an irresistible offer: Become engaged to soccer star Diego Torres to hide that he's gay and in return get a life of luxury. The simple decision soon becomes complicated. Diego is being blackmailed, and Amy needs to find the culprit. It doesn't help that Casey, his pretty assistant, is a major distraction. Will Amy watch her from the sidelines or find the courage to get back into the game?

Where the Light Plays

C. Fonseca

ISBN: 978-3-95533-421-5
Length: 285 pages (97,000 words)

Dr. Caitlin Quinn is a sophisticated, self-assured Irish art historian visiting Australia on sabbatical. That doesn't mean she can't enjoy the local scenery—especially sun-kissed Surf Coast artist Andi Rey. Their attraction is unstoppable, but their lives are moving in opposite directions. Andi doesn't need distractions, and a woman that eschews commitment spells trouble, with a capital "T".

The Brutal Truth

Lee Winter

ISBN: 978-3-95533-898-5
Length: 339 pages (108,000 words)

Aussie crime reporter Maddie Grey is out of her depth in New York and secretly drawn to her twice-married, powerful media mogul boss, Elena Bartell, who eats failing newspapers for breakfast. As work takes them to Australia, Maddie is goaded into a brief bet—that they will say only the truth to each other. It backfires catastrophically.

A lesbian romance about the lies we tell ourselves.

Code of Conduct
© 2018 by Cheyenne Blue

ISBN: 978-3-96324-030-0

Also available as e-book.

Published by Ylva Publishing, legal entity of Ylva Verlag, e.Kfr.

Ylva Verlag, e.Kfr.
Owner: Astrid Ohletz
Am Kirschgarten 2
65830 Kriftel
Germany

www.ylva-publishing.com

First edition: 2018

Credits

Edited by Sandra Gerth
Proofread by Paulette Callen
Cover Design and Print Layout by Streetlight Graphics

CPSIA information can be obtained
at www.ICGtesting.com
Printed in the USA
FFHW01n0832230618
47184279-49859FF